SECRET HEIR

DYNASTY VOLUME I

MJ PRINCE

For my own heir, my motivation for everything

"Here's much to do with hate, but more with love.
Why then, O brawling love, O loving hate,
O any thing, of nothing first create."

1

Today my life is going to change.

I tell myself that every day. Sometimes, it's the only way that I can keep myself sane, the only way to get through the shit show that is the life of Jazmine Woodson—my life.

But today—today, it feels like it's actually true. There's something different about today, something in the wind. A whisper of premonition in the sea breeze that's currently whipping mercilessly against my cheeks.

I instantly shoot the ridiculous thought down. A whisper of premonition in the breeze? Something in the wind? *God, I'm really starting to lose it.*

But it isn't the first time. This isn't the first time that I've felt ... something. Because all my life, I've felt like there's something just dancing on the edge of my consciousness, waiting in the wings, just beyond my grasp. Sometimes I feel like I can almost grasp it, but it slips away again, like a dream that you can never remember after you wake up.

Then there are those times of quiet when I feel like I can almost sense the pounding of the waves crashing against the shore, as if it's the pounding of my own heart or when I'm looking up at the sky at night and I can almost *feel* the glow of the stars or the moon pulsing above me. In those times of quiet, it almost feels like they're a part of me, watching me, waiting for me.

In those times, I feel like if I just reach out, I'd be able to hold the moon itself in my hand—of course, I never let myself do that, because that would make me certifiably insane and as messed up as my life is, I'd like to think that at seventeen, I have a way to go before I lose my mind entirely.

So, just as I always do, I sweep the crazy feelings out of my mind. I busy myself with packing away my sketch book and pastels, dusting off the sand from my worn jeans as I stand and look out at the achingly familiar scene.

Rockford Cape. It's been one year since I've been back here and it feels too long. The four-hour bus ride from foster home number ten and the price of a roundtrip bus ticket, means that coming here is no easy feat but I never let a year go by without coming back to this place. I've lived in ten different towns, ten different foster homes since I was seven. A different foster home each year, to be precise, but this place is the only real home I've ever had.

The place where mom and I lived before she died. Before the car accident that took everything from me. Before the world became this lonely place with me wandering lost through it. Because that's how I feel most days—lost.

On this day ten years ago, in this town, my life changed forever and on this one day each year, I come back to this place. I visit my mom's grave and sit on this beach for hours, losing myself in my sketchbook. Capturing the blue-green waves crashing against the sandy shoreline, the silhouettes of the lifeguard outposts dotted along the coast, the rickety pier jutting out onto the water with the multi-colored lights of the equally rickety amusement park reflecting off the water.

I can still remember coming here with my mom most evenings, and for the few hours each year that I spend here, I can almost imagine that the last ten years were nothing but a bad dream. In a life that is full of temporary places and faceless people, this place is the only anchor that I have.

After one last look, I turn away from the past and make my way back to the bus station. To the bus that will take me back to Brockton, to foster home number ten in the little backwater town that is my present.

I make it back just in time to start my evening shift at Rodeo Ricky's. Not a Rodeo as the name suggests, but a diner with a difference—an undoubtedly seedy difference. The first few shifts had left me feeling ashamed and dirty. But then I shut those feelings out. I'm good at that.

Still, as I stand in front of the rusted staff bathroom mirror and slip on my uniform, consisting only of a pair of hot pants and a bra, I can't help but feel a bitter stab of disappointment at what I see.

Get it together, I tell myself.

I need this job and I'm not exactly spoiled for choice in a small town like Brockton. The job pays well and the tips are even better. I'm saving for my future—in less than a year, I'll be out of the foster system, out on my own. I'm hoping to get a scholarship to art school, but if that fails, then I'll have to pay my own way. I'm providing for myself and that is nothing to be ashamed of.

I let out a long breath and stride into the dimly lit diner with renewed determination.

Tonight's especially busy—the diner is packed with the usual seedy patrons, leering at the scantily clad waitresses sauntering between the tables, myself included. I paint on the smile that gets me the most tips and head to my first table of the night. Not that I need the smile to get the tips—I'm not vain by any measure, but I know I've inherited my mom's looks. Long, jet black hair falling like a silken waterfall down my back, delicate features, full lips and perfectly arched brows. My body is my mom's, too—slim, yet curved in all the right places.

But it's my eyes that set us apart. No one has my eyes—it isn't a good thing either, because most days I wish that I didn't have these eyes.

As I approach my first table for the night, I'm reminded of exactly why. People usually give me two looks and as if on cue, the middle aged, balding man seated at the table in front of me gives me those exact two looks that I've grown so used to.

The first is appreciative and the second startled, once he sees my eyes. Wide and doe-like, they almost seem innocent, although the color is anything but. *Uncanny* is probably the closest word to describe the startling coloring—the vivid violet with smoky silver rings. Even the thick black lashes can't shield my freakish eyes.

I'd say that the eyes probably belong to my father, but I wouldn't know—I've never met the bastard who abandoned my mom and me before I was even born and my mom never talked about him. I don't care, the asshole may as well be dead. I hope that he is, at least then I won't have to think about the fact that he's out there somewhere being a father to another daughter while I'm rotting in this hell hole without one.

The man in front of me gets past that initial shock pretty quickly, though, as he takes in the abundance of bare skin on display. *Dirtbag.*

"Ready to order?" I ask, ignoring the urge to wince at the sound of my own false tones.

The man leers at me, as if I'm the meal and not the triple cheese-burger, chilli cheese fries and pitcher of beer that he's ordering. I feel like ripping his eyeballs out and feeding them to him. But instead, I grit my teeth and flash a well-rehearsed smile, playing out an equally well-rehearsed routine. I'm a good actress.

The way this sleazebag is looking at me, only reminds me of the aversion that I have towards the opposite sex.

Whenever I think of men, it only makes me think of my asshole of an absentee father and the perverted men who frequent this fine establishment, like the one seated at the table in front of me right now. Then, of course, there was foster father number six, the sick bastard who thought it was a good idea to try to grope his sixteen-year-old foster daughter. Asshole. I'd quickly put him out of commission, kneeing him squarely in the balls before reporting his ass to the police. But the memory of his sweaty hands on my skin still makes me shudder.

I scribble down this loser's order and make my way to the kitchen. I'm halfway across the diner when I pass by a crowded table of rowdy jocks. Although I pay very little attention to my fellow students at my latest high school, these faces look familiar. Guys from my high school, most of them on the football team, I think, but I don't pay close enough attention to be sure. Not the usual clientele and all clearly under-aged but tonight, they're here all the same. *Great.*

I don't expect them to recognize me. I keep a near invisible profile at school and working at a place like this doesn't exactly make me popular at high school number ten or it makes me popular for all the wrong reasons. Frankly, I don't care.

I stopped caring what other people think a long time ago. I've never stayed in one place long enough to make friends or to care what the kids think of me in whatever high school I happen to be.

I walk past their table without so much as a hint of recognition in most of their faces, although I don't miss the word *whore* being whispered by one or two who apparently are aware that I happen to be a fellow student.

It's not the first time and I can't even bring myself to feel offended. But if only they knew. I haven't even so much as kissed a guy before and I sure as hell haven't had a boyfriend or even gone on a single date. I've never once been tempted. Without my even noticing, something like a stone wall has built itself up around me. Hell, I'm starting to think that my heart itself is made of stone.

"Jazmine, can you take table six?" Ricky calls out from behind the counter. Ricky is just as bad as his patrons, but that works well for me —he probably knows I'm under-aged, but is too much of a sleaze to care and had given me the job anyway.

"Sure," I call back, walking over to the far corner of the diner. As my gaze falls on the table, something inside me twists in discomfort. Even in the dimly lit room, I can see that there is something different about this man.

His silvery grey hair and the creases around his eyes tells me he's somewhere in his late fifties. His strong jaw and well-defined features tells me that he must have been handsome in his younger days, but it's his eyes that really get to me. They're dark grey but the pigmentation is so striking, strange in a way that is almost otherworldly and there is a knowledge in them that doesn't belong in this place, in this world even. In fact, everything about this man feels alien. Like those eyes have seen things, know things that weren't of this world.

What the hell? Am I being serious right now?

But there's no denying that this man is totally out of place. He doesn't belong here anymore than a god, if they exist, belongs on Earth. I can see the way his presence affects the people around him, too—they glance his way before quickly averting their gazes. As if they can sense, just as something inside me can sense, that there is something about this man that stirs the very air around him.

Yeah, sure, because this man is really a being from another world who just wandered into this seedy diner in the backwater town of Brockton of all places. Shaking my head in annoyance, mostly at myself for thinking such stupid thoughts, I stop in front of the man's table.

"What can I get you …" I trail off when those startling grey eyes meet mine. *He knows me.* Is my immediate thought.

Stop it. I tell my overreactive imagination, as I struggle to paint on my usual smile. I brace myself for the perverted comments, but they never come. In fact, contrary to the depraved looks I get from the usual clientele, this guy is pointedly not looking at my tits or my ass or any of the usual places that the customers usually ogle. The expression on his face seems almost … sad?

"I'll have a whisky, no ice." The man's voice is gentle, kind. Not something I'm used to.

"Coming right up," I say, trying to keep my voice light, despite my growing discomfort. I open my mouth to say something else, although I have no idea what. But thinking better of it, I walk away instead, feeling the man's eyes on me the whole time.

I get through the rest of the shift feeling like I was two seconds from running out of the diner. The man at table six stayed until an hour before closing, watching the whole time. Again, not in that perverted way that I'm used to, but watching all the same, and I've never felt more uncomfortable in my entire life. I could feel something like shame prickling down my spine as I batted my lashes and flashed the usual smile to the customers under that watchful gaze.

I'd gotten rid of that shame a long time ago, but for some reason, in the presence of this total stranger, I suddenly wanted to cover up and get the hell out of there.

The shiver of premonition returns. Those eyes see things, know things that I'm sure I never want to find out.

2

*A*s I walk through the derelict neighborhoods that make up Brockton, I can't shake the feeling that I'm being watched. I tell myself to stop being so paranoid—it's been a strange day, and my nerves are fried, but it's no excuse to start imagining things. Still, I can't shake the feeling.

My eyes dart around the decrepit houses, peering into the darkened woods surrounding the low-rise buildings, but I see nothing. There are no lights on in any of the houses, which is not unusual given the time of night, and also the fact that most houses in this part of town sit abandoned. I almost jump out of my skin when a dog barks loudly in the distance somewhere. I reprimand myself and force my breath to calm.

I round the corner and head towards the trailer that is foster home number ten. I feel the usual pang of bitterness whenever I lay eyes on what's meant to be my home.

I hate this place. Not that I'd particularly liked any of the other foster homes. They had each been different—some with normal families, nice houses, well-intentioned foster parents, and others not so nice or well-intentioned. After the third foster home, the quality started to steadily decline—nobody wanted to take in a rebellious teenager who had a history of getting kicked out of multiple foster homes, other than the less well-intentioned people who just wanted me around so that they could collect a monthly check. Foster home number ten is definitely that kind of home, or trailer, to be precise.

I'm reminded once again of my lonely existence. It's not that I set out to be a loner, but I just don't see the point of forming any attachments, when I know that I'll inevitably be packing up and moving again once my current foster family gets fed up with my bad attitude. Because they always do—no one has ever cared enough to put up with me for more than a year, no one has ever wanted to keep me, and I can't blame them.

In truth, I know it's more than just that, though. For as long as I can remember, I've always felt … different. Like, even if I did try, I could never really fit in. Maybe it's because my mom's death ripped away my childhood or because having to worry about how to provide for my own future makes my life very different from that of a normal teenager. Or maybe it's something else, something that I can't quite put my finger on that makes me feel like I just don't belong anywhere —not here in this shit hole of a town, not in any of the other towns that I've lived in, nowhere, and something inside me knows that I could travel the entire earth and still never find somewhere to belong.

There are times when I'm standing in a room full of people and still feel alone, like if I scream at the top of my lungs, no one would even hear me. The thought is a depressing one and maybe a tad melodramatic, but it's true.

Feeling something like defeat wash over me, I fling open the flimsy trailer door and step inside. Thankfully, my latest foster mother, Janice, is out. Probably getting trashed as usual, using the money that she's meant to be spending on food and supplies for me, no doubt. I remind myself that it doesn't matter—I'll be out of here in less than a year, then I'll be on my own. The thought is a scary one, but not scary enough to want to stick around here for longer than I have to.

The trailer is a mess, as usual. Dirty dishes are piled up in the sink and the place reeks like alcohol and tobacco. Normally, I'd get to tidying up, I'm the only one who ever does. But tonight, I'm exhausted. The eight hour round trip to Rockford Cape and the five hour shift at Rodeo Ricky's, has left me shattered.

Flopping down on my cramped bed, I don't even bother to change out of my jeans and sweater, as I squeeze my eyes shut in an attempt to shut out my surroundings. It's the first day of my senior year tomorrow, and it's nearly midnight, so I need to get some sleep. But despite feeling tired, sleep seems out of reach tonight. Sighing, I get up and pull out a small metal tin from the drawer beside the bed.

The trailer is dark, the only light coming from the silvery light of the moon streaming in through the single window. Looking up at the lone silhouette against the sky, I feel drawn to it somehow.

Feeling the invisible tug, I step back out into the night, walking aimlessly until I find myself at the abandoned playground that separates the trailer park from the nearby woods. I sit down on one of the rusted swings and it creaks in response. I open the battered metal tin that I'm clutching. I have very few personal belongings, everything in my life is disposable. Everything apart from the contents of this tin.

I run my fingertips over the tattered photographs—my mom smiling widely at the camera. It's almost like looking into a mirror.

A strip of photo booth shots from the booth at the amusement park back in Rockford Cape. Another photograph of a six year old me walking along the beach, the amusement park lights in the background, as my mom trails behind.

Then there are the drawings—it isn't just my mom's looks that I've inherited, it's her talent, too. Every drop of artistic skill I have, comes from her. I've looked at these sketches countless times throughout the years, but no matter how many times I've seen them, they're just as beautiful each time.

The way she captured the loneliness of the night, the vivid colors amongst the darkness that most people never really notice. I look up at the night sky and see those same deep hues in the darkness—the midnight blues and deep purple blending into black, embellished by the blanket of starlight, which makes the scene look almost mystical.

I love the night—the stillness of it, the quiet. When I look up at the night sky, the vastness of it makes me believe, for just a moment, that there is so much more than this place, this life. I feel the quiet of the night quieting the discontent in my own life and I feel something like peace wash over me. Momentary as it is, it's the only peace I have.

The faint whiff of rotting garbage floating on the night breeze from the nearby dump reminds of my reality, though, and that peace is swept away in an instant. There is nothing more than this life and *this* is my place in the world.

I suddenly get that feeling again that I'm being watched, and something like primal instinct is whispering through my veins, telling me to get my ass back indoors. I find myself looking into the woods beyond the playground. In the darkness, it's difficult to see anything amongst the trees, but I can make something out in the shadows. A figure standing in the darkness. Watching. The night air is cool, but I'm suddenly sweating. I can hear the pounding of my own heartbeat in my ears.

Run. Run. *Run.*

My mind is screaming at me now, trying to shake me out of the trance.

"Jazmine." The sound of my name startles me and I can't help the scream that rips out of my mouth as I jump to my feet.

I look up to find the man from earlier that night standing in front of me. The man with those knowing eyes. I try to gather my senses, trying to make sense of the scene. My eyes dart back to the woods, but the figure is gone.

Was that figure in the forest this man? I can't be sure, but I doubt it, there's no way he could have made it here so quickly, and there was something distinctly different about that figure. Something I can't sense in this man in front of me. Still, the mixture of fear and panic doesn't recede. In fact, it only grows stronger, because what I'd seen before was only a shadow, perhaps only an imagined threat, but this man standing before me is very real.

"What the hell are you doing here?" I demand, backing away slowly.

If I turn and run, he can just grab me from behind. He may look like an old man, but something about him tells me that he doesn't move like one.

I'm suddenly aware of how alone we are out here and my gaze darts around in panic, trying to find anyone or anything that might save me from a potentially bad situation, but there's not a soul in sight and I'm completely alone in the darkness with this man.

"Wait—how do you even know my name?" I ask. He could have overheard it back at the diner, but I can't be sure.

The man is calm in contrast to my own panicked state.

"Sit, please." He gestures to the swing that I had just vacated. His voice is as gentle as it was back in the diner, but I'm not fooled.

"Listen, asshole, I don't know how you found me here, how you know my name or what you want, but if you don't get the hell away from me right this minute, I'm going to scream and call the cops." I realize as I say those last words, that I didn't bring my cell with me. *Dammit.*

Those strange grey eyes look unfazed by the threat, which only makes the sickening feeling in my gut worse.

"I'm not going to hurt you," the man says. I don't believe him.

"Bullshit."

"So you just happen to follow me from the diner, find me out here alone in the middle of the night and expect me to believe that you have nothing but honorable intentions?" I scoff, although I don't know why I'm still standing out here conversing with this total stranger, who is likely a rapist or deranged serial killer.

I decide that I need to distract him long enough to make an escape.

Something like sadness crosses the man's face.

"That's exactly what I expect you to believe—because it's the truth. I'm not here to hurt you," the man repeats. I still don't want to believe him, because no sane person would, but there's something about his expression that eases my panic a fraction.

"Then what do you want?" I demand, still continuing to inch away.

The man notices and lets out a long breath.

"My name is Magnus Evenstar," he says.

"And I'm your grandfather."

I don't think I heard him right, because that can't be true. I stare at him in disbelief.

"What?" I've stopped moving completely now. Shocked into stillness. Well, that's not what I was expecting. At all.

He doesn't say anything, letting me digest his words.

"You're not—you're not my grandfather. He's dead," I retort when I can speak again. Both of my mom's parents died before I was born.

"Your father was my son," the man replies.

I blink at him, taking in his appearance, that strange aura surrounding him, making my skin prickle.

I don't miss the word *was*.

"He's dead," I say flatly. I had always acted like my father was dead, but hearing it confirmed … I don't know how to feel.

"Yes, he died a few months ago." There's that sadness again.

"Let's say I do believe you, which I *don't*—what does it have to do with me?" I say then, narrowing my eyes at the man claiming to be my grandfather.

"It has everything to do with you," he replies.

"I want you to come with me."

Indignation shoots through me. Who the hell does this guy think he is?

"Excuse me?" I sputter.

"I'm here to take you away from this." He gestures to the trailer park in the distance.

"Listen, *Magnus*, I'm not going *anywhere* with you. You may think that I'm somehow related to you, but the only family that I had died when I was seven.

"My *father* was nothing but a deadbeat who wanted nothing to do with me or my mom, so I want nothing to do with him or his family."

"That's not true—your father did want you, but he …" He seems to be struggling to find the words or the right excuse. I don't care.

"He couldn't—it was forbidden".

Forbidden? I have no idea what the hell that means, but I'm not about to stick around to find out.

"Whatever. Thanks for the offer, but I'm fine where I am," I say, standing up a little straighter and meeting those grey eyes straight on.

It's a mistake. I feel that whisper of premonition again, like whatever it was that lay in the shadows, just beyond my reach, is now washing over me, suffocating me. It feels like I'm standing at the doorway to something so terrifying, that if I let myself step through the threshold, nothing will ever be the same again.

"Oh, really? You're fine with baring your body in order to survive? You're fine with this?" He gestures to the trailer park again and anger spikes through me.

"Screw you, asshole. You don't get to judge me or where I live. You don't know what I've been through, you have no idea what I've had to do to look after myself. Firstly, you can't just expect me to believe that you're my *long lost grandfather* without any proof—"

He cuts me off then.

"You want proof? I have more than enough—DNA tests and your birth certificate amongst them. You think I would risk coming here for the wrong person? No. There is no mistaking who you are."

I gape at him in shock. How the hell did he get hold of my DNA? And my *birth certificate*? I shake my head, sweeping those thoughts away. Never mind. It still doesn't change anything.

"I don't know what you'd risk doing—I don't know you, remember? You're a total stranger. Secondly, even if you *think* you have proof, you can't just waltz in here after seventeen years of *nothing*—no phone calls, no visits, not even so much as a birthday card and expect me to what? Come and live with you? Sorry, but you're about seventeen years too late. I'm not interested".

The calm expression flares into something like anguish.

"Your father only found out about you shortly before his death. He kept it a secret at first, and I only found out after his death."

I didn't think I'd care, but the words feel like needles in my chest.

"Of course, he did. A dirty little secret. Let me guess, he didn't want his perfect little family knowing about his little mistake?"

"There's so much you don't understand, Jazmine, so much you don't know. But I'm here to show you. It's taken me months to track you down and now that I've found you, I'm not leaving here without you".

I shoot him an incredulous look.

"Which part of *I'm not going with you*, didn't you understand? Let me say it again—*I'm not going anywhere with you*. So, you can leave now." I fix one of my most merciless glares at him. The one that makes most people pale under its intensity. But my uncanny violet-silver eyes don't seem to faze him at all.

"You have your father's eyes," he says wistfully, and I feel like scratching them out of my face.

I can't stand here for a second longer. I need to get the hell away from here. Now.

"Fine. Don't leave, stand there all night, if you want. I'll leave and if you even think about following me, I'll call the cops." I make the empty threat again.

I turn my back on him, and start walking away, but his next words stop me dead in my tracks.

"You need to come with me, Jazmine. It's not safe for you here anymore, Jazmine."

Not safe? What the hell?

He's lying, I tell myself. Why the hell should I believe a single word coming out of this guy's mouth and even if he is telling the truth, it doesn't change the fact that this man is still a stranger to me. A total stranger.

Leave. I order myself, but instead of getting the hell out of there, I open my mouth instead.

"What are you talking about?" My question is barely a whisper in the night, scared to hear the answer.

"You need to trust me".

Everything happens so quickly then, but at the same time, it feels like everything is moving in slow motion.

The man grabs my arm and before the scream working its way up my throat can rip out of my mouth, I'm being blown away by what feels like a hurricane. Only it isn't.

I can feel my eyes widen as the very air around me shifts, comes to life, crackling with fire and lightning. Then the atmosphere itself is *opening*. I'm out of my mind with fear, but through the haze of blind panic, I can see the endless expanse beyond the opening. The never-ending star-filled universe against a prism-like spectrum of colors. So many colors, so vivid, it's difficult to look at.

I can feel myself thrashing and kicking, but it's no use, this man is far stronger. He's pushing me into the opening and I can do nothing but let myself fall through it.

I'm flying then, flying through what feels like time and space, which is *crazy*. But it's difficult to keep a grip on reality when you're *flying through starlight and rainbows*. I can feel myself screaming, but the sound is lost in the vast expanse. Traveling at what feels like light-ning speed, I'm too paralyzed to be terrified. I'm beyond all thought and reason. After what feels like an eternity of falling, the universe stills and thankfully, I feel and see nothing.

3

I wake up to a crashing headache.

Am I hungover? No—I wasn't drinking last night. I was working at the diner.

The memories come flooding back. The man with the knowing eyes at the diner. The same man showing up at the playground near my trailer in the middle of the night, telling me that he's my grandfather—Magnus Evenstar, he'd called himself.

My eyes focus on my surroundings, but I can't make sense of it. I'm lying on a bed—not my cramped bed in the trailer, which is foster home number ten, but a huge ass bed with silk sheets and pillows that feel like clouds. If that isn't enough to convince me that I must be dreaming, the white marble floor and onyx walls definitely are. I jolt out of the bed and feel a wave of dizziness as I stand at the center of the palatial room. As I gape at the large onyx fireplace and the plush purple velvet furniture dotting the room, my confusion only grows.

Where the hell am I?

The scene outside the floor to ceiling French windows is of an impossibly blue sky, meeting an even bluer ocean. It's paradise. *Am I dead?*

A loud knocking at the large double doors makes me jump out of my skin. I look down at my attire to make sure I'm decent, only to find myself clothed in grey silk pajamas—sure as hell not mine. I don't own anything silk.

The man from the diner steps into the room.

"Where the hell am I?" I demand instantly, feeling both disoriented and furious.

"I told you I wanted you to come with me," Magnus replies simply in the infuriatingly calm tone.

"So you *kidnapped me?*" I'm shouting now and I don't give a shit who hears.

"Calm down, Jazmine. I can explain. We have a lot to talk about."

I stare at him in disbelief, I can feel my panic rising, but I stamp down on it, forcing my breaths to slow. I'll need to stay calm, if I'm going to have any chance of getting the hell out of here.

"Explain," I say through gritted teeth, although I have no interest in knowing. I just want to keep him distracted while I look for an escape route.

Magnus takes a deep breath then, before walking over to look out of one of the large windows. I keep my eyes trained on him the whole time, in case he tries to grab me again.

"In the beginning, there was Eden—I'm sure you're familiar with the story, like most humans are. But what humans do not know, is that Eden is real and it isn't just a garden, it's an entire world. It sits alongside Earth in another realm, running parallel alongside Earth, but never touching.

"Its inhabitants are the Seraph—the first beings to ever be created. We are mortal just like humans but unlike humans, we have the power to influence the elements, to control them. Every season, every raindrop, every gust of wind, the rising of the sun each morning and the painting of the night sky each night—it is by the hand of the Seraphs. Adam was once a Seraph until he fell from grace, was stripped of his powers and banished to Earth. From him, the human race was birthed. Humans know nothing of our true existence, though they have told tales about us throughout the ages, worshipped us through many guises. We are their gods, angels, higher beings, apparitions, deities. These are all just human interpretations of the Seraph.

"So, to answer your first question—you are in Eden, the royal city of Arcadia, to be precise."

Oh god, I've been kidnapped by a lunatic from a cult, and now he's going to kill me.

I don't know what I was expecting him to say, but it sure as hell wasn't this. All efforts at finding an exit fall away as my entire universe focuses on trying to process Magnus's words.

"What the hell are you talking about? I can't even ..."

I'm shaking my head in utter shock and denial. My mind can't even begin to fathom the meaning of his words. Because it's crazy. Nonsense. It has to be.

"You don't believe me," Magnus says flatly.

"No shit. Did you hear the crazy shit that just came out of your mouth? A world called Eden in *another realm*? Another race—the Seraph or whatever they're called that can *influence nature*? It sounds *insane*."

He seems displeased by my profanity. I don't give a shit.

What he does then, shuts me up entirely though. One minute he's standing with the morning sun encasing his solitary figure, the next, the daylight around him *disappears*. There are actual *shadows* seeping out of him, *swallowing the light*.

I back up frantically, stumbling as I go, and nearly landing on my ass.

Then as quickly as they had appeared, the shadows vanish again. Leaving only the daylight in their wake.

"What—what the hell was *that*?" I almost shout.

He turns to me, those knowing grey eyes taking in my flabbergasted expression.

"A demonstration of the power of the Seraph. I forget that humans will only believe what they see," he says.

"Except you're not human, Jazmine. At least not fully—your father was a Seraph, so that makes you half Seraph."

If I thought I was shocked before, it's nothing compared to what I'm feeling now.

"And not just any Seraph. The Dynasties are the ruling class of Eden—the strongest Seraph bloodlines. In the beginning, there were eight Dynasties, but after the fall of Adam and his Adonis Dynasty, seven remain. Of those seven Dynasties, the two most powerful Dynasties are known as the sovereign Dynasties, the two royal blood-lines—the St. Tristan Dynasty and the Evenstar Dynasty. The rule of Eden has always fallen to one of these two sovereign Dynasties and before your father died, he was the King."

He fixes his eyes on me.

"The blood that runs through your veins is the royal Evenstar blood which can be traced back to Eve herself. You are the heir of the Evenstar Dynasty, Jazmine. The last and only heir."

I let out a loud laugh, that sounds manic, even to my own ears, but what other reaction could I possibly have to those words?

"You're nuts," I choke out, once the laughter subsides. But there is no humor in Magnus's expression.

"You know what I'm saying is true."

I sober up then.

"No. I don't. What you're saying is *crazy*. I live in a *trailer*, for god's sake.

"You expect me to believe that my asshole of a father was a *King* and that I'm the *heir to his royal Dynasty*, next in line to the *throne* of a world which exists in an *alternative realm?*"

Magnus looks back at me calmly, although I feel like I'm losing my goddamn mind, no scratch that, I must have lost it already, because I'm still standing here, listening to this nonsense.

"When a King dies, the seven Dynasties rule together until the next sovereign heir comes of age to ascend to the throne. It is ... expected that the next in line to the throne will be the heir of the St. Tristan Dynasty."

"Oh, well *thank god for that*. Now, that we're clear that I'm not about to be the *next ruler of this alternative realm*, you're still expecting me to believe the rest of that bull? Well you've definitely got the wrong girl—because that *thing* that you just did? I can't do anything even remotely close to that."

"Oh, really? You've never looked up at the night sky and felt like you were connected to it somehow? Never felt like you could control the stars and moon with just a single sweep of your hand, if you just only reached out? You've never felt like you could touch the wind or feel the pulsing of the waves in the ocean?"

His words are like a punch to my gut. Because I can't deny the truth in them. It's as if he's pried open my mind, read my deepest thoughts and is reciting them back to me. I have never been so unnerved in my entire life.

"You may not know how to use them yet, but you do have these powers within you—it runs in your blood," he says.

"And if your foster home records are anything to go by, it would seem that you're far more aware of your powers than you'd like to admit," he adds.

My jaw drops, but at this stage, I don't even know why I'm so surprised that he's managed to get his hands on my foster home files. I shudder at the memories of my time at those first few foster homes. I'd been too young to make sense of the strange things stirring inside me. Too young to separate reality from what couldn't possibly be real and in my innocence, I hadn't yet learned how to hide those parts of myself that no one could ever accept, myself included. After the first few therapy sessions and foster home changes, I'd learned pretty damn quickly, though. I'd learned to accept that I didn't belong, but that I should never again let anyone see exactly why.

"All your life you've felt like you don't belong—not in any of your previous foster homes, not anywhere on Earth. You've always felt like there was something just waiting in the wings, dancing at the edge of your consciousness. Something that you can't grasp in your waking hours, but you know it's there."

I don't want to hear more, but with some kind of morbid fascination, I can't stop myself from listening. Because I'd been right about him. Those eyes see things, know things that no one in this entire universe should know.

He steps towards me, and I know I have to get the hell out of here, although I have no idea where I am. But I can't make my legs move.

"There's a reason why you've always felt like you didn't belong. It's because you didn't—you don't belong on Earth, Jazmine. You never will,"

"I don't know what you're talking about," I manage, but my voice sounds as shaken as I feel because right now, the entire universe feels like it's spinning—and everything I've ever thought I believed, everything I've ever thought I'd known, feels like it's being swept away in the storm.

"You've always wanted more than your life on earth could ever offer you. It's because you were made for something greater than a human life."

I can only stare at him in silence, not a single coherent thought left in me as he approaches.

"I'm sorry for all you've been through, Jazmine, all the loss, the loneliness, the years you felt like you had nothing and no one. I can't change that.

"Your father was sent to Earth on a mission and fell in love with a human while he was there—your mother, but he knew it couldn't be, because the law forbids it and your father had his duty to his Dynasty, to his throne. He knew that he would be the King of Eden and his people needed him. He didn't find out about you until just before his death. His dying wish was for you to be found and brought here to Eden, so that you can claim your rightful place as heir to the Evenstar Dynasty."

"What was his name?" I find myself asking, although every fiber in my being doesn't want to care.

"Arwen—your father's name was Arwen Evenstar."

There is another question echoing through my mind and again, I don't want to care. I bite the inside of my cheek to keep from speaking, but the words come out anyway, although I am sure I don't want to know the answer.

"How did he die?"

Magnus is silent for a long moment and the sadness that I glimpse in the depths of those grey eyes in that moment is so unending, that it makes it difficult to breathe.

"He committed suicide."

The words floor me and I want to know more, but something about Magnus's closed off expression tells me he already knows the questions I'm about to ask and the answers are not for me to know.

"Your father was a brave man, Jazmine. A good King," he says after a moment.

"I can't change the past, Jazmine. But I can change your future—you're an Evenstar now. You always have been and from now on, things are going to change. I promise you that."

I'm silent for what seems like an eternity.

"Let's say I believe you—do I get a choice in any of this? What if I don't want to live here in *Eden*. What if I don't want to be a Seraph, an Evenstar heir or whatever? What if I just want my life back?"

I feel the lie in those last words, because he'd been right earlier—I've always wanted more than my old life was able to give me. I was always searching for that *more*, although I never knew what it was—and now it's being revealed to me ... I feel like someone's placed the entire universe in the palm of my hand, and I have no clue what to do with it.

"You don't have a choice, Jazmine," came his simple reply, but before I can speak, he continues.

"It's not safe for you on Earth anymore."

I remember that he had spoken those same words to me in the playground.

"What do you mean, it's not safe for me on Earth?" I demand.

He only shakes his head and turns back to look out at the morning sky.

"There is so much that you don't know. So much that I can't tell you. Even the other Dynasties don't yet know about this threat and it must stay that way for now. But just know that I'm telling the truth."

"What the hell is that supposed to mean?" I feel my anger rising again.

He turns back to me.

"I know that after all you've been through, it's hard for you to trust people. But you can trust me, Jazmine. I'm your family, your blood. So, trust me when I tell you that Eden is the only place where you will be safe now."

He's right. It's not easy for me to trust people—and I sure as hell don't trust this total stranger who is claiming to be my long lost grandfather from another *realm*.

"Sorry, no deal," I snap back. The words feel harsh on my tongue, but I swat the misplaced guilt away. Seventeen years without a single word and now he shows up and wants to play happy family? Granted, he didn't know I even existed until a few months ago, but still. Then there's the fact that this man has, effectively, *kidnapped* me. He's telling me it's because it's not safe for me on Earth anymore, which in itself sounds insane, but added to that, he won't tell me why. Yeah, we aren't off to a great start here.

The image of the shadowed figure in the woods flashes through my mind. For a split second, I consider telling Magnus. But I sweep the thought away. In light of everything that's followed, the strange encounter seems even more surreal. From imagined threats to imagined worlds, I clearly haven't been thinking straight since I left the diner. I expect to wake up from this surreal nightmare any minute now.

"I'll take my chances on Earth. So, if you don't mind, I'd like to go back," I say instead.

Those eyes look sad again, but determination is mixed in with it.

"Well I'm afraid that's not going to be possible, Jazmine—you remember the way you came? That is also the only way back and this …" he says, holding up what looks like a key made of burnished gold, "is the only way a portal can be summoned.

"There are only seven keys—one for each Dynasty and the Dynasty heads are the only keepers."

I notice the symbol of a crescent moon engraved into the bow and I wonder what it means.

For a moment, I consider snatching the key and making a run for it. But after witnessing the shadows that Magnus seems to have on tap, I'm not that foolish. In any case, even if I am successful in my snatch and grab, I still have no idea how to use the damn key. A feeling of helplessness washes over me as I look out at the sweeping expanse of sea and sky.

I feel the irony of it all. Only a few hours ago, I'd been standing on the beach in Rockford Cape, thinking that today my life was about to change—and it has.

Ten years ago, on this day, my life was turned upside down when my mom was ripped from my world, and on the same day, ten years later, my life is being turned upside down again.

But this time, as much as I want to deny it, it feels like something is being given to me, *given back* to me, and I can only hope, but it feels like life is done taking things from me and maybe, just maybe, I can let myself live again.

4

(M)y first thought as I walk along the rocky shoreline is that everything is so much more beautiful here. The colors so vivid, they're almost alive or maybe it's just because *I* feel more alive in this place. It feels like whatever it was that had been lying dormant inside me, is now stirring and all the senses that I've long since learned to dull, are now coming alive.

I haven't entirely accepted the overwhelming truths that have just been revealed to me. I keep expecting to wake up back in my bed in that shit hole of a trailer, to find that all of this was nothing but a dream.

But it never happens and something inside me is resigned to my fate. At least until I can get my hands on one of those keys, figure out a way to open up one of those portals and go back.

But back to what? I ask myself. Back to the life that I hated? Back to the trailer park? Back to my friendless high school existence? Back to serving greasy meals and alcohol, wearing practically nothing but my underwear, to perverted, just to make a few dollars? As much as I hate to admit it, there isn't anything for me to go back for. It's a sad thought, because it's basically the same as saying that up until now, my life has been utterly meaningless and that *I have nothing to live for.*

I try to sweep the dark thoughts from my mind as I look out at the water. The sea has always been beautiful to me, and I've always loved the coastline, but the scene here is like no other I've ever seen. It's wondrous, breathtaking, almost surreal. I itch to capture the scene with the stroke of my paintbrush, and with my artist's eye, I can see the colors blending together to make up the picturesque scene.

From this viewpoint, I can see that Arcadia is an island surrounded by a cluster of other smaller islands. I can see what seems like the smallest of the islands in the distance. A mountainous isle surrounded by sandy shores with a large cluster of regal looking buildings sitting atop the highest plateau. I wonder what it is.

Magnus had told me earlier that Arcadia is the royal city. Looking up at the structures atop the mountains behind me, I can see why.

Two large palaces fill the horizon—the one that I'm standing closest to, and also the one that I had woken up in earlier, is the Evenstar palace as Magnus had told me. Then there's another palace gleaming pure gold in the distance, which Magnus had said is the St. Tristan palace. There are other large manors and mansions in between, five of them, to be precise. Each one as impressive as the next.

The afternoon sun is blazing high in the clear blue sky and I tilt my face up to feel the heat of the sun against my cheeks, closing my eyes for a moment.

It's then that I feel someone watching. I open my eyes to see what I think at first is a flare of sunlight atop one of the ledges overlooking the shore where I'm standing. I squint my eyes against the white light and as it fades, I can make out a figure—a very tall and broad shouldered figure against the daylight. I feel the breath catching in my throat because even from this distance, I can see the face looking down at me, and it is the most beautiful face I've ever seen. Handsome is too weak a word.

His perfectly chiseled features could've been carved from the stone that he's standing on and his lips are sensual in contrast. Ash blonde hair gleams in the sunlight, forming a halo around that stunningly beautiful face. I find myself thinking that this is how the human stories about angels must have started, because this guy looks exactly how I think an angel might. Except in place of angelic white robes, this guy is wearing faded jeans and a white t-shirt, which accentuates his powerfully muscled body. The sight is surreal—he looks like a guy around my age but of course, I know he's no normal guy. He's a Seraph. Effectively, a *god*.

I notice his eyes then. Even from this distance, I can see that they're blue. But not just any blue—a shade of blue as endless as the sky above me, so vivid, that it's difficult to look at for too long without feeling disoriented. I can feel myself burning under the intensity of those eyes as they look at me, look into me, travel the length of me, leaving a trail of fire in their wake.

There is something uncanny about those eyes. I wonder what they look like up close. I find myself thinking that it's the same thing that people thought about my own eyes. I find myself having to blink a few times, partly because I can't quite figure out whether what I'm seeing is real, but also because looking at that face is like looking directly at the sun—you can't do it for too long without being dazzled by the intensity of its beauty.

I can tell nothing from this guy's expression. It's totally shuttered, like a stone wall. I catch a fleeting look of something indecipherable in the depths of those uncanny eyes, but it's gone before I can even blink.

Time seems to stop as I stand there staring at him. He has such a strange effect on me—I feel like I've been sleep walking up until now. Looking at him is like waking up.

A split second later, there's another flash of blinding light and when the light clears, the figure is gone.

What the hell was that? I think to myself, once my sanity returns and I'm capable of thinking again. I convince myself that I must have just imagined it—nothing more than a figment of my already crazed mind. But I can't shake the feeling that the image has already been burned into my mind, never to be erased.

~

"**You** look wonderful, Jazmine." I can hear the twinge of pride in Magnus's voice as he looks me over.

"I feel ridiculous," I grumble in response, although it isn't entirely true. I can't deny that when I looked in large floor to ceiling mirror earlier, in what is now my bedroom, even I couldn't help but be stunned by what I saw. I hardly ever wear makeup but the beauticians that Magnus had forced on me earlier this evening have worked their magic to bring out the angle of my cheekbones with a light blush and the fullness of my lips with a rose-colored stain. Dark eyeshadow lines my eyes and my already thick lashes look even darker. Even my eyes somehow look less unnerving or maybe it's because the vivid violet with the startling silver rings isn't so out of place in this world of equally vivid colors and uncanny beauty.

Then there's the dress—even I can't help but appreciate how utterly beautiful this dress is. The violet fabric is rich and finely made, hand tailored, no doubt. It's elegantly cut and clings to my curves in all the right places. The back is cut low, leaving the skin at my back exposed, shielded only by the sparkling gossamer fabric trailing from the shoulder straps of the dress. I don't think I've ever owned a dress other than when I was a little kid, let alone an evening dress like this.

I don't know how money works out here in Eden, but I have no doubt that this dress likely cost ten times more than all my belongings put together—not that I have many belongings, or any at all, now that I've had to leave it all behind. I'm glad that I was clutching my mom's tin when I was pushed into that portal. Everything else can be replaced, but not that, never that.

"I don't feel comfortable wearing this dress—it's not mine," I say.

Magnus just shakes his head in response, as he leads me through the cavernous marble halls. This place is like nothing I've ever laid eyes on before and I can feel myself gaping at my surroundings.

"It is yours—everything in that dressing room that I had stocked for you, is yours. All of this that you see before you, is rightfully yours.

Because as I said before, Jazmine, you are the heir to the Evenstar Dynasty."

I shake my head in disbelief. The same disbelief I'd felt earlier when I walked into the dressing room which adjoined the palatial room that is now my bedroom. There were endless rows of clothes, shoes, bags and jewelry. Something occurs to me then.

"The clothes—they look like things that humans would wear … you know on Earth."

Magnus shoots me an amused look.

"What were you expecting?"

"I don't know, space suits? Togas? Victorian dresses? Animal skins?" How the hell am I supposed to know? I'm clearly new to this whole world or realm or whatever. But the last thing I expected was to find a walk-in closet full of fashionable clothes. I find myself thinking about the guy I'd seen on the beach earlier. He was wearing normal clothes, too, although of course, that was about the only thing about him that was normal.

I notice Magnus's own outfit then—a finely made tux with a midnight blue sash running from his shoulder to his waist and various insignia pinned to his lapel. He carries himself with a quiet elegance which belongs to some dashing senator or president even. Definitely not what I'd have expected my grandfather to be like, if that's really what he is. I would have expected him to be more like a grumpy old man, smoking a pipe and sitting in a rocking chair in the corner. Total cliché, I know. But clearly, my expectations of life and what now appears to be my reality, are completely out of sync.

"Like I said before, Eden sits parallel alongside Earth—in many ways, it is a mirror of it. You will find that there are many similarities between the two worlds. Of course, we have these grand palaces and opulent balls, but you will find similar things amongst the royals on Earth, too."

"Yeah, sure. Because I've spent lots of time with royalty on Earth," I say, rolling my eyes.

"Well, you are royalty here, Jazmine."

The words were difficult to digest. Because how can I be?

Yesterday I was living in a trailer—a real nothing and no one, and today I'm living in a palace, being told that I'm the heir to one of the sovereign Dynasties of another world, in an alternative realm. It's not exactly easy to take in.

The realization of how surreal all of this is, threatens to drown me in that moment and I feel like I'm going to be sick.

Magnus notices my expression.

"You'll get used to it. In time, and I hope you'll grow to like it here. It's where you belong."

The sane part of me still refuses to accept that any of this is even true. I mean who's to say that this man didn't just pick me out randomly and kidnap me under the guise of being my long lost grandfather? That sounds like the most likely explanation. But not when he knows things about me, about my thoughts, the things that lay dormant inside me, that no one in this entire universe could possibly know.

Then, of course, there was the fact that he happens to be in possession of a conclusive DNA test. He'd shown it to me earlier and it looked genuine enough, apparently issued by the hospital lab in Brockton itself. But how am I meant to know for sure that it's not some forgery? The birth certificate would have been easy enough to get a copy of, too, if he knew what he was looking for. But who would go to all that effort for a nothing and no one like me? An orphan with no past and no future? The doubts rage in my mind, but I'm reminded that none of it even matters, I'm stuck in this place regardless. At least for now.

Then, as if reading my thoughts, or maybe my expression is just that transparent, Magnus's gaze lands on me.

"If you're still in doubt about your lineage, then maybe this will help ease your mind."

At the exact same time as he says those words, we pass by a large, gold framed painting, the sight of which makes me stop in my tracks.

The portrait is of a king. But not just any king. I know, even without being told who that man in the portrait is, with the dark hair and gentle features. I know, because just as Magnus had said before, this man has *my* eyes. The freakish violet color with the uncanny silver rings which I know no one else in this entire universe could possibly possess. Looking at those eyes staring back at me from the portrait, is like looking in the mirror and I feel chills racing down my spine at the very sight.

I examine the skillfully painted portrait for what seems like an eternity, my eyes taking in the crown of sapphires atop the man's dark hair, the midnight blue velvet cape draped on one side of his tall frame. But even without those symbols of royalty, even through the painting, the air of authority that I can feel radiating from this man's face, is unmistakeable. There's a sadness in those features, too. A loneliness. Some part of me wonders that if, perhaps, for as long as I had been alone, he had been, too.

But I say nothing and when I'm able to move again, I turn away from that face and continue to walk in silence.

Something occurs to me then.

"Were you the King before …" I can't bring myself to call the man I never knew, my father. But Magnus seems to understand.

"No. the rule of Eden didn't fall upon me in my generation," he replies.

We reach another hall then, as vast as all the others. But instead of white and black marble, every inch is covered with intricate murals—richly colored and startlingly life-like. The hall is so large, that I imagine it would take months to examine every depiction. As if drawn, I walk up to one of the walls and run my fingertips over the cool surface.

"Ah yes, while trying to track you down, I learned that you are a very talented artist. You'll appreciate these murals."

"I inherited my mom's talent." I reply, semi-distracted, as I peer up at the masterful mural.

"What are these?" I ask, as I continue to stare.

"These murals depict the history of Eden, going back to the beginning of time itself. I believe that recreations can be found in some of the grandest Cathedrals on Earth, but these are the originals."

Magnus gestures to the image of a beautiful landscape. The tumultuous scene is so real, that I can almost feel myself being immersed in the spectrum of elements portrayed.

The landscape begins with the image of night. The blanket of stars and the lone moon almost glow against the backdrop of the midnight sky. The night turns into a storm as lightning rages through the frozen landscape with snow topped mountains shooting up into the dark grey sky.

The harsh landscape gives way to a raging sea, as the storm turns into a tempest. The landscape changes then. The sky remains overcast, but the dark green waves give way to a windswept scene with autumn leaves sweeping through the brown and gold landscape. Autumn turns to spring, as roses bloom amidst the lush green hills and sparkling lakes.

The last scene is the total opposite of the first. In place of night and winter, the scene is of clear blue skies and summer. The sun gleams in the impossibly blue sky, encasing everything with its golden light.

"This landscape represents the full spectrum of the powers of the Seraph. All Seraphs can influence the elements with varying abilities, but as I said before, the members of the seven Dynasties are the most powerful.

"The sovereign Evenstar bloodline rules over the night with the moon and stars as our allies. This is why you feel such a connection to the night. The Aspen Dynasty has its strength in winter and ice, the Aldebran Dynasty in storm and sea. Then there is autumn, which is the domain of the Oaknorth Dynasty, and spring which belongs to the Hemlock Dynasty. The last two Dynasties have always been the closest of allies—the Delphine Dynasty who rule summer, and finally the St. Tristan Dynasty, the other sovereign Dynasty, which lords over the sun and daylight.

"Whilst the members of each Dynasty have the inherent ability to influence all elements, each Dynasty has a particular affinity to a particular set of elements and seasons. The exception is, of course, daylight and night, which are the two most potent powers. Only the St. Tristan Dynasty can summon and influence daylight and only the

Evenstar Dynasty can influence and summon night. These two sovereign Dynasties have always been the furthest apart in their powers."

I struggle to keep up as Magnus condenses what seems like the legacy of an entire race into a five-minute explanation and I can't help but feel overwhelmed.

I come across a section which looks like a scene of darkness and bloodshed. I can almost feel the tragedy emanating from the deep colors and the painting of a naked male figure falling into what looks like a never-ending abyss.

"This is the depiction of the fall of Adam and the banishment of his Dynasty—the Adonis Dynasty."

"The story of Adam and Eve being banished because they had sex?" I ask.

Magnus shoots me a look.

Right. I forget that I'm talking to someone who is meant to be my grandfather. Talking about sex probably isn't appropriate.

I feel puzzled as I stare at the scene, because it doesn't depict that at all. Something occurs to me—in the stories that I'd heard as a child, both Adam and Eve fell, but Magnus had only spoken of Adam falling and that the Evenstar bloodline could be traced directly back to Eve herself.

"The human stories are wrong about the fall. Adam and Eve loved each other, this is true. But Adam became obsessed with power—he wanted to usurp the Evenstar bloodline, take the power for his own. Seeing his evil intentions, the seven Dynasties banished Adam and the Adonis Dynasty to Earth, stripping them of all power."

A shudder runs through me as my eyes travel over the scene one last time before turning away.

Magnus continues to walk and I follow.

"Tell me again about what the hell this ceremony is about?" I ask, as we approach what looks like the center of the palace. I don't know why I care, seeing as, for the most part, I still fully intend on getting out of here the first chance I get. But I figure that I might as well be prepared for whatever I'm about to get myself into.

"It is a ceremony to present you as the heir of the Evenstar Dynasty to the other six Dynasties."

"Is this absolutely necessary?" I ask, unable to hide my lack of enthusiasm.

Magnus shoots me a firm look. "Yes. It is. You will find that the Dynasties have many traditions, all of them are of great importance in keeping the order here on Eden. The people depend on us to lead. These are your traditions now, Jazmine, your people."

I don't agree with him, but I don't see the point in arguing, so instead I ask, "What exactly are you expecting me to do?"

"The heir of each Dynasty will be presented to you by the head of their respective Dynasty. Each heir will then pay their respects to you —all you have to do is stand. You can manage that, right?" Magnus replies dryly.

He gives me a second glance.

"And try not to swear."

I crack a smile, despite myself.

"Nope. Sorry, can't promise that."

$\mathcal{W}$e reach the top of a large marble staircase and I feel anxiety prickling through me. From this viewpoint, I can see the vast hall before me, filled to the rafters with unfamiliar faces. Every one of those faces turn towards me and I can feel myself bristle in discomfort. I hate being the center of attention and suddenly, I'm wishing that I can open one of those portals right this minute and disappear back to Earth. Suddenly, my pitiful excuse for a life there seems a thousand times better than what I'm about to get myself into. If the reality of the situation hasn't fully sank in before, it does now. I'm way out of my depth here.

Magnus notices my rigidity and takes my arm gently. I jump at the touch, because I'm not used to being touched. Not at all.

"It's going to be fine, Jazmine." I don't want to feel any reassurance from his words, but the calm in his voice is contagious and I can feel my own breath slowing. *Breathe. Just Breathe.* I tell myself.

Magnus leads me down the sweeping marble staircase and I can feel my every move being watched. The silence is deafening.

The walk down the red carpeted aisle to the large platform at the other end of the vast hall feels like the longest distance that I've ever walked in my entire life. But I make it there. I put steel in my spine as I hold my head up and look out at the crowd. I decide right then and there, that as out of my depth as I may feel, I can do this. This is nothing compared to what I've been through. If I can withstand being ogled by a room full of sleazy men as I serve them wearing practically nothing but my underwear, then standing in front of this crowd in this finely-made gown, should be a walk in the park. *I can do this.*

My gaze sweeps over the front row and I can identify what appear to be the heads of the other six Dynasties easily. The finely made clothing and aura of authority is difficult to miss. Their expressions are neutral, but I can sense the quiet scrutiny. As if every breath that I take is being watched, observed.

My gaze falters, as it lands on what I assume are the six Dynasty heirs. They all seem to be around my age, but the way that they carry themselves, and the air of confidence surrounding them, is like nothing I've ever seen. I also notice that each one of them is impossibly good looking. They belong on the cover of a fashion magazine or on screen in the latest teen blockbuster. People like this don't exist in real life. Normal people don't look like this.

But I remind myself that there is nothing *normal* about these people. They are the heirs to the six Seraph Dynasties. Royalty. Gods. The air of entitlement surrounding them, tells me that each one of them is very much aware of this status, too. If Magnus is expecting me to be anything like these brats, then he's going to be sorely disappointed—I'm about as different from these people as the trailer, which was foster home number ten, is from this grand palace.

My gaze travels from one face to the next. The girl standing closest to me has dark hair like mine, but it's cropped short in a sharp angled bob cut and there are blue streaks throughout. Her face is pixie-like, much like the rest of her petite frame, but the scowl that mars her pretty face, tells me that this girl is anything but delicate. Her grey eyes look back at me in a mixture of boredom and annoyance. I feel myself bristling in response.

The next face belongs to a guy with dark brown hair and bright aquamarine eyes, who can only really be described as utterly gorgeous. The eye color is so strange, that it takes me a moment to peg down the shade. He's tall, and even in his tux, I can see that he's well built. I narrow my eyes as I notice the not so subtle way that those eyes sweep over my body. He makes a point of letting his gaze linger on my chest before flashing me a cocky grin. It doesn't take a genius to figure out that this guy is a Grade A creep. But that handsome face probably means that girls around here still fall all over themselves to get a piece of this jerk.

The guy next to him is equally handsome. His hair is also brown but my artist's eye sees the threads of deep red and burgundy mixed in with the dark mahogany. He's also tall, but his build is leaner, although no less toned. His vibrant amber eyes are just as bored as the first girl's, but they turn thoughtful for a moment as they look back at me before reverting back to disinterest.

In keeping with the theme, the next girl is also startlingly gorgeous. Her light brown hair is set in perfect waves and her make up is immaculate, although I can see that she would be equally beautiful without it. Clearly, she doesn't think very much of me, though, because the disapproval is clear in those light hazel eyes as they regard me. She turns her nose up and whispers something to the girl beside her, which I'm certain is not a compliment. I feel my cheeks flaming, but I don't allow myself to drop my gaze.

The other girl lets out a low chuckle and when my eyes shift to her, I find myself looking at possibly the most stunning girl I have ever seen. Her bright blonde hair, cascading in a silky curtain down her back and her emerald green eyes belong to a model. As does her tall, slim figure. The rose-colored dress with the gold accents is possibly the most beautiful dress that I've ever seen or maybe it's just the way this girl wears it that makes me think that. Everything about this girl screams perfection. But what's also clear, is that this girl sure as hell knows it. The scathing look that she gives me is harsh enough to shred rainbows, and I instinctively return the look with a merciless one of my own. I don't know this girl, but I sure as hell won't let her give me the look of death without returning the favor.

I notice then that there's an empty spot next to the girl. I eye the empty spot curiously, but not for long, because the curiosity is replaced with *utter shock* when my gaze lands on the tall figure walking in from the wings.

My brain processes the scene at a frustratingly slow pace.

That golden blond hair, the uncanny blue eyes and that impossibly beautiful face. Handsome is too weak a word. That tall and powerfully muscled frame looked good in faded jeans and a white t-shirt, but in a dark tux, he is utterly devastating. The way that he carries himself, makes it seem like the tux was tailor made for him. It probably was. He moves with such elegance, that it's difficult not to watch him.

The guy from the beach, who also happens to be the most beautiful guy I think I've ever seen, looks back at me, those vivid blue eyes locking onto mine. His expression is cool, assessing, and just like on the beach, I can feel my skin burn under that gaze. But other than that, his face is as closed off as when I saw it last.

He stops when he reaches the empty spot beside the model-perfect blonde girl and stands beside her. I don't miss the way she loops her arm around his, although I'm not sure why I'm surprised or why I care. Of course. The laws of science and of the universe itself dictate that these two perfect specimens would be drawn to each other. Nothing would make sense otherwise.

I snap to attention as Magnus begins calling up each heir to the platform.

The girl with the short black hair is first and Magnus announces her as Keller Aspen, heir to the Aspen Dynasty. Next is the heir to the Aldebran Dynasty, Baron Aldebran, who is the dark haired guy with the aquamarine eyes. The second guy with the reddish brown hair is Lance Oaknorth, heir to the Oaknorth Dynasty. The girl with the light brown waves and impeccable make-up is Ivy Hemlock, heir to the Hemlock Dynasty.

I suffer through it all with a smile which is as rehearsed as the one I paint on for the patrons of Rodeo Ricky's but far, far more difficult to maintain. Because although each heir dutifully bows in greeting, they each make it subtly clear that I'm not welcome. Not here on this planet, not here in their royal world of riches and privilege. I didn't expect them to go as far as rolling out the welcome wagon, but their clear disapproval is surprising. Not least because I don't even know these people, and they sure as hell don't know me.

The perfect blonde is the most scathing of them all. I didn't think it was even possible to smile courteously at someone and make them feel like you want to scratch out their eyes at the same time. But Layla Delphine, heir to the Delphine Dynasty, manages it perfectly.

The guy from the beach is as courteous as the rest, when it's his turn to greet me, but those vivid blue eyes are like glaciers as they regard me. Much like the rest of his icy demeanor. When Magnus announces his name, I think it's ironic that the heir to the sovereign Dynasty that lords over the sun and daylight, is in fact, colder than the harshest winter night. Raphael St. Tristan, heir to the sovereign St. Tristan Dynasty, and if Magnus was correct earlier, next in line to the throne of Eden.

I'm grateful when it's all over, although not so grateful when Magnus carts me around to meet countless other 'nobles,' as he calls them, during the evening reception which follows the ceremony.

"The Dynasties have always kept our houses small in order to preserve the potency of our bloodlines," Magus explains to me as he maneuvers around the groups of nobles littered throughout the vast hall.

"There is only ever one heir of each Dynasty in each generation, this is to prevent infighting within a Dynasty and it is why the heirs to each Dynasty are so important."

I roll my eyes at that. No wonder those over privileged brats act like they're so damn special. Any doubt left in me as to whether I should get the hell out of this place as soon as I possibly can, is obliterated by the thought that these spoiled pricks will one day rule this entire goddamn planet. No, this is not the place for me. Not at all.

"Within the Evenstar Dynasty, as I said before, you are the last and only heir. My wife, your grandmother, died in childbirth and your father was my only child. You do have distant relatives within the Evenstar Dynasty, though."

With that, he proceeds to introduce me to some of those distant relatives. It feels so alien to me—going from having no family whatsoever, to being introduced to a whole host of supposed distant relatives, who seem to know all about me, although I have no idea who the hell they are.

He moves on to introduce me to other nobles outside the Evenstar Dynasty and I can't keep up with all of the names and faces. But I don't miss the way that they all look at me—like I'm a new species of insect that's just been discovered. Interesting, but beneath them all the same.

A few people express their condolences at the death of my father, which I find bizarre, because they must all know that I didn't even know him. I also get the feeling that although the words seem sincere enough, they are not entirely genuine. There's a hint of something like disgrace hidden in the words, because although I've only just walked into this world, even I can gather that a king who commits suicide must be a pretty scandalous thing. For about the hundredth time since I was hauled onto this planet, I wonder what the hell I've gotten myself into.

I manage to slip away when Magnus gets called over by one of the other Dynasty heads who I recognize from the ceremony as the head of the Aspen Dynasty. I can see where the scowling girl gets her looks from, because her mother is equally striking.

My steps are hurried and I keep my head down, as I make my way to the nearest exit, until I find myself standing on one of the large balconies which flank the vast hall. I tilt my face up to the night sky for a moment. The blanket of starlight twinkles against the midnight blue sky and the crescent moon reflects off the equally dark waters. I'm grateful for the cool night air, and the stillness of the night. As always, it has a calming effect on me.

The calm doesn't last long though, as I sense someone approach. I turn away from the peaceful night scene and find myself face to face with the guy who can only be described as the personification of daylight. Even in the darkness, he glows with some ethereal light. As if he carries the sun with him wherever he goes.

I realize that I had been hoping that the image of perfection that

I'd seen on the beach would turn out to be too good to be true. That up close, I'd see that he isn't, in fact, the most beautiful person I've ever laid my eyes on. But I'm sorely disappointed, because this guy is just as beautiful up close as he was from afar, even more so. He's the kind of guy that could break hearts with just one look. I notice the little details that make his perfect face even more devastating—the sexy indent on his top lip, the even sexier dimple on his chin and his impossibly long golden lashes, so thick, that it's sinful. I find myself thinking again that he looks exactly like an angel might.

But when he opens his mouth to speak, that image is quickly banished.

"You don't belong here." His harsh tone is as cutting as his words.

My initial surprise quickly fades and I return his icy glare with one of my own.

"Oh, yeah? Says who?" I say, although in the back of my mind, I'm sure that I agree with him. I *don't* belong here. I knew it from the first moment I stepped foot on this planet and the less than welcoming ceremony only reinforced that fact.

"Says *me*."

I didn't pick up on his arrogance earlier, but I don't know how I could've missed it now. Everything about him screams privilege and wealth and the way he carries himself makes it clear that he is well aware of it. This guy has an entire world at his feet, and when he speaks, it's with the authority of a crown that's his by birthright.

Because I know it'll infuriate an arrogant prick like him, I say, "And sorry, who are you again?" I'm pleased with the cool disinterest in my tone.

Those sensuous lips twist in a mocking smile as he takes a step closer, disrupting the air around me.

"Oh, I think you know who I am, *Jaz*."

"Jazmine," I correct him.

He pretends to think something over.

"Naah. Too many syllables for someone so insignificant. It's a waste of breath. I think I'll call you *Jaz*."

The insult stings and I can feel the swell of indignation in response.

"And *I* think I'll call you *a fucking bastard.*"

I see the surprise flare in those piercing blue eyes. I expect him to be offended but he seems ... oddly fascinated instead. He's probably never been insulted before in his life. Probably used to girls just throwing themselves at his feet and is expecting me to follow suit. Well, he has another think coming.

He cocks his head to the side as he regards me.

"No. that would be you—you're the bastard here, remember?"

The indignation turns into white hot rage at his words. This guy may have the face of an angel, but he has the mouth of the *fucking devil*. It figures that someone so hot would be such an asshole. It only makes perfect sense. I guess I hadn't been wrong about what I hoped I'd find up close after all—because his face may be even more beautiful up close, but his personality certainly isn't. This guy is the biggest asshole I've ever met in my entire life. Some part of me is glad. Because if he hadn't turned out to be such a bastard, I'm pretty sure that I'd be in trouble.

"*Fuck you,* asshole," I hiss, giving him a look that could kill birds in mid-flight.

His eyes travel the length of me and I'm suddenly aware of his closeness. His scent engulfs me, making me think of citrus and cool winter mornings. My traitorous body responds to him on an almost primal level, which surprises the hell out of me, because I haven't even so much as looked twice at a guy before, regardless of how good looking.

But there is something about this guy that makes me feel like my body has a mind of its own, something about him that makes me feel like the whole room, hell, the entire universe disappears in his presence, leaving only me and him in the vastness of time and space.

The smirk on that impossibly beautiful face tells me that he is well aware of the effect that he has on me.

"Are you offering to *fuck* me, Jaz?"

I think my jaw hits the floor at the outrageous question. Then I throw my head back and let out a harsh laugh. *Is he being serious?*

When I turn back to him, he looks far from amused. In fact, he looks pissed.

"I'd rather *swallow glass* than go anywhere near you."

His gaze rests on my neck where my pulse is fluttering just beneath the surface, and he flashes me another arrogant smirk.

"You sure about that, Jaz?"

"Hmmm. Let me think." I tilt my head to the side, and narrow my eyes before looking at him straight on.

"Yeah, pretty damn sure." I meet his gaze unflinchingly, although it's a struggle to keep eye contact when those impossibly blue eyes make me feel like I'm *falling through the sky* if I let myself look into them for too long.

"I think you're a liar."

"And I think you're *delusional.*"

"Because you're new here, I'll let you insult me this one time. *Once.* But let me get one thing straight, Jaz—around here, *I* run shit. One word from me and I can make your life a living hell. This is my planet, my world—and *you don't belong here.*"

His words are like a slap to the face, but I school my expression into staying blank.

"And let *me* get one thing straight, *you spoiled prick*—I don't give a *shit* who you are, I'll talk to you however I want. I didn't choose to come here. I was *kidnapped* and now I have no other choice but to stay. But just because I have to be here, doesn't mean I'm going to put up with threats from a spoiled asshole like you. You have no idea what I've been through or who I am. You want to make my life a living hell? Go ahead. I've been there, done that."

Something flickers in the depths of those vivid blue eyes just then, and his gaze seems to falter for a moment. But he recovers quickly, flashing me a cold smile.

"Watch yourself, Jaz, you're not in the trailer park anymore."

I'm not sure how the hell he knows about foster home number ten, and I don't even want to think about what else he knows. I make sure that my expression betrays nothing.

"Wow. So, not only are you a total dickhead, you're stalking me, too."

He bares his teeth in what would be a smile, if it didn't look so menacing.

"Don't flatter yourself, baby."

I almost gag in response.

"Urgh, trust me, there is *nothing* flattering about the thought of an ass-wipe like you stalking me. In fact, the thought gives me nightmares."

He narrows his eyes at the insult and I can feel the venom in his gaze. But there's no way I'm going to let this asshole intimidate me.

"You don't know what you're messing with, Jaz. This world may seem beautiful, but you have *no idea*."

"No—*you* have no idea. If you think you can just threaten me and bark orders at me, then expect me to roll over and obey, you're in for a surprise, you *royal asshole*. I'm not sure how things work around here in *Eden*, but where I come from, you can't just treat people like shit for no reason at all."

"That's because you come from the *gutter*," he replies and I want to wipe that arrogant smirk off his face. The rage inside me builds to an almost frightening level.

But I force myself to calm. He's goading me and for whatever reason, he wants me to lose it. But I won't give him the satisfaction.

"Yeah? Well, I'm here now and I'm not going anywhere, so you might as well get used to it." I'm impressed at the coldness in my own voice, although I have no idea why I'm even saying these words. I don't have any other choice but to be here right now, but, it sure as hell doesn't mean that I've permanently resigned myself to my fate. I don't let any of that show, though, my face a perfect mask of stone.

"You can start by welcoming me to Eden," I add sarcastically, mirroring his earlier arrogant smirk. Take that. Asshole.

My words seem to have the desired effect. His eyes blaze like twin flames. He thrusts his face close to mine, and I make to shove him away, but he grabs my hands to stop me. I don't miss the way my skin burns under his touch, and it makes me even angrier.

"Just stay the hell out of my way, Jaz, or I swear to God, I'm gonna *break you.*" The words are less of a threat than they are a warning, a premonition. But they're unnecessary, because I have no interest in going anywhere near this asshole.

He drops my hands, all but throwing them back at me and stalks off, leaving me to stare after him in utter shock.

I let out a breath I didn't even realize I was holding. But the relief is short lived, as he stops in mid stride and turns back to look at me one more time.

"Oh and, Jaz?" he says, although not waiting for a response.

"Welcome to Eden."

His eyes are as dark as the midnight blue sky above us, and what I see in them makes it clear that I'm far from welcome here.

6

"Hell. No." I cross my arms over my chest as I glare at Magnus.

"You need to finish your senior year, Jazmine," Magnus replies firmly. I'm starting to think that he has something to do with my own stubborn streak.

"And I'm all for that, but I'm not going to a *boarding school*."

I don't know what I surprises me more—the fact that they have boarding schools here in Eden, or the fact that Magnus is telling me that the educational system is practically identical and that my high school credits would count here. I can't even begin to figure out how that works.

Magnus lets out an exasperated sigh. I kind of feel sorry for him— he's clearly never had to deal with raising a teenage girl before. He's going to have some hard lessons to learn. I automatically scold myself for the thought, because I'm not actually thinking about sticking around here, am I? Especially not after the welcome that I received last night from his royal prick highness.

"Like I said, the Dynasty heirs have *always* attended Regency

Mount Academy. It is tradition. Your father went there, I went there and then my father before me and so on.

"It's the most prestigious boarding school on the entire planet. You'll get the best education there. They also have a first-rate art program, which is perfect for a talented artist like yourself."

"I still don't get it—so the subjects are just like a normal high school? No, I don't know, spellcasting, potion making or levitation lessons?"

Magnus lets out a chuckle then.

"I think you watch too many films. There is no such thing as witches and warlocks, Jazmine."

"Right. Of course. Because there *are* beings called the Seraph which exist in an alternative realm but it's ridiculous of me to even consider that witches and warlocks exist."

"And to answer your question, yes—the subjects are the same as what you'd expect to find in a normal high school on Earth. However, there are *some* differences. Most notably, elements class."

"Elements class?" I ask, as I take a sip of my coffee. We're having breakfast in one of the many palace gardens and I can't get over how beautiful my surroundings are. The ornamental gardens, with the picture perfect rose bushes, the white and black marble terraces, even the fine china on the marble table and the butler serving us; it's a scene right out of a fairy tale.

"Elements class is where students learn how to use their powers."

That response makes me bolt upright in my chair.

"What? But *I don't have any powers*—I told you this before."

Magnus looks frustrated again.

"Yes, and I told you before that you do have them, you just don't know how to use them yet. You'll be behind at first, of course, but the teachers have been made aware and you'll catch up in time, no doubt."

I cover my face with my hands and groan, although I really feel like screaming.

～

*T*hat evening, I find myself in the back of a limousine being driven to what is going to be my new boarding school. Two things strike me as totally surreal in that sentence. The first is that I'm in an actual limousine—I don't think I've ever even seen one in real life before, let alone been in one. Second, I'm going to be attending a *boarding school*.

All ten of the schools that I'd attended had been public. I can remember that there had been a prep school in the same town as foster home number eight, and the kids I'd seen around town who attended it were insufferable—rich brats who wore fancy clothes and drove around town in their even fancier cars. I have a feeling that this boarding school is going to be ten times worse.

But I don't bother to argue anymore. Magnus made it clear around half an hour into the drive, that it isn't going to make any difference. So, I sit in silence and stare out of the tinted window instead.

Despite my mood, even I can't deny how scenic the route is. The limousine crosses one of the many bridges which connect Arcadia to the neighboring islands. I realize that we're heading towards the small island with the cluster of majestic looking buildings atop a plateau that I had seen from a distance that first day on the beach.

The bridge seems to go on forever, the silhouette of the island in the distance, not seeming to get any closer. But finally, like a veil being lifted, I can see the moonlight illuminating the small island at the end of the bridge. There is a large forest on one side of the island and a wide, rocky beach on the other. The only road through the island is the one leading from the bridge, winding up over tall cliffs to the large plateau overlooking the beach and ocean beneath it. The island appears uninhibited, apart from the large, sprawling buildings on the plateau. From this angle, the tallest building seems to almost touch the moon.

The scene is like a picturesque postcard of a deserted island getaway. But of course, I know that it isn't an island resort on top of that cliff, but a boarding school for the insanely wealthy.

When we reach the plateau, I can see that the buildings look very much like how you'd expect a boarding school to look. Not that I'd actually ever seen one, but it isn't difficult to envisage.

There are trees lining the buildings which are separated by sprawling lawns and green spaces. The tall building that I saw from a distance, looks like the main campus building and it's flanked by smaller buildings on each side. There is what looks like apartment blocks, which are probably the student dorms, near the main building. Further away, just at the very edge of the plateau, I can see that there is a large mansion overlooking the rocky beach beneath. I find myself wondering what the building is.

I notice as we pass through the campus grounds, that the place is deserted and silent, apart from the sound of waves crashing against the cliffs below. Magnus tells me that classes don't start until tomorrow, so most students won't be arriving until then.

I find myself thinking that it all looks so normal. I don't know what I'd been expecting. Maybe a medieval castle with a drawbridge and a moat, with magical dragons circling and students flying around on broomsticks, learning how to slay dragons. But instead, you could mistake the campus for some ivy league university, or at least what I think an ivy league university looks like.

I expect the limousine to head towards the student dorms but it heads in the opposite direction instead. Towards the mansion at the edge of the bluff.

"Where are we going? The dorms are over there, aren't they?" I ask.

"You're not staying in the dorms." Magnus replies.

"I'm not?" I shoot him a puzzled look.

"No. Dynasty heirs have always had their own halls of residence."

I look up at the large mansion up ahead as the realization dawns on me and I think I feel sick.

The limousine stops in front of the large marble-paved drive way, but the last thing I want to do is get out of the car.

"This is Sovereign Hall. It's where you'll be staying," Magnus says, although through the churning in my gut, I'm finding it difficult to concentrate on his words.

I can't believe I didn't make the connection up until now—*the Dynasty heirs have always attended Regency Mount Academy*. Magnus had said this earlier, but I'd been too busy protesting about the very idea of going to a boarding school, that I didn't even consider that I'd be going to the same boarding school as the spoiled brats that I'd met at yesterday's ceremony. The very same brats who each made it clear that I'm not welcome here in Eden, let alone their high school.

I feel like hurling when I realize that not only will I be going to the same school as that asshole who had basically threatened me yesterday, but I'll be living in the same halls as him, too, along with all of the other rich pricks who apparently hate me for just existing.

"Here are the keys to the Evenstar suite. I arranged for your things to be sent in advance and your class schedule should be on your dresser."

"Oh, god." I cover my face with my hands.

"What's wrong?" Magnus asks.

"I can't go here—I can't live *there*." I gesture to the white marble pillars and the large gold leaf double doors.

"I don't belong here."

Magnus sighs in frustration.

"We've been over this, Jazmine. This is exactly where you belong."

"You don't understand." I'm almost pleading now.

"The Dynasty heirs *hate me*—they made that pretty clear at last night's ceremony."

Clearly the courteous bowing had fooled everyone but me, because Magnus looked utterly perplexed.

"What are you talking about?"

I'm silent for a long moment as I deliberate whether to tell him about the less than friendly welcome that I'd received last night from the heir to the throne himself. But something inside me is stopping me. I'd taken care of myself since I was seven and I sure as hell don't need Magnus to start fighting my battles for me now. I can handle myself.

"It's nothing," I say finally. You're right. I'll be fine."

Magnus regards me for another moment, suddenly looking uncertain.

"Are you sure it's nothing?"

"Yeah, I'm sure. Don't worry about it."

"Good. Here, take this." He hands me a cell phone and I don't even know why I'm still surprised. I begin to ask how the hell they have cell phones here on Eden, but why wouldn't there be? This place being a mirror of Earth and all.

"I'll call to check up on you. But I've added my number on here, so call me if you need anything."

It feels strange having someone care enough to actually check up on me or to have someone give a damn about me at all. I haven't had that since I was seven and although it feels alien, I can't deny that it chips away at my walls and I can feel some of the icy exterior that has built up around me throughout the years, thawing.

"Thank you," I mumble. The words are barely audible, but Magnus hears it.

"You're very welcome, Jazmine," he replies with a wistful smile.

$\mathcal{I}$’ve never set foot inside a boarding school before, but I'm pretty sure that Sovereign Hall is like no other student hall. The gold leaf double doors open out onto a cavernous, marble-floored reception room. A modern, all-white open plan kitchen and dining room flanks the reception on one side, and a living area with plush velvet couches and a large marble fireplace flanks the other. The far wall is lined entirely with glass and opens out onto what looks like an indoor swimming pool, with another wall of glass beyond that looking out onto the coastline below.

I crane my neck to look at the glass chandelier which hangs over the reception hall and the curved white marble staircase leading up to the rooms above. The ceiling is impossibly high and I wonder where it stops.

Upstairs, the first floor splits into two wings. I take the left wing and read the gold plaque on each set of double doors as I pass. Aldebran, Aspen, St. Tristan and finally Evenstar. I'm guessing the other heirs are rooming in the other wing. I'm less than thrilled to find that the St. Tristan suite is directly across from the Evenstar suite. In fact, the thought that I'm going to be living across the hall from the jackass that is Raphael St. Tristan for the entire year, makes me sick to my stomach.

I step into my quarters to find a large suite which is three times larger than any bedroom I've ever had in all ten of my previous foster homes. In fact, the room is probably larger than most apartments. A king size, four poster bed fills the middle of the room. A plush purple velvet chaise lounge sits between the large floor to ceiling mirror and marble top dresser. But the best feature has to be the black marble fireplace at the center of the living area, with the plush black faux fur rug sprawled in front of it.

I'm also pleased to find that in addition to stocking the closet, Magnus has also arranged for a full array of art supplies. A pile of blank sketch books perch next to a large wooden easel and there are shelves full of pastels, paints and blank canvases.

I drop down onto the enormous bed and for a moment, I can *almost* feel grateful. But there remains the fact that no matter how nice my surroundings, there is no changing the reality that I'll be spending the entire year living with a bunch of spoiled pricks *who hate my guts*.

~

I hate the first day at a new school. I should be used to it by now, this being the eleventh one. But I'm not. In fact, this one is probably the worst one yet by far. I expect the curious glances, but what I don't expect are the whispers and the open disapproval. I expected to just drift through this place in the usual way—keeping my head down and being as invisible as possible. But it becomes painfully clear, from the first moment, that it isn't going to happen. Not here.

I'm puzzled, because no one here knows me or at least they shouldn't. But I have a sinking feeling that the spoiled pricks who are now my new hall mates, have something to do with my notoriety. Thankfully, I haven't seen any of them yet, and this place is big enough that I can hope that I can get through the year without crossing paths with any of them. All I have to do is sneak in and out of

Sovereign Hall when they aren't around. It was easy enough this morning, because the mansion was still empty when I left for class.

I let out a sigh as I pass through yet another hallway where the students literally step back as I walk past, as if I'm the carrier of some contagious disease. I school my expression into staying blank. But I can't shake the feeling that I really don't belong here.

Everything about this place screams wealth and privilege—from the marble floors and wood paneled halls, to the prissy uniforms. I've never worn a school uniform in my life, but here I am walking through these fancy halls wearing a crisp white shirt, black pleated skirt and dark grey blazer with a golden Regency Mount crest embroidered on the front pocket. It's the same uniform as all the other students are wearing, and yet I still feel like a total outsider.

My first class is calculus, and I feel eyes on me as I walk through the room. I take my seat at the back, and I'm not surprised when the desks around me stay vacant.

"This seat taken?" a quiet voice startles me and I look up to see a brown-haired girl standing at the desk next to mine. Her dark brown eyes dart around nervously as she shifts from one foot to the other.

"No, it's all yours," I reply, eyeing her curiously. I'm not sure why she's choosing to sit next to me, when the rest of the student body seems to be treating me like a leper.

I turn back to my blank notebook, but I'm surprised when the girl next to me speaks again.

"I'm Dani Larch," the girl says after a moment, as she settles into the desk next to me.

I don't reply at first, trying to figure out this girl's intentions. She has the kind of honest face that makes you want to trust her instantly, but my trust issues make it difficult for me to do that.

"Didn't you get the memo about staying away from me?"

The girl looks perplexed.

"No …"

She looks around the room, and notices the looks being thrown my way. I expect her to get up and find another desk. But she doesn't.

"Oh, you must be Jazmine—Jazmine Evenstar, right?"

"How do you know my name?" I ask, quirking an eyebrow.

She looks slightly guilty then.

"Word spreads fast around here—and the word is that you're the secret heir of the Evenstar Dynasty that they've been trying to track down, for months now."

I nod slowly. It still doesn't explain the less than welcoming behavior.

"Is that all?" I ask. I've never particularly cared what people thought of me, but I may as well know what I'm dealing with here.

Dani looks guilty for a moment, but I give her another nod of encouragement.

"Look, I don't give a damn what people think of me. But I guess I should know now, so I can prepare myself."

She lets out a sigh.

"Okay, well the Dynasty heirs …"

She trails off as she looks towards the classroom doorway. I follow her gaze to see the flawlessly beautiful girl with the bright blonde hair saunter into the room. Her skirt is about three inches too short, making her impossibly long legs look even longer and the guys in the front row are practically salivating at the sight. The girl is clearly aware of it, too—she knows she's beautiful, and she knows how to use it to her advantage.

Those gem-green eyes fix themselves on me as soon as she enters the room, and a look of distaste mars her otherwise flawless features. So, the girl clearly still hates me for whatever unknown reason. Fine.

I return the look with a pitiless glare of my own, and those green eyes flare with indignation. As if she can't believe that I would even dare to look her in the eye. Well, she has no idea who she's messing with. Part of me thinks that I probably shouldn't be doing that to someone who is probably more than capable of blasting me away with some freakish power in the blink of an eye, without even breaking a sweat. But I've encountered enough high school mean girls to know that the only way to deal with them is to nip the power trip in the bud from the get go.

I notice that the bitch queen isn't alone. The short haired girl, who

I remember from the ceremony as Keller, flanks her on one side and the other girl, who I think is called Ivy, is on the other. They both flash me a look of displeasure as they spot me at the back of the room. I don't look away.

Beside me, Dani is visibly cowering. She probably regrets taking the seat next to me.

"That's Layla Delphine—the heir to the Delphine Dynasty," Dani whispers as Layla turns away. She's like the queen bee here at Regency Mount."

"Yeah, I guessed that part," I reply, rolling my eyes.

"Keller Aspen and Ivy Hemlock are her two BFFs, and they're also Dynasty heirs."

"Right. Got it—queen bitch and her two cronies."

Dani's eyes widen in response, and I can't help but smirk.

The teacher walks in then and the class quietens down.

All of the desks in the front row are taken, but Layla chooses an already occupied desk, and immediately, the offending student gets up and scuttles away to the back of the room like a terrified mouse. Keller and Ivy follow Layla's example.

I look up at the teacher, who is a middle-aged, stern looking, woman. She watches the scene with a passive expression, as if this sort of thing is totally normal.

"If you didn't already know—the Dynasty heirs rule Regency Mount. They're untouchable—even the teachers are scared of them."

I didn't know. But I guess now I do, and with that realization comes the sinking feeling that it's going to be one hell of long year.

We have a pop quiz for the first lesson, which means no talking and I'm grateful for that. I find out pretty quickly that Magnus hadn't been lying about the schooling being the same as on Earth. Calculus sucks ass on both planets, it seems.

When the bell rings, signaling the end of class, I pack up my stuff and walk hurriedly towards the door. I'm no coward, but I'd like to avoid any sort of altercation on my first day.

Unfortunately, Layla has other ideas. I don't see that Dani is following me until I hear Layla's voice behind us in the hallway just outside the classroom.

"Well, if it isn't the pauper and the bastard whore."

I feel myself bristle at her words and I turn slowly to face her.

"Say that again, *bitch?*"

I hear a round of audible gasps, and I then I notice that an audience has formed around us, as students on their way to their next classes stop to gawk at the showdown.

I feel my face burning at the attention. I was hoping to avoid this, but if she wants to bring it, I'm not about to back down.

She steps closer to me, and I stay rooted to the spot. Dani has moved to stand beside me, but is visibly shaken.

"I said, you're a whore and a bastard," she replies, crossing her arms over her perky chest.

I roll my eyes in response. I really don't have time for this shit.

"You don't know anything about me."

"I know that your daddy fucked a dirty human, and that you're his dirty little half-human bastard.

"I also know that you're a *whore* and that before you came here, you were turning tricks for a dollar. God, I knew the Evenstar Dynasty was desperate for an heir, but I didn't think it would ever sink this low."

I don't know why her words surprise me. After my encounter the other night with the king of all pricks, I'd guessed that these bastards had clearly been trying to find some dirt on me. Still, I feel like ripping this girl's hair out and clawing that smug smile off her perfect little face. But I force my breath to slow instead. She wants me to lose it, but I'm not going to play into her hands. It doesn't mean I'm going to let her get away with it either. So I step forward until I'm toe to toe with the bitch.

"Please, honey, the only *whore* I see around here is you. Pull your skirt down and button up your shirt, because no one wants to see your ass and tits—it's tacky as hell."

To accentuate my words, I reach out and button up one of the buttons on her gaping white shirt, smirking as I step back.

Layla's face turns crimson with rage, and I hope embarrassment, too. Next to her, Ivy looks just as furious, but Keller just quirks an eyebrow. I get the feeling that nothing much shakes this girl.

Layla is sputtering, grasping for a comeback, as whispers break out in the crowd around us. I don't wait around for the response as I turn on my heel and walk away.

Screw these bitches. I'm hoping that it will be enough to put them in their place and make them leave me the hell alone for the rest of the year. But I have a sinking feeling that this is only the beginning.

8

"*J*azmine, wait up!"

Through the roaring of my own heartbeat in my ears, I almost don't hear Dani calling after me as she follows me down the hall.

"Are you crazy?" she asks, once she catches up with me.

"You can't just go around insulting the Dynasty heirs unless you have some kind of death wish."

I shake my head in response.

"I couldn't care less about the stupid Dynasty heirs," I retort.

"Look, what I was about to tell you in class—the Dynasty heirs have basically marked you as an outcast and like I said before, they rule this place. What they say goes."

I roll my eyes, because I don't care. I remember what that asshole from the ceremony told me—*one word from me, and I can make your life a living hell.*

I guess the jerk actually followed through with that threat. But it'll take more than a couple of bitchy insults to get to me.

"I don't get it, though. I mean, you're one of them right? You're the heir to the Evenstar Dynasty."

I turn to Dani then.

"Yeah, I guess that's what I'm supposed to be. But trust me, they've made it crystal clear that I'm not one of them and that I don't belong here."

Dani purses her lips together and I fully expect her to walk away. I mean, why would she want to hang around with someone with the mark of social death on them.

"Listen, I like you. I've never seen anyone stand up to Layla and her cronies like you just did. I actually don't think anyone has *ever* done that before. You think it'll be okay if I hang with you?"

The surprise is clear on my face.

"Why would you want to do that? You said it yourself, I've been marked as an outcast, whatever that means. If you hang with me, it'll make you one, too."

"It doesn't make a great deal of difference in my case. What Layla said about me being a pauper? I'm a scholarship student, I ... don't come from a noble lineage. So, that doesn't place me very high up on the social ladder. It pretty much places me at the bottom, actually."

"You'll see soon enough that lineage and wealth mean *everything* here."

Dani catches the hesitant look on my face.

"Look, I don't have any friends here—pathetic, I know, and I have a feeling that you're going to need one, so ..."

I've gone through seventeen years without forming a single friendship and as sad as that might sound, forming attachments has always been pointless for me. Just another person to lose. I definitely don't want to form any attachments now, seeing as for the most part, I still don't plan on sticking around for long. But Dani's earnest look makes it difficult to say no and I agree with her about having a feeling that I'm going to need a friend in this place.

"Okay," I say finally with a small smile, which only grows as Dani beams back at me in response.

~

J have English second period and I'm grateful that Layla isn't in that class, too. I'm not so grateful to see that the dark haired guy from the ceremony, Baron, I think his name is, and the one with the reddish brown hair, Lance, are in that class. Thankfully, they ignore me completely.

I don't miss the way that they command the room—girls flock around them and guys greet them enthusiastically as they pass. I also don't miss the way they seem to be above class rules—talking in class and openly hitting on girls without so much as a warning from the teacher. This place is insane.

"I'm not really a fan of the cafeteria scene," I say to Dani, as she leads me towards the large glass double doors leading into the dining hall.

I was hoping to be able to avoid the cafeteria for the whole year. I always found somewhere else to eat in my previous high schools—either out in one of the sports fields or in an empty classroom.

"You can't do that here—rules are pretty strict. Students are only allowed to eat in the cafeteria," Dani replies.

I consider foregoing lunch altogether, but the grumbling in my stomach demands food. Letting out a sigh, I follow Dani through the glass doors.

The scene that greets me is like no other cafeteria I've ever seen before. Marble floors and a glass ceiling with finely made tapestries hanging on the walls, makes this place look more like a high class restaurant, than a high school cafeteria. The food is also nothing like normal cafeteria food either. There's lobster and caviar on the menu, for god's sake.

We find a table near the large French doors leading out to the patio, which is a little quieter than the rest of the large room. I can feel eyes on me as I walk past, this time accompanied by whispers. No doubt about the earlier show down with Layla. I sit with my back to the room, but I still feel the eyes on me.

"So, tell me about Earth," Dani says, as we settle into our seats. "That's where you've been living, right?"

She's whispering, as if talking about Earth isn't something that people usually do in good company.

"You've never been? And also why are you whispering?"

"Of course, I've never been. It's forbidden for the Seraph to visit Earth, unless it's for a mission or the heads of all seven Dynasties give special permission."

"It's ... okay, I guess," I reply with a shrug. I let out a long sigh.

"Truthfully, my life there kind of sucked. I've lived in a different foster home each year since I was seven." I'm not usually one to spill my guts to someone I barely know, but there's something about this girl that makes me feel automatically at ease, or maybe I'm just tired of being alone.

Dani looks stunned.

"God, I had no idea. I'm sorry," she says.

"This may be a really forward question—but word is that you were a, you know, um ... some kind of stripper waitress back on Earth."

I choke on my food.

"What the hell?"

Dani looks sheepish then. "Yeah, I mean, no judgment if you were. I think it's kind of cool."

"Firstly, there was no stripping involved—just hot pants and a bra," I say, although I don't think it's really any better. "Secondly ..."

I let out a long sigh.

"There was nothing cool about it. I needed the money because I was saving up for art school. It was good money and I needed to do what I had to do."

Dani nods, then sensing that I don't feel comfortable talking about it anymore, she changes the subject.

"They say that Earth is like a mirror of Eden, only humans are ... lesser beings."

I think her words over before replying.

"I've only been on Eden for two days, but from what I can see so far, the part about it being a mirror is probably right—Eden looks like paradise, but it also looks like the same drama and bullshit exists here as on Earth.

"And for that very same reason, I don't agree that humans are lesser beings at all."

Dani looks thoughtful, but says nothing.

I can see from her expression that she wants to say something else, but is hesitant. I look at her expectantly, although I'm not sure I want to hear.

"I—I just wanted to say that what happened with you father ... he was a good king. The people loved him, most thought he was one of the best kings that Eden has ever had.

"What happened was a tragedy—the biggest tragedy that Eden has known for centuries."

I was right to not want to hear. Because although this man was a stranger to me, hearing about what a great king he was, and how he *committed suicide,* makes my insides squeeze painfully.

I have no response and Dani senses that it's not something I'm ready to talk about.

So, we eat in silence for a little while, and I've had two spoonfuls of the gourmet pasta, when Dani's eyes dart towards the patio.

"*Oh my god.* There's Raph St. Tristan."

The name makes the hairs on the back of my neck stand on end, but my eyes follow Dani's gaze to where that asshole is standing, or leaning against the patio railing, to be precise.

He's wearing a white shirt and black trousers like all of the other male students, but I don't think anyone here pulls it off the way he does. The dark grey Regency Mount blazer makes his broad shoulders look even broader and his black tie hangs loose around his neck. He looks like he's just walked off a GQ photoshoot. The midday sun encases him with a golden glow, but I know that there's nothing angelic about that perfection. This guy is sexy as hell. *He's an asshole.* I remind myself. The biggest asshole I've ever met. It shouldn't matter how beautiful he is, because he's thoroughly ugly on the inside.

Just then, I see two girls saunter over to where he's lounging. One is wearing her uniform skirt so short, that I can almost see her panties, while the other has her shirt unbuttoned low enough to show the lacy top of her bra. Both are gorgeous. It's clear from their flirtatious body language, that they think he's irresistible. It would've been less obvious if they'd just taken their shirts off and started lap dancing on him.

The smile playing on those sensuous lips is irritatingly charming and his gaze is hooded, golden lashes drooping low over his brilliant eyes. He looks like he's in his element. The girls are giggling loudly now at something he's saying, the sound traveling in through the open patio doors. I'm sure that it probably isn't that funny. One of the girls is resting her hand playfully on his arm, while the other one is whispering something in his ear suggestively. So, I was right, he does have girls throwing themselves at him wherever he goes, and he probably expected me to do the same that night of the ceremony. It makes me all the more glad that I showed him otherwise. The whole thing makes me feel disgusted, and suddenly I instantly lose my appetite.

"He's an asshole," I tell Dani, who's still looking star struck.

"Sure he is," she replies. "But he's still hot as fuck."

I almost choke on my water.

I don't particularly want to hear any more about this guy, but Dani continues regardless.

"I told you before that the Dynasty heirs rule Regency Mount. Well, Raphael St. Tristan is the *King* of Regency. The Dynasty heirs do nothing without his say so. It's like the biggest cliché, but all the girls here would drop their panties for him in a heartbeat, and every guy is either scared of him or worships him—but they *all* want to be him."

None of it surprises me. Not at all.

"He's the captain of the soccer team, heir to the sovereign St. Tristan Dynasty, wealthier than *God*, the most powerful Seraph in recent history and of course, he's next in line to the throne of Eden. In the same way that Seraphs are like gods to humans, Raph is basically a god compared to everyone else here."

"Wow. He sounds like the perfect mix of spoiled prick and arrogant ass," I retort. Dani chuckles in response.

"And wait, they have *soccer* here? Also what do you mean he's the most powerful Seraph in recent history?" I ask, despite myself.

Dani looks at me like I'm from another planet, which would be correct—I am.

"Of course, they have soccer here—it's the biggest sport on the planet and the Regency Gladiators are the best high school soccer team in the country. Raph is the star striker and captain of the team.

"And the part about him being the most powerful Seraph—you'll see in elements class. We all have powers, the Dynasty heirs strongest of them all, but Raph's power is something else. The guy has never been beaten in a duel."

I cover my face with my hands and groan. Perfect. Not only does this guy hate me, he can probably also snap me in half without even breaking a sweat.

"Too bad he's the biggest jackass to ever grace the face of the universe," I mutter.

"I'm guessing you've met him then?"

"Yeah, unfortunately. He spoke to me at this stupid presentation ceremony a couple of nights ago."

"Wait—he *spoke* to you?" she looks shocked, and I roll my eyes in response.

"Yeah, but trust me, I wish he hadn't."

"What did he say?"

"Nothing much—it went something along the lines of I'm not welcome here, and I should stay out of his way."

"What the hell?" Dani hisses.

"I know. He's a real charmer," I say dryly.

"No, I mean like what the hell—Raph doesn't speak to people outside his circle, and he sure as hell doesn't speak to outcasts."

"Urgh, will you stop with this social hierarchy bull already. It's making me want to throw up my lunch. Besides, the only reason I've been marked as an *outcast* in the first place, is because of that asshole."

"No wonder Layla laid into you in calculus this morning," Dani says. I grimace at the memory.

"Layla and Raph have been dating since they were like—in kindergarten or maybe even before that. I think they've basically been betrothed since *birth*."

I remember how Layla had curled her arm around Raph's at the ceremony, and the memory makes my stomach churn.

"Good for them. An asshole King and a bitch Queen ruling over their kingdom of mindless followers. A match made in heaven Although Layla might want to keep an eye on her man, because he's clearly not keeping his hands to himself," I add, as I observe Raph's hand reaching around one of the girls plastered to him and cupping her almost bare ass.

"Yeah, Raph isn't exactly Mr. Faithful, but Layla is hardly the princess of purity either. Raph and Layla are always breaking up and getting back together—one week they're on, the next they're off. It's like this epic love story. I'm guessing they're in one of their off periods."

Speaking of the she-devil, Layla emerges from one of the side buildings and is stalking towards the patio where Raph and his groupies are standing. Her eyes are narrowed, furious.

I watch the sequence of events unfolding like a soap opera, playing out right in front of my very own eyes.

"Oh, no, here comes Layla. Girl fight," Dani mutters. I notice that other people in the cafeteria are also now looking out at the patio.

First, the girls look up to see Layla approaching, and they look like they might try to stand their ground. But they're clearly terrified, or at least visibly intimidated by the authoritative and much more menacing girl. So, I watch with interest as they scurry away like little white mice.

Layla is in front of Raph now. He's looking at her sardonically, like a cat visibly displeased that the creatures it had been toying with have been taken away. But instead of yelling at him, Layla leans in, pressing her body close against his, whispering something in his ear. She's stroking his cheek sensually. I feel an odd tightening in my stomach.

Raph appears utterly disinterested. He's saying something to Layla now, his expression cold, dismissive. Whatever it is, makes her storm off in an apparent rage. I realize then that she's heading towards the patio doors and that she'll pass our table when she steps through. But I don't let myself look away.

She glares at me as she storms past, but thankfully, she doesn't stop. I don't think I'll be able to handle any more of her bitchiness today without punching her in the mouth.

A second later, Raph walks through the patio doors and I do drop my gaze then. Because the last thing I need is for him to notice me and start threatening me again. This time in front of the entire school.

He does notice me, though. All eyes turn to him as he passes, but I can feel his eyes on me. Dani was talking, but falls silent as Raph passes.

I let out a breath I hadn't been aware I was holding, when I see his back in the corner of my eye.

Dani and I eat in silence for a few minutes until she starts whispering furiously at me.

"Holy shit. I have no idea why, but Raph was like full on *staring* at you when he passed our table, and he's still staring."

I can feel my hackles rising.

I flash a casual glance over my shoulder and indeed find that those vivid blue eyes are locked onto me. His expression is as closed off as ever, and I can almost feel the arctic wind blowing from his direction.

"It's a stare of death—he's probably trying to kill me with his eyes."

Dani chuckles, but she eyes me thoughtfully. I shift in my seat uncomfortably.

I throw another glance at Raph's table, which is at the center of the cafeteria. It doesn't take a genius to work out that it's the popular table. All of the Dynasty heirs are sitting at the table—Keller and Ivy sitting on either side of Layla, Baron and Lance sitting next to Raph. They're surrounded by other students who are clearly the crème de la crème of Regency—perfect hair, perfect make-up, expensive shoes. They scream wealth and privilege. Students at neighboring tables are looking longingly at that central table, as if begging for an invite, or as if to catch even a few words of conversation. It's pathetic.

"That's Baron Aldebran," Dani says, looking over at the dark-haired guy who would probably be the most gorgeous guy in Regency, if it wasn't for Raph.

"Midfielder on the soccer team. He's Raph's wingman and an even bigger player than Raph, if that's possible. Or maybe they're equal. Either way, all the girls here want a piece of that and I think he's slept his way through most of them here—or at least the ones worth doing."

I roll my eyes then. God, it sounds like the raging hormones in this place are out of control. My tactic of keeping to myself in all of my previous high schools means that I've almost forgotten what a hot bed of sex and scandal high school can be. Except this place is like high school on steroids—I guess it must be the obscene wealth that makes these kids think they can do whatever the hell they want.

"And that's Lance Oaknorth next to him. He plays defense on the team and he's also super hot. He's probably the nicest out of the three guys, but it's too bad he's been dating Ivy Hemlock since junior year, who, as you've already seen, is kind of a bitch." I catch a tinge of wistfulness in Dani's tone as she eyes Lance, but I hope I'm just imagining it. Dani isn't the type of girl to knock guys on their asses, but she has a girl next door look which makes her undeniably pretty. Plus, she seems to be the only decent person here in Regency. She's much too good for any of these Dynasty heir pricks.

"You're living in Sovereign Hall, right?" Dani asks then.

"Unfortunately, yes."

"God, that's amazing. You'll get to go to all of the crazy parties that they throw there."

I don't like the sound of that.

"What parties?"

"The Dynasty heirs are always throwing parties at Sovereign Hall. The school has a strict curfew, but they turn a blind eye to the parties, if they're being hosted by the Dynasty heirs."

"Of course, they do."

"In fact, I think there's a party tonight—first day of semester and all."

I let out a frustrated groan. Great. I'm going to have to make sure that I get upstairs and lock myself in my room before it all kicks off.

"I wouldn't know. I'm not invited."

Dani shakes her head in disbelief again.

"I really don't get why they hate you so much. I mean you're meant to be one of them and your father was the King, for god's sake. I get the fact that you being half human and the whole stripper waitress rumor doesn't exactly put you on the A-list. I guess there's also the age old rivalry between the two sovereign Dynasties—yours and Raph's. But to have the Dynasty heirs actually decree that you're an outcast— that's like giving you the kiss of death. It's some pretty serious shit."

"I'm not one of them," I repeat. I don't know what she means about the rivalry part, but I have no interest in asking for any further details.

"They've made that clear and you know what? I couldn't care less. They can hate me. Screw them."

Dani gets that thoughtful look again.

"It's a shame though—because I know that every guy here probably thinks you're the hottest thing to set foot in Regency Mount since ... Layla herself."

"And if it wasn't for the Dynasty heirs' school-wide decree, you'd probably have at least a dozen guys over here right now, asking you out."

I can't help but laugh in response.

"What? That's crazy."

Dani looks at me like I'm dense.

"Oh, god, you're not one of those hot girls who knows that they're hot but puts on the fake modesty, are you? Let me guess—you were like the hottest girl in your last school?"

I laugh again.

"No, not even close. I'm not being fake modest, but I've had more important things to think about."

Dani looks at me like I'm crazy, or like life suddenly doesn't make sense.

Her eyes travel from the popular table, where Raph is still staring, to me and back again. Then a small smile forms on her lips.

I catch Layla following Raph's eyeline, the look of displeasure on her face is clear. She gets up and walks over to where Raph is sitting, and drops her ass onto his lap. He doesn't push her off as she pulls his face to hers. I look away then, not wanting to throw up my lunch.

"I think I get it now," Dani says, her smile growing wider and with a knowing gleam in her eyes.

I don't ask her to spell it out because frankly, I really do *not* want to know.

9

*T*hankfully, the next period goes by uneventfully, mostly because there are no Dynasty heirs in my theology class. Dani is in my class, though, and when we compare schedules, we find that we actually share most of our classes. I find myself liking that. I've always walked the high school halls alone and never thought anything of it. But Dani is right—having a friend does make things more bearable and I like her. She seems different from the rest of the spoiled rich kids at Regency. Maybe it's because she understands what it's like not to be born with a silver spoon in your mouth. We're from two totally different planets, but in some ways, our backgrounds aren't that far apart.

When I walk into my last class of the day with Dani, I'm not so glad to find that sociology isn't so Dynasty heir free. The first thing I see when I walk in is Raph, sitting, no, more like lounging, in one of the front row desk chairs. Layla is perched on the desk in front of him, sitting in a very deliberate angle, so as to expose as much of her long legs as humanly possible. I think I might throw up my lunch.

Those blue eyes fix directly on me as I enter the room. His face was utterly blank just a moment ago as he regarded Layla's peep show.

A block of stone would have been more expressive in comparison. But those irritatingly perfect features draw together in a scowl when he sees me. Great. He hates me so much, that even his stone cold mask can't hide it.

Layla follows his line of sight and her pert nose wrinkles at the sight of me, as if she's just caught a whiff of a dead animal. Nice.

I purposely ignore them as I try to find some seats. We're the last to arrive, so I'm expecting only the seats at the back to be free. But I'm surprised to see two spare seats at the front. In the same row as Raph.

I'd rather chew my own arm off than sit in the same row as the asshole King and his bitch Queen. But I don't have the luxury of being able to make other students move with just a look. Not that I'd want to do such a dickish thing. So, I take the seat at the front and Dani drops down next to me.

When the class starts, I keep my eyes fixed to the front, at Professor Gorman, as he drones on about this year's syllabus. But I can feel Raph's eyes burning a hole into me all the while. I ignore him completely, not wanting to give this asshole the satisfaction of thinking I've even noticed that he's in this class, or in the same school, for that matter.

We're halfway through class when Professor Gorman asks everyone to open their textbooks to this week's topic. I follow the instructions on autopilot and I can hear my own scream when an explosion of pure white light flares from my open textbook, blinding me in an instant.

I feel my ass hit the cold hard floor with a painful thud as I fall off my chair in an attempt to get away from the death lights. Laughter explodes around me, and when my vision returns, I can see that my ass is sprawled out on the floor. The whole class is in hysterics. Everyone, apart from Dani, who is looking at me with concern.

I'm not laughing, though. I'm furious. I get up from the floor with as much dignity as I can muster. My eyes shoot directly to Raph. The mask of stone is gone, replaced by a cocky as hell smirk, which just infuriates me all the more. He looks like he's having the time of his life. Next to him, Layla looks as pleased as a cat being rewarded with its favorite treat. She's almost purring with delight.

A stream of obscenities rings through my mind and I'm not even thinking straight when I pick up my five hundred page text book and hurl it directly at Raph's smirking face. The laughter stops immediately, and I hear some gasps as the book, which is as heavy as a brick, flies through the air towards Raph.

I must have a good arm because it looks like that brick is going to smash straight into that perfect face of his.

But his reflexes are impossibly fast. He snaps out a hand and catches the projectile in mid-flight, just a hair's breadth away from his face. An instant later, my text book explodes into a ball of flame in his hand.

I watch in disbelief as the inferno engulfs his bare hand, my text book turning into ashes as his gaze locks onto mine. He's not smiling anymore. The deathly calm in those glacier-like eyes, coupled with the fact that he can apparently summon an inferno in the blink of an eye, is positively unnerving. I feel a chill race down my spine when I finally understand exactly who and what I'm up against here.

My gaze falls on Professor Gorman who is watching the whole thing passively. Again, as if this sort of thing happens in class all the time.

"Are you just going to stand there?" I ask, feeling my own outrage.

"This *asshole* almost blinded me and he's just set my text book on fire!"

I catch Raph snickering in the corner of my eye, because I must look totally naïve. Of course, Professor Gorman isn't going to do anything. As Dani told me earlier, even the teachers are scared of these spoiled pricks.

"Sit back down, Jazmine," Professor Gorman replies flatly, completely unfazed by my outburst.

I think I lose whatever fraction of calm I have left then. Without another word, I pick up my bag and get the hell out of there, because if I have to look at Raph's mocking smile or Layla's equally smug expression a moment longer, I'm going to lose my shit.

~

*A*fter spending the rest of the afternoon in the library, I finally muster the courage to head back to Sovereign Hall.

As I approach the sparkling white mansion, the first thing I notice is the cars on the white stone driveway. The garage on the side of the mansion, which was empty last night, is also now occupied. There's a sleek black motorcycle at the front of the driveway. Next to it is an equally sleek matte black sports car, which looks like it costs more than the price of most homes. A large blacked out Range Rover is behind it, along with a white convertible. There are two other cars in the garage. I can't make out what they are. But one thing is clear, the spoiled brats are home.

I seriously consider trying to climb in through my bedroom window. But I shake the thought away. I live here, too, and I'm not going to hide from these bastards.

I take a deep breath and step through the front door. Conversation stops as I enter, and I can feel eyes on me as I walk through the reception hall. I don't make eye contact with anyone, I but can see Baron and Lance turn from the video game that they're playing on the massive flat screen TV, to look at me. Ivy, who is sitting on Lance's lap, gives me the look of death. Keller is propped up on the kitchen island, where Layla is sitting on one of the stools. Both are clearly not happy to see me.

I don't say a word as I try to walk up the spiral staircase as calmly as possible. I'm not going to run, but it's an effort to keep my pace unhurried and my face blank.

Focusing much too hard on putting one foot in front of the other, I don't notice the tall muscular figure coming down the stairs until I crash into a rock-hard chest and find myself looking up at a pair of impossibly blue eyes.

I push myself back, as if I've just hit a wall of fire, but that's not a great idea, given that I'm standing on a staircase. I feel myself losing balance but before I go plummeting backwards down the cold marble steps, I feel a solid arm around my waist, keeping me from falling. I can feel all eyes in the room staring, but they suddenly feel so far away.

Raph says nothing as he pulls me against his chest. Even through his white shirt, I can feel the heat of his skin. In the same way that he almost seems to glow with the sun's light, he seems to carry the warmth of it, too. We're standing so close, that we're sharing breath and I know he can feel my heart thundering against my chest. The feel of his hard body flush against mine makes warmth pool in parts of my body which makes me hate my traitorous reaction.

I can feel the flush creeping into my cheeks and I'm embarrassed as hell. Not to mention furious at myself for the insane reaction, because only a few hours ago, this asshole almost *blinded me.*

I place my hand against that rock hard chest to push him away and I think I might just be imagining it, but I can swear that I can feel his heartbeat racing as fast as mine. I squash the thought immediately and remind myself that it's impossible, because *this asshole doesn't have a heart.*

"Get your hands off me, asshole," I hiss. My voice is quiet, but everyone in the room hears it.

Just like that night after the ceremony, I expect him to be pissed at the insult. But he flashes me a cocky smile instead. *Like a Cheshire cat.* For a second, I find it hard to remember that this guy is the devil incarnate himself. I find it hard to even *think.* Because that smile. It takes my goddamn breath away. It's the kind of smile capable of making even angels fall in love on the spot. The kind of smile that is capable of illuminating even the greyest of skies. Like the goddamn sun coming out after a storm, which is fitting, given that this asshole lords over the *sun itself.*

But when he opens his mouth, sense and reason return with a vengeance.

"Somehow, I'm finding it hard to believe that's really what you want, Jaz," he says, those luminous blue eyes traveling over every inch of my flaming face.

I can feel said flaming face burn even hotter in response, in a mix of anger and embarrassment. Because he's right. My traitorous body is emitting all the wrong signals right now and I want nothing more than to set the record straight.

"That's because you're a *delusional narcissist,*" I retort. I hear a chuckle from somewhere in the living room, reminding me that we have an audience. But I couldn't care less. Let them see me put this prick in his place.

Raph only smirks in response. Smirks. He's clearly enjoying himself. But I'm not, and this conversation needs to be over. Now.

I'm also well aware that his arm is still wrapped firmly around my waist and I hate the fact that I can feel every ridge of chorded muscle, even through my blazer.

I open my mouth to make myself blindingly clear, ready to break his arm if that's what it will take for him to let me go. But he's already speaking.

"We're having a party here later tonight."

I stare back at him in silence, because I have no idea why he's telling me this. I can tell nothing from his expression and for a split second, the ridiculous thought springs up in my mind that this is some kind of invitation.

But his next words make it crystal clear that it's not. Not at all.

"You're not invited," he adds flatly, as if it's obvious.

I have no desire to attend his stupid party. But still, his words feel like a slap to the face.

It's enough to sweep away any lingering embarrassment or any other thought or feeling which isn't hate, for that matter.

"Screw you, asshole," I hiss, with enough venom that I feel him loosen his grip. Only slightly, but just enough.

He's too distracted, by god knows what, to react when I shove him back so that he lands on his ass on the cold marble step.

I stalk up the rest of the steps, leaving Raph laid out on his ass in the same way that he laid me out on my ass in class earlier. But I don't miss the hoots of laughter coming from Baron and Lance's direction and Raph's responding growl, telling them to shut the hell up.

I turn into the left wing hallway and something feels off, although

I have no idea what. I try to shake off the irrational feeling. My nerves are probably still fried from that run-in with the king of all assholes.

But when I open the double doors to my suite, I find that the whisper of premonition was not unwarranted.

It takes a moment to register what I'm seeing. There are flyers plastered on the walls and what was once immaculately white marble has been replaced with pictures of naked women—escort flyers. Tits and ass. All over my walls. Every square inch.

I stand deathly still as the anger simmers in my veins, boiling over until it's all I can feel and the lewd images plastered all over my walls blur into a haze of anger.

It's eerily quiet in the halls. As if those bastards downstairs are gleefully listening, waiting to hear my reaction.

My mind brings up the image of Raph coming down the stairs earlier, that icy gaze burning through me as he caught me. Why he didn't just let me fall, I have no clue, because clearly, he loves seeing me suffer.

That motherfucker.

But I stifle the scream of frustration that's working its way up my throat and calmly walk across the hall towards the St. Tristan suite. The door is locked but I don't let that stop me.

I kick the door down, surprised by my own strength. I guess what they say about anger and adrenaline is true—it really does give people superhuman strength.

I'm surprised that no one comes running upstairs at the loud bang. They probably think I've keeled over and died and there's no way any of those fuckers downstairs would even consider rushing to my rescue. No, they probably can't even imagine that I've just kicked down Raph's door or what I'm about to do. That's because they have no fucking idea who I am.

That same adrenaline pumps through me as I scan the room. It's as large as my suite, larger maybe. It's surprisingly tidy for a guy's room and the whole place smells like him—citrus and cool winter mornings. It only fuels my anger. My gaze falls on the shelves lined with soccer trophies—way too many to be normal. I look at the plaques on some of the trophies – MVP, Arcadia High School League Cup, Eden High School League Cup and it goes on and on.

Well, well, well, I guess Dani was right—this asshole is some kind of soccer star. I can't help the smile that breaks out on my face as I look across the room.

There's a set of large double doors leading out to a balcony which overlooks the ocean. Perfect.

Armed with Raph's precious trophies, I walk over to the French doors, fling them open and proceed to hurl each trophy out to sea. Every single one.

When I'm done with those, and the trophy shelf is satisfyingly bare, I grab an armload of Raph's no doubt very expensive clothes and sneakers, then add those to the cargo now floating across the ocean.

Ten minutes later, I'm standing on the balcony with a face splitting grin on my face as I look out at the beautiful view—Raph's precious belongings, scattered on the rocky beach beneath and floating out to sea.

∿

I spend the next couple of hours trying to rid my walls of the flyers. But there's way too many of them and the high ceiling makes it impossible to reach all the flyers without a ladder.

I finally give up just before midnight, staring hopelessly at the discarded flyers piled high at the center of my room, and the still covered ceiling and higher sections of the walls.

With the anger and adrenaline gone, I'm exhausted as hell and I want nothing more than to hide in my room forever. But the bass pounding through the very foundations of Sovereign Hall and the music blaring out at a merciless volume, makes sleep impossible. I don't know how it's even possible to hear the music from downstairs, when all the walls in the place seem to be made of marble.

I twist and turn on my bed for what seems like hours, although my bedside clock tells me it's only been twenty minutes since I climbed into bed. Maybe it's because with each passing minute I can feel the anger returning. Anger aimed at one person in particular.

I don't know what compels me to leave my room. But I only know that I can't stand to be in my room a moment longer, my walls plastered with images of tits and ass. A reminder of what these people clearly think of me.

A part of me knows that it's also because staying hidden in my room like some kind of shameful secret is just what Raph wants. He gave his orders and he expects me to obey. But I'm not one of his little subjects and he has another think coming if he's expecting to be able to lord over me, like he seems to over every other person in this goddamn place.

I'm already immersed in the sea of bodies crowding the entrance hall when I realize that I didn't even bother to get changed. I'm still in my sleep shorts and vest. But it's quickly apparent that I'm showing far less skin than most of the people at the party.

Sovereign Hall is heaving with people. Everyone on campus seems to be here tonight, or at least those popular enough to be invited, and everyone looks like they're dressed to go to a beach party, where there'll be a *swimsuit competition* taking place, instead of a house party. But of course, this isn't any normal house party. It's a goddamn mansion and of course, there's an indoor pool the size of a tennis court.

I expect to slip through the crowd unnoticed. Everyone is either too busy getting wasted on the dance floor, or making out on every available surface. But I'm sadly mistaken. I can feel eyes on me as I pass, people visibly backing away. I couldn't care less and in fact, I'm glad. It makes it far easier to cross the packed hall when the crowd parts like the *red sea* for me.

I find myself at the sweeping marble topped bar in the natatorium and I ignore everyone and everything as I perch on one of the bar stools and proceed to pour myself a drink. Thankfully, the bar is all but deserted.

I realize that this is my very first high school party. Not much of a first, but I drink a bitter toast to that. It seems that alcohol tastes the same even in Eden, and I drink another toast to that.

I scan my surroundings, and it's clear what goes down in these parties—making out. Lots of it.

Members of the soccer team paired off with one, or more, scantily-clad girls, doing god knows what, and it's everywhere I look. Not just in the dark corners of the hall.

The Dynasty heirs are easy to spot, even among the heaving crowd. Even with the excessive wealth and opulence surrounding this place, they stand out as the most privileged of them all. The most beautiful. The most powerful.

That distinct air of power and cruel beauty makes them utterly unapproachable. Unattainable. But all eyes are drawn to them, like moths to a goddamn flame. Those privileged enough to associate with them, hover close by, but not close enough to truly be a part of their world. They own this place, they're the very reason why everyone is here tonight. All desperate for even a single look, a word, from one of the Dynasty heirs. And it makes me sick.

I see the queen bitch herself standing with Keller and Ivy, along with a group of girls I recognize from their oh so popular lunch table. They're surrounded by guys from the soccer team who seem utterly enthralled by these stunningly beautiful girls.

Layla eyes me with distaste as she notices me across the natatorium. As if my very presence is equivalent to a stray animal wondering into the party; and it's clear from the look on her face, that she can't quite believe said animal would even dare to show its face. Keller follows her line of sight and the look on her face is equally disbelieving. Clearly disobeying the royal asshole's orders is something entirely alien to these people.

My eyes travel to where Lance is standing with Baron by the pool edge. Again, both are surrounded by the opposite sex.

I almost roll my eyes at the cliché of it all. But then my gaze falls on something, or more accurately, *someone*, that makes me regret my decision to come down here at all.

Raph is lounging on one of the poolside recliners, surrounded by what looks like a cast of teen supermodels, all clearly on the list of the most beautiful girls on campus. Although, Raph, too, looks like he's just walked off the runway of some international fashion show. That, or off the cover of some goddamn magazine. It's sickening as hell, but I can't seem to look away.

He has one girl pressed to each side of him, whilst two other girls dance with each other in front of him. Actually, dancing is a polite way of putting it, because they're more like *grinding*. Dirty grinding, which given the fact that they're both wearing string bikinis, makes it akin to stripping. The only thing missing is the pole. *Christ*, and they think *I'm* the stripper.

My gaze flicks to Layla momentarily and needless to say, her expression is one of pure venom as she watches her betrothed acting not so betrothed, although unlike the cafeteria scene earlier, she doesn't make a move to stop him.

The entire scene makes me sick to my stomach and it's a wonder I'm able to keep my drink down.

He chooses exactly that moment to look my way, and as soon as his eyes lock onto mine, I feel my stomach sink. *What the hell was I thinking coming down here?*

His expression is unreadable, but I can see from the fire blazing in the depths of those luminous blue eyes, that firstly, my presence is entirely unwelcome and secondly, that he knows exactly who is responsible for throwing his precious trophies in the ocean.

I fully expect him to cross the vast natatorium and drag me upstairs to his balcony, so that he can throw me off it—so that I can join his belongings as they float out to sea. But he doesn't make a move.

I force myself to turn away and I down the rest of my drink, although I'm all too aware of the way those eyes are boring a hole into me. If only looks could kill, I'm sure I'd be dead by now.

I let out a long breath as I slam my glass down on the marble bar surface. Whatever restless rebelliousness was in my system earlier, is now long gone, and I want nothing more than to crawl back into bed and disappear. Even if I probably won't be able to sleep a wink until this goddamn party is over, and the deafening bass stills.

Unfortunately, I've barely made it off the bar stool when I'm faced with those blazing blue eyes up close, as Raph glowers down at me.

"I specifically recall telling you that you weren't invited." His voice is as cold as ice in contrast to that fire.

Although I'd been only all too ready to leave this party, his tone makes me change my mind pretty damn quickly. If only to prove a point to this asshole.

"And I specifically recall telling you that if you think you can threaten me and bark orders at me, then expect me to roll over and obey, then you have another think coming, *asshole*."

He smirks in response and I want nothing more than to wipe it off his perfect face.

His eyes travel the length of me and despite feeling overdressed earlier in comparison to the swimwear-clad crowd, I suddenly feel exposed in my vest and sleep shorts.

I'm equally aware of his lack of clothing as he stands much too close, wearing nothing but black swim shorts. But I refuse to look and it's probably the most self-control I've ever had to exert.

"I think your exact words were *royal asshole*, actually."

I'm both surprised that he actually remembered what I'd said, that he's capable of remembering anything other than his name being spoken in praise and chanted in glory, and at the same time, I'm pissed as hell that he has the gall to throw those words back at me.

I open my mouth to give him something else to remember, but he's already continuing.

"I'll give you one chance to get the hell out of here. One. Go back upstairs. Now. And I'll pretend I never saw you down here."

My answer is simple.

"No."

"No?" He says it as if he's never heard the word before, which is probably true. I can't imagine anyone having the balls or in the case of every single girl on this damn planet, the self-control, to ever refuse him. The heir to the goddamn throne. He's probably never wanted for anything in his entire life. Well, I'm more than willing to educate him.

"No." I repeat. "N.O. As in I won't be following your orders, *your highness*," I mock.

His perfect features twist in displeasure. Then he cocks his head to the side as he regards me thoughtfully, like a formation on a chess set. Considering his next move before he goes in for the kill.

I wonder why he hasn't yet brought up his goddamn trophies. But I'm not about to give him an opening to do just that, so I continue before he can fill the space between us with more of his poisonous words.

"Seeing as you insist on cranking the bass high enough to wake the dead, and seeing as you thought it would be a good idea to plaster my walls with pictures of tits and ass, hiding away in my room isn't much of an option right now."

He flashes that infuriatingly arrogant smile then.

"I thought you'd be used to seeing tits and ass everywhere. Does it remind you of home?"

Bastard.

I bite down on the responding insult working its way up my throat because he's just not worth it.

"Is that the best you've got?" I ask coolly, quirking an eyebrow.

I can see from the heat in his expression, that it has the desired effect.

"Because if that's the case, then I think I'll just sit down and pour myself another drink. I'd ask you to join me, but I don't drink with assholes, so if you don't mind ..." I add, sounding much braver than I feel. Because right now, I feel intimidated as hell. But there's no way I'm about to let him see that.

The heat in his gaze blazes to an almighty inferno and I was right to feel intimidated. I'm suddenly all too aware that I'm feeding a fire that will most likely burn me alive.

"I do mind, actually," Raph replies, his eyes darkening.

I open my mouth to retort, but we're suddenly interrupted.

"What do we have here?" Baron's voice travels from behind Raph.

I look up to see those striking aquamarine eyes peering at me from over Raph's shoulder. He flashes me that panty dropping smile. But with the two of them towering over me like a pair of line backers, it's impossible to feel anything other than intimidated.

Across the natatorium, I can see Lance looking over at us from the pool edge. The flash of alarm in his expression tells me that if I'm not already worried, then I sure as hell should be.

Raph's eyes me coolly, and the ruthless glint in those impossibly blue eyes is impossible to miss.

"No one important," he replies casually, but his eyes never leave mine and clearly those words are directed at me.

"Just someone who needs to be taught a lesson."

Baron's smile widens in response. But before I can tell both these assholes to go to hell, I feel the ground falling away beneath me. It takes me a moment to realize that I'm being carried over someone's shoulder. Raph's very broad and powerfully muscled shoulder.

I start thrashing against the iron grip, although I'm still too disoriented to truly understand what's happening.

Raph lets out a low growl in response.

"You think you're funny throwing my stuff into the sea—my trophies?" he says, finally alluding to my earlier act of revenge.

"Let me go!" I scream, although it's lost in the pounding music. Put me down, you fucker!"

Before I can say anything else, I feel myself flying through the air and the shock of wetness as I plunge into water. Acting on instinct, I kick my way up to the surface, spewing out chlorine water as I break through. Laughter echoes through the glass walled natatorium.

Any residual disorientation fades when I realize that the asshole has thrown me into the swimming pool.

I smooth my hair back with shaking hands. I'm so furious, I can't even see straight. But through the haze of rage, my eyes lock onto Raph, who is standing over the pool, his arms crossed over his perfectly tanned chest and looking all too pleased with himself. I want to wipe that smile off his face.

I can hear the distinct sound of Layla and Ivy cackling in the background.

"Damn girl, you look sexy as hell all soaked through like that." Baron is standing closest to the pool edge with Lance and both of them are smirking down at me.

My face is burning now, because I can feel that everyone is staring. What looks like the entire soccer team is gathered around, pissing themselves with laughter, at the sight.

My temper explodes and I grab the two closest people to the pool edge—Baron and Lance, pulling them into the water by their legs.

Baron glides through the water effortlessly, *like a shark*, and surfaces quickly, laughing as he breaks through. Heir of the sea, indeed. I can feel his arms wrap around me as he tries to help me out of the pool.

"Chill, sweetheart, it was just a joke," he says, still laughing. His arm wraps tighter around my waist as he leads me up to the pool steps. I make to push him away, but Raph is already speaking.

"Get your fucking hands off her, B," Raph growls. He suddenly looks furious as he glares at Baron, and I have no clue why. It only makes me angrier.

I climb the pool steps and march over to where Raph is standing, painfully aware that my white sleeping shorts and vest are soaked through, leaving little to the imagination. I hate myself for not wearing a bra to bed tonight.

Raph's eyes are like blue flames as they rake over my body and it only adds fuel to the anger boiling inside me.

Something inside me snaps then and I feel the sharp sting of flesh against my palm as I slap Raph across that smug face of his.

The room falls into silence and I can hear audible gasps coming from the soccer team. Raph looks stunned, but recovers quickly. He's beyond furious. Good. So am I.

"Are you crazy?" Raph seethes.

I force my breathing to calm, and I step closer as I bring my face up to his.

"Yeah, I am—and if you keep messing with me, you'll see just what a crazy bitch I am. You think this was funny? Well laugh it up, because you won't be laughing when I return the favor."

Feeling brazen then, or just feeling like I have nothing left to lose, I bring my lips up to his ear.

"And I *always* return the favor."

I think I'm imagining it, but I swear that I feel a shudder go through that powerfully muscled body. Either way, he seems at a loss for words, as I turn on my heel and walk away into the stunned crowd.

I can feel his eyes burning a hole into the back of me. It isn't until I get back upstairs and see my reflection in the full length mirror that I realize my soaked white sleeping shorts are so see-through, that I may as well have been walking away bare assed.

10

I wake up the next morning, totally regretting the promise of pay back. Who am I kidding? I may not take shit from anyone, but that doesn't mean I have any experience in revenge tactics, or any other form of high school terrorization. The trophies in the ocean stunt was purely a onetime thing.

I wake up extra early for school, planning to sneak out while everyone is still asleep. I know that I told myself that I'm not going to act like a coward, but I don't think I can handle seeing any of the assholes who happen to be my hall mates this morning, without losing my shit entirely.

It occurs to me as I step out onto the driveway and my gaze falls on the matte black sports car, that I'm pretty sure it belongs to a certain angel faced devil. I can't help the smile that breaks out on my face when I notice that someone has left the keys in the ignition. It's almost as if the universe is telling me to do this. I say a silent thank you and walk towards the car. The paint job is so flawless, that it's almost a shame. Almost.

I don't know what I'm going to do at first, but again, as if being guided by the powers that be, I notice a half empty vodka bottle from last night's party on the front steps. A few feet from that there is a discarded t-shirt and a packet of cigarettes with a lighter. I'm suddenly extremely thankful for that damned party last night. Best idea ever.

I start up the engine and as it roars to life, I'm scared that it'll wake up my demonic hall mates. Thankfully, no one comes out. I drive away from Sovereign Hall, towards the edge of the bluff.

I've never made an alcohol bomb before, but I've seen it done on TV enough times to get the gist. I hope that the method shown on TV is actually correct.

I launch the vodka bottle, with the flaming t-shirt shoved into the neck, through the open driver's side window, and don't stick around to watch as Raph's sleek black ride goes up in flames.

My phone rings as I walk towards campus with a renewed spring in my step.

"Jazmine, just calling to check on you. Everything okay?" Magnus's voice says, as I pick up on the second ring.

"Everything's great," I reply cheerfully. In fact, it's more than great.

"What are you up to? Anything interesting?"

Oh, nothing much. Just finished blowing up Raphael St. Tristan's car.

"Just going to class," I reply innocently and I'm glad he can't see the shit-eating grin on my face.

~

I'm still wearing the same shit-eating grin all through first period physics and second period algebra. I can tell from the way that Dani is eyeing me, that she's totally confused by my sudden good mood.

"You seem ... awfully cheerful this morning," she says tentatively, as we pack up at the end of algebra.

"Do I?" I reply innocently.

"I would've thought that you'd be upset. I heard that Raph threw you in the pool at last night's party. In front of everyone."

The memory still makes my blood simmer, but it's hard to stay angry when I'm still feeling the high of my earlier act of revenge. All morning I've been half expecting Raph to come bursting through the classroom door and to drag me outside by the hair to face a public firing squad. But it doesn't happen, so I let myself ride the wave of post-revenge satisfaction for a while longer.

"It was no big deal," I reply with a shrug.

"No big deal?" Dani echoes, looking perplexed.

I contemplate telling her then, but I don't for a minute think I'm going to get away with what I did this morning and I don't want to implicate Dani. She'll find out soon enough.

Soon is sooner than I think. We stop by my locker on the way to the cafeteria, so that I can drop off my books.

I'm in mid-sentence, opening my locker, when I feel the heat of an explosion rushing towards me. I grab Dani and duck just in time to avoid the roaring flames. Dani gets up and I can feel my eyes widen as she releases a stream of wind and water from each palm, dousing the fire. I guess having elemental powers comes in handy in the face of a locker bomb.

I scramble to my feet and it's at that exact moment that Raph walks past with Baron and Lance flanking him on each side. The crowd that's formed in the hall parts like the red sea for them. I catch Baron's smirk as he glances my way.

But I stop breathing altogether as Raph fixes that icy glare on me. He says nothing, not even stopping to look at my charred locker. But the look in those eyes tells me everything I need to know. It was him.

I feel like running after him and launching myself on his back. But I force myself to stay calm.

"What the hell was that?" Dani asks, her eyes wide as she comes to stand beside me.

"A death wish," I mutter.

Dani looks alarmed as she follows on my heels into the cafeteria. I maintain my calm as I pick my lunch. I go for the fancy looking soup and fill my bowl to the brim.

"That's a lot of soup," Dani says, as she eyes my overflowing bowl.

"I'm hungry," I reply simply, schooling my expression blank.

The cafeteria is packed full of people as I maneuver the room, Dani following close behind. But instead of heading towards the patio doors, I turn towards the center of the room.

Raph is sitting on his throne, surrounded by his loyal subjects, with his queen bitch sitting on his lap. Baron, Lance and Keller notice me standing behind Raph. One of them, I think it's Lance, opens his mouth to say something. But it's too late as I pour the contents of my overflowing bowl of soup over Raph's golden blonde head.

The cafeteria plunges into silence and the only sound is Layla's screech of death as she clambers off Raph's lap. I wish I had two bowls of soup so that I could have doused her, too.

Raph shoots up in his chair and turns to face me. Everyone is staring now. *Everyone.* Beside me, I can hear Dani let out a whimper, but she sticks by my side.

"What the *fuck?*" Raph shouts. Even with soup running down his face, he still looks impossibly beautiful. It makes me angrier. I'm not the only one though, because he looks like he's about two seconds from exploding. I should be scared, he's meant to be freakishly power-ful. He can probably set me on fire with just a snap of his fingers, but I stand my ground and look him dead in the eye. I realize then that *I hate this guy.* I don't think that I've ever actually hated anyone before, but I completely, totally and utterly hate him.

"You firebombed my locker," I reply flatly, glad for the deathly calm in my tone, although I feel far from calm.

"And you *blew up my car!*" He hollers. A round of gasps followed by whispers break out around us.

"Because you tried to *drown me* last night!" I scream back.

"And why was that, Jaz? You think feeding my trophies to the fishes is cute?"

Another round of gasps.

We stare each other down in silence, and no one else makes a sound. It's so still, I can literally hear my own breathing.

"Well, I guess we're even now," I say finally, my voice a ragged whisper.

Raph seems to calm down then and it makes him all the more

dangerous. He flashes me a smile which is as beautiful as it is disturbing.

"Oh, no, baby, we're *far* from even." The promise echoes through my ears long after he stalks off out of the cafeteria and I take my seat at the table in the remote corner.

Dani and I eat mostly in silence as conversation around us resumes. But I can still feel eyes on me. I half expect one of the other Dynasty heirs, Layla in particular, to come and mouth off at me or worse. But nothing happens.

"I can't believe you blew up Raphael St. Tristan's car," Dani says, as we finish eating.

"And threw his trophies in the ocean."

She throws back her head and laughs then. After a moment, I join in. It was pretty damn funny. Too bad I don't think I'll be laughing for very long.

11

I sleep with one eye open, still convinced that the pay back that Raph has waiting for me is going to be the mother of all pay backs. But a few days go by and nothing happens.

I'm exhausted as I step out of my room that morning to grab some breakfast before getting ready for class. I've barely made it two steps down the hallway when I hear giggling coming from across the hall. A girl? No, sounds like *girls*, plural.

I roll my eyes and eye Raph's room in disgust, just as the double doors fling open. Raph walks out into the hall dressed in nothing but his black boxer shorts and I think my jaw hits the marble tiled floor.

He was wearing swimming shorts at the party a few nights ago, but I was too furious to see anything other than red. I do notice now though that this guy is seriously ripped. His abs and chest are so defined, that they could be carved from the marble floor that we're standing on. He's cut like a diamond—not a shred of fat on him. Combine that with his flawless golden skin, defined arms and the powerfully muscled thighs of a soccer player, and this guy is like sex on legs. I stamp down that thought because since when did I have such a dirty mind? Add to that the fact that *I hate* this guy.

I'm suddenly all too aware that, again, I'm only wearing a pair of barely there sleeping shorts and a grey vest. The way that those uncanny blue eyes rake over me, makes me want to run back into my room and grab a dressing robe. But I stay rooted to the spot.

"Not planning on sneaking out to blow up someone else's car this morning, are you?" Raph asks, as he leans back against the doorframe of his room.

"No, not today. I think I'll wait until you get a new car," I retort, although I know I sound distracted. It's not easy to stay focused when the sexiest guy I've ever seen in real life is standing practically naked in front of me.

He flashes me one of those impossibly beautiful smiles, as if he knows exactly where my mind is. *In the gutter*, that's where.

I notice then that he's got a dimple on each cheek and it only adds to his infuriating perfection.

"See something you like, Jaz?"

My gaze travels behind him to the not one, but two naked girls lying on his enormous silk sheeted bed. I suddenly feel sick. This guy is a total pig.

I purposefully rake my eyes over every square inch of his rock hard body before flashing him a frosty smile.

"Naah. There's *nothing* here that I like."

He smirks in response.

"Sure. Is that why you keep staring at my chest?"

"You're *disgusting*—go back to your orgy, you pig."

Those vivid blue eyes flash like twin flames.

"Jealous, Jaz? You know you're always welcome to join."

I gape at him in a mix of outrage and embarrassment, because I really can't stop staring at him and it pisses me off. I notice that he has a row of tattoos along his left rib cage. It looks like a row of suns with their rays intricately woven together. No doubt a tribute to the element that this prick lords over. So really, just a tribute to himself. Typical. But the artist in me can't help but admire the skillfully etched tattoos and the foolishness in me can't deny that they look sexy as hell on him. *Stop staring.* I command myself.

"'I'd rather have *all my teeth pulled out, then fed back to me.*"

"Lying again, are we? There isn't one girl on campus that wouldn't drop their panties for me. All I need to do is look their way. You're no exception."

I think I throw up a little in my own mouth.

"I can see that confidence is clearly *not* an issue for you," I reply. "But unfortunately for you, the only way you'll ever get to see *my* panties is if you …" I trail off suggestively, because I think I'm going to enjoy shattering that odd fascination in his eyes.

"Kiss my ass first," I finish sweetly.

His smile grows wider.

"I'd love to, Jaz, but only if you *suck my dick* after."

"*What?*" I gasp. "*What did you just say?*" I gape at him in shock, not quite able to believe that he'd be so damn crude. But then again, this *is* Raph.

He quirks an eyebrow in response.

"Would you like me to say it again?" His voice is perfectly casual, as if he's merely discussing the weather and not asking me to *suck him off.*

My face goes up in flames because I'm suddenly imagining doing just that and I'm mortified when my gaze drops down to the package bulging in his black boxer shorts. Holy shit, is it meant to look that big?

Stupid hormones. Before I can embarrass myself, I turn on my heel without another word, and stalk off down the hall, all too aware of those heated blue eyes glued to my ass as I take each step.

~

I sit in elements class later that morning feeling anxious. Magnus had warned me that I'd have to take this class, but I'd forgotten about it until now, too caught up in my ongoing feud with Raphael St. Tristan and the other Dynasty heirs.

"I don't think they'll call you up on the first day," Dani whispers to me as we sit up on the bleachers with the rest of the class. Professor

Roman is standing on the grassy field below, waiting for the last stragglers to take their seats.

Unlike the other classes, everyone in the senior year seems to be in this one class. From where we're sitting, I can see Raph sitting on the first row with Baron and Lance to his left. I see Layla's perfectly straight golden blonde head of hair to his right, with Ivy and Keller next to her. One perfectly manicured hand curls around his shoulder and I feel something twisting in my traitorous gut. He shakes her off after a second and I can see her flash him a hurt look.

"Looks like they're on the outs again," Dani comments, following my gaze.

I roll my eyes, because the last thing I need is to hear a running commentary on Raph and Layla's 'epic love story.'

"Makes sense—I mean I did see him walk out of his bedroom this morning with two naked girls in his bed. The guy is a pig."

"Holy shit. Was that awkward? What did he say?" Dani asks.

Only because I think it'll shock her even more, I say, "He asked me to suck his dick."

Dani's eyes go as wide as saucers, and she chokes on her next breath.

Thankfully, Professor Roman starts speaking then.

"Welcome to the first elements class of your senior year.

"We'll start off today with the usual—opening duel between two Dynasty heirs.

"Raph and Baron, you're up."

I watch as Raph gets up from the front row, followed by Baron. They make their way to the center of the large field, shaking hands formally in what looks like part of the duel etiquette. But I see the grin that the two exchange. They clearly enjoy this and something tells me that these two are probably the best at it.

I have no idea what 'it' is until the duel starts. I expect Raph to make the first move. But he hangs back, waiting with the patience of a predator.

The bleachers are silent in anticipation, until Baron unleashes what looks like a water tornado. I hear my gasp of surprise because of course, I've never seen anything like that in my life. *People on Earth didn't just summon water tornados.* It's a reminder of exactly where I am and who I'm surrounded by.

Raph easily intercepts the cyclone of water with a burst of pure fire. You'd expect the water to put out the fire but in this case, it's the other way around. The heat of the flames seems to *vaporize* the water until there's nothing left but mist. I don't know how the hell it happens, but I have a feeling it's because of what Dani told me the other day—Raph is the most powerful Seraph that Eden has seen in generations. As I watch the duel, riveted, I can see that it has to be true.

The crowd roars with excitement as the two fighters exchange water for fire, thunder for wind, lightning for storm. I remember then what Magnus told me that day in the hall with the murals. The Dynasties each have their set of elements that they're closest to—Baron, being an Aldebran, is clearly all about sea, storm and wind, whereas Raph, being St. Tristan and also a sovereign heir, could pretty much use any element. But it's clear that fire and light are his forte.

Baron is good—there's no doubt in my mind that he can wipe the floor with any of the other students here. But Raph is just *better*. Faster, sharper, tactically masterful and far, far more powerful.

The duel ends with a blinding flash of white light which consumes the entire field. For a split second, I'm totally blinded and can see nothing but white.

When the light clears, Professor Roman declares Raph the winner and the bleachers erupt with cheers. I feel like I should be clapping, too, but I remind myself that Raphael St. Tristan is an asshole whose sole purpose is to make my life a living hell. So, I keep my hands firmly at my sides.

Raph's gaze travels up to the top row and those vivid blue eyes lock onto mine as he walks back towards the bleachers. He flashes me that frighteningly beautiful smile. A taunt. I know then that the inferno he unleashed in class that first day was barely a flash compared to what this merciless asshole is capable of and he was using this duel to demonstrate the full extent of his power to me. To let me know exactly what and who I'm messing with.

My stomach twists painfully. Not just because I realize that this feud with Raph will clearly end in defeat, but also because I realize he was right—I can't do anything remotely close to what he and Baron just did on that field. I'm no Dynasty heir. Hell, I'm not even a full Seraph. I'm a nothing and no one, just like I always have been and *I sure as hell don't belong here.*

✤

"*P*lease come tonight—you're going to love it," Dani asks, as she rifles through my overflowing closet.

I still can't get used to the fact that I now own more clothes than I've ever owned in my entire life. I was more than happy to agree to let Dani come over and pick out an outfit earlier. But I'm not so happy about the fact that she's pleading with me to go to a gig tonight.

Granted, it's a Friday and it's a gig that she'll be performing at. But I'm not exactly a social butterfly and going to a gig on a Friday night where there would, no doubt, be other students from Regency, doesn't sound very appealing.

"Please—you're like my only friend here at Regency. You have to come and support me tonight."

Dani pulls a mock sad face and I can feel myself relenting. It's her next words that seal the deal, though.

"Besides, you don't want to stick around here on a Friday night. The Dynasty heirs might throw an impromptu party and you'll have to suffer through it locked in your bedroom."

I jump up from my huge ass bed and begin looking through my closet, too.

"Fine. You've convinced me," I reply, rolling my eyes.

Dani gives me an excited hug in response.

"You'll love it. Battle of the bands at Twisted is insane and the band I sing with is pretty damn good, if I do say so myself."

"Where'd you meet them?" I ask, as I try to find something sensible to wear. I'd never been to a gig before, so I have no idea what's appropriate.

"I take music lessons during the summer in Arcadia. These guys are from the same music center as the one I go to, and they kick ass on stage.

"I still can't believe this is your room and that I'm actually in Sovereign Hall. I never thought I'd get to step foot in here. I also can't believe how many clothes you have. You're so lucky."

I can't help the sadness that creeps into my smile then.

"It wasn't always like this, Dan," I reply. "Most days I still don't really believe any of it is really mine."

Her eyes turn serious then.

"But it is yours—all of it. So, you need to own it, girl."

I feel myself smiling in response.

"And the first step to owning it, is to wear this tonight." She holds up a tiny black dress which looks so tight, that it's almost indecent. I have a feeling that Magnus didn't have much involvement in picking out the contents of his seventeen-year-old granddaughter's closet. Because if he did, this tiny black dress would definitely *not* have been included.

"Oh, no—no way," I reply.

Dani just smiles back at me in response.

12

Clearly under-aged drinking isn't an issue here in Arcadia, or at least not at Twisted.

The DJ is still playing as the first band sets up on stage, when Dani orders a second round of drinks. We're with two of her band mates—two alternative rocker type guys and a red haired girl with tattoos covering one arm. Just like Dani, they're laid back, cool and utterly normal. A welcome break from the spoiled brats at Regency.

They don't suspect that I'm not exactly one of them—i.e. half human and supposedly a Dynasty heir. But then again, why would they? That makes me relax all the more, which is no easy feat, given that I'm wearing the tiny black dress that Dani coerced me into wearing. Paired with sky high black heels, I may as well be back at Rodeo Ricky's.

Dani's band goes off backstage and I'm in mid-conversation with Dani, when her eyes widen as she looks at something behind me.

"Can I get you a drink?" The voice behind me is familiar and the smile drops off my face when I turn.

Aquamarine eyes look down at me and I find myself face to face with Baron. Dressed in a grey t-shirt and black jeans, he's undeniably gorgeous. Too bad he's best friends with my arch-enemy.

"What the hell are you doing here?" I demand, aware that I'm being rude. Dani is gaping at me, as if I've just lost my mind. I scan the crowd then, because if Baron is here, then it means that Raph must be close by. But I don't see him.

"Relax, sweetheart, I'm not stalking you. Lance is playing in the battle tonight. I'm here to support."

Dani lets out a yelp.

"Lance is playing?" she asks.

Baron notices her standing next to me then.

"Yeah, he's playing with his band—you know the Ten Knox Nails."

"No way! Lance is in Ten Knox Nails?" Dani's forgets her usual star struck demeanor whenever she's around one of the Dynasty heirs and it's replaced by her enthusiasm for music.

"Yeah, they rock. You're Dani, right?" Baron says, flashing that smile that no doubt makes all the panties on campus drop.

Dani and I are both surprised that he knows her name. Somehow it makes him less of an ass in my eyes.

"Yeah, nice to meet you," she replies, reverting back to shyness.

He regards her curiously for a moment.

"Do I know you from somewhere?" he asks, and we're all confused now.

"Yeah, she goes to your school, remember?" I say, sarcastically.

Baron only shakes his head and his eyes look like they're trying to piece together a puzzle. Clearly thinking makes his brain hurt, because he doesn't look like he's enjoying it.

"No—I mean somewhere else?"

I see Dani flush then and now I'm curious.

"Well, ah … my parents are workers on the Aldebran estate so …"

My eyes dart to Dani in surprise. I wonder why she hadn't mentioned this before. But then I know all too well what it's like not to want to tell people about your background, because you don't want anyone judging you. I get that and I can respect that. I remember then what Dani told me on the first day of school, about not being of noble lineage. But I find myself admiring her courage all the more now—all these years she's had to go to school with these privileged pricks, all of them probably looking down their noses at her because her parents are the hired help.

I feel myself stiffen as I watch Baron's reaction, ready to tell him to get lost if he says anything even remotely derogatory. But he just flashes that easy smile, not a hint of snobbery.

"So, about those drinks—can I get you girls one?" He asks.

Despite his surprisingly cool reaction to Dani's revelation, the invitation still makes me eye him suspiciously, and my guard is back up.

"Why? Are you going to piss in them?" I ask, eyes narrowed.

Baron throws his head back and lets out a loud laugh, which is kind of infectious.

"No, of course not. Call it a peace offering," he replies, eyes twinkling.

"I need to go help the band set up, but you guys go ahead," Dani says then.

"You're playing?" Baron asks.

"Yep. Gotta go—you'll be okay here, right, Jazmine?"

I want to say no and beg her to stay, but I know that would be ridiculous. So, I nod and force myself to smile.

"Well …?" Baron prompts, gesturing to the bar.

I think it over. I still don't trust him, but I guess a truce with at least one of the people responsible for making my life a living hell, can only be a good thing.

"Fine. But I'm going to the bar with you—just in case."

He looks offended.

"Jeez, you think I'd drug your drink? Got trust issues much? I may sleep around, but I don't need to drug girls to get them into bed with me. I can do that with just a smile."

He flashes me what must be his most charming smile, and I let myself laugh in response. This guy is incorrigible, well aware of his reputation and proud of it. Somehow, it doesn't infuriate me like it does when it comes to Raph.

"Not that this is me trying to get you into bed—I mean unless you want to."

His eyes travel the length of me, and I can see that the little black dress has got his full attention.

"Because I mean—damn, sweetheart, that dress is … just *damn*."

I roll my eyes then.

"Just get me the damn drink," I retort. "I'll have a vodka and soda."

We stand at the edge of the dance floor with our drinks. The place is rammed and I don't see anyone else I know. A group of guys who Baron says are from the soccer team greet him with some fist bumps and macho hugging as they pass. But other than that, I don't see anyone that I know. I'm still not convinced that Baron is here alone, but I don't ask about the other Dynasty heirs. Mostly because I don't want to know.

"Look, I know you haven't exactly been welcomed with open arms. I've played my part in that. But you're one hell of a fighter and I guess what I'm trying to say is, that I respect you for that."

I find myself smiling in response to that.

"Thanks—I think."

"Besides, anyone who has the guts to throw their lunch on Raph in front of the entire school, is okay in my book."

I let out a laugh then, because in hindsight, it was pretty damn funny.

"And don't even get me started on how pissed he was when you blew up his ride."

I laugh even louder, and he joins in.

"Man, he was so pissed, I think he busted an artery. I wouldn't be surprised if there was a solar eclipse on Earth as a result.

"Throwing his trophies into the ocean is probably my favorite, though."

I cover my face, and let out a groan. Not that I feel bad for what I did. The fucker deserved it.

"Couple your kickass attitude with the fact that you're drop dead gorgeous, and I think you're pretty much every guy's dream girl."

I get the feeling that Baron probably gives compliments out to girls like candy—everyone gets one. But I'm not offended by that, Baron doesn't pretend to be anything other than he who he is—he's fun and I guess in that moment, I'm long overdue for that. Plus, there's the fact that he doesn't make my skin feel like it's on fire whenever I'm within two feet of him or make me feel like my insides are being put through the grinder whenever we lock eyes.

I roll my eyes in response to his words.

"Oh, come on, don't tell me you don't know how fucking gorgeous you are?" He echoes Dani's words from a few days ago.

"Because, I know that every guy at Regency sprang a boner that first moment you walked onto campus."

"Ew." I cringe and Baron laughs in response.

"If that were true, then I wouldn't be standing here all alone with you. Most guys at school treat me like I've got some contagious disease."

Baron winces then. "Blame that one on Raph—he pretty much warned every guy to stay clear."

I think that's odd. But Baron is probably referring to the school-wide outcast label that I've been given and for that, I do most definitely blame Raph.

Baron and I get through two more rounds before Dani's band starts playing. I'm no battle of the bands expert, but they're pretty damn good.

"Your friend Dani's an amazing singer," Baron says as the band moves into their second set. I agree with him. she's absolutely amazing and on stage the girl next door is replaced by a star who's difficult to look away from.

"Wanna dance?" Baron asks. I hesitate at first, but the alcohol in my system, coupled with the irresistible beats blaring from the stage, makes me want to get on the dance floor. Plus the fact that, pervy jokes aside, Baron is surprisingly a pretty decent guy.

We move to the upbeat tempo, singing or more like shouting along to the songs. Baron keeps his hands to himself, apart from twirling me around a few times. It's during one of those twirls that I spot something, or someone across the room which makes my stomach drop.

Raph is walking in through the club entrance, Layla in tow. I look over to the far corner, which looks like the VIP section and see that Keller and Ivy are already there, along with a group of people who I recognize from the popular table.

Heads turn as Raph enters. I don't think the guy can even help it. He's that irritatingly beautiful. It's almost impossible not to look his way. Plus of course, there's the fact that he's next in line to the throne. I realize that he probably can't go anywhere without people knowing who he is.

Tonight he's wearing a plain black sweater and dark jeans. His golden hair and skin glow, even in the dim light. Those impossibly blue eyes lock onto Baron and me almost instantly. Layla is raging at him about something. Clearly they're in the middle of some kind of argument. If I think that my dress is indecent, then Layla is practically naked in her nude, skin tight dress, with so many cut outs, that she actually does just look naked. Guys are visibly drooling in her direction. But Raph, who her attention is fixed on, isn't paying her a shred of attention as she grabs onto his arm. He's too busy giving Baron and me the look of death. He looks like he's fuming and I have no clue why.

Dani's band finishes their set and bows before going backstage. The crowd erupts with applause and I see Lance walk on stage next with a group of four other guys. The song which starts up is a slow one.

I feel awkward at first but Baron's easy going manner makes it difficult to stay that way. He draws me close, but keeps a respectful distance as we begin to sway to the lead singer's raspy vocals. Lance is playing electric guitar, and even in the midst of the other instruments, I can hear how good he is.

I'm so busy trying to block out a certain pair of burning blue eyes, that I don't sense Raph approaching, no, more like stomping towards us, until he's standing right in front of me.

"*What the fuck is this?*" he demands. If his expression from afar looked like he was fuming, then up close he looks positively furious.

I stare back at him in confusion, because I have no idea why he's so pissed. Not one. I can feel people beginning to stare. Most notably, the people in the VIP section, Keller, Ivy and Layla included. Layla's eyes are narrowed to slits and she looks like she wants to claw my face off.

Baron looks alarmed by Raph's apparent rage. But I'm not. I'm just angry.

"What does it look like?" I snap back.

"It looks like you're standing here in not enough clothes, with your tits on display and your hands all over *someone else*."

I try to block out his words, but his insult stings and at the same time, I'm utterly baffled by his reaction.

"Fuck you, asshole—and what do you mean by *someone else?*" I shout back. "*As opposed to who?*"

"Raph, calm down," Baron is interjecting now, trying to pull Raph away.

"Sorry," Baron shoots an apologetic look my way and he's looking between me and Raph, as if Raph has lost his mind. I think I agree with him.

"Just stay the hell away from us," Raph seethes.

I don't know what makes me do what I do next. I could blame it on the alcohol, but I think it has more to do with the way those impossibly blue eyes burn into me.

I walk over to Baron, closing the distance between us as I pull his head down and kiss him. Baron is surprised at first, no, more like *utterly shocked*. He recovers quickly and kisses me back after a second, taking control of the kiss as his tongue sweeps into my mouth. I have very little kissing experience. In fact I have *none*. But Baron clearly has plenty for the both of us. He lives up to his reputation, because he is a damn good kisser. There's no butterflies or fire or any of the other crazy things that you hear about in romance novels. But it's a damn good kiss.

I break away and Baron looks a little dazed. Raph, however, looks like he's about to lose his shit.

I don't stick around to watch. Fuck him.

I turn on my heel and walk away, well aware that everyone is witnessing this floor show.

I catch a glimpse of Baron and Raph as I walk out of the bar, still standing in the middle of the dance floor, locked in some heated argument. What the fuck ever.

I send a text to Dani to tell her that I left early and that I don't need a ride back to campus when I realize that I have no idea where I am and I also think I'm drunk. I contemplate going back to the bar, but I can't bear the thought of seeing that asshole's stupid face again.

I'm just about to text Dani again, when I hear the rumble of an engine behind me, following me down the otherwise deserted street.

I can feel my skin prickle with panic, but I force myself to stay calm. I command myself to keep walking, my gaze darting around for any sign of safety. The shops lining the darkened street are all closed, and there doesn't seem to be any houses on this street.

I can see a gun metal sports car in the corner of my eye. I don't recognize it. I hear the sound of the electric window lowering and I almost scream when someone says my name.

"Jaz, get in."

I whirl around to find that infuriatingly perfect face looking back at me from the driver's seat of what is probably his new ride.

I let out a harsh laugh as my nerves calm.

"No. Fucking. Way."

Raph lets out a growl of frustration.

"Get in the car, Jaz," he repeats.

"Are you deaf?" I shout back. "I said *no*."

"If you think I'm going to leave you out here when I know that you're drunk and you have no idea where you are, then you're wrong."

I stare back at him in confusion.

"What the fuck do you care, asshole? You hate me, remember?"

He gets out of the car himself then and all six foot three of him towers over me on the sidewalk.

"Please, just get in the car." I don't know whether it's the alcohol making me hear things, but his voice sounds different—gentle in a way that I don't think I've ever heard him speak before.

My confusion only grows; but he's right—I am drunk and I have no idea where I am. The stubborn part of me would rather get lost and mugged than get in the car with the guy who has made my life here in Eden a living hell so far. But I know I'd only be punishing myself. Plus, I fully believe that this equally stubborn asshole will just continue to follow me if I don't get in.

I say nothing as I let Raph open the passenger side door for me and I climb in.

The silence in the car is both painfully awkward and deafening. The atmosphere in the small compartment is so charged, that I'm finding it hard to breathe, even though the window is fully open.

"I'm sorry for what I said earlier. I was …I was just pissed and I didn't mean what I said," Raph says haltingly, as if apologizing is a foreign concept to him. It probably is.

Once I get over my initial shock, I turn to him. I don't ask him for an explanation of why he was pissed, because I don't think I want to know the answer.

"Did that hurt?" I ask instead.

"Did what hurt?" he replies, frowning.

"Apologizing?"

He surprises me by laughing. I don't think I've ever seen him genuinely laugh before and it makes him look almost innocent. *Almost*.

We fall into silence again and I look out at the darkened streets as we pass, once again surprised by how similar everything looks to Earth.

I don't know what makes me ask the next question. It could be the alcohol in my system or the darkness of the night that makes it feel like it's safe to bare something.

"Isn't your girlfriend going to be super pissed that you just walked out on the gig and left her there?"

Raph is silent for a long moment.

"If you mean Layla, then she'll be fine. There's plenty of other guys there to keep her entertained … and she's not my girlfriend anymore. It's not like that between us."

I don't really know what that's supposed to mean, and I don't know why I care.

I wait for him to bring up my kiss with Baron, but he doesn't. I don't know why I feel disappointed. Of course, he doesn't even give a shit, because as I have to remind myself, he hates me. This uncharacteristic act of mercy doesn't change that.

Neither of us speak again until Regency Mount looms on the horizon. The sight reminds me that while there seems to be a temporary cease fire tonight, tomorrow we'll still be enemies. Still, while we're still under the cover of the night, I bare another piece of myself.

"Most days I think you're right, you know."

I can feel those blue eyes turn to me, burning bright, even in the darkness.

"I don't belong here."

"When I saw you in elements class today—what you did … I can't do anything like that. I don't have those kinds of powers. I shouldn't be here. I mean I've gone through ten different foster homes, ten different towns and I didn't belong in any of them. I don't know why I thought that this place would be any different."

I look over at Raph and find him gripping the steering wheel so tightly, that his knuckles are turning white.

He closes his eyes for a split second, rubbing his brow in a gesture of frustration.

"Dammit, Jaz," he lets out a frustrated groan, but says nothing else.

Eventually, I feel my eyes drifting shut and I let myself float into the darkness.

13

"*W*hat the hell happened last night?"

Dani's voice is way too loud in my ear and I hold my cell away from it. My head is pounding with what is definitely a hangover.

I start to explain myself, although I actually have no idea how I got back into my bed. I remember dancing with Baron, *kissing Baron*, Raph being furious, me walking out of the club, Raph following me, then taking me home.

I think I must have fallen asleep in the car, because I have no recollection of how I got back to my room. Only that I woke up this morning still fully clothed, and tucked into bed. Did Raph do that? The thought of it makes my head spin in confusion, which is the last thing I need, given my hungover state.

"I heard that Raph saw you dancing with Baron and he completely lost his shit, then *you and Baron kissed,* and he started laying into Baron right in the middle of the club.

"Is that true?"

"Yeah, that happened," I reply slowly. I didn't really think of it like that. "Although it was more like him laying into me than Baron."

"Well, after you left, I saw him and Baron get into a big fight and Raph stormed out, too."

I feel suddenly guilty. Baron is fun and turns out, he's an okay guy. He didn't deserve to get caught up in the middle of what happened last night. Whatever *that* was. I make a mental note to apologize when I see him next.

"How did you get home?" Dani asks.

"Raph took me home," I reply and brace myself for Dani's exclamation of surprise. But the line goes silent. As if she's so shocked, she can't even speak.

"Sorry," Dani says after a moment, "I just fell off my chair and dropped my phone."

I laugh despite myself.

"But seriously—what the *hell?* Raph took you home? As in, drove you home in his car? As in, he actually took you home? That makes no sense, isn't he meant to hate you? So much so, that he's labeled you an outcast to the entire school?"

I cover my face with my pillow for a second, wanting to *smother myself*.

"Yeah. It was really weird. What's even weirder, is that I think I must've fallen asleep in the car, because I woke up this morning fully clothed and tucked up in bed, with no idea how I got here."

"So, what you're saying is, that Raph *carried you to bed and tucked you in?*"

Dani is laughing now, but I don't see the funny side to this. Not at all.

"I *knew it.* I guessed it from that very first day in the cafeteria."

"Knew what?" I demand.

Dani just laughs in response.

"Oh, girl, you're in deep shit."

❧

I spend the entire day in bed on Saturday, nursing my headache and generally just not willing to face any of the people that I happen to share Sovereign Hall with. I'm avoiding one person in particular, and I'm not sure what scares me more—facing Raph's usual icy and cruel self, or the uncharacteristically decent guy who took me home last night. The guy who had Raph's impossibly beautiful face, but who was kind and seemed like he actually cared in a way that was totally at odds with the asshole I had come to know. It's impossible to believe had I not seen it myself, and I have a feeling that it's the latter that's far more dangerous.

By Sunday afternoon, I feel like it's safe enough to leave my room. I listen to the sounds of people getting ready and leaving and only when I'm sure the halls are empty, do I leave my room and make my way to campus.

I'm armed with a canvas and some paints. I've also brought the little metal tin containing the only memories that I've ever had worth keeping.

I guess I could've stayed in my room to paint, but I'm starting to get cabin fever and I want to check out the art studios ahead of art class on Monday.

The campus grounds are mostly deserted as I head towards the art building on the outskirts. The building is right next to the sports fields and I realize that I'm not the only one on campus today.

Soccer practice appears to be in full swing as I walk past the large soccer field. I've never been a jock chaser, but the sight of the players doing their drills on the field, some of them shirtless, I might add, isn't exactly painful on the eyes.

I pick up my pace when I realize that Raph is probably on that field. No, he's definitely on the field because of course, he's the soccer team captain. The last thing I want is to bump into him. Hell, he's such an egomaniac, that he might actually think I'm stalking him or something if he sees me here.

I'm almost at the entrance of the art building when I hear someone call out my name.

"Jazmine, wait up." I curse under my breath, but I feel less apprehensive when I turn and see that it's not Raph jogging towards me, but Baron.

A sweaty and very shirtless Baron. God, he really is sexy. I almost don't blame him for having slept with nearly all the girls on campus, if I looked that good, then maybe I'd be a slut, too.

"Hi," I say tentatively, suddenly feeling awkward as I remember how I'd laid one on him last night.

"So … about that kiss …" Baron says, those aquamarine eyes dancing playfully and it's difficult not to smile back. He really does have a great smile.

"I'm sorry," I blurt out.

His smile just grows wider.

"You don't have to apologize. In fact, feel free to kiss me whenever you want. I'm always open for business, if you want to do that again."

He tilts his head to the side playfully.

"Or anything else …," he adds, wagging his eyebrows.

I can't help but laugh. This guy.

"Thanks. I'll keep that in mind."

"Although, next time maybe don't kiss me while Raph's around—I kind of value my life."

"Yeah, sorry about that," I reply with a wince.

"I've known Raph since we were in diapers, and I've *never* seen him so pissed … something going on between you two?"

I balk at his words.

"No. God, no," I reply quickly.

He eyes me thoughtfully, and I catch a flash of light in the corner of my eye. Raph is standing in the middle of the soccer field, all golden hair and golden skin, looking like the sun itself. And he's staring right at us.

"Speaking of which, I think I should go."

Baron follows my gaze to Raph, who is now stalking across the field towards us. He doesn't look happy.

Baron turns back to me with a shit-eating grin on his face, but I don't listen to what he has to say as I rush inside into the safety of the art building.

~

*W*hat I love most about painting is that it's the only time when I can truly lose myself. When I sweep my paintbrush over the canvas, creating colors and contours out of nothing, I feel like I have some semblance of control and direction in my otherwise meaningless existence. The gnawing thoughts in my head quieten and any doubts seem to vanish. When I paint, I'm the master of what I create, the master of my own fate. All the loneliness, all the pain, all the anger of the past vanishes, leaving only me in the vastness of time and space.

I lose track of time as I work on the canvas, building the colors and layering the scene. I don't know what inspired me to recreate this image, but I feel like it's something that I need to do, something that I need to see.

So lost to the world, I don't notice that I'm no longer alone until a voice snaps me back into the present.

"You did that?" I recognize Raph's voice, but at the same time, it sounds nothing like him. There's no anger, no sarcasm. He sounds tired almost.

I turn to face him, and it hits me for like the millionth time how utterly beautiful this guy is. He's wearing grey sweats and a plain white t-shirt that's similar to the one he wore that first day on the beach. It clings to his muscled body like a second skin. His golden hair looks damp and freshly showered and even with the backdrop of the dimly lit studio, he glows with some ethereal light which I wouldn't be able to capture, even if I tried for months, years. It's difficult to remember that I hate him.

"Yeah, I did," I reply simply, holding my paint stained hands up to show the evidence.

He looks past me and studies the freshly painted canvas for a moment. Those impossibly blue eyes looking thoughtful.

I wait for him to insult the painting—the scene of the sun setting over the beach back in Rockford Cape, the pier in the background with the amusement park lights reflecting off the still waters. But he doesn't, he looks oddly stunned instead, his throat working as he takes in the rich colors.

"It's—it's beautiful," he says and then I'm the one who's stunned.

"Thanks," I reply tentatively, still waiting for the scathing follow up remark.

"Who's that?" He asks then, gesturing to the two silhouettes walking along the shoreline. A small girl next to a slender woman, walking hand in hand into the sunset.

I suddenly feel like this is all too personal. Like I'm baring a part of myself that no one should see, least of all, Raphael St. Tristan. This painting, this memory, it's sacred to me.

Still, for whatever reason, I find myself answering.

"That's my mom and me," I say.

"She used to take me to this place almost every afternoon when I was little.

"When she died … it's all I really have left of her."

As soon as the words leave my mouth, I regret them. I usually hate telling people about my mom's death. I hate the pity that I see in their eyes, the awkward moment that follows, because they don't quite know what to say. As I look up into those vivid blue eyes, I see none of that. Instead, there is something like understanding in those eyes and it confuses the hell out of me. Because what the hell does a spoiled brat like Raphael St. Tristan, born into privilege and who has never wanted for anything in his life, know about loss and loneliness.

He doesn't say he's sorry, which is always the worst thing that someone can say, because of course, the car accident that changed my world wasn't anyone else's fault.

He walks towards the table next to the wooden easel instead, where my mom's sketches and photographs are laid out.

"Is this her?" he asks gently, touching the edge of one of the photographs. It's the strip of photo booth shots that my mom and I took one evening at the amusement park.

I nod, unsure of what to say, because this moment is so surreal, that I'm not even sure it's real.

He looks at me then and those sensuous lips curl up in a small smile. A genuine smile that I don't think I've ever seen before.

"You look like her," he says. "Actually, the likeness is scary."

I feel myself smiling, despite myself.

"Yeah, I'm like her doppelganger."

He lets out a chuckle.

"She was an artist, too," I say then, fingering the sketches inside the metal tin.

"I got that from her, too."

Something flickers in the depths of uncanny blue eyes as Raph turns to me.

I'm suddenly aware of how close he's standing, and of how alone we are in the dim space. The air in the room suddenly seems too thick, and the sound of my heartbeat too loud in my own ears.

His eyes travel over every inch of my face, and I feel it like a burning touch.

"You've got paint on your cheek," he murmurs.

Then, before I can stop him, Raph's fingertips are brushing against my cheekbone in the lightest of touches. They feel cool against my flushed skin, but at the same time, everywhere they touch, I feel my skin burn and come alive.

What is happening here? I know that I should move away, but my body isn't listening. All I can do is stare into those eyes, which have now darkened so, that they're as blue as the bottom of a flame. And fall into them.

"What are you doing?" I manage to say, my voice barely a ragged whisper in the space between us.

"I don't know," he replies as he draws even closer, so close that I can feel the words almost on my lips.

"Raph—are you in here? Teague says he saw you go in here …" The voice is an unwelcome one in this strange world that we've created between us.

It takes a moment for me to register that Layla is standing by the doorway and she looks furious.

Those merciless green eyes travel from Raph to me and back again, narrowing into slits as the displeasure on her face intensifies.

Raph drops his hand, as if he's been burned. Although, I'm the one who feels the burn from his sudden apparent desire to get as far away from me as possible.

"Raph—what are you doing here … with *her?*"

He doesn't even look at me as he picks up his duffel bag and walks towards Layla.

"Nothing," he replies and I feel the knife which seems to have lodged itself in my chest twist even deeper.

"Let's go."

I watch as he leads Layla away from the room, without even so much as looking back at me.

As I force my breathing to slow and clamp down on my out of control emotions, I remind myself that I hate this guy. Hate him completely, totally and utterly. Layla may be a total bitch, but she did me a favor just then. A huge favor. If she hadn't shown up to remind us all where we stood in this damn place, I can't even begin to imagine what the fallout would have been.

14

a few weeks pass without a single incident. Life almost seems … normal. Well, I'm still being treated like an outcast, but the whispers and looks are starting to die down. In fact, some people now even seem scared of me—like I'm some kind of psychotic bitch. *I guess blowing up the King of school's car will do that for your reputation.* If there's one thing you can count on—whether it's on Earth or I guess on Eden, people always get bored.

Raph seems to be avoiding me completely. Which is good, because I sure as hell am avoiding him, too.

Still, I see him on campus several times and I'm not pleased to learn that we share more than just a few classes. Each time I see him, he either has Layla plastered to his side or some other girl or girls, plural. Good. Because it just reminds me that I hate him.

Gym class is one of the few classes that Dani and I don't have together. I'm running late to the lesson because it's swimming today and I have no idea where the pool is, although Dani tried to give me directions as we were both leaving first period chemistry. Her second period class is in the opposite direction, otherwise she said she would've shown me the way.

The girls' locker room is empty when I finally find the gymnasium where the pool is located. *Great, I'm late.*

I yank open my gym bag and root around inside for my black, Regency-issued uniform swimsuit. I hurriedly strip down and pull on the black Lycra one piece. But something feels off.

I catch a reflection of myself in the locker room mirror and I swear I almost scream.

The black one piece is not exactly a one piece anymore. There are massive cut outs across my midsection and ass, so that it's basically a bikini—a very crudely put together and very revealing bikini. With all the body parts on display through the ruined swimsuit, I might as well be naked.

My vision slowly turns to red as I gape at my reflection in the mirror, knowing exactly who would be responsible for something like this.

I make to take off the suit but then I think twice. Fuck them. Fuck them all.

I march through the locker room and I'm feeling deathly calm as I push open the double doors leading to the indoor swimming pool.

The lesson hasn't yet started and the class is gathered at the edge of the pool nearest to the door. Conversation comes to a complete halt and everyone turns to stare at me. Every damn person.

Keller's eyebrows shoot up in surprise. Lance's mouth drops open and next to him, Baron's stunned expression is almost comical. There is nothing funny about how I feel in that moment. Nothing.

The expression on Raph's face is equally serious, though, those blue eyes burning like twin flames as they track my movements.

It's Layla who catches my attention, as she walks towards me, her black swimsuit perfectly intact.

The gleeful look on her face only makes my temper burn hotter.

"Do you like my little present, slut?" she asks.

"God, why am I even asking? Of course you do—you probably miss walking around half naked. Too bad I don't have any cash to throw at you right now, but you're such a whore, that you'd probably be happy to suck off all the guys here for free."

I'm so angry, I can't even see straight and when Layla lets out a vicious laugh, I can feel it shredding away the last of my self-control.

"I can't believe you actually *wore it*—you really are a shameless whore. *Just like your mother*—you filthy human bastard."

I lose it then. My intention was to come here and give these fuckers a piece of my mind but Layla's words make me lose my shit. In fact, everything about her smug little face does.

I pull my fist back and punch her squarely on the mouth.

There's a round of gasps and the room erupts with movement, but I don't register any of it.

"You little bitch!" Layla screams, clutching her bloodied mouth.

She lunges for me and someone shouts, "Cat fight!"

I dodge her easily, then throw another punch. This time my fist lands squarely on her throat and she's choking and gasping for air as she hits the tiled floor.

I jump on top of her then, straddling her as she thrashes underneath me.

"Don't you ever talk about my mom, you fucking bitch. *Ever.*"

She's screaming as she's trying to claw at my face. The entire class is gathered around us now, and I can hear people calling out, but I can't make out a single word through my rage. I think I see the teacher standing there, but he does nothing to stop the fight, which is typical of this place. The rules don't apply to the Dynasty heirs.

"Get off me, you crazy whore."

I land a punch to her perfect little nose and I feel wetness on my knuckles. Blood.

I feel something shift in the air then, something gathering. My eyes dart to Layla's hand where a ball of flame is building. *Shit.* It's then I remember exactly what I'm dealing with here. I may be able to hold my own in a fist fight, but these people aren't normal people—they are fucking gods and this girl is about to incinerate my ass.

I feel a pair of strong arms pull me back, just as the ball of flame is about to turn into a flamethrower. My back hits a solid wall of muscle and I hear Raph's voice from behind me.

"Layla, put the fire out."

I'm too shocked to register that Raph is intervening on my behalf, and my shock is mirrored in everyone else's faces.

Baron doesn't seem too surprised, but Lance and Keller are both looking at Raph as if *he's* the one standing there practically naked.

Layla scrambles to her feet and she looks furious.

"Are you kidding me—you're sticking up for this bitch? *Have you lost your goddamn mind, Raph?*" she screams. The fire is out, but she's lunging for me again. Something in Raph's eyes makes her stop short.

"Don't fucking touch her, Layla. I swear." His voice is deathly calm, but I know that that's when he's at his most dangerous. Everyone here seems to know it, too.

My whole body is shaking with adrenaline and I think that Raph must be able to feel it, because his arms tighten around me momentarily and I think I must be imagining it.

"What the fuck is going on here, Raph? You started all of this—*you hate this whore!*"

He ignores Layla and takes the towel from around his neck, draping it over my body.

Her words snap me into action then. Because she's right—Raph did start all of this. He's the fucking King of this place, he put the label on me, he made the promise to make my life a living hell. If it wasn't for him, none of this would even be happening. So what if he just stopped his bitch girlfriend from flame throwing my ass. He probably only did it because he wants to get the killing strike in himself.

Fuck him. Fuck them all.

"Get your fucking hands off me," I shout as I push Raph away. "I don't need your help. All of this is your fault in the first place. So, just *leave me the fuck alone.*"

Raph looks stunned and his eyes darken to a midnight blue. He looks angry, though I couldn't care less.

Turning on my heel, I walk away from the mess.

∼

"*W*hat the hell, Jazmine?" Dani whispers. We're in the library after classes, studying for tomorrow's trigonometry test—it's one of those times when I wish that Eden wasn't so similar to Earth. I mean who would've thought that you could move to a whole different *realm* and still have to take the same exams?

But Dani doesn't seem to be interested in passing tomorrow's test, she's more interested in grilling me about my earlier fight with Layla instead.

"I'm not saying that Layla doesn't deserve it. God, if anyone here deserves a punch to the mouth, it's definitely her. But she's the queen bee for a reason—she's going to *kill* you, Jazmine. Like gut you from head to toe and eat your insides for breakfast."

I grimace at the mental image.

"Gee, thanks for the vote of confidence, Dan."

"Although, she's only the queen bee because Raph's always had her back ... but now I hear he's backing someone else."

She looks at me pointedly, and I duck my head to pretend to study the formula on the page.

"Are you fucking him?"

My head snaps up as I stare at her wide eyed. Totally stunned at her choice of words.

"*What?* Of course not!" I hiss back. I'm blushing so furiously, that Dani starts eyeing me curiously. I don't like it.

"Wait—you're not a—"

I say nothing as I go back to pretending to analyze the formula in the textbook.

"Oh my god. You are! You're a *virgin?*"

Dani is staring at me wide eyed.

"Well, if you must know, I am."

"How is that even possible? I mean look at you," she replies.

I let out a long sigh then.

"I told you I moved around a lot. Not exactly ideal for dating or forming any attachments. Add to that my many trust issues ..." I trail off.

"And anyway, since when are you such an expert?" I mutter.

Dani just smirks at me in response.

"Hey, I may be a friendless loser around here in Regency but I'm in a band, remember—I get up to all kinds of things off campus," she replies with a wink.

Now I'm the one to look at her in shock.

"Kidding. But my first time was with a guy from my last band. We dated for a year back in sophomore year but long distance relationships are too hard to maintain," she adds.

"So, there's *nothing* going on between you and Raph?" Dani prods. "Not even a little kissing, groping, touching ..."

I make a face which is meant to be a grimace.

"You mean apart from the fact that the asshole hates me and he's likely going to murder me in my sleep one of these days?"

Dani waves her hand dismissively.

"You know I'm not entirely sure he does anymore—or if he did at all. You know what they say about love and hate ..."

"No, I don't," I lie.

"Well, whatever is going on—"

"Which is nothing," I interrupt.

"—just be careful. Getting in with the Dynasty heirs is a dangerous game. No one comes out unscathed."

I let out another sigh.

Dani says nothing as she squeezes my hand. She's looking at me like I'm a dead woman walking and every fiber in my body agrees with her.

❧

*L*ater that evening, Sovereign Hall is blessedly still as I walk through the golden double doors.

My fists are throbbing and I can see the bruises beginning to form around the open cuts which still sting like a mother.

Letting out a long sigh, I head over to the kitchen and open the double doors to the freezer. I grab a handful of ice from the ice tray and dump it in a tea towel.

I'm in the process of putting together a makeshift ice pack, when the front doors fling open. I stiffen at the intrusion and prepare myself for another confrontation, although this time, I'll probably end up putting my hands out of commission for at least a few weeks, which isn't ideal, given that I need them to paint.

But instead of Layla's hateful face, I see Baron walk in. He's laughing at something and is in the middle of throwing a comeback when I realize that he's not alone. Raph is with him.

I consider getting up and bolting to my room. But why the hell should I? I live here, too.

Baron surprises me when he walks over and flashes me that wide smile.

"You kicked ass today," he says and I feel my eyebrows arch. Baron's been pretty decent to me the last few times I've seen him, but the Dynasty heirs have known each other since birth, so I would've thought that his loyalties would lie with Layla.

"Really?" I say tentatively.

"Yeah, sure. Seeing the two hottest girls in Regency rolling around on the floor in their swimsuits was the hottest thing I've ever seen."

The excitement in his eyes makes me burst out laughing, despite the fact that his words totally gross me out.

"I think every guy in class sprang a boner. Hottest catfight ever."

"You're always so in tune about when the guys at Regency are getting boners—is there something you need to tell everyone?" I quip.

Raph, who has been standing in the entrance hall watching until now, walks over to us, and throws a smirk at Baron.

"Ha. Ha." Baron replies, rolling his eyes.

I feel all laughter drain from my body and I'm suddenly on my guard again.

Raph had been furious the last time I saw him in swim class. I expect to see the same anger when I look into those impossibly blue eyes. But I think I see something like concern instead as his gaze falls on my swollen hands, which is ridiculous, because why the hell would he care? He hates me.

What he does then surprises everyone, including, it seems, himself. I can see the conflict raging in those midnight blue eyes as he takes both of my hands in his and presses the makeshift ice pack to my knuckles.

I feel like I'm two seconds from falling off my stool as I gape at him, and Baron looks like he's about to keel over in shock.

The room is deathly silent and the air feels so charged, that it's difficult to breathe.

Baron coughs and I turn to find him shifting awkwardly on his feet, looking like he'd rather be anywhere else but here. Raph doesn't seem to notice though, as he keeps his gaze locked onto my face.

"God, as much as I'm enjoying standing here choking on all this sexual tension, I think I'll go upstairs and drill holes into my teeth—because that'll be more bearable."

Raph doesn't say a word as he keeps the ice pack pressed onto my knuckles, and neither of us speaks as he takes out a first aid kit from one of the kitchen drawers.

I say nothing as he dresses the cuts on my knuckles, his expert fingers applying the antiseptic deftly and with surprising gentleness. I don't move a single muscle, I don't think I even breathe.

When he's finished, he still says nothing as he walks away. As I stare after him, I don't think he needs to.

15

*I*t's a few days after my showdown with Layla and the bizarre encounter with Raph in the kitchen. I've spent the entire afternoon after class and the early part of the evening in the art studio, distracting myself with my latest project.

It's dark by the time I walk the tree lined road from campus to the edge of the plateau where Sovereign Hall perches.

I can hear the music blaring from midway down the road, and there is indeed another party in full swing. Great, this is the last thing I need.

I let out a long sigh and shoulder my way past a group of drunken students. Just like at the last party when Raph tried to *drown me in the pool*, I'm forced to witness the hormone fest surrounding me. I think I throw up in my mouth as I see a couple practically having sex on the kitchen island. Gross. I had my breakfast on that only a few hours ago.

I spot Baron in the pool, surrounded by a group of perky blondes. Totally in his element. Keller is also in the pool area, making out with a cute guy from the soccer team. He seems enthralled and intimidated by her at the same time.

I try not to look for Raph as I climb the stairs, but my eyes seem to have a mind of their own. I spot him in the packed living area. He's with Layla, which is perfect. Of course. I notice though, that they seem to be locked in some heated argument. Raph looks furious. Whatever.

I feel Layla's eyes on me as I continue up the stairs, but I don't turn to look. The bitch can kiss my ass.

I open the double doors to my room and straightaway I notice that there's a fire blazing brightly in the fireplace. *What the hell?*

I feel like I'm moving in slow motion as my gaze falls on the metal tin lying open on the plush black rug in front of the fire place. I run over to the orange and white flames just in time to see my mom's sketches and photographs *burning in the fire.*

I feel like I've been punched in the chest and I can't seem to get any air into my lungs as I stare at the fire. And stare. And stare.

I can't tear my eyes away from the horrific scene of every single memory that I've ever had worth keeping, going up in flames. *The only pieces of my mom that I have left.*

I feel so utterly useless in that moment, because if I could summon water or wind, or *anything*—I could try to salvage what's left of my mom's memories. But I can't even do that.

Panic spurs me then and I think I've lost my mind because I try to reach into the fire itself, not caring that I'm about to *burn my own hands off.*

I'm yanked back forcefully by strong arms and I thrash against them as they hold me back.

"Let me go!" I scream.

"Jaz, don't," Raph's voice in my ear is oddly soothing and I can hear something else mixed with it—sadness?

"Get the fuck off me!" I whirl around to face him.

"Put out the fire—please!" I don't care that I'm begging the guy who most likely is responsible for this for help.

He shakes his head and there's that sadness again.

"It's too late, Jaz—they're gone."

"No!" I cry out.

"I hate you—I fucking hate you!" I'm lunging for him now, but he holds my arms to stop me.

"It wasn't me, Jaz—I had nothing to do with this, I swear."

Those blue eyes look so sincere. But I don't believe him. I don't trust him.

"I don't believe you." I'm shaking my head as I back away from him, my voice barely a ragged whisper.

I turn on my heel and run.

I can hear him calling after me, but I don't stop.

I see Layla's satisfied smile as I run past the living area and I want to punch her on the mouth all over again. But it won't bring my mom's memories back.

So, I keep running. Out of Sovereign Hall, away from the crowd where I don't belong, away from the people who will never accept me.

I keep running until I reach the rocky beach beneath and I collapse onto the sand, feeling like all of the fight in me is gone.

It's only then that I cover my face with my hands and let the tears that I've been holding back since I stepped foot in this godforsaken place, fall. I let myself cry then—for myself, for all the lost memories.

I don't sense his presence until he's sitting next to me on the sand. I want to tell him to leave, but there's nothing left inside me anymore. Nothing in me that cares.

I draw my knees up to my chest then, hugging them to me.

We sit in silence for what seems like an eternity, watching the silvery beams of the crescent moon reflecting off the waves as they lap against the rocky sand.

"I have no idea why I even decided to stay here," I say finally. "I mean, Magnus basically kidnapped me and the only way back is with some key I can't get my hands on and even if I could, I'd still have no idea how to summon a damn portal. Although I've been telling myself that I'm going to leave the first opportunity I get, so far I haven't even bothered to try to find a way back. I guess some part of me was hoping that I'd finally found the place where I belong."

I don't know why I'm telling Raph all of this. I'm almost just saying it to myself. He listens though, not saying a word as he sits there beside me.

"After my mom died, I felt like I was drifting from place to place. Lost. Like there was nowhere on Earth where I could possibly belong. I felt so different from everyone else around me. I could be in a room full of people and still feel like I was the only one there. Like even if I screamed at the top of my lungs, none of those people would hear.

"When Magnus showed up with this promise of a different life, I guess part of me was sucked in. Part of me hoped that it would be different. That the connection that I sometimes feel to the moon, the stars and the night isn't just me being crazy.

"But I was wrong—I don't have those powers, I'm not one of you. *I don't belong here.* I think the saddest part is that all along, I've known that there was nothing for me to go back to Earth for. My life on Earth was utterly meaningless—I was nothing, no one. Those memories of my mom in that tin? It was all I had left."

I get up then, brushing the sand off my jeans.

"Now it's all gone. And now, I'm done," I say.

"I'm so done."

I'm almost at the path that leads up the side of the cliff back up to Sovereign Hall when Raph's voice stops me.

"Don't go."

His words are quiet, but the night breeze carries them to me.

I turn slowly and find him walking towards me, the blue of his eyes so dark, that they are almost the same color as the night sky.

"What?" I ask, my voice barely a ragged whisper.

"I said, don't go," he repeats.

I stare at him in confusion.

"Don't you get it? I said *I'm done*—you win."

He lets out a long breath, and those uncanny eyes lock onto mine, looking into me, through me.

"I'm sorry for … everything. Everything that's happened to you since you've stepped foot here. All of it is my fault."

The apology floors me and I don't even know what to think. I should tell him that I don't believe him. I should tell him that the apology doesn't matter, not after all he's done. But those words don't come out and I can only stand there in silence.

"I don't know if I've lost my mind and I have no idea why I'm stopping you right now... But I want you to stay. I ... *need* you to stay."

I'm utterly baffled now as I look back at him and I have no words.

"What you said about not being able to use your powers? I can help you with that."

I start to shake my head, but he's going on.

"Please let me help you with that."

I'm silent for a long moment as I look at that impossibly beautiful face. For the first time since I've met him, he looks ... scared almost.

It feels like I'm standing on the precipice of something so profound, that if I let myself look over the edge and see, things would never be the same. *I* would never be the same.

I'm aware that I feel terrified in that moment, but something about the fragile look in those uncanny eyes strikes a chord inside me and if anyone were to ask me why I did what I do next, I know I won't be able to explain.

"Okay," I say quietly.

He holds his hand out to me and I take it and in that moment, it feels like we're the only two people in the vastness of time and space.

*a*s I stand on the rocky beach at an ungodly hour a few days later, I regret that I ever accepted Raph's offer.

"God, when you said that you were going to help me with my powers, I didn't expect you to be such a drill sergeant."

He smirks at me in response.

"I have soccer practice every morning, so this is the only free time that I have in the mornings."

"But it's 5:00 a.m." I groan.

"I know. Thanks for letting me know the time, but I have a watch for that."

"You're an asshole," I grumble.

"A very kind and helpful asshole who is giving up his time to help you because I'm that amazing," he replies, flashing that cocky smile.

He's clearly a morning person because even at this ungodly hour, he looks devastatingly handsome in a grey t-shirt and black sweat-pants. It figures, he is, after all, meant to be the bringer of day.

I, on the other hand, look like the walking dead.

He puts on his official training face as he fixes those bright blue eyes on me.

"We'll do water again today."

I've been working on summoning water for the last few sessions and I managed to make the shoreline swell on the first day, but it was hardly impressive. Nothing like Baron's water tornado from that first elements class. I haven't managed to do anything since.

Some part of me still thinks standing here with him is totally surreal. Only a few days ago we were at each other's throats, trying to come up with new ways of torturing each other every other day and now here we are training together? It's beyond weird. But I'm slowly getting used to it and to Raph's special brand of arrogant charm. Now that I don't hate him, *as much*, I'm actually starting to find his cockiness surprisingly entertaining. I wouldn't go so far as to say I like it, though. He still irritates the hell out of me.

I'm not foolish enough to trust him. I keep expecting him to revert back to being that asshole who made my life on Eden a living hell. I keep thinking that this is some sick joke and I keep waiting for the punchline, but it doesn't come.

I don't expect Raph to notice the flicker of uncertainty in my eyes as the doubt eats away at me. But he does and he pauses mid-instruction, taking a step towards me as he studies my face. I feel unnerved, because he's done this a few times now and it surprises me each time how perceptive he is. I'd always thought of him as a self-centered prick, who cares about nothing and no one but himself. Those uncanny blue eyes are surprisingly observant as they watch my expression in that moment and something inside me whispers that perhaps he's always been watching.

"What's up, Jaz?" he asks, his voice surprisingly gentle.

I shake my head slightly then.

"I keep thinking that any moment now you're going to turn around and firebomb my ass or unleash whatever sick payback you have waiting for me next."

His brow furrows and I think I must be imagining it, but Raph seems genuinely offended by that.

"You still don't trust me," he says flatly.

"Do you blame me?" I ask warily.

He lets out a long breath then.

"No. I promise you, Jaz, this isn't some kind of sick payback. I offered to help you, so I'm here—helping you."

I stare back at him, the confusion from that night on the beach when he floored me with that very offer, returns.

"Why are you doing this?" I ask. I don't think I've even allowed myself to ask him this yet.

He looks away then, turning his gaze to look out at the crashing waves.

"I don't know," he replies honestly.

I don't push him. Partly because I can see that he doesn't have the answer himself and also because maybe I don't want to know it.

The moment passes and Raph begins the session with demonstrations in the usual way. When it's my turn, I feel the knot of apprehension in my stomach tighten.

"Come on, Jaz—you need to get past this first one so that we can move to the other elements." Raph puts on his team pep talk voice and I can see why he's the captain of the soccer team. He's good at this.

"So, I'm expected to know how to use all the elements?" I ask again.

"Yes, all of them. Of course, you won't be able to summon daylight, only I can do that," he replies with a flourish, and I roll my eyes in response.

"In the same way that only members of the Evenstar Dynasty can summon night. Exclusive sovereign Dynasty powers and all that."

I walk closer to the edge of the water and I can feel my frustration burning as I try to focus on hearing the pounding of the waves against the shore, feeling the movements of the water. Just as I feel the connection beginning to snap into place, I feel a wall coming down around my senses.

"Argh—it's no use," I cry out as I come up empty again.

"Calm down," Raph's says evenly.

I squeeze my eyes shut in frustration, but I can feel Raph's eyes on me. I turn to him finally, to find him watching me, trying to read me. I don't want him to.

"What is it?" he asks quietly.

My answer is one that I'm certain I hadn't let myself admit until that moment.

"My first foster parents were nice people. They couldn't have kids of their own, so they took me in after my mom died. I was only seven, but I could sense the expectations they had for me. I'd be their little angel—sweet, perfect, *normal*. I guess they soon found out that I was far from any of those things, even then. Things would happen which nobody could explain—the shadows, the shifting elements. Things that I was too young to control, secrets that I was too young to know how to hide."

I'm vaguely aware that I'm telling Raph things that I've never told a single soul. It feels like a damn bursting inside me and I can't stop the words from breaking through.

Raph doesn't say a word. He just listens and in that moment, it's what I need.

"They put me through endless therapy sessions, convinced there was a way to *fix* me. But it was no use. Their good intentions turned to doubt, then to disappointment and even fear. It's as if they were scared that I'd one day kill them in their sleep." The memory of it burns through me, but I force myself not to let it show. The way those endlessly blue eyes are watching me, though, tells me that Raph sees it anyway.

"I was shipped off to foster home number two in less than a year and it went on like that until I learned how to hide my curse. Until I learned how to hide who I was. I guess that after a lifetime of hiding those powers, of blocking them out, the thought of finally unleashing them, scares the *shit* out of me."

I turn back to the sweeping horizon, watching the waves lap against the shore as I feel Raph watching me.

"Your powers aren't a curse, Jaz. They're a *gift*," he says finally. His words touch some part of me I didn't even know existed until this moment and when I turn to look at him, the look in his eyes is not one I've seen before.

He steps closer to me, and although I'm certain that I should, I don't step back, standing rooted to the spot instead.

"You were born a *god* and made to live like a human. There is nothing *normal* about you and you should be fucking proud of that — because there is *nothing* good about being normal."

He says every word with a conviction that floors me, as if he wants me to believe every word in the deepest, darkest parts of me. In those broken parts that I long ago learned to hide.

I open my mouth to say something, but nothing comes out because in that moment, I have no words.

"Are you ready to try again?" Raph asks then.

This time, there isn't a shred of hesitation in me, not a shred of doubt left. As if by just those words, he was able to change something inside me that I'm certain will never be the same.

I nod silently and take a deep breath. I follow his instructions as he guides me through the first few moments again.

Nothing happens at first. I search for the connection, but this time, I hold onto it, getting past the initial apprehension. The connection comes to life inside me, like an almost visible chord, drawing me to the water.

I don't realize what's happening until Raph's hand grabs mine, and he's dragging me up the beach, away from the shore. We're not fast enough though, as an impossibly large wave comes towering over us before crashing down.

My scream is drowned out by the waves, and the only thing stopping me from being swept out to sea, is Raph's arms around me, pulling me away from the water.

As the waves retreat, I find myself pressed up against Raph's muscled body, his very wet, muscled body.

His t-shirt and sweats are soaked through, as are my hoodie and leggings.

I can't stop the laugh that bubbles up my throat and Raph is laughing along with me. So, we stand there laughing like a pair of lunatics, although I almost just drowned us both.

"God, Jaz—next time, try *not* to aim for yourself—or me for that matter," Raph says, once the laughter subsides.

There's an awkward moment, when we both realize that we're still holding onto each other and neither one of us seems about to let go. Every inch of his body is solid muscle and the feeling of his hard body pressed up against the softest parts of me feels too good. I desperately try to smother the raging hormones rising inside me, but it's difficult when Raph's impossibly blue eyes are burning like twin flames as they look into mine.

I pull back first, aware that my face is on fire.

"I think we should get back," I say after a moment.

Raph hesitates, but nods after a moment.

"Okay," he replies, his voice sounding gruff.

Baron, Keller and Lance are sitting around the kitchen island, in the middle of having breakfast, when we walk through the front door.

Conversation stops as they notice two things—one, that I'm laughing at some lame joke that Raph's just made, like we're old friends instead of enemies, and two, that we're completely soaked.

"And where the hell have you two been?" Keller asks, still eying our soaked through clothes.

"Training," Raph replies evenly, walking towards the kitchen island and swiping a piece of toast from the pile that Lance is buttering.

"*Training?*" Keller repeats. "Care to elaborate?"

I'm still standing by the door, unsure of whether to follow Raph to the kitchen or go directly to my room to change. Raph and I may have called a truce, but I have no idea where I stand with the rest of the Dynasty heirs. Although, of course, I know that they take his lead.

Raph makes the decision for me.

"Come here and get some breakfast in you, Jaz. I've been listening to your stomach grumbling all morning."

I roll my eyes. He's right though, I didn't have time to eat before we left the house at *5:00 a.m.*

"I've been helping Jaz catch up with elements training," Raph says in reply to Keller's earlier question.

All three of them look at Raph as if he's just announced that he's renouncing his throne, and running away to join the circus.

"Right," Lance says slowly.

"So … is this a new thing now?" Keller adds, quirking an eyebrow.

I admire Raph's unruffled demeanor because I sure as hell feel awkward under their scrutiny.

"Yeah, sure," he replies with a shrug, draping an arm around my shoulders casually.

"We're like best friends now."

I choke on my next breath and Baron grins at my reaction.

"Er—I think that's taking it a bit too far," I say, stepping away from Raph's grasp. His arm drops to his side and I think I might be imagining it, but I catch a glimpse of disappointment in his eyes.

"Raph's just offered to help me out and I've accepted," I add, as I walk round to the only empty stool which is on the opposite side of the island.

It also happens to be next to Baron, and I don't miss the look in Raph's eyes as he watches Baron pass a piece of toast to me.

"Except, aren't you two meant to hate each other?" Lance says.

"Is that what it was?" Raph says innocently, although I'm confused by his choice of words. Baron doesn't seem to be, though. Neither does Keller.

"Yeah, I distinctly remember that Jazmine here blew up your car," Lance replies with a smirk.

Baron and Keller snigger at that. Raph shoots them a filthy look.

"Well I guess that explains where you two have been sneaking off to every morning," Baron says with a shrug.

"Layla is going to lose her shit when she finds out," Keller mutters. I stiffen at the mention of the girl's name, but Raph just waves the comment off dismissively.

"Anyway, if you need any help—I don't mind teaching you a thing or two about winter and ice," Keller adds after a moment. She catches the look of surprise on my face.

"Raph here may have the reputation of being the best of the best, but don't listen to all the hype. No one does winter and ice like I do," she adds with a grin, which I feel myself returning.

Raph just rolls his eyes in response, devouring another piece of toast.

"What the hell, me, too," Lance says. "I can help you with autumn, fire and earth."

"I can help with water, sea and storm," Baron adds. "Although, conveniently, it looks like you've already started on that."

My eyes dart to Raph, who looks back at me innocently.

"I think I've got that covered," he replies and Baron just rolls his eyes.

Conversation moves on to an upcoming soccer match and parties as we finish our toast and coffee. It strikes me how surreal it is that I'm sitting here having breakfast with the same people that, a few weeks ago, I thought were going to kill me in my sleep. I can't deny that I like sitting here with them and that their company, although alien, makes me feel something that I haven't felt in a hell of a long time.

~

The next few weeks fly by and it feels like my feet don't even touch the ground as I go from training with Raph at the crack of dawn, classes, staying after school in the art studio, hanging out with Dani and also now training with Baron, Lance and Keller after classes.

It's not like Raph and I have started hanging around together at school, but I get the feeling that word about our truce has spread throughout Regency pretty quickly anyway, because the distasteful looks are gone. People no longer avoid me as I walk down the halls and some people that have never even spoken to me before, stop to say hi. It's surreal to say the least. The guys at school still keep their distance, though, and although I try to quash it, I have a sneaking suspicion that Raph has something to do with that. Although I don't miss the looks thrown my way—whenever he's not around, of course.

Layla still makes it clear that she despises me whenever I have the misfortune of bumping into her. In fact, now that I'm spending all this time with Raph, she seems to hate me more than ever. Frankly, though, I couldn't care less.

"So, Raph is helping you with what exactly?"

"Elements training," I reply for like the millionth time. Dani has been grilling me almost every day at lunch since I've started training with Raph. She's convinced there's something more to this. But I'm not. Raph is well … *a king* in this place—he can have anyone he wants and that includes Layla, the most beautiful girl in the school, who also happens to hate my guts.

He seems to have calmed down with the orgies and groupies, for whatever reason lately, and strangely, Layla also doesn't seem to be glued to his side like she usually is. But I haven't forgotten that he's *a player*. Pure and simple. His offer to help me out with elements training means just that, and I'll be damned if I'm going to let myself read any more into it.

I mean, it's not like Raph doesn't flirt with me. In fact, every other thing that comes out of his mouth is some kind of innuendo. That's because when he's not being a scary as hell asshole, being charming is part of his nature—flirting, to him, comes as easily as breathing. He probably isn't even aware that he's doing it. There are still days when I think it's completely surreal that we're no longer at each other's throats. Things do, undeniably, feel … different. I peg it down to the sudden absence of animosity. I heard once that hate, once gone, can leave an empty hole in a person. I feel that now, I guess, but what that hole will be filled with, I don't yet know, or at least I'm not ready to know.

"That's all—are you sure there's nothing else you want to tell me? *Come on,* Jazmine, you spend almost all of your free time with Raph St. Tristan now—the hottest guy in this entire school, no wait scratch that, on this *entire planet,* and you're trying to tell me that there's nothing else?"

"There's nothing to tell because *nothing* is going on."

A shadow falls over our table and I look up to find a guy that I recognize from our calculus class standing over me. I can't remember his name, but I think he's also on the soccer team. He has light brown hair and hazel eyes—really good looking in that wholesome, clean-cut way.

"Can I join you?" he asks. Dani and I exchange baffled looks, but I nod dumbly in response.

"Devon, right?" Dani asks.

"Yep, I'm in your calculus class."

I nod again, pretending I knew his name all along.

He gets straight to the point then.

"Jazmine, I was sort of wondering if you know, we could go out some time. If you're free."

I gape at him, because I don't think anyone's ever asked me out before.

"Like on a date?" he adds, flashing a brilliant smile.

I open my mouth to answer, but I'm interrupted by Dani who is staring at something behind me.

"What the hell …" she trails off, as another shadow falls over our table.

I follow her gaze and look up to see Raph standing over our table. I notice that the tables around us have gone quiet, too.

He looks pointedly at Devon, who now looks visibly paler. I look on in confusion, as he gets up without another word, and goes back to his table.

I turn back to Raph, who is looking back at me nonchalantly, as if he hasn't just scared off some poor guy who was in the middle of asking me out on a date.

"Hi …?" I say tentatively, although I have no clue what he's doing here. We may now be spending most mornings, and if I'm honest, most afternoons together, but we still sit at our respective lunch tables. Him at the table in the center of the cafeteria with the popular crowd, me with Dani in the corner near the patio doors.

"That seat taken?" Well, it clearly was taken before he scared off that poor guy.

He's usually so confident or just downright cocky, but he seems oddly uncertain just then as he stands over our table.

"Are you feeling okay?" I ask.

He looks confused for a second.

"Yeah, why?"

"Because you're asking to sit with me at lunch? I think you might be lost?"

He rolls his eyes as he drops down on the seat next to me.

Dani gapes at him, as if God himself had just deigned to grace our lunch table.

Her eyes grow even wider as he drapes an arm around the back of my chair, as if he owns it.

Everyone is staring at us, and I'm all too aware of Layla's eyes burning a hole through my back. Raph seems oblivious to it all, but I suddenly lose my appetite.

That's great for him, though, because he takes it as a signal to start helping himself to my lunch.

Dani is watching him eat from my plate, when he turns to her and flashes that smile that makes all the girls fall at his feet. I can see it has the like effect on Dani.

"Hi, you're Jaz's friend, Dani, right?"

"I'm Raph," he introduces himself with a straight face, although I think it's totally ridiculous, because there isn't a single student in the entire school or a single person on this entire planet most likely, who doesn't know who he is.

"*Jaz?*" Dani repeats, quirking an eyebrow at the nickname. I shoot her a look of death.

Raph smirks in response.

"Yeah, it's my nickname for her." I'm about to tell Dani that the only reason he calls me that is because he thinks my full name has too many syllables for someone so insignificant. A waste of breath is what he called it. But I get the feeling that it's no longer the reason. The nickname has irritatingly stuck and I feel like I wouldn't like it if he did actually start calling me by my full name.

"I like it," Dani says.

"Me, too. Best friends should have nicknames for each other."

I frown in response, as Dani grins from ear to ear.

"We're not best friends," I say quickly.

"I get why you'd want to deny that in front of Dani here, but I'm sure she won't be offended. We can both be your best friends."

I cover my face and groan in frustration.

"By the way, what was Devon Waldorf doing at your table?" Raph asks, after a moment, and I don't miss the pointed look that Dani gives me.

"He was asking me out on a date," I reply coolly.

A frown mars that otherwise perfect face.

"He's a jackass," he replies harshly.

"Isn't he one of your teammates?" I reply incredulously.

"Yeah, that's why I can say that he's a jackass."

"What did you say?" he asks and I can sense the tension in his voice.

"I didn't get to say anything, because for some reason, he ran off," I reply through gritted teeth.

Raph doesn't notice my irritation or at least he pretends not to.

"Hmm. Must be your garlic breath from this pasta."

Dani bursts out laughing.

I cut my eyes at her and Raph in response, and his smile only grows wider.

"Anyway, it's a good thing. You don't want to go out with that asshole."

Something about his tone pisses me off.

"How the hell would you know what I want?" I ask, my voice rising.

He has the gall to wink at me. "As your best friend, it's my job to know and it's also my job to make sure you don't go out with any assholes."

I get up, glaring at him all the while.

"Urgh. Screw you. The only asshole I see around here is you." And with that, I stalk out of the cafeteria, well aware of Raph's laughter following me and Dani joining in, too.

~

"*U*rgh, I'm so beat right now," I groan as I follow Lance and Raph through the large golden doors of Sovereign Hall. I stayed behind after classes to finish off some work in the art studio while Lance and Raph had soccer practice. Then we headed over to the woods on the far side of the island to practice fire and earth.

Now, I'm exhausted. But there's no rest for the wicked, because I have some serious studying to do.

"You did good, though," Lance says, as he heads towards the living area. Baron and Keller I've gotten to know pretty well so far, but I haven't spent much time with Lance. Dani was right about what she said on the first day of school about him, though, he does seem like the nicest of the three guys who basically rule Regency. He's drop dead gorgeous, but doesn't seem to know it, or at least he doesn't use it to his advantage to get into girls' panties. He's also got a wicked sense of humor, which is definitely refreshing. I have no idea what a guy like him is doing with someone like Ivy Hemlock. Ivy is the only one of the heirs who still seems to agree with Layla about hating me. I don't see her around much, but when I do, she's right by Layla's side, giving me the look of death.

"You mean apart from the part where she almost burned down that tree and started a forest fire?" Raph quips, and I give him a withering look in response.

I head upstairs and expect Raph to join Lance in the living area. Lance is powering up the console, and it looks like he's settling in for another night of gaming. The three guys seem to do that often, and it's so human-like and just so plain *normal*, that it's easy to forget that these guys aren't actually normal people at all—they're freaking gods. Gods teaching me how to influence the elements.

I shake my head at the thought, though I can't help the smile on my face.

"You going to bed?" Raph's voice behind me startles me. I hadn't realized that he was following me up the stairs.

"I wish. I have to study for my Eden introductory exam," I say, stifling a yawn. Up until now, the only difference between the subjects at Regency and those that I studied back on Earth, has been elements class. Even the history and geography topics are centered around Earth. Because the two worlds are so aligned, or so I'm told.

But when Magnus called me a few days ago, I found out that it's because everyone else learns Eden history, geography and politics much earlier on, with the Earth-based topics studied during high school. I'll have to catch up by private study, taking exams along the way. None of which, I'm looking forward to. Despite my ongoing uncertainty about my place in Eden and my willingness to stay, some part of me is curious to learn more about this world.

"I can help you with that," he offers, as I reach the door to my suite and I stare at him surprise.

He shrugs and looks almost shy for a moment. It's strangely adorable.

"I mean, if you want."

"I don't know …" I begin to say. It's one thing to take him up on his offer of elements training. But studying together? Spending time alone in my bedroom with him? That feels like something entirely different. I realize then that I'd drawn a line somewhere between us and hanging out in my room with Raph would definitely be crossing it.

He flashes that impossibly beautiful smile.

"I'd like to think that I know a fair amount about my own world. Heir to the throne and all. And I'm not just a pretty face, you know."

I laugh then, despite myself.

"Who said your face was pretty?" I reply, raising an eyebrow.

"You did," he says, that cocky smile growing wider.

"I don't think I've ever said anything of the sort," I retort.

"You don't have to, it's written all over your face—I mean, why else aren't you be able to keep your eyes off me?" He flashes me a wink, as I gape at him in outrage.

"You have got to have the biggest ego in the world—no, both worlds. Earth and Eden."

What comes out of his mouth, makes my own mouth drop open

and I wonder again how the hell I could've mistaken this devil for an angel.

"That's not the only part of me that's big—I'm told that I also have the biggest dick in the word—both worlds, to be exact."

I hide the tell-tale flush on my cheeks by turning my back to him as I open the doors to my suite.

"Ew. Just *ew*."

I turn back to him and realize that he's still waiting for my answer. Am I going to let him in?

I try to picture that line that's been drawn, but all I can see is that smile, those vivid blue eyes and I find myself nodding, when I should be saying no.

17

*F*our hours later, I'm lying on my front, on the plush faux fur rug, which is in front of the large fireplace at the center of my room.

My Eden textbooks are scattered in the space between where I'm sprawled out and where Raph is sitting, his back leaning on the plush velvet couch at the edge of the rug.

"I hate to say this, but you *are* pretty smart," I say, as I close my history textbook, feeling all studied out for the night. I hate to admit it, but I'm certain that Raph's help tonight has cut down what could have been days of studying, to a few hours.

The introduction to Eden history section was pretty much everything that Magnus had told me on my first day in Eden, but in far greater detail. Eden geography is entirely new to me, though. Eden, it turns out, is indeed a mirror of Earth, even down to the countries and cities. The only differences being the names and of course, the fact that the Dynasties rule *everything*. The entire goddamn planet. Raph mentioned though, that there are other parts of Eden which do not mirror any place on Earth. The royal city of Arcadia being one of them.

"Why do you sound so surprised?" Raph asks, raising a golden eyebrow.

"Because you're an *ass*," I retort, unable the resist the opening.

He laughs in response, and I have to shift my focus to the open pages of my Eden politics book, in an attempt to distract myself from the way that laugh lights up his whole face, making him look innocent almost. Something he definitely isn't.

The book is open on the modern politics section and my gaze falls on a diagram of the current Dynasty heads. Magnus's face looks back at me and the other faces on the page are familiar, too. I'd seen those faces watching me at that first ceremony, the disapproval in their eyes veiled, but there all the same.

The book must be outdated though, because the image at the head of the diagram is the face of the man who was meant to be my father, Arwen Evenstar. The image is small compared to the wall to ceiling portrait that hangs in the Evenstar palace. But those eyes, so like mine, are just as piercing.

I can feel Raph's eyes on me, trying to read me. But I don't want him to. I divert his attention to the space where the heir to the throne should be instead. It's blank, Raph's destiny yet to be written, although there's no doubt as to what that is.

"I guess you're not so important after all, if they neglected to include your picture here," I say mockingly.

Raph just flashes me that infuriatingly cocky grin.

"Hardly. It's just because it's near impossible to capture this image of perfection."

The gagging gesture that I make is only half pretend. His expression is as arrogant as ever, but I think I glimpse something beneath that is at odds with everything he seems to be trying to portray.

I don't know what makes me ask him the next question.

"Do you want the throne?"

My question catches him off guard, and for a moment I feel stupid for even asking it. Raph is regal in every sense of the word. He was made for that throne, he exudes it, emanates it. He carries himself with the air of a throne that is his by blood and a crown that is his by birthright. To question whether he wants it is, absurd, yet I can't help but think otherwise, when I catch a glimpse of something unreadable in those endlessly blue eyes.

"I'm sorry, it's a stupid question," I say when he doesn't respond.

He shakes his head then.

"No ... it's just that I don't think anyone has ever asked me that before."

That doesn't surprise me, as just seconds ago I'd felt stupid for even asking, when the answer is so obvious. But his next words aren't what I expect to hear.

"I've been raised to want the throne, taught since birth to want it above all else. It's all I've ever known."

There is so much left unspoken in those words, and I have no idea how to respond. But I try anyway.

"I guess you're lucky then," I say, although the words don't feel true.

His eyes darken as he looks away into the fire that he'd started in the fireplace earlier. He looks different just then. It's not just the glow of the fire warming his already golden features, but something tinges those devastating features—sadness?

"Things aren't always what they seem," he says quietly, almost as if he doesn't want me to hear it.

"Everyone always assumes that my life is perfect—but they have no idea."

I stare at him in confusion, and I want to ask what he means. But something inside me holds me back. Believing that this impossibly beautiful guy is shallow, conceited and couldn't possibly understand all the loss and loneliness in my life is easy. It's safe. I don't want to believe that there's anything more to it, that there's some deeper side of him that maybe understands those painful parts of me only too well. So, I keep my mouth shut as I shift to lie on my side.

Raph seems to sense the unspoken decision, too.

When he turns back to me, that easy charm is back and I'm glad, because that glimpse of what lies beneath it is downright dangerous.

He flops onto his back beside me and we talk about classes and other things which don't really matter. As much as I hate to admit it, I like having him here. With me. I'm so used to being alone, that the feeling should be alien. But it's not, it feels strangely right, like some part of me has known him my entire life. It's difficult to remember that only a few weeks ago, I hated this guy.

My eyes are starting to drift shut when I feel Raph shifting beside me. The fire in the fireplace goes out. Before I can register what he's doing, I feel his arms around me, lifting me up and carrying me across the room to my bed.

"I can walk, you know," I protest, but it's a weak one. I'm half asleep and I find my arms looping themselves around his neck, as if they have a mind of their own.

"I know. But where's the fun in that."

He carries me like I weigh nothing. A reminder of the strength contained in that powerfully muscled body. His arms are oddly gentle around me. I must really must be half asleep and I think I might be imagining it, but as he lowers me onto the bed, he lays me down almost tenderly, as if I'm made of glass.

I expect him to leave then, but he flops down next to me on the bed instead, and he looks like he's settling in for the night.

"What are you doing?" I ask after a moment. I'm now fully awake and painfully aware that Raph is lying next to me. On my bed. The bed is huge, so there's plenty of space between us, but his presence is still overpowering.

I turn to look at him. The room is dark, the only light coming from the silvery moonlight streaming in through the floor to ceiling windows. Of course, Raph always glows with his own light. God, he's beautiful, I find myself thinking, and at the same time, trying to stamp the thought out because no good can come of it.

"What does it look like—I'm sleeping in your bed. Duh," he replies, flashing me that insufferably charming smile.

"No, you're not," I reply. "You have your own bed across the hall in *your* room."

"I know. But I like *your* bed."

He looks back at me all wide-eyed and innocent.

"Best friends have sleep overs all the time."

"That would be true, but we're *not* best friends so ..."

I'm fully aware that I'm lying there with my arms crossed over my chest, looking stiff as a board. I'm glad that I changed into a t-shirt and sweats earlier instead of my usual sleeping shorts and vest.

Raph picks up on my extreme discomfort and laughs. He actually laughs.

"Oh, come on, Jaz, I had no idea you were such a prude—don't tell me you've never slept in the same bed as a guy before."

I clamp my lips together and Raph's eyes flare in surprise as he interprets my silence.

"No way—"

I cut him off with an indignant look.

"Well, if you must know, I haven't," I say, through gritted teeth. I hope that it's enough to shut him up. But of course, Raph doesn't drop it.

"You haven't what?" he prods, his smile growing wider. I want to wipe it off his face, but I say nothing.

His voice is oddly gentle when he speaks again.

"Are you a virgin, Jaz?"

My face is flaming and for a second I consider lying and telling him that I've slept with plenty of guys before. But why would I do that? It isn't true and it would just feed into the rumors that the Dynasty heirs have spread around school about me—that I'm some kind of whore.

The memory of it burns in my mind, and I'm suddenly angry.

"Yes. I'm a virgin."

His eyes darken and there's something there that I can't read, but I'm too angry to care just then.

"Ironic, isn't it? Those rumors about me being a whore—rumors that you probably orchestrated, couldn't be further from the truth, because I've never even had sex before."

"But you've done other stuff right? I mean, back on Earth you ..." He trails off, but I know what he's referring to.

"I took the job at Rodeo Ricky's because I didn't really have a choice. I was one year from being out of the foster system and out on my own. I was saving up for art school and needed to be able to support myself. You wouldn't understand what it's like to be in that situation, where you have to do whatever you need to, just to provide for yourself. Sure, I had to wear a skimpy outfit and serve burgers and beers to a room full of perverted old men. But I sure as hell didn't let any of them touch me and I wasn't sleeping around."

The expression on Raph's face when I turn to him is not one I've ever seen before.

"How is that even possible?" he says after a moment, and hurt spikes inside me at the insult.

"How is what even possible? You think that just because I had to bare my body just to provide for myself, that I'm some kind of slut that—"

He cuts me off.

"No, that's not what I'm saying at all."

"What I mean is—I mean *look at you*, you're *gorgeous*, Jaz. I …"

He trails off, and I'm stunned into stillness, because I can't believe my ears. Did he just call me gorgeous? And the way that he's looking at me just then as if …

I turn away to look at the ceiling, because this is all just too much. We're straying into dangerous waters, and I feel the tide threatening to pull me under.

He doesn't finish what he was saying. I let out a long sigh.

"I moved around a lot. Ten different high schools in ten different foster homes and I have some serious trust issues," I say.

That last part makes him smile.

"Really? I never would've guessed that you have trust issues."

I roll my eyes in response, and I don't know what makes me say what I say next.

"When I was fifteen, my foster father tried to …" I try to find the words, because other than telling the cops, I've never spoken to anyone about this and I have no idea why I'm telling Raph, of all people, now.

"He tried to sexually assault me—"

The waves of palpable anger that I feel rolling off Raph cuts me off. He looks so furious, that he's almost glowing with anger.

"But it didn't get that far. I kicked him in the balls and called the police."

He chuckles then.

"But it meant that for a long while after, I didn't like to be touched. I guess I still don't," I say.

"So, to answer your earlier question, I haven't done other stuff. I hadn't even kissed anyone before until that kiss with Baron that night at Twisted."

Those blue eyes burn like twin flames in the darkness, and he looks almost angry. Why would Baron being my first kiss even matter to him?

"What's the matter?" I ask.

"Firstly, I'm going to kick Baron's ass."

I gape at him in response.

"Secondly, I feel like a total dick. I had no idea. I'm so sorry, Jaz."

I smile then, despite myself.

"Well, like I said before, you are an asshole."

He laughs.

We're silent for a long while and he seems to be thinking something over in his mind.

"I haven't ever slept with a girl either, by the way."

Now, it's my turn to laugh. When I turn to my side to face him, his expression is dead serious.

"Sorry. I don't buy that. I saw you post-orgy only a few weeks ago, remember?"

He rolls his eyes.

"That's not what I meant. I've fucked girls before—plenty of girls."

"Gross," I interject.

"But I don't ever sleep with them. I usually get them to leave straight after."

I gape at him in shock and I don't like the strange warmth spreading in my core at the confession and all that it means.

I'm sure that I don't want to hear the answers to the next question, but I ask it anyway.

"But what about Layla?"

Raph doesn't even blink at the mention of her name, although I feel my own extreme discomfort at having mentioned it.

"I have never slept in the same bed as a girl," he repeats.

Still, I don't want to believe him.

"Okay, what about that *morning* when I saw those two girls in your bed—*naked* girls."

I have to admire Raph's cool in the face of these questions that would make most people flush crimson. I sure as hell feel embarrassed at even asking them.

"What you saw that morning, those girls came to my room that morning. They didn't sleep there."

The image of what I saw that morning is still burned into my mind, and I remind myself that this guy is a total pig, so I should tell him to get the hell out. But when I open my mouth, something else comes out.

"So, what are you doing here then?" I ask quietly.

"I don't know," he replies honestly. The same thing he said to me in the art studio and on that training session on the beach.

"Do you want me to go?" he asks, turning to me.

Yes. Should be the answer. But I can't seem to make myself say it.

We're not touching, though there's something strangely intimate about the way we're laying across from each other, eyes locked.

"No."

Something flares in his eyes, something that I don't recognize. It stirs something inside me which I'm not ready for. So, I close my eyes.

I'm almost asleep when I hear Raph's words. So gentle, that I think I must be dreaming them.

"Goodnight, Jaz."

∼

"*Y*ou have to come to Friday night's game—it's our first one this season."

Raph has been bugging me to go to his stupid game for the past two weeks and it's driving me bananas.

"Dani, help me out here." He really knows how to lay on the charm, because to my annoyance, Dani joins the chorus.

"You *have* to go, Jazmine. The Regency Gladiators are the *best*."

I narrow my eyes at my traitorous friend. But part of me is kind of glad that she and Raph have been getting along so well. I've learned pretty quickly that Dani is good at reading people, so I guess I thought that she'd see right through Raph's charm pretty quickly, and see him for the arrogant asshole that I still like to think he is. But she seems to think that he's a genuinely good guy. I guess I was wrong about her being able to read people after all. Because I refuse to acknowledge the alternative.

"But I don't even like soccer. I went to one game before, only because they needed someone to work the concession stands for the night and it was dull," I say, helping myself to another spoonful of my frozen yogurt.

"Trust me, this is like no other soccer game you've ever seen before," Raph says. "It's not the same as the kind they play on Earth. Plus, you get to see me in all my glory."

I choke on my next spoonful of yogurt.

"How could I say no to that," I reply sarcastically.

Raph leans over to me and I don't miss Dani's smirk as Raph's thumb wipes a drop of yogurt off my bottom lip. The simple touch sears my skin and I jump back as if he's just held a lighter up to my lip.

I hear Dani stifle a laugh with a cough.

Ever since that first night in my room, Raph has been acting like we're attached at the hip. In the classes that we have together, he either sits next to me or behind me and of course, it doesn't stop him, if those desks happen to be occupied. One look from him and the offending person promptly gets up and finds somewhere else to sit. He is also now a permanent fixture at Dani and my lunch table, much to Layla's annoyance, and to the confusion of the rest of the student body. Everyone, apart from Baron, Keller and Lance, that is. Because whenever they see Raph and me together, they exchange looks which tell me that I desperately need to set the record straight about whatever they think is going on.

Because nothing is going on. I mean, sure Raph has now taken to sleeping in my bed like it's his own, much to my annoyance. But nothing ever happens, and we both keep to our respective sides of the bed. Although, even I haven't failed to notice that Raph is *always* trying to touch me—surprisingly, nothing perverted or sleazy. Just a brush of the hand here, an arm around me there, wiping food off my lip like he just did. I always push him away but I get the feeling he understands why. Especially since I told him about foster father number six a few nights ago. I also get the feeling that he's doing it to make me at ease with his touch, and the flutters that it causes inside me aren't entirely unpleasant. Shit, I'd rather gouge my eyes out than admit it, but something tells me that I'm straying into dangerous territory.

"God, Jaz, you really know how to chip away at a guy's ego," he says. His tone is light hearted, but I think I see a flash of hurt in those blue eyes, although I'm probably just imagining it.

"Which is perfect for you, because your ego could use some chipping."

He chuckles at that.

"Anyway, about the game …"

I throw my hands up in frustration.

"Oh god, okay, if you stop bugging me about it, I'll go."

His smile lights up his entire face and those perfect dimples pop out, making it impossible for me not to smile back.

He pulls me in for a hug and although I don't return the hug, I also don't pull away. I try not to notice the deafening silence that has descended on the tables around us or Dani's shit-eating grin.

I think I must be fast asleep and dreaming, but I can hear Raph's voice in the night. I can't make out the words but I hear the anguish in his voice.

Consciousness taps at my senses and I drag myself out of sleep as the impact of Raph's large frame tossing and turning causes my bed to quake.

I look over to the other side of the large bed where he's lying with the sheets tangled around his waist. It's dark in my room, but the silvery moonlight beaming in through the large French windows illuminates the bed just enough so that I can see that Raph's bare chest is gleaming with sweat and the beads of moisture glistening on his face.

Alarm spikes inside me and I don't even stop to think before I reach over to him. I take his face in my hands, telling him to wake up. He's having some kind of nightmare and I don't know why, but the sight of him like this affects me in a way I can't understand.

He continues to thrash for a moment longer before those startlingly blue eyes snap open. They're hazy and out of focus at first, though. Dazed as he grasps for consciousness. The flash of vulnerability in those eyes, so at odds with his usual arrogance, does something to me that I can't explain.

He blinks up at me for a few seconds. Neither of us says anything. Neither of us moves. His eyes register my face above his and I might be imagining it, but it's as if the sight chases the shadows from his eyes.

The darkness is thick with something that I can't even begin to understand or maybe it's just that I'm not ready to. My hands are still holding his face and when he reaches up to cup my elbows, I don't stop him. We're so close, that I can feel the running stag clamor of his heart. I can feel every breath he takes against my skin, as he attempts to steady his breathing.

"You were dreaming," I say finally, in an attempt to slice through the charged air.

He's silent in response.

"Do you want to talk about it?" I ask quietly, although I'm not sure that allowing myself to delve beneath Raph's surface is entirely safe for me.

He shakes his head then. "Not right now." His voice is husky with sleep and with the memory of whatever it was that haunted him in it.

He slowly pulls me closer after a moment, until my head is resting on his chest. His arms circle me, holding me to him.

I don't know whether it's the glimpse of a part of Raph which I'm sure no one in the entire universe has ever seen, or whether it's the merely the cover of night which makes me feel like every secret is safe in this dark place. But I don't make a move to pull away. There are a million reasons why this shouldn't be happening, but in that moment, I don't allow myself to hear them. I don't allow myself to even think.

We stay that way for what seems like an eternity.

"Is this why you don't ever sleep with anyone?" I find myself asking finally. I don't know where the question came from and I don't expect Raph to answer. But he does.

"Yes." He says simply and it feels like he's saying a great many things with just that one word. But I'm not ready to hear them. I force myself not to think about what any of this means, closing my eyes instead, as I force myself back to sleep.

~

I wake up to the feeling of something solid wrapped around my waist and my back pressed up against a wall of warmth.

I think I must still be dreaming, as I look down and see golden skin with a dusting of fine golden hairs—an arm? It's wrapped around my waist. I feel something tickling my ear and my throat. The feeling sends a shiver down my spine.

"Hmmm." I hear Raph's voice in my ear and then the feeling of something brushing against the side of my neck. It feels like he's breathing in the very scent of me.

As consciousness taps against my senses, I feel Raph's bare skin against mine and my own skin burns everywhere it makes contact with his—which is in a lot places. His bare chest is pressed up against my back, with only the thin material of my too small sleeping vest between us. His bare legs are tangled up with mine. My goddamn hand is resting on top of his.

I'm jolted awake when I feel his other hand against the bare skin at my abdomen, where my vest has ridden up. I feel something long and hard pressing against my back which makes heat pool in my core, and muscles I didn't even know existed, clench tightly.

I bolt upright and Raph rolls sleepily onto his back. It strikes me again how young he looks when he's asleep, innocent almost. But there was nothing innocent about what I'd just felt pressed up against me.

"Quit staring at me like that or you're going to make me blush," he says, those blue eyes opening to look up at me. God. Seeing those eyes first thing in the morning is like a shock to the senses, which is more effective than any alarm clock.

"I'm staring at you in *outrage*," I retort.

I still can't believe that just moments ago I'd woken up to his body tangled up with mine. God. *Did we fall asleep like that?* Were we sleeping like that *all night?* The memory of last night floods my mind then. Waking up in the middle of the night to find Raph thrashing in his sleep. The way he'd looked at me, as if I was the one thing that could chase the nightmare away. The way he held me to him afterwards and what I'd let myself feel. Seeing Raph so vulnerable had done something to me. Something that had stripped me of my good senses, clearly.

But there isn't a trace of that vulnerability in his face just now. Only his usual arrogant smirk.

A part of me expects him to bring up whatever it was that happened last night. But he doesn't. There isn't even a trace of the memory of it in those luminous blue eyes. Either that or its carefully hidden in a way that only Raph, with his years of being raised in the public eye, could achieve. It's almost as if last night was nothing but a dream, it sure as hell feels like it. Unfortunately, the memory in my own mind is as clear as day and it's very much real.

"I don't appreciate you *groping* me in my sleep," I snap with more force than necessary.

"Me groping you? I don't appreciate being *molested in my sleep* either."

I stare back at him, sputtering as I try to find a response, because I can't actually believe this guy is serious. But I'm glad because the way he's infuriating me just now makes it easy to promise myself that whatever it was that came over me last night, will never happen again.

"Urgh. Don't flatter yourself. I wouldn't even look twice at you, let alone *molest* you."

"Then stop staring at my chest." He flashes me that cocky grin which sets my temper on fire and damn those dimples.

I can feel my face flaming because I realize that I *am* staring at his perfectly cut chest. *Dammit.*

A rush of disbelief hits me, because how in the world did we go from hating each other's guts to sleeping next to each other every night? I'm literally in bed with my enemy. I have no idea how I let myself get into this situation and I can't help but feeling like I'm riding on a runaway train, about to hurtle over a cliff to my death.

"It's not my fault you sleep practically naked," I snap.

"I'm not naked—I'm wearing my boxers. Although, if you want me to sleep totally naked, I'd be down for that, too."

"God, you're such a pig. You have a bed of your own, in your own room across the hall—you can sleep there shirtless, naked or however the hell you want."

"But I told you, I like *your* bed."

"Well, then, keep your hands to yourself or you won't be sleeping in it much longer."

"Likewise," he winks.

I notice something then as I look at the covers. Something which I'm sure was the same thing pressed up against my ass just a few moments ago.

The horror in my face must be apparent, because Raph bursts out laughing.

"Relax, Jaz—it's only a little morning wood."

I'm totally mortified. Firstly, although Raph's basically moved himself into my room, this is the first time that either of us has strayed past our respective sides of the bed. Secondly, I'm pretty sure I've never seen *that* happen before. Either that, or he's been hiding it pretty well to stop me from freaking out. Which he was right to do, because I am freaking out. I can't stop looking at it, though, and Raph smirks at my reaction.

"Stop staring at my dick, Jaz."

"God. I hate you so much." I almost scream in frustration as I leap off the bed and stalk into the en-suite bathroom, slamming the door behind me to block out Raph's laughter.

~

*W*e're walking out of Sovereign Hall, on our way to class, when Raph stops me.

I look over at him and I can't ignore the pang of concern. He's been oddly sullen since I walked back into my bedroom after my shower. His usual cocky charm replaced by the faraway look that I can see in those impossibly blue eyes now. I wonder if it has something to do with his nightmare last night.

"Will you … will you go with me somewhere today?" he asks; he looks uncertain in a way that's at odds with his usual confidence.

"What—*now?*" I ask, feeling a mixture of surprise and curiosity.

"We've got class," I add, stating the obvious.

"Forget it," he says, shaking his head, as if berating himself for asking. He turns to walk away. I should let him. But I find myself calling after him instead.

"Wait—what is it?" I ask. "Where do you want to go?"

He hesitates for a second.

"There's just something I need to do today," he replies simply. "And this year, I guess I don't want to do it alone."

I'm intrigued now despite myself. But that doesn't mean I should be skipping class to go to god knows where with Raph.

Still, when I open my mouth, I find myself saying exactly the opposite of what I should.

"Okay."

He smiles in response, but it's not that usual infuriatingly arrogant smile. He looks humbled almost, and I don't think I've ever seen that look on him before.

We drive in silence for most of the way, Raph seemingly lost in his own thoughts. I find myself sneaking glances at his profile. A strange sadness touches those impossibly perfect features and for the hundredth time, I wonder where he's taking me and why. But I don't push him. Something about that sadness reminds me of the quiet times when I think about my mom and I know the only thing I want in those moments is to be left to my own thoughts.

We finally reach a secluded mountain trail in what Raph tells me is the outskirts of Arcadia.

I don't question Raph as he leads me up the mountain trail. If this had been only a few weeks ago, I'd be certain that he was leading me out into the wilderness so I could get lost and never return. But I realize then, as I follow him blindly to an unknown destination in this distant place, that there isn't even a hint of suspicion in me. The thought is unnerving, because surely I don't actually trust him? How can I, when he's the same guy who threatened to break me and made my life miserable when I first arrived?

Raph stops when we reach a narrow cliff, overlooking a vast expanse of ocean beneath. I look down and see the terrifying drop to the rough waters beneath. Suddenly, I'm not so trusting.

"What are we doing here?" I ask, unable to keep the suspicion from creeping into my voice.

But Raph looks lost to the world in that moment. Something about his silence moves something inside me.

He sits down on the edge of the cliff, and then motions for me to sit with him. I hesitate for a second, but find myself sitting and I wait for him.

"I was ten when my mom died," he says finally, and I can feel the surprise reflected in my expression when I turn to him, but I say nothing as I let him continue.

"She battled with depression for years. I guess I was too young to really understand what that meant, but I remember knowing that she was always so sad. She never spoke about it, but I think she hated the pressures of being part of a sovereign Dynasty, being married to the head of the St. Tristan Dynasty and the mother of the future heir to the throne. The constant scrutiny, always being watched, living life in the public eye. My father's attitude didn't help things either—he's all about appearances and preserving the St. Tristan Dynasty. Having a wife who was severely depressed was a scandal that he didn't want anyone knowing. So it was kept a secret and all the while, she deteriorated, pulling further and further away. Until one day, her body was found washed up on the rocks down there."

The revelation floors me and I feel like I can't even breathe. In that moment, I let my guard down, just as Raph seems to have done, and I feel the sadness and loss wash over me. Feelings which are only too familiar but totally unexpected coming from this guy who I've always believed lived a perfect life and had never wanted for anything, who didn't know what it was like to lose someone he loved.

But I was wrong because he does. He knows only too well. I feel something shifting inside me, although I haven't moved an inch. It's the same feeling I got when Magnus unveiled this whole new world to me. The feeling like the whole universe is shifting, that everything I know to be true, everything I believe is changing and the feeling that some part of me would never be the same again. I keep those thoughts to myself as Raph continues to reveal parts of himself that I'm sure no one else in this entire world has seen.

"My father made sure that everyone believed it was an accident—she was out here hiking and fell. But he knew better, and in time, so did I." There's a tinge of bitterness in his voice then.

"Your nightmare last night ..." I begin to say.

He nods slowly.

"I have them sometimes. It's different each time, but she's always falling and it always ends the same—her body lying twisted amongst those rocks." Just like last night, I get the feeling again, like his words mean so much more than I'm letting myself hear.

"I come here every year on her death anniversary. I've never brought anyone with me ... but I wanted you here with me today."

This shocks me into stillness, but I don't let the meaning of it sink in. I don't ask why, because I'm sure that I don't want to know the answer.

"I do that, too," I find myself saying instead.

"On my mom's death anniversary, no matter which foster home I'm in, however far, I go back to Rockford Cape where we lived. I visit her grave and spend a few hours at the beach where my mom used to take me. I visit the tacky amusement park that she used to love taking me to and walk along the stretch of beach that she loved. I don't know why I do it, I guess because all of the different foster homes felt so temporary and that place, our place, was like my only anchor."

I can feel Raph's eyes studying my profile as I look out at the overcast sky above and the tumultuous waves below.

"Your painting that day in the art studio, of the beach—was that the place?" he asks.

I nod silently. Magnus had told me on that first day that Eden was in many ways a mirror of Earth and in that moment, in the face of Raph's confession about his yearly commemoration of his mom's death, I'm surprised to find that there are parts of his life which are a mirror of my own. It would have been impossible to believe only a few weeks ago that his perfect life could be anything like mine, but I realize that there is darkness hidden in the depths of his light. A darkness that I recognize. A loss so deep, that you need to bite the inside of your cheek just to keep from crying out.

"Hey, I guess we're both screwed up then," I say finally, trying to lighten the mood, because the air between us feels so thick right now, that I'm finding it difficult to breathe.

"But I still think I've got the worse deal—my mom being killed in a car crash, then finding out ten years later that my absentee father was, in fact, a king of an alternative realm, who recently killed himself, is pretty difficult to beat."

Raph smirks in response and something inside me is glad that I'm able to make him smile. Even if it is that smirk that usually infuriates me.

His face grows serious then.

"Did Magnus tell you how it happened?" Raph asks. "Your father's suicide, I mean."

His words cause pinpricks of discomfort to race through me, because I'm not ready to talk about this.

"No," I reply quietly.

Raph watches me for a long moment.

"Do you want to know?" he asks finally.

I shake my head in response, not trusting myself to speak. We're both silent for a moment.

"One day, I think I might," I say finally. My voice is hoarse, even to my own ears.

"But right now ... I'm not ready."

Raph just nods in response. He doesn't push me, doesn't force the subject.

We sit there next to each other for what seems like an eternity, watching the rhythmic movements of the waves below.

After a while, Raph gets up and surveys the tide. When he turns back to me, there's a mischievous twinkle in those impossibly blue eyes which tug at my curiosity.

"The last thing my mom said to me was to live like I was alive. I didn't know what it meant back then. But I know now.

"So, when I come here each year, I do something to remind myself of what it feels like—to be alive."

That mischievous glint coupled by those last words, make me think that I'm not going to like what comes next, not one bit.

"What is it that you do?" I ask anyway, the hesitation clear in my voice.

Raph grins back at me, the earlier sadness fading, or just retreating back into wherever he keeps that part of himself hidden.

He holds out his hand to me.

"Do you trust me?" he asks.

There's a million reasons why I shouldn't, even if he has just shared something with me which he's likely never shared with anyone else.

But I find myself taking his hand and letting him pull me up to my feet.

We're both standing at the edge of the cliff, looking down at deadly drop, at the waves crashing against the rocks below. The height is dizzying from this angle.

"Jump with me," Raph says simply.

Alarm and panic shoot through me because I think he must have lost his goddamn mind.

"*Are you crazy?*" I almost shout.

Raph just looks amused.

"No. Trust me, it's safe," he says.

He holds out his other hand and the waves beneath us swell higher. I can see what he's doing, making sure the tide is high enough to break the fall. But that doesn't mean I'm about to willingly agree to jump off this cliff with him.

He's watching me as I freak out internally. But I don't feel any pressure from him. I could say no and I'm certain he wouldn't force the subject.

I'm terrified as hell at the sight of the drop. But something inside me feels the thrill of the risk, the danger.

I think I may have lost my mind, too, because I find myself nodding silently.

Raph flashes me a daredevil grin and doesn't give me a second to chicken out, because the next thing I know, I'm hurtling off the edge of the cliff, down towards the crashing waves beneath.

My scream is lost in the wind whipping crazily at my face as I fall. I can barely register my own body parts but distantly, I can feel Raph's hand still gripping mine. The fall is terrifying and exhilarating at the same time. Every fiber of my being buzzes with awareness and I know I've never felt so alive in my entire life. For the few seconds that we're falling, my mind blanks completely and there's no loss, no pain, no anger. There's just the feeling of falling.

Our hands separate as we crash through the surface of the ocean beneath. The water is ice cold and my whole body feels like it's been plunged into the Antarctic.

I panic for a second, but it's enough for the tide to pull me under and then I'm *really panicking*.

Raph is there in an instant, though, grabbing my hand again as he kicks up to the surface, taking me with him.

When we finally break through the surface, I'm sputtering and coughing. Sea water is spewing from my mouth and I'm pretty sure it's not a good look.

Raph is just laughing at me, though, and his impossibly blue eyes blaze even brighter with excitement and adrenaline. The shade is so vivid, that I find it hard to breathe for a second, although that could just be the sea water in my lungs.

"Oh, my god! You *asshole*. I can't believe you talked me into doing that!" I cough out.

He laughs harder in response.

"Don't tell me you didn't enjoy it."

"Urgh," I reply in exasperation. He might be right, but I sure as hell don't want him knowing it.

I turn and start swimming towards the shore without another word, afraid that if I had to look at that smug face a minute longer, I'd end up drowning him.

I reach the shore and if I thought I was cold in the water, the feeling of the chilly breeze against my already frozen skin, is even worse. I'm seriously thinking that I'm going to get hypothermia. Raph reaches the shore a few seconds later and although the sea is Baron's element, Raph himself looks like some kind of ocean god as he emerges from the waves. He belongs to the elements and they belong to him—every ray of sunlight, every crashing wave, every gust of wind, within his control.

The image is swept from my mind though, when Raph opens his mouth.

"Nice bra, Jaz." He smirks as he fixes his eyes directly on my chest. I look down and to my horror, I find that my light pink bra is clearly visible through my soaked white school shirt. I can feel my face flame in embarrassment when I realize that the lollipop pattern on the bra is clearly visible, too. I kick myself for choosing to wear this bra today of all days and seriously, I wonder for the hundredth time, who the hell Magnus got to stock my wardrobe. But it's not like I had any idea that I'd be *ocean diving off a cliff* today instead of going to class.

"Stop staring at my bra, you asshole," I reply through gritted teeth. But it just makes Raph's smile grow even wider.

"Urgh. You're such a pig!"

He chuckles as he shrugs off his school blazer, and he surprises me by dropping it around my shoulders, over my own blazer. I'm even more surprised to find that although his blazer is soaked, it's as warm as a heated blanket. I pull it tighter around me instinctively.

Raph notices the fine tremor which is now racking my body and wraps an arm around me as he guides us back to his car. I want to push him away, but he's so goddamn warm, that my heat deprived body protests at the very thought. I'm horrified at myself when I feel my body snuggling closer to his. The infuriating grin on Raph's face tells me that he senses both the snuggling and the horror.

"Just so you know, I'm only doing this to stop myself from turning into an icicle," I snap.

"Sure, Jaz. Don't worry, I won't hold it against you."

My apprehension eases a fraction but his next words just make my temper rise again.

"But I can't promise that I won't make fun of you for it."

"I think I preferred it when we hated each other," I grumble.

"Aww, are you finally admitting that you don't hate me anymore?" he teases.

"No. I still hate you," I reply quickly, although I know it's not true. There's no doubt that Raph still irritates the hell out of me, but as much as I'd still like to think so, I know I don't hate him anymore. I let myself admit that maybe I'd been wrong about him. He's still a spoiled prick and an insufferable asshole most of the time, but the other parts of him that I've glimpsed tell me that there is so much more to him than the shallow, self-centered prick that he seems to want everyone else to see. That maybe our worlds aren't so far apart after all. It's a heretical thought, and not one that I want to entertain, so I shove it away quickly, because letting myself believe it feels dangerous.

"Well, I don't hate you," he replies, as we reach his car.

He turns to me then. His arm is still around me and I'm suddenly aware of how close we're standing, so close that I can feel the warmth of his breath on my chilled skin and when those vivid blue eyes lock onto mine, I feel the heat in them, too.

"I don't hate you at all." His voice sounds strangely husky, and I can feel alarm bells ringing in my mind.

Our eyes lock and for what seems like an eternity, yet no time at all, I see him. Not the heir to the throne of Eden. But a contradiction, wrapped in a puzzle, topped with riddle, and all over it are warning labels telling me to *stay the hell away*.

I force myself to step back, cold panic replacing the chill racing through my flesh.

"We should go," I manage to say, although I can hear the tremor in my own voice. I tell myself it's the cold.

His eyes burn into me like twin flames for a moment longer before his golden lashes sweep down, shielding the intensity of his gaze.

He nods finally, and as I get into the car, I try to remind myself of the lines I've drawn between us, but somehow, I can't see them anymore and although my feet are now firmly on the ground following the earlier cliff dive, somehow, I feel like I'm still falling.

"*W*atch this," Keller says as she dips her fingers into the large lake. It's a few days after the insane cliff dive and Keller has taken me deep into the forest at the far edge of Regency Mount Island.

I watch wide eyed as something forms on the surface of the clear blue lake, a pattern like fine white lace. Starting from the spot that her fingers are touching, then spreading out to the rest of the lake.

"What the hell ..." I hear myself saying, but my voice sounds distant, even to my own ears because I'm too busy gawking at Keller *freezing this lake over* with just one touch.

"That's amazing," I add.

She stands back, surveying her work proudly.

"Know how to ice skate?" she asks.

Before I can answer, she gestures to my leather boots and I watch in astonishment as blades of pure ice materialize at the soles.

"Thanks for offering to help me out by the way." I realize then that although we're on our fifth session, I haven't even bothered to thank her yet.

She waves her hand dismissively.

"It's nothing. Call it me making amends for the part I played in all that crazy shit that happened at the beginning of semester."

It feels like an age away now, but something occurs to me then.

"Isn't Layla pissed at you for even speaking to me?" On my first day at Regency, I saw Keller walk into class with Layla and Dani was categorical about her description of Keller as one of Layla's cronies. Although, after getting to know her, it's difficult to imagine this girl being anyone's lackey. She's tough in a way that tells me she doesn't take shit from anyone, Layla included.

"She can be as pissed as she wants, but she can't tell me who I can and can't speak to. I mean I've been friends with Layla since forever and she can be nice when she's not being a bitch. But that doesn't mean I can't make other friends. I like you—you've got guts and you're not scared to speak your mind. It's a rare thing around here, when practically everyone is so caught up in social status and wealth."

I'm surprised at her insightful response.

I follow Keller onto the ice then and we skate a few rounds before she stops me at the center of the lake.

"Here, try to create something from the ice—like this." She sweeps her hand up and I watch as the ice beneath us extends upwards to form an elegant spiral figure.

"I can't do that!" I reply.

We've worked on doing snow and wind the past few sessions and I managed to create some icicles last session, but this is entirely different.

Keller's not taking no for an answer, though, and she's not someone I want to argue against.

So, I focus on the connection to the ice beneath me and I sort of just lose myself as I begin to move. It feels like nothing I've ever experienced before, but at the same time, it feels so familiar—like the feeling of abandonment and calm that washes over me whenever I paint. I realize that it's because I'm doing the same thing—I'm creating something. But rather than creating it on canvas, I'm using the element of ice itself, bending it to my will to form the beautiful sculptures.

I lose track of space and time as I move and when I stand back to look at my creation, I feel stunned.

Even Keller seems speechless, as we look up at the ice garden that I've spun—rose bushes, fountains, statues, intricate railings and terraces all made entirely of ice.

"Whoa ..." I hear Lance's voice behind me and I turn to see that he's standing on the ice behind us with Raph. I wonder how long they've been standing there.

He wonders off to inspect my work and Keller follows him, still looking impressed and proud of her tuition.

I turn to Raph, and the expression on his face touches something in my core.

"That's amazing, Jaz," he says quietly. His voice is different than I've ever heard before.

"Thanks," I reply, smiling shyly at him. Something flickers in his eyes as he watches me.

I feel the blush creeping on my cheeks, so I skate away towards the center of the lake where there are twin arches of ice and a canopy of delicate icicles hanging between them.

Raph follows me and I know that Lance and Keller are somewhere in the ice garden, too. But I feel like we're the only two people in the forest, on this planet even.

"I think there's one thing missing, though," Raph says, as he moves closer to me in this sanctuary that I've created.

"What?" I ask, though it's a wonder that I can speak through the pounding of my heartbeat in my ears.

"Snow."

I look up to see the blanket of snowflakes falling around us. I close my eyes as I let the flakes of snow fall around me, feeling the cool kiss of the snowflakes against my cheeks.

I hear a sharp intake of breath and when I open my eyes, I see Raph staring at me. Like fully staring. The way he's looking at me, reminds me of that first night in my bedroom when I told him about my past. The look has the same confusing effect on me now, as it did then. Maybe I shouldn't be confused. Maybe I just need to see it for what it is. Because what it looks like is that he wants to kiss me.

I should be alarmed at that. The thought should make me run as far away from him as possible. This guy hated me not so long ago. He made my life a living hell. The hate is gone, but it doesn't change who and what Raph is—so devastatingly beautiful, that it's almost unreal, and he has an entire planet at his feet. He could have anything and anyone that he wants. I'm way out of my depths with this guy. I have zero experience with any of this and testing the waters with a guy who has the ability to shatter my heart into a million pieces if I let him anywhere near it, is a dangerous idea. One that I shouldn't even be considering.

And yet ... yet I can't stop myself from looking up into those impossibly blue eyes as they look into me, through me. I don't pull away when he draws closer, although I feel like the air around us is so charged, that I'm finding it difficult to even breathe.

He does something that surprises me, as he brushes those sensuous lips against my closed eyelids, the sensitive skin of his lower lip brushing against my lashes.

When I open my eyes to look at him, those blue eyes are so intense, that it's difficult to keep looking without feeling like I'm falling through the sky.

"You had snow on your lashes," he murmurs and he's so close, that I can feel his words almost on my lips.

I realize that he's going to kiss me. *Oh God*. Panic and something like fear races through me, but still I don't move.

His mouth brushes against mine in the softest of touches, once, twice. It's nothing more than the brushing of lips, but oh God, it's *everything*. Everything I didn't feel in that kiss with Baron—the fire, the flutters, the heat. It's all there and it's insane, because it's not even really a kiss.

I can hear the sound of my own pulse roaring in my ears and my heart is pounding so hard, it feels like it's going to come out of my chest.

But everything stops when Raph pulls back as if he's just been burned. He looks at me in something like horror, and then I'm the one who feels like I've been burned.

He curses, as he takes another step back, and it feels like a slap to the face.

"Shit. That was a mistake. I shouldn't have done that," he says.

I take a step towards him, although I have no idea why, because it feels like I'm stepping into the path of an oncoming train.

"What—" I have no idea what I'm even trying to say, but Raph cuts me off as he holds his hand up to stop me and I clamp my mouth shut, feeling the humiliation wash over me.

His eyes take in my stricken expression, and he runs his hands through his hair in frustration.

"Dammit—*I can't do this with you.*"

His face becomes shuttered, closed off like the first time I'd seen him on the beach. I can't ignore the clawing that I feel in my chest or the feeling like someone has just stabbed me right in that same spot. When he speaks again, his voice is as cold as the ice surrounding us.

"This can't happen."

I'm saved from having to say anything as the delicate snowflakes falling around us turn to large droplets of rain, pouring down on us in what is an entirely appropriate representation of everything I'm feeling. Because I sure as hell feel like I might cry.

"Sorry to interrupt this touching moment," Lance calls over to us from another section of the ice garden, which is now starting to melt. There's a wry look on his face which is mirrored on Keller's.

I tear my eyes away from Raph, who is still just standing there, stone faced.

Something like anger washes over me, and I focus on it because it's familiar. It's safe.

"You weren't interrupting anything," I call back to Lance, although I'm really speaking to Raph. Take that, fucker.

I walk away from him and join Lance and Keller on the edge of the lake.

I don't bother to wait for Raph.

Keller walks ahead with me and is watching me in a way that

tells me she can sense something is wrong. But I tell myself that there's nothing wrong. No, in fact this is just right. *What was I thinking?*

That was a mistake. His words echo through my ears and I feel like screaming. But why should I be mad?

Raph probably realized, just as I should have realized, that whatever it was that happened, is *wrong.* He probably just remembered that he's the future king of Eden and has the entire planet in his hands, whereas I'm a half human nobody who can't even use her powers properly. But fuck him. Because he started this. He asked me to stay, he offered to help me learn how to use my powers, he was the one who started sleeping in my bed, sitting with me at lunch and in classes, touching me and making me feel like I was actually beginning to trust him.

Then I laugh at myself for my own naiveté. Because it's my own fault for reading too much into things. Raph was probably being just *Raph*—flirting is like breathing to him. He's charming without even trying, he can get girls to fall for him without even meaning to. So, the joke is on me. But I feel that familiar wall of stone closing around me because I will *never* let that happen again.

"Did something happen back there between you and Raph?" Keller asks, as we near her motorbike. Yes, that's right, this kickass girl actually has her own motorbike.

"No," I lie. But she, of course, doesn't buy it.

"Well, it sure felt like it, because I haven't felt so much awkwardness in the air since that time in sophomore year when Lance walked in on Baron balls deep in Lance's Winter Ball date."

I laugh at the mental image, despite myself.

Keller looks at me expectantly.

"It was nothing," I say.

"I just forgot for a second who Raph is," I add, after a moment.

Keller looks at me thoughtfully.

"You know, most people think that they know Raph—he's got this perfect life and he's untouchable. Every girl wants him, every guy wants to be him or is just scared shitless of him, etc.

"But I don't think anyone really *knows* Raph. He puts on one hell of a front. That's what being next in line to the throne does."

I don't want to hear anymore, because I was in a good place just a few minutes ago—resolved not to let myself get caught up in Raph's twisted web again. I don't want to think about the glimpses of him that I've seen beneath the self-centered and arrogant façade, the parts of him that I'm almost certain no one else has seen and all that it means. I don't want to think about the fact that I know that his life isn't perfect, that although our lives couldn't be more different, he understands the loss and sorrow that's plagued me for almost my entire life. That he understands it only too well.

But I don't stop her when she continues.

"Even Layla never really knew Raph. But then again, it was never like that between them."

I clamp my mouth shut but the question comes out anyway.

"What do you mean?"

"It's not for me to tell you about Raph's business. I can only tell you what I see—and I've never seen anyone get to Raph the way you do," she replies.

"I mean, like back at the beginning of semester—I've never seen him actually *hate* someone. He normally just doesn't give a shit."

"So you're saying that you've never seen Raph hate someone as much as he hated me?" I say flatly. "Gee, thanks. That's good to know."

Keller rolls her eyes.

"No, I mean I've never seen someone get under Raph's skin the way you do," she says.

"Whether it's hating you for blowing up his ride..." she laughs and I can't help but laugh with her at the memory.

We stop in front of her motorbike and her grey eyes turn somber.

"... or whether it's something else ..."

I say nothing as I take the spare helmet that she hands to me.

"But I get that it's Raph, and nothing about that guy is simple," she says.

"So, just be careful," she adds.

I nod silently, but something inside me already knows that the warning has probably come too late.

~

That night, I lock my bedroom door, although that foolish part of me waits to hear the sound of knocking. It never comes.

I tell myself that I should be glad. That it's the smartest thing I've done since that night that Raph asked me to stay. But I don't think I sleep a wink that night and the feeling like my chest is being shredded to pieces doesn't go away.

~

"But you said that you were coming," Dani's voice pleads from the earpiece of my cell.

"I know I did, but I changed my mind," I reply, as I stare up at my bedroom ceiling.

It's two hours until kick off of tonight's soccer match and I'm still firmly refusing to leave my room.

"Does this have anything to do with the way that you and Raph have been avoiding each other all day?"

I feel a pang in my chest at the reminder of the look on Raph's face when he walked into first period trigonometry earlier. He wouldn't even look at me. As if the sight of me alone was an unwelcome reminder of that *mistake*.

Unsurprisingly, he didn't show at Dani's and my lunch table and when I saw him in the hallway after classes, he turned and went the other way as soon as he saw me. As if he couldn't get far enough away. I tell myself that I should be glad, but still, I can't deny that I felt it like a knife to the chest.

Dani sighs then, interpreting my silence correctly.

"Look, whatever's happened between you two, if you don't show up to tonight's game, it'll look like you're letting him get to you—and I know how much you'd hate that."

Her words aren't wrong, but I don't think I can stand the sight of Raph right now without doing something stupid or embarrassing, like trying to kiss him again. For real this time. I stamp down on the traitorous thought. I remind myself that I should be thankful because this was exactly the sort of thing that I needed to avoid. I remind myself that not too long ago, I hated Raph, hated him with a ferocity which was beyond reason. What in the world would possess me to want to kiss him or to feel that stabbing in my chest, when he acted like he'd been burned by that almost kiss.

This is a mistake. His words play themselves over in my mind and I tell myself that he's right—it was a mistake. Letting him draw me in was a mistake, letting him gain my trust was a mistake. Because Dani hadn't been wrong when she told me that getting in with the Dynasty heirs was a dangerous game and no one came out unscathed. It's good that this happened now because god only knows what would've happened if he'd actually kissed me.

Raph swore to me once that he'd break me if I didn't stay away. I realize now how true that promise was, because I know deep down, that Raph St. Tristan does indeed have the ability to break me. But I won't let him. I've lost too much already.

"He sort of kissed me, Dan," I say finally.

I can hear Dani's responding gasp down the line.

"What do you mean sort of?" she asks, once she gets over her initial shock.

"It wasn't really a kiss, more like lip brushing," I say, trying to find the right words.

"Lip brushing?" Dani repeats, incredulously.

"Like when two lips touch? That's called a kiss," she says flatly and I almost want to laugh, if it wasn't so tragic.

"Okay, so you ... *lip-brushed.* That's great, right? I mean this is Raph St. Tristan we're talking about. Every girl at Regency wants to *lip-brush* with this guy."

"Yeah, except he acted like he was horrified and then told me it was a mistake." I feel my voice waver as I say it out loud and I hate myself for it.

I love Dani, though, because as much as she seems to like Raph and has clearly been rooting for him, she goes into loyal friend mode almost instantly.

"Well, screw him. Who does he think he is? Raph St. Tristan is a loser.

"Okay, maybe not a loser because that would be impossible. But still, if he wants to act like an asshole, then he sure as hell doesn't deserve you."

"Thanks, Dan," I reply, smiling despite myself.

"I mean I told you before that you're like the hottest girl in Regency right now. You can have anyone you want."

I don't agree with her, but I keep listening.

"So, tonight, you're going to go to that soccer game, act like you don't give a shit about Raph St. Tristan and then go to the beach party after and enjoy yourself," she says.

"Screw Raph St. Tristan," she adds.

I agree with those last words. Screw Raph. It was a mistake. Fine. I can agree with that and tonight I'm going to show the asshole that I won't be making the same mistake again.

2 0

*D*ani was right about one thing—soccer games in Eden are nothing like the soccer games that I've ever seen on Earth.

It's the same concept, with the two teams trying to get the ball into the goals at opposite sides of the large field. But that's where the similarity ends, because the players on the field are using their powers to tackle, dribble and lob the ball across the field.

I watch wide eyed as the flaming soccer ball sears a hole through the back of the net on the opposite side of the stadium and the crowd goes wild.

"Wow," I manage.

"I know, right? The Regency Gladiators are killing it tonight. I almost feel sorry for the Gramercie Prep Raiders."

I try not to look at Raph on the field, but that's kind of impossible, because as striker and team captain, all eyes are on him and Raph is irrefutably the star of the team. In the same way as he is in a duel, he is just *better* than everyone else on the field. Faster, sharper, tactically masterful and far, far more powerful.

Raph always glows with his own light, but tonight, he *shines*. It's difficult to look at him without feeling like I can't breathe, but at the same time, it's impossible to look away. *God, I'm really twisted.*

But every person in this stadium seems to agree, because they all worship him. Everyone. The whole team got cheers when they ran out onto the field earlier. Baron and Lance were both greeted with an almost deafening roar. But Raph—when he ran out onto that field dressed in his Regency Gladiators navy blue and gold kit, the whole stadium stood on its feet and it felt like there was an earthquake with all the stomping and cheering.

The whole thing just makes the knot in my chest feel even tighter and I suddenly wish that I hadn't come tonight.

Dani notices my expression because she reaches over and gives my hand a reassuring squeeze.

"Don't worry, the night is young. There's plenty of players on the team and every single one of them is dying to ask you out on a date."

I roll my eyes.

"How do you even know that?"

"I like eavesdropping," she replies, matter-of-factly.

"And I can second that." I look up to see Keller standing in the aisle next to our seats.

I'm surprised to see her and the look on Dani's face tells me she is, too. I spotted Layla in the VIP seats earlier with Ivy and the rest of the popular kids, so I expected Keller to be there, too.

"I'm bored of the usual crowd. I feel the need for a change tonight," Keller says with a shrug, as if reading our minds.

Dani scoots over to make space for her.

"Anyway, what were we saying? Oh yeah, I totally agree with Dani about the soccer team lusting after you. I sit with most of them at lunch and the amount of salivating is kind of gross."

"Ew," I reply, as Dani bursts out laughing.

"Baron mentioned that Raph—"

Keller cuts me off with a dismissive wave.

"That Raph put out a warning that no guy can touch you? Yeah sure, but boys will be boys. They think with their dicks, even if it'll get them killed, and that won't stop them from trying when Raph's back is turned."

Her words surprise me, because although I had a sneaking suspicion, I didn't actually know for sure what the warning actually was. I told myself that Raph has just spread the word that I was an outcast, not to be associated with. What Keller is saying, though, is entirely different.

I don't know whether to be pleased by the possessive and utterly confusing gesture, or pissed. Pissed, I decide. Because who the hell does he think he is? He clearly doesn't want me, yet he warns other guys to stay away from me? Screw him.

"Oh, yeah, I mean Devon Waldorf tried to ask Jazmine out on a date just the other day. That was before Raph showed up and scared the poor guy off," Dani says. I glare at her in response.

Keller flashes me an approving smile.

"Devon's hot and the Waldorfs are one of the oldest noble bloodlines. They're old money. Ivy tried to get with him the beginning of junior year before Lance, but he wasn't interested. He's kind of picky."

Perfect. I think to myself. He actually has standards—not just willing to sleep with any girl that drops her panties for him. Unlike someone else. As I'm thinking it, I know the judgment isn't entirely accurate, because I'm pretty sure Raph is pretty picky himself—all of the girls I've ever seen him with are model hot. Not that it's much comfort.

Keller and Dani keep my mind off Raph with their jokes and pervy comments as they ogle the other players on the field. It's probably the first time they've ever spoken, but they get on like a house on fire. It's not surprising, because they're both real and grounded in a way that not many students at Regency are.

When the match is over, Keller leads us down to the field where some of the players are all still celebrating their victory. My stomach twists when I see Raph standing in the middle of the field. Shirtless. Sweat glistens from his golden skin and it's difficult not to stare, because the guy is cut like a diamond.

The twisting in my stomach turns into a sickening feeling when I realize who's standing next to him.

Layla is wearing a tight, hot pink, dress that shows off her cleavage and slender figure perfectly. It strikes me as a bit much for a soccer match, but none of the players seem to be complaining as they ogle her.

I can't deny that I'm pleased to see that Raph isn't one of those guys ogling. But he is standing with her and he doesn't push her away when she places a hand on his forearm in what's clearly a possessive gesture. Great, they're back together no doubt—not that I ever knew what was really going on between them. Only that Raph indicated that they were over but as Dani had told me before—one minute they're off, the next they're on. Bitterness creeps into me because maybe he was just using me to distract himself from whatever drama he had going on with Layla and I hate the fact that I've become a footnote in their 'epic love story'.

Raph doesn't notice me standing there with Keller and Dani. But Baron does and he jogs over to us.

"Good game, B," Keller says when Baron reaches us, slapping him a high five.

"Hey, Dani, nice seeing you again" he greets her with that lady killer smile and I think I see Dani blush.

"Jazmine, I feel like I haven't seen you in ages, too. You're always staying after class or holed up in your room with Raph."

Dani is staring at me in shock, because I haven't exactly mentioned that up until yesterday night, Raph had effectively moved himself into my room and that we'd been sharing a bed for the past few weeks. In fact, I was hoping that it had gone unnoticed. But Baron and Keller's rooms are in the same wing, so clearly they have noticed.

I still try to deny it though, letting out a forced laugh.

"What? That's crazy—Raph doesn't hang out in my room."

I want to wipe the shit-eating grin off Baron's face.

"So, I *haven't* seen him sneaking out of your room every morning and he *hasn't* been sleeping in your room every night?"

He looks back at me nonchalantly, like he hasn't just dropped a truth bomb about something that I would've cut off my own arm to keep other people from knowing.

Dani looks like she's about to explode with the questions that I know she's dying to bombard me with. Keller doesn't look surprised, though, because like Baron, she clearly hasn't been oblivious to the new rooming situation on our wing.

I'm saved from saying anything as a familiar face comes into view.

"Who's been sleeping in whose room every night?" Devon asks, clearly having overheard those last words. I hope that it's the only thing he overheard.

He looks pretty damn good, freshly showered and in his soccer jacket. That boyish smile, hazel eyes and clean cut wholesomeness makes him the kind of guy you'd want to bring home to meet the family. Not that I have any apart from Magnus. But still, I can appreciate that wholesomeness.

"No one," I answer quickly. Maybe too quickly. I'm well aware that my face is flaming.

Baron looks like he's enjoying this too much.

"Anyway, if someone had been ... doing *that* ..." I say hurriedly. "It's not happening anymore and it will never happen again. Because *that* is now over. Before anything even started."

Devon looks totally baffled. But that's a good thing because no way do I want this guy, this cute guy, who is potentially interested in me and doesn't come with a million complications, thinking that I've been rolling around in bed with Raph St. Tristan.

Baron throws a smirk at me.

"Are you sure about that? Because *Raph* is staring at you so hard right now, those big blue eyes look like they're about to fall out of his pretty head."

Shit. So much for not naming any names. I shoot Baron a look of death as he flashes me another shit-eating grin before jogging off to join his groupies.

Dani throws me a look and mutters something under her breath that thankfully I think only I can hear.

"*Lip-brushing,* huh?"

Keller is almost pissing herself with laughter. But I'm not laughing as I look over at Raph, who is indeed staring. Staring hard.

Screw him.

I turn to Devon, giving him my full attention.

"So, are you coming to tonight's after game party?"

He looks nervous and it's kind of sweet.

I hesitate because inexperience means that I don't know what the proper etiquette is —is he just asking if I'm coming to the party generally or is he asking me to come with him? And all of this is difficult enough without having to focus on blocking out a certain pair of uncanny blue eyes which are still trying to burn a hole into me.

Dani answers for me.

"Yes, Jazmine would *love* to go to the party with you, Devon."

Now, it's my turn to feel embarrassed.

He smiles back at me, and I find myself thinking that he really does have a great smile. He doesn't have dimples and it's not so beautiful that it's difficult to look at, but then again, he's also not an asshole who's likely to break my heart in two.

"Great. Do either of you girls need a ride there, too?" he asks Dani and Keller.

"Nah, I drove here," Dani replies.

"I hitched a ride with B, but it looks like his car's gonna be full with all his groupies, so mind if I catch a ride with you?" Keller asks Dani.

"Sure, no problem."

And with that, the two of them are walking off, leaving me alone with Devon.

I catch a glimpse of Raph over Devon's shoulder and I notice that he still hasn't moved and that he's still staring. His eyes narrow as he notices that Devon and I are by ourselves and I almost hear the cogs in his mind whirring as he probably realizes that we're going to the party together.

To my horror, I see him start to walk towards us, no, more like stomping. Layla is still next to him, but he isn't paying her a shred of attention and she looks furious.

I quickly grab Devon's arm to steer him off the field and he looks perplexed by my sudden rush, but goes with it.

Devon's arm drapes around me casually and I stiffen at the touch, but there's no way I'm about to give Raph the satisfaction of seeing me push Devon away. So, I lean into Devon instead as we walk off the field.

"Is this okay?" he asks after a second.

I catch a glimpse of Raph, who has now been intercepted by Baron, and Baron is clearly trying to talk some sense into him.

Not that Raph has any right to be angry. None at all.

"It's fine," I reply. "Great, actually."

"Hey, D—got a death wish?"

I tell Devon to ignore the taunts from the other players as we walk off the field, but I'm not sure I believe my own advice, because Raph really does look like he's about to murder my date.

~

*D*evon is the perfect gentleman during the drive from Gramercie back to the beach just beneath Regency Mount, where the party is tonight.

He doesn't try to hit on me and doesn't make a single inappropriate comment as we chill together at the beach party. We hang out with Dani, along with some other guys from the soccer team, who all look at Devon as if he's a dead man walking. Then we dance a little on the makeshift dance floor, and sit by one of the bonfires. The whole thing feels so normal, like the typical high school date that I've missed out on all these years and part of me is really enjoying it.

But despite myself, I can't deny that I can't fully enjoy myself because part of my mind is elsewhere. It's on Raph. Just like he was on the field and at school, he's the center of attention at the party. Star player and team captain—everyone is congratulating him and paying their respects to the king. What the fuck ever.

He's surrounded by at least half a dozen girls at all times and I don't fail to notice that Layla never leaves his side.

I don't know what Baron said to him back on the soccer field, but whatever it was, has stopped Raph from murdering Devon, although I do catch him glaring at my date several times throughout the evening, as if he would very much like to kill the guy. The whole thing is so twisted, that it just pisses me off even more.

"So, I'm guessing you know this but I'm kind of taking a big risk by being here with you tonight," Devon says, as we sit by the bonfire, watching the flames flicker and dance.

"Oh you are?" I reply in a teasing tone.

"Yeah, I mean Raph's been giving me the look of death all night."

"You noticed that, huh?" I say, with a grimace.

"Kind of hard not to and I'm sure soccer practice isn't going to be much fun for the next few weeks."

"Sorry."

"But I guess what I'm trying to say is that it's worth it. Because I like you, Jazmine, and I want to get to know you better."

His words surprise me and at the same time I don't know how to respond. I mean, Devon is good looking, funny and seems like an all-around decent guy. But do I like him? Do I want to get to know him better? I have no clue. My stomach doesn't flutter when he's around, my heart doesn't pound like crazy. But he also doesn't irritate the hell out of me or make me feel like I'm standing on the edge of a cliff about to fall to my death. He's open, honest and uncomplicated. He's being up front about how he feels and what he wants from me—and maybe that's the most that I can expect.

The uncertainty must show on my face.

"Look, I'm not sure if something's going on between you and Raph ..." he starts.

"There isn't," I interject quickly. "I mean, he used to hate me and now he doesn't and that's it."

Devon pauses for a moment, then nods.

"Okay, well, if you ever want to hang out—on a date or otherwise, I'm here," he says then.

"And in particular, if you don't have a date to the Fall Ball yet, then I'm also here," he adds.

Dani's mentioned the Fall Ball a few times, but I'd forgotten that it's coming up. Raph didn't mentioned it at all before I started avoiding him, but then again why would he? It's not like he was ever going to ask me to be his date.

I'm saved from having to come up with the right response, though, when someone calls over to Devon, asking him to move his car, because it's blocking someone else in.

Devon sighs before turning back to me.

"Hold that thought, I'll be right back."

I nod as I watch him go. My eyes find their way to Raph. He's sitting closer to the cliffs, with Layla next to him. Ivy and Lance are there, too. The four of them look so right together, they fit together perfectly, like they *belong*. It's me who doesn't.

I get up and find myself walking away from the party, towards the water. I don't know where I'm going, but I keep walking until the orange lights of the bonfires are replaced by darkness and the silvery glow of the moon. I walk towards the shore until I feel the cool water lapping against my bare feet. In the distance, I can see people from the party swimming and splashing around.

"Can we talk?" Raph's voice makes me jump. I didn't sense him approaching but now that he's here, his presence is all that I can feel. I hate how he does that—makes the whole universe narrow until it feels like we're the only two people in it.

I turn to look at him and school my face to stay blank, although it's difficult as hell. In a white t-shirt and denim cut offs, he cuts a sexy figure, even in the darkness.

"What's there to talk about?" I ask, keeping my voice flat.

I can see that it irritates him. Good.

"Well, for starters, do you mind telling me why *Devon Waldorf* has been glued to your side the entire night?"

He looks pissed, but I am, too.

"What happens between *Devon* and me is none of your business."

Those blue eyes flare in the darkness.

"Like hell it isn't." He has the gall to say.

"It isn't," I reply.

"Look, I have no idea what twisted game you're playing. I thought we'd called a truce, but it looks like you've just come up with a new way to torture me. Whatever it is. I'm done being your pawn."

Raph looks back at me in confusion, but I can't allow myself to believe him.

"What are you *talking about*, Jaz?"

I lose it then—the control that I had been trying to maintain vanishes, and there's only anger and hurt left.

"I'm talking about the fact that you've been acting all nice to me— pretending that you want to help me, sleeping in my bed, making me believe that you're not actually an asshole, but that you might actually be a decent guy, trying to make me feel that I can actually begin to *trust* you, trying to get me to *like* you."

I'm aware that I'm ranting and that I'm probably embarrassing myself with the words that are coming out of my mouth. But I don't care.

"Then you almost *kiss* me. But then tell me that it was a *mistake* and you've been avoiding me ever since. Now, you're here with *Layla* acting like, I don't know. Like you're back together or maybe you always were together. Because that's the thing with you—I have no idea what the hell is even going on."

I throw my hands up in frustration and turn my back to him so that he can't see the shine in my eyes. I'm angry at myself, because I have no idea why I even care. I *don't* feel anything for this guy but hate, I *don't* even like him. So, why does it feel like my chest is being ripped open? Why does every fiber of my being want him to turn around and tell me that it wasn't a mistake? Raph St. Tristan is nothing but a heartache waiting to happen, I shouldn't want anything from him other than for him to stay the hell away from me.

I force my breathing to calm as I look up at the stars and the night sky. But even that does little to comfort me just then.

I feel Raph coming up behind me and my body stiffens at his presence but because I'm stupid and weak, I don't move away. I feel his solid chest against my back and the warmth that he radiates causes me to shiver. It reminds me of that morning when we woke up tangled up in each other's arms. His hands are gentle as they caress my arms and move down to my waist. I want to push him away, when he wraps those strong arms around my waist but I lean back instead, letting him support me. He must be able to feel my body tremble under his touch, and I think I must be imagining, it but I can swear I feel his body quake, too.

I hate him for how good this feels. How wrong it is and at the same time, I want it to be right.

"It's not like that," he says, his voice sounding hoarse.

"Then tell me what it's like." The question is barely a ragged whisper in the night, and I'm not sure if I'm even ready to know the answer.

He lets out a long sigh which makes my skin tingle, and I swear I can feel his face hovering over my neck, over my hair, breathing me in. I feel the ghost of his lips brushing against my shoulder and it's barely a touch, yet it shakes me to the core.

"It's complicated—Layla, the throne, this world."

He doesn't offer up any other explanation. He doesn't seem to be able to. But those words alone are enough. They tell me everything I need to know and I feel them like a punch to the stomach. I feel every inch of my body locking up, the stone walls starting to close up again.

I wrench myself out of his arms, hating myself for feeling the loss of his warmth. When I turn to face him, my face is like stone, because I'm made of stone.

"What are you even doing here?" I ask, with a deathly calm that scares even me.

Those impossibly blue eyes lock onto mine and I see the anguish in them, but it doesn't matter, because he still can't answer the question.

"I don't know," he says finally.

I take a deep breath and I feel the stillness settle inside me as we look at each other in silence for what seems like an eternity. Because he doesn't seem able to say the words to make the silence go away.

Fuck this. I can't bear to stand there a moment longer. I turn on my heel to walk away. He speaks then. But his words make me wish that he hadn't.

"*Dammit*, Jaz—it's complicated. There's so much you don't understand."

"You keep saying that," I reply flatly.

"I didn't ask for any of this. Everything was fine before you came along."

He runs a hand through his hair, in a gesture of frustration.

"But then you show up here, mess things up, turn the world upside down."

He steps closer to me, so close that we're sharing breath. It reminds me of that day in the forest, the feeling of his lips brushing against mine and I want to scream.

"I don't want you, Jaz."

I don't think he could've hurt me more if he'd slapped me in the face just then. I need to walk away. Right now. But I stand rooted to the spot and let him dig the knife in deeper.

"I can't want you—I can't give you what you need. None of this can ever matter."

And just in case those words aren't painfully clear enough, he stabs me in the chest one more time.

"This—it can *never* happen."

I feel like the wind has been knocked out of my lungs for a moment. But I don't allow myself to feel the loss. I've had too much of that in my life already. So I let the anger in instead.

"*So, what the hell are you doing here?*" I demand, because it makes no sense. He's looking at me like's he's the one who's being torn to pieces, when it's him doing the tearing.

"I don't know," he repeats those words and I force myself to look him in the eye, although the sight of him makes me feel like my insides are being shredded apart.

"Then why don't you just leave me the hell alone." I fill my words with venom and ice because ice can't feel.

Raph looks like I've just slapped him in the face, which again makes no sense, because he's just made it painfully clear that he wants nothing to do with me. But I'm glad to see the hurt. Good, because I want both of us to hurt.

Something seems to snaps inside him then.

"Because I can't leave you alone!" He's almost shouting now.

"I'm not blind—I see the way the guys at school look at you. From the first moment you stepped on campus, they *all* wanted you. I have no right or claim to you. But the thought of another asshole touching or so much as looking at you, makes me want to set something on fire."

I stare at him in utter shock. When that fades, I'm left only with anger. Not the red hot anger that cares, but a deathly cold anger that numbs every fiber in my being. The whole thing is so twisted, that it makes me sick. He makes me sick.

"So, let me get this straight," I say with a voice as cold as the stone that I'm made from and his eyes darken until they are almost the color of the night sky.

"You don't want me. You can't want me. None of this matters. But you don't want anyone else to be with me either?"

Raph looks stricken, but I force myself not to care.

"Is that right?" I demand.

He doesn't answer. His silence is answer enough. The look in those now midnight blue eyes tells me that he can't stand to let me go, but his silence tells me that he can't say the words to make me stay either.

"Well, you're right about one thing—you have no right or claim to me." My words are harsh, but I want to hurt him.

"Jaz—" He walks towards me but I hold my hand up to stop him because I can't stand it. I can't stand to be near him, to even look at him.

"Don't. Please, just don't come near me. I swear to God, I don't ever want you to come near me again."

The plea stops him in his tracks, and this time as I walk away, he doesn't stop me.

21

*R*aph respects my wishes and keeps his distance, although the stupid part of me wishes that I had never asked him to stay away, which is utterly pathetic, given that he was clear when he told me that he didn't want me.

It's not like the thing between us, whatever it was, lasted for very long. It was only a couple of months, for god's sake. But it feels like I can't even remember a time when Raph wasn't part of my daily routine—whether it was hating him or ... otherwise. It feels like my life hadn't really started before him and now going back to that time when Raph wasn't a part of my daily life, feels like I'm trying to be someone that I no longer am. I've experienced too much loss in my life not to recognize the familiar feeling.

I keep myself distracted with classes, homework, painting, hanging out with Dani and when Raph isn't around, with Baron, Lance and Keller, too.

But at night, I can't deny that I miss his warmth. It's weird that you don't realize how alone you are, until you know what it's like to miss someone. At the same time, the realization makes me hate myself for missing someone who clearly wants nothing to do with me.

I'm sitting in elements class like a zombie, Dani and Keller sitting next to me, trying to pay attention to what Professor Roman is saying. My gaze travels to Raph on the front row with Baron and Lance next to him. Layla is sitting in her usual spot beside him and my stomach feels the usual burn.

"Layla, you're up."

Almost immediately, she stands and saunters towards the middle of the field, her expression is almost gleeful.

"Pick your opponent," Professor Roman says then.

I feel sorry for whoever would have to go up against this girl. Everything about her tells me that she's merciless in a duel.

"I choose ..." Layla pauses dramatically, seeming to enjoy the attention as the other students wait in anticipation.

"Jazmine."

I don't think I hear her right. Why would Layla choose me, knowing that I'm probably the least experienced person here? It's hardly going to be a challenging sparring match. But then I realize with a sickening feeling that it's exactly why Layla has chosen me. Of course, she knows that I'll be no match for her and she clearly hates me. She's going to use this as an opportunity to humiliate me and tear me to pieces in front of the whole class. Payback for what happened in swim class a couple of months ago.

"That's hardly a fair match, given that Jazmine has just started her training," Professor Roman says with a scowl.

Layla turns to look up at me, her eyes fierce with challenge. I see Raph getting up, his eyes cold as he turns to Layla. He opens his mouth to say something but Professor Roman is already speaking.

"You don't have to do this," he says looking up at me.

The rational part of me knows that I should take the out that's being offered. There is no way I'm going to come out of this unharmed. But something inside me is not letting me back down. I raise my eyes and meet Layla's stare unflinchingly.

"I accept," I say simply, putting steel in my spine as I hold my head high and climb down the bleachers.

Dani and Keller are gaping at me like I've lost my mind. Baron and Lance have similar looks on their faces as I pass them.

Then I meet Raph's eyes and something like concern flashes in them. But I don't need his concern. I don't want him to care.

I shoot him an icy look. He's the reason why Layla hates me so much in the first place. The hate that I should feel for Layla in that moment, I direct at Raph, putting as much venom as I can muster in my stare. Raph's lips clamp shut and he scowls as he sits back down.

I meet Layla in the middle of the field, feeling strangely calm. She looks like she's having the time of her life. Her eyes are bright with excitement, eager to start tearing chunks out of me.

My heartbeat is roaring in my ears. My legs feel like jelly, but I won't let Layla see that.

Layla leans over, her perfectly manicured talons digging into my forearm as she speaks.

"I'm going to enjoy this, you little slut," she whispers.

"Now I totally understand why your poor father killed himself when he found out about you. The shame of finding out that he fathered a dirty human bastard who was selling her body must have been too great a shame to bear. No King would have been able to survive it."

I can feel my self-control being shredded to pieces. But I force myself to breathe. She's trying to get to me, trying to make me lose focus and it's working, because I can barely see straight through the rage. I shake off her arm and thrust my face up to hers so that we're breathing the same air, so that she can feel that I mean exactly what I'm about to say.

"I'm going to tear you to pieces."

But as soon as I say the words, I have no idea why I've said them, because I'm no match for her in an elements duel and we both know it. The only one that's going to be torn to pieces is me, with Layla doing the tearing.

She just smiles at me before turning to walk away towards the other side of the field. I didn't think it was possible for a smile to convey how much you want to kill someone. But Layla manages it.

I stand on my side of the field, desperately trying to remember everything that I've learned so far. Layla is pacing like a caged animal on her side of the field, ready to strike at any moment.

I clear my mind and gather my focus. The field falls away, as does the crowd watching from the bleachers. There is only the humming of power in my veins and the connection I feel to the elements around me.

Layla lashes out first, with an arc of fire which rivals Raph's own flamethrower that I'd seen in that first elements lesson. The flames surge towards me and I only have a split second to react.

I hold my hand out, focusing on summoning a whirlwind to engulf the fire and the power rushes from my veins, connecting with the air around me to form the whirlwind. I hear the startled shouts from the crowd and I stare dumbfounded, because we definitely didn't cover that in the training sessions. No one has taught me that and yet the knowledge of it is somewhere inside me.

Layla's expression is shocked for a moment, but she quickly recovers and is moving again.

She retaliates with another blast of fire, this time there's wind swirling it and she creates her own whirlwind but this one is made of flame. I react almost instantly, some primal part of me holding a knowledge that my conscious state is not aware of. I summon a wave of water which swallows the fire, extinguishing it in less than a second.

Barely conscious of my own actions, I summon lightning as thunderbolts hurl down from the sky. Ice hails down on the field as the ground rumbles and quakes. Another round of gasps breaks out from the bleachers.

The fear is clear on Layla's face as I step forward, the storm around me raging stronger. I'm not in control of my own body. I can feel nothing, can think of nothing but the connection, the storm raging around me until I *become* the storm. The power is dizzying, I can feel the danger in it, something that I have never felt before because in that moment, it feels like the entire universe is in my hands and such power is infinitely dangerous.

I should stop then. But I don't. I stretch out both my arms and the power recedes like a tsunami pulling back before unleashing its final wave of destruction. I can feel the air shifting, changing. What came before feels like nothing compared to what's roiling in my veins in that moment.

The sky above the field darkens until day becomes night and the gasps and exclamations from the crowd becomes dead silence. Tapping into the power of night, the power which runs most potent in my blood feels exhilarating and terrifying at the same time. It feels like skydiving through the air or like drinking water for the first time after months in the desert or like taking the first breath after suffocating underwater. It feels like all of those things and none because nothing can really describe the raw power that I feel coursing through me in that moment.

I feel the shadows gathering around me, like a mist creeping along the ground, it thickens. The tendrils of darkness curl around me, ready to act on my command. The shadows are so dark that I know that if I were to release it from this darkness, none would emerge.

The power is consuming me, demanding that I release it. But something inside me stops me cold. This isn't me. I'm not this person. I look over at Layla, let myself see what I'm about to do. The girl is frozen in place, her eyes wide with terror, the earlier venom replaced by a look of helpless fear.

Something inside me fractures as I drop onto my knees, the shadows receding and dissipating. The ground stills and the darkness disappears as I drop my head into my hands. *What am I doing?*

What comes next happens so fast, that I barely have time to register. The air thickens again as another arc of fire blasts towards me. I look up and catch a glimpse of Layla, her face contorting in fury as she directs the wave of fire towards me. Then there's a flash of blinding light and something comes between me and the wall of flames, shielding me from it, moving faster than humanly possible.

It takes a moment to register that Raph is kneeling on the ground in front of me. His arms are around me as he shields me and he holds my head to his chest. His back absorbing the fire.

I pull away in shock and look up at him. Our eyes lock and something undefinable passes between us. Raph's eyes are as dark and unfathomable as storm clouds, his expression unreadable.

Everything happens so quickly after that, Professor Roman, who had been standing paralyzed, is moving towards the field. Chaos breaks out on the bleachers.

Layla is moving towards where Raph is kneeling in front of me, a look of deadly heat in her eyes. Not a trace of the earlier helpless fear. Professor Roman is holding her back as he tells her to get off the field.

Raph doesn't turn to look at them. His eyes are still intent on my face. I expect him to get up but he doesn't pull away. His arms are still around me and something akin to fear spreads through me like wildfire.

"Are you okay?" Raph asks, his voice raw and thick with some emotion that I don't understand.

"I'm fine." I force myself to reply and at the same time force myself to let go of him.

Professor Roman dismisses the class early right then and everyone hurries away. I can see Dani and Keller waiting by the bleachers along with Lance and Baron.

"God, what the hell was that?" I ask as I stare up at Raph wide eyed and for a moment I forget how much I'm meant to hate him. That power, so raw, so potent. I've never felt anything like it. There was a seduction in that power, too, which made me feel like I was teetering on the edge of a knife blade. Goosebumps rise on my skin at the memory.

Raph's eyes are as dark as midnight as he looks back at me.

"I don't know, Jaz. I've never seen anything like that ..."

Neither of us speaks, but we're still standing there and it seems like neither of us wants to walk away either.

"It looks like you didn't need all of that training after all," he says finally, the ghost of his usual teasing smile playing on those sensuous lips. I can see that he's still shaken, but I don't know why because he's made himself pretty clear about just how little he cares.

Except the way he's looking at me just then, as if the shock of what just happened has stripped something away from him, leaving him raw and for a moment, it seems like whatever control he had been exercising all these months has finally dissipated.

Part of me is aware that we're standing in a field with crowds of people around us, but it's one of those moments between us when it feels like we're the only two people in the vastness of time and space.

I feel like the entire universe is watching just then, waiting, and time seems to stop as I feel like I'm standing at the edge of that precipice again.

"Jaz, I—"

I wait for him as he seems to be battling with something in his mind. Something seems to win out and when he turns to me again, it's with that face of stone that I saw that first day at the beach. His eyes are like glaciers, his gaze shuttered.

"I can't do this," he says, finally, as he turns and walks away.

I can do nothing but watch his retreating figure as the gaping hole that had opened up inside me that night of the bonfire, widens until it swallows everything in its path, leaving only the emptiness that resonates in the wake of loss.

Part of me thinks that I should be happy that it turns out I have powers worthy of a Dynasty heir after all. But I don't feel that. I only feel fear at the danger that comes hand in hand with power and something else, something like fear as I watch Raph walk away.

$\sim$

"I'm not going to the Fall Ball," I say for what must be the tenth time.

"Yes, you are," Dani insists, for what must also be the tenth time.

Keller and Dani have dragged me to one of the shopping districts in Arcadia where they're in the middle of dress shopping and ganging up on me about the Fall Ball.

They've become fast friends and I'm glad because, having never had even a single friend before, I don't actually know how I ever got through the week without these two.

"You are," Keller adds as she steps out of the boutique dressing room in a silver ball gown which suits her coloring and frame perfectly.

"I don't even have a date," I remind them.

"That's not true—is it, Dani?" Keller says, with a smirk.

"Nope, Devon Waldorf asked her to go."

"He didn't ask me to go," I correct. "He just said that if I didn't already have a date, then he would go with me."

Dani and Keller exchange incredulous looks.

"That sounds like he asked you to go," Keller replies flatly.

"Urgh. It was weeks ago now and I haven't spoken to him since. So he's probably found himself another date by now."

"Nope. Not true," Keller says, as she unzips the silver dress and reaches for another one from the plush velvet couch next to me.

I realize then that this is my first dress shopping trip. Ever. Buying clothes was always a luxury I couldn't afford. Now, it feels so strange not even having to think about how much any of these clothes cost. All I have to do is present the Evenstar card that Magnus has given me.

"I know for a fact that Ivy asked Devon to go, but he turned her down. He said he didn't have a date yet, though, because he was waiting for a certain someone to accept." Keller looks at me pointedly.

Something occurs to me.

"Wait, what? Isn't Ivy going with Lance?"

At the mention of Lance's name, Dani suddenly looks uncomfortable and suspicion knifes through me.

"You never told me who your date was Dan—you mentioned it was some guy, but I don't think we got to the part where you told me his name."

Dani clears her throat and acts all nonchalant, but her words are like a bomb.

"Oh, it's Lance."

Keller's eyes look like they're about to pop out of her head. As do mine, probably.

Had I been so caught up in my own spiral of self-pity, that I hadn't even noticed what was going on around me? I mean it's not like I track the comings and goings of Lance and Ivy. But I had no idea they had broken up and how in the hell didn't I know about Lance and Dani going to the Fall Ball together?

"Whoa. Okay. Can you say that again and explain how the hell all this happened right under my nose without me even noticing?"

"Well, Lance and I have been in the same music class since like freshman year. But it's not like we run with the same circle—well until now, sort of. I had no idea that he and Ivy had even broken up until he asked me to go to the Fall Ball with him last week. I think I almost died with shock.

"I didn't tell anyone it was him, because I don't want it to be a big thing and I have a feeling Ivy is going to blow her top when she finds out."

"She will," Keller replies honestly. "But it's fine. Ivy isn't Layla—her bark is worse than her bite."

"Although, there's no way you're going to be able to keep it under wraps for long. You showing up to the Fall Ball on Lance's arm is going to be pretty hard to ignore."

"Especially because, you know ..." Keller trails off.

"I'm not of noble blood or whatever. I get it. But Lance asked me and he doesn't seem to care, so I'm not saying we're going to run off together and make babies. But it'll be a fun night, I guess." Dani shrugs casually, as she slips on an electric blue number.

I admire her level headed and cool approach. I wish I could adopt the same approach when it comes to a certain someone who shall not be named.

"Well, at least it's not the Oaknorth Dynasty hosting the Fall Ball this year like they usually do, because that'd be even more obvious. The Oaknorth estate is undergoing renovations, so the ball's going to be at the St. Tristan palace instead," Keller adds.

"God, Dani. You're always beating me up over keeping secrets, but all this time you've been hiding juicy secrets of your own," I interject then.

Dani rolls her eyes.

"It's hardly the same thing. Lance asked me to the Fall Ball. That's not the same as him rolling around in my bed behind everyone's back."

I groan and cover my face with my hands. The last thing I need is to be reminded of Raph St. Tristan in my bed. I'm like a recovering addict and any mention of him is bad for me.

I bite down on my lip to stop myself from asking the next question, but I must be a glutton for punishment, because I ask it anyway.

"Is Raph going with ...?"

God. It's so pathetic, that I can't even say it out loud.

Keller's expression falters and my stomach drops because I know that look. It's the look that someone has before they tell you that although you've survived the terrible accident, the person that was in the car with you hasn't.

Keller picks up a beautiful red dress, made of pure silk and lace.

She hands it to me and closes my hands over the hanger.

"Call Devon and tell him you'll go to the Fall Ball with him."

~

Sovereign Hall is quiet that night when I get home. Keller stayed behind in Arcadia to meet some friends and Dani went back to her dorm after dropping me off.

There doesn't seem to be anyone else home as I drop my dress bag on the kitchen counter and start making myself a sandwich.

I hear footsteps coming down the marble stairs and I feel my blood freeze when I look up to see Raph walking towards the kitchen. He's wearing grey sweats and nothing else. The sight of his golden skin and ripped chest makes me think of his body lying next to mine all those nights. Not touching. But then again, he never did need to. Every fiber of my being comes alive at just his presence and it's probably the most pathetic thing in the entire universe.

I don't pay him any attention as I continue making my sandwich, not even when I feel those blue eyes on me.

"So, we're not even speaking now?" he says finally, and his tone irritates me because why the hell should he be pissed? He's the one who's been toying with me like a freaking yo-yo.

"I thought we were meant to be friends."

I laugh harshly then.

"We were never *friends,* asshole. You hated me, made my life a living hell. Then for whatever reason, you stopped with that form of torture, and came up with another way to break me."

"What? Jaz, I told you that's not what it was."

"Okay, but you also told me that you don't want anything to do with me. So clearly you have some kind of split personality disorder, because I don't know what the hell you're doing talking to me right now."

He falls silent then.

"What are you doing here?"

Still silence.

"Okay. Well then, there's nothing for us to talk about."

I turn back to my sandwich. But he doesn't leave and I can feel myself getting angrier all the while.

From the corner of my eye, I see his gaze fall on the dress bag on the counter.

"Are you going to the Fall Ball with Devon?" he asks, and my temper hits the roof.

"That's none of your business," I reply. I haven't called Devon yet and honestly, I'm not sure if I'm going to go through with it. But Raph is sure pushing me in that direction.

"Just answer the question, Jaz."

"Sure, I'll answer the question. If you answer mine—who are *you* going to the Fall Ball with?"

I shouldn't give a damn about who he's going to the Fall Ball with. I don't want to care. But some stupid, weak, naïve part of me is wishing that he'll say no one or that, even more pathetic, he'll ask me to go with him right then and there.

But of course, he doesn't, and the flash of guilt in his eyes tells me everything I need to know.

"God, you're so twisted. I can't even look at you without feeling like I want to hurl."

"Jaz—" He reaches out for me, but the look burning in my eyes makes him drop his hand to his side. Because if he so much as touches me, I think I'll explode.

"You told me that you can't do this, that this can *never* happen, that anything that did happen was a *mistake*. So *what do you want from me?*" I'm almost screaming now.

He doesn't answer and I make to walk away, but his words stop me.

"There's so much you don't know, Jaz. So much you don't understand about this world, about who I am in it."

"Then make me understand. Tell me."

Those blue eyes sear into mine and I wait for him.

"I can't," he says finally, turning away from me.

"And it won't make a damned bit of difference anyway, because I can't give you what you need."

I'm done.

"You're so *messed up* and I'm done letting you mess with me. You hate me one minute, you sleep in my bed and try to kiss me the next, then you're telling me how it's all a mistake, that you can't be with me. That *you don't want me*. But you're warning every guy at school off me and you don't want me going to this stupid dance with someone else? Do you know how messed up you are?"

"Yes!" He shouts. He moves towards me then, quick as a flash of light. His hands are holding my face, his fingers devastatingly gentle, although his words rage like fire.

"I know how messed up I am. Trust me, I know. I'm fucked up because when I'm around you, *I can't think straight*. Because the thought of you with someone else makes me feel like I'm going to *lose my goddamn mind*."

His words floor me and at the same time, they make me come alive. My heart is pounding so fast, it feels like it might burst out of my chest. There are a million questions roaring through my mind, but when I look into those midnight blue eyes, I see the answer, and everything inside me stills.

"But none of it matters, right? Because you don't want me?"

He closes his eyes then and lets go. That impossibly beautiful face is a picture of defeat. But he's not the only one who's lost, we both have.

"It *can't* matter, Jaz. I can't want you. You deserve ..." he lets out a long breath. "*More*. So much more. But it doesn't matter, because I can't give you more—I don't have *more* to give."

It was almost cruel for him to tell me all of that, only to say that none of it even matters, that it could never matter.

There's nothing left in me as I pick up the dress bag and turn to face him one last time.

"Okay," I say quietly. "Then, to answer your question, I am going with Devon."

I don't stay to listen to what else he might have to say, because as we've both just admitted to each other, none of it can matter anyway.

22

I'm grateful for Keller's choice because even I can't deny that this red dress is smoking hot. The dress clings to my curves and is cut low in all the right places, so as to entice a little, but not too much. The silk makes the ensemble look elegant, while the lace makes it just the right kind of sexy.

My jet black hair falls like a silken waterfall down my lace covered back and is swept back from my face by diamond encrusted clasps.

I almost died of shock when Keller dragged me to Ivy's room earlier to have my make-up done, because I would have thought that the girl would sooner claw her own face off than help me in any way.

But Keller had been right about Ivy—her bark was worse than her bite and she isn't Layla. She didn't say much as she applied the powders and tints in all the right places, but she didn't need to. I got it —her loyalties are with her friend, but it didn't need to be anything personal against me. I can respect that.

I expected her to bring up Dani and Lance. But weirdly, she didn't and I wonder how much she actually cares.

I have to hand it to the girl, though, Keller is right, Ivy knows how to work a make-up brush. The dark brown, grey and black powders are perfectly blended around my eyes in what has to be the best smoky eye look I've ever seen in real life. I usually hate drawing attention to those violet eyes with the silver rings. But tonight, the kohl lining makes that unnatural coloring look almost beautiful, stunning. The hint of blush across my cheekbones is just the right flush and the deep ruby red tint that Ivy expertly applied to my lips makes them look both sensual and demure.

"Jazmine—get your sexy butt down here."

I take a deep breath because despite the dress and the make-up, I'm nervous as hell or maybe it's because of them that the nerves are jangling through my body. Is it too much? I hate being the center of attention, eyes on me. I'm so used to just trying to stay invisible, drifting from place to place, observing life around me with my artist's eye, rather than living it. But that all changed when I came to Eden, the looks, the attention and even though I've felt hate, been hated, had my hopes and maybe even my heart crushed, I realize that at least, I've been *living*.

And tonight, as I walk down the sweeping marble staircase at Sovereign Hall, every fiber in my being does feel alive.

The large reception hall falls silent as I descend the marbles steps. Baron is standing on the side nearest to the kitchen, pouring drinks for his not one, but two dates. He misses one of the glasses and vodka sloshes onto the counter as his jaw practically hits the floor. I almost want to laugh, despite feeling embarrassed as hell.

Lance is standing with Dani, near Baron. Both of them are looking at me like they've never seen me before.

Keller's date is trying hard not to stare, but Keller doesn't seem to mind, she picked this dress after all, so she's to blame. Ivy and her date stand next to Keller and I'm surprised to see the pride in Ivy's face as she surveys her work.

I try not to look at the figure by the door. But clearly, I'm a glutton for punishment because my eyes find Raph anyway. They always do.

This isn't the first time I've seen him in a tux. The dark tux he's wearing tonight is similar to the one he wore at that first ceremony— finely made and elegantly cut to fit his tall, yet powerfully muscled frame. But tonight, his beauty is utterly devastating and I feel an ache in my chest as I take in that golden hair, those uncanny blue eyes and that impossibly perfect face. The face of an angel. He carries himself like he knows that he has the world at his feet, and in that moment, he looks every inch the heir to the throne that he is. His aura emanating the authority of the crown that is his by birthright.

Those blue eyes burn into mine and something flickers in their depths as he takes in the sight of me. I see the way his throat works, the way his lips part slightly and the way his chest hitches as he takes a sharp intake of breath. He steps forward, as if almost involuntarily drawn and I feel the universe narrowing so that nothing exists but the two of us standing there in the vastness of time and space.

But something stops him in his tracks, and the illusion is shattered. My gaze falls to Layla's hand on his forearm, holding him back and I feel the touch like a stab to my own chest.

Layla is a vision of white and gold, with her golden blonde hair, emerald green eyes and perfect face. She fits so perfectly with Raph, that it's painful to look at. They look so right together, made for each other. She's his queen and has been since the day he was born. I don't know what, for a second, made me think otherwise. I can't think about Raph's words just then—*when I'm around you I can't think straight.* Because I think, in that moment, I understand what Raph wasn't able to say. The reason why it can *never* matter. Layla is what matters and she will always be the one by his side.

I'm horrified to feel the moisture pooling in my eyes and I blink it away rapidly before anyone can see.

"You look beautiful, Jazmine," Devon's voice startles me as I reach the bottom of the staircase. I hadn't seen him standing there and I feel a flash of guilt as I look up at that wholesome face. He looks handsome tonight in a tux jacket and black pants and the look in those clear hazel eyes tells me that there is nowhere else he'd rather be than taking me to this dance. It's uncomplicated, simple, nice. It's safe and that should be enough for me.

So, I paint on a smile as I let him pin my corsage to my dress. Raph says nothing, but I can feel him watching the way that Devon's fingertips graze the bare skin just above my chest. But I can't care about the fire in his eyes. He's made it clear where he stands, so now I have to do the same.

~

*T*he limo ride to the St. Tristan palace helps ease my nerves. Baron and his two dates, Lance and Dani, Keller and her date rode in the same limo as Devon and me. Raph, Layla, Ivy and her date plus two other guys from the soccer team and their dates rode in the other.

By the time we reach the St. Tristan palace, I'm almost enjoying myself. Devon is the perfect date. He's polite, laughs at my jokes, opens doors for me, doesn't taunt me or make fun of me. I should be enjoying myself.

When we step into the decadent ballroom at the St. Tristan palace, I feel like I've stepped into a fairy tale. Everything is gold and the ballroom gleams like a jewel in the night. Orbs of firelight float high in the rafters of the impossibly tall ceiling, as silk and lace swirl on the vast dance floor beneath.

This is my first high school dance, but I'm pretty sure this is far and above a normal high school dance. Not least because the Dynasty heads seem to be in attendance. Magnus called a few days ago to ask if I was coming, but said that he wouldn't be here because he's away attending to official business, whatever that means.

I realize as I look at my opulent surroundings, that this place is Raph's *home*. I mean, of course, the Evenstar palace is just as decadent, but I still don't really consider that as mine and I sure as hell didn't grow up there. The thought only makes me realize all the more that Raph did the right thing by cutting things off before they could even start. Things are better this way, because we both know that nothing could ever come of whatever that was between us.

I willingly take Devon's arm, as he leads me to the dance floor and at the same time, I see Raph lead Layla in a waltz. I follow Devon's lead, holding my palm out to meet his and my hand touches his at exactly the same moment as Raph's hand closes around Layla's.

I try to focus on Devon as we dance together and considering my inexperience with any kind of waltzing, he does a great job of leading us through it. But my gaze travels to Raph and Layla more than once. I'm not the only one though, because everyone is watching them. Together, they shine brighter than all the gold and jewels surrounding them. The future king of Eden and his queen. I can't bear the sight of it, but at the same time, I can't look away.

My stomach twists irrationally at the sight of Layla's hand in his and his hand resting on her perfectly curved hip. Raph's face is like stone, his eyes shuttered—the face of the heir to the throne of Eden.

After a few more beats, the pairs on the dance floor shift and I find herself passing from the safety of Devon's arms to Raph's.

Something like fear races down my spine and I can feel the slight tremor in my hand as he takes it in his. His touch is devastatingly gentle on the bare skin at the small of my back, and I'm all too aware of the way his fingers flex as he draws me closer. The contact of his bare skin on mine at such a sensitive spot, is almost too much to bear.

I can feel how equally affected Raph is in the way that his breath hitches as he draws closer, seeming to inhale the very scent of me, in the running stag clamor of his heartbeat against my own.

Neither of us speaks as Raph leads us through the dance, but when my eyes lock onto his, I can see the way they darken as they travel over every inch of my face, drinking in the sight of me.

Everywhere our bodies touch, I feel the fire. His powerfully muscled body presses against mine and I feel my body respond, as if it has a mind of its own. Heat pools deep in my core and I feel something primal and raw course through me.

The traitorous feelings are insane and wrong in every sense of the word. Looking at someone like this, feeling these sensations, mean something and I shouldn't be allowing it to happen.

Raph raises a hand to my face, as if helplessly drawn. His fingertips are gentle on my cheek, barely a ghost of a touch, but I feel it in every part of me.

"What are you doing?" My voice is a ragged whisper and I'm barely able to speak.

He closes his eyes, and touches his forehead to mine.

"I don't know." He repeats those words, and it's enough to draw me out of the trance. I'm aware of my surroundings again and I can see that people are starting to stare. Devon is frowning as he watches us, and Layla looks like she's about to walk over here and pull us apart.

There are another pair of eyes on me, too, which I don't recognize, but I think I've seen once before. I look over to the edge of the dance floor and find a man with blonde hair, a few shades lighter than Raph's and amber eyes looking over at us. His expression is neutral, but I sense the displeasure in the depths of those eyes. I can't place that face, but his attire tells me that he is one of the Dynasty heads. The realization comes to me then that he's Raph's father. I recognize him because not only does he share some of Raph's handsome features and imposing stature, I also recall that veiled look of disapproval from that first ceremony.

I look away from the man and gathering what control I have left, I turn to Raph and step away from him.

"This isn't a good idea," I manage to say, although I can hear the tremor in my own voice.

I don't wait for Raph to respond as I walk away from him and find a quiet corner of the hall to gather my thoughts.

I'm not alone for long though.

"Jazmine, it's a pleasure to see you again, and settled into Regency Mount so well." I turn to find Raph's father in front of me. His tone is pleasant enough, but his words seem oddly hollow.

"Jethro St. Tristan," he says, holding out his hand. I take it after a moment, although I can feel the levels of discomfort rising inside me. I find myself thinking about that day on the cliff and Raph telling me about his mother's depression which eventually took her life. How his father, this man standing before me now, hid it, was ashamed of it and cared more about his Dynasty than his own wife. The thought of it makes me sick and it's a struggle to take his hand without letting the disgust show on my face.

"We didn't get to speak properly at the presentation ceremony, but you've met my son, Raphael St. Tristan? I see you two seem to have gotten to know each other quickly."

I blink at his words, because I know that they aren't what they seem.

"Yeah, he's in some of my classes and of course, we both live at Sovereign Hall."

"Yes, so you will have seen how unruly he is."

I stare at him in surprise.

"I'm not sure what you mean ..." I reply, tentatively.

"Oh, I think you do. I have eyes everywhere when it concerns my Dynasty."

I feel a chill race down my spine.

"I'm well aware of my son's indiscretions—the girls, the partying, the unruly behavior.

"Most of it is his way of rebelling against me. But it won't last long —Raphael is going to be the king of Eden, his life has been planned for him since the day he was born. He was raised for the throne. His life has purpose, meaning, in a way that you wouldn't understand."

I feel insulted by that, although I know the words are true. My life so far has been a meaningless blur, I can't even begin to imagine what it would feel like to have it all planned out for me the way Raph does. But I'm not sure if it's a good thing or a bad thing anymore.

"I must admit that the motion to bring Arwen's secret heir to Eden was not one that I initially supported. You are half human after all, and being raised on Earth with your *background*—well, one could only conclude that you wouldn't belong here in Eden, let alone be suited to the life of an heir to a sovereign Dynasty."

His tone is diplomatic, but his words are cutting all the same, and I can feel myself bristling.

"But I don't suppose it matters, because nothing will change the fact that Raphael is next in line to the throne, wouldn't you agree, Jazmine?"

"Yeah, of course—why would anything change that?" I look back at him in confusion, because I have no idea what he's trying to say.

Before he can respond, I feel Raph's presence.

"Father," he says. He's wearing that shuttered expression again.

"Raphael. Always a pleasure to see you, my son."

Raph nods stiffly and I feel a strange tension in the air between him and his father. Everything is so formal, so emotionless.

"I was just telling Jazmine here about how much you're looking forward to ascending to the throne and how nothing will be getting in the way of that," he says. Again, his words are full of some other meaning.

I don't think I've ever spoken to anyone so seemingly pleasant and yet so cold. I get the feeling, though, that this is what is required of those in power. They spin a tangled web and their pleasant words are laced with deceit. But Magnus isn't like this, or at least he doesn't seem to be.

I catch something like anger flash in the depths of Raph's eyes. But it's gone in an instant, retreating beneath that mask of stone.

"Of course," Raph replies evenly. Not a shred of feeling in his voice. He's so closed off, that he may as well be one of the stone pillars lining the ballroom.

"And of course, there's your impending betrothal ceremony to Layla." The words sound casual, but they are very deliberate.

"Did you know, Jazmine, that the St. Tristan Dynasty and the Delphine Dynasty have been linked through marriage for generations?"

I feel my levels of discomfort rising to record levels.

"Really? It sounds kind of incestuous." As soon as the words leave my mouth, I can't believe that I've spoken them. But then again, Raph's father is right, I'm not cut out for this sovereign Dynasty bull. I say what I mean and suddenly, I don't want to waste any more energy trying to sift through the hidden meanings or trying to pick the roses amongst the thorns.

I get the message loud and clear. Raph is going to be King, his life has meaning, his life has a purpose. I'm a nothing and no one. A half breed who doesn't belong here and I should stay as far away from Raph as possible so that he can ride off into the sunset and continue the interbreeding tradition of his Dynasty. Message delivered.

I feel like saying so out loud, but the look on Raph's father's face is outraged enough that I think saying anything else would probably push him over the edge, and as much as I'd enjoy seeing that, I just don't have the energy.

I don't even bother to excuse myself as I walk away because I don't think I can spend a second longer in this place without feeling like I'm going to break apart.

23

I don't even bother to take the dress off as I flop down onto my bed. After that insightful talk with Raph's father, I asked Devon to take me home early. He said he was fine with it, although I could sense his disappointment. I felt bad because it wasn't fair for me to agree to go with him in the first place. I've spent the past ten years alone, I don't need someone to hold my hand or to be by my side. I don't need to settle for someone, even if they feel nice enough or safe. I'm better off alone.

So, I lie in my bed alone. I'm too lost in my thoughts to sense footsteps down the hall until I hear someone knocking at my door.

I don't answer at first, and consider pretending I'm not here. But my lamp is on, so they'll be able to see the light under the door. I have no idea who it could be, because the ball was still in full swing when I left and everyone seemed to be settling in for a long one. I checked up on Dani before I left, but she seemed to be having the time of her life with Lance and I was glad for her, for both of them. Baron, despite having two gorgeous girls on his arm didn't seem to be having as much fun as I thought he would, though, and something about the way he was looking at Lance and Dani made me wonder.

"Come in," I say finally, sitting up. I regret my words almost instantly when the door opens and Raph steps into my room.

"Shouldn't you be at the ball with Layla, you know showing your subjects how amazing and perfect their future king and queen are?" I mean it to sound harsh, but I'm too tired for it to come out that way and honestly, he's the last person I expect to be here right now. I'm aware that I sound bitter and pathetic. But I'm past caring.

Raph flinches at my words, but I get no comfort from that.

"I should be," he says. "But I'm not."

I stare at him, well aware of how alone we are right now. He's waiting for me to ask him a question that I don't know I even want the answer to anymore. But I ask it anyway.

"Why are you here?"

He lets out a long breath, then as he walks towards the bed. I don't stop him.

"Because I *want* to be here."

I have no idea what to say to that. But Raph is already talking.

"You met my father today," he says.

I let out a sharp breath, not exactly a laugh.

"I did and what a pleasure it was," I reply.

"You spoke to him for all of five minutes, so maybe now you understand at least a fraction of what it's like to be me."

Something in Raph's face chips away at my defenses, although I don't let my guard down completely.

"All my life, my father has told me that being born into privilege comes with responsibilities. So, my whole life has been mapped out for me—what schools I went to, what skills I needed to have, what sports to play, what friends to have, who I should be with. Even down to what I should say, how I should act, who I should *be*."

"Are you expecting me to feel sorry for you? Because your life is all about wealth and privilege? Because you're the heir to the throne of an entire planet? Is that it?" I ask.

"No, all I want is for you to understand that my life—it doesn't belong to me. It belongs to my Dynasty, it belongs to the throne. People envy my life because they think the crown belongs to me, but

216

they're wrong—it's *me* who belongs to the crown. I told you once that this world may seem beautiful, but it's not. Beneath all the wealth and privilege, there are lies, deceit, shackles, traps."

I'm silenced by the raw truth that I feel in those words, and I don't want to feel anything other than hate for him. But I do.

"Do you know what it feels like to know that your life isn't yours? Not to have a choice? In anything? You told me that night on the beach when I asked you to stay, that there are times when you're standing in a room full of people and still feel alone, like if you screamed at the top of your lungs, no one would even hear you.

"I've felt like that for almost my entire life—most days I feel like that. Like I'm alive, but I'm not really living."

I'm surprised that he remembers my words from that night and more so that he's admitting he knows what that feels like.

But we both fall silent then and I'm not sure if there's anything either of us can say that could matter.

"Look—why are you even telling me this?" I ask. I know it sounds harsh but I can't let myself care. "You've just said yourself that what you want doesn't matter. So you *wanting* to be here, *wanting* to tell me all of this—it doesn't change anything. Because it can't. Your father was pretty clear on what does matter—you, ascending to the throne and your *impending betrothal*. So, I think you should go."

Raph turns to me then. I don't expect any explanation other than what he told me before, which is that it's complicated. But his words surprise me.

"My betrothal to Layla was decided the day I was born. I never had a choice in it. The St. Tristan Dynasty and the Delphine Dynasty have always been the closest, the union maintained through the genera-tions by marriage.

"Everyone expects us to be together. But it's more than that, the alliance between our Dynasties depends on it."

I feel sick and I don't think I can listen to anymore. I open my mouth to tell him to leave, but his next words silence me.

"But I don't love Layla. I never did.

"I tried being with her, for the sake of duty, but she always knew I was never really there. I've never been anything other than honest. So, we have an understanding."

Anger spikes inside me and at the same time, I feel sick to my stomach.

"And what kind of understanding is that? That you get to fuck other girls because you don't love her? Is that what this was? You wanted to mess around with me so I could keep your bed warm at night, while you sit on your throne with Layla by your side during the day? Well, you didn't get very far, because we've barely even kissed!"

He looks almost distraught then.

"No! God, Jaz, that's not what it was about at all. It isn't what this is about. You said so yourself—we barely even kissed.

"Because I knew from the minute I saw you, that it would never be about just that with you. Layla knew it—that's why she hated you so much.

"I couldn't even let myself kiss you, because I didn't want to lead you on, only to tell you that nothing can ever come of it. I knew that I could never give you what you wanted, what you *deserve*. Because you deserve more—you deserve *everything* and I don't have that to give. *It's not mine to give.*"

I laugh harshly then.

"But that's exactly what you did. We may not have slept together, but you did sleep in my bed every night. You made me almost trust you, when you know I find it hard to trust anyone; you made me almost like you, then you told me it was a mistake. That you don't want me. Yeah, you did a great job. So save your explanations for someone who believes you—because you sure as hell didn't care about leading me on."

He loses it then.

"God, Jaz, you have no idea. If I didn't care, I would have treated you like all those other girls—fucked you, then tossed you aside."

The intensity in those blue eyes and the rawness of his words burn into me.

"But you're not like those other girls. You deserve more than I would ever be able to give you, so I couldn't even go there.

"Since that first minute I saw you on that beach, I couldn't stop thinking about you. God, I wanted you so bad. I felt like I was going crazy. Baron sure as hell thought I'd lost my goddamn mind."

I'm shocked into stillness, and my mind blanks. I don't know what I'd been expecting but I sure as hell hadn't expected this.

"You're so goddamn beautiful, Jaz, it's almost unreal. And not just in the superficial way—*everything* about you is beautiful. Your sass, your strength, your kickass attitude. You've been through so much, but you're so tough. You don't let anyone give you shit. I mean you blew up my car for god's sake. You're so different—different from anyone I've ever met. In a world that's all about appearances and status, you're so real. Everything about you is real.

"At first I tried to drive you away. Because *I had to* but also because I couldn't bear to be around you without ..." He trails off then, seemingly unable to finish as he shakes his head. "I thought that if I got you to leave, it would fix everything. But then I couldn't stand to see you go."

His breathing is ragged, as if every word has been ripped out of somewhere deep inside him.

When I'm able to speak again, my voice is as unsteady as I feel.

"But you told me that you don't want me. That you can't want me. That this can never happen."

"All my life I've been programmed to want only what I've been told to want. It's all I've ever known."

He lets out a sharp laugh, but there's no humor in it.

"I've grown so used to it, that I didn't even question it. None of it ever felt wrong ... until now. Because for the first time in my life, I want something that I know I shouldn't. And I know I'm wrong for ..." He trails off then, shaking his head in a helpless gesture.

I shouldn't want to hear the rest. But I can't stop myself from asking him anyway.

"For what?" I say finally.

His hands reach out to cup my face then, his fingers achingly gentle against my cheekbones. I feel the touch in every fiber of my body. Then when his gaze locks with mine, I feel the entire universe falling away.

"For wanting what I want," he replies finally, his voice barely a whisper in the space between us.

"I shouldn't want you. I *can't* want you. But I don't think I care anymore, because I can't stay away from you, Jaz."

His words floor me and I feel like I can't breathe as I look at that impossibly beautiful face.

"I want you. I want you so much."

I'm stunned speechless as I stare back at him. He drops his hands from my face and takes my hands in his.

I think he's going to kiss me and I don't think I would stop him. But he sits next to me on the bed instead.

"Can I stay here with you? Tonight?" he asks.

I can hear my sharp intake of breath, because I'm not sure what he's asking.

"Just sleeping," he says quickly.

"I just want to sleep next to you tonight."

No, should be my answer, but something else comes out of my mouth.

"Okay," I say quietly.

He kicks off his shoes and shrugs off his tux jacket but is still fully clothed as he stretches out on the bed next to me. I hesitate at first, then reach over him to turn off the lamp, before lying back.

We lay in silence for what seems like an eternity.

I don't know what possesses me to do what I do next, but I shift over to rest my cheek on his chest. I hear his breath hitch in response, but a moment later his arms are around me and I let myself feel his strength, let his warmth seep into my bones, let it chase the cold away.

He presses his lips against my hair, breathing me in and at his next words, I feel my own sharp intake of breath.

"God, you were so beautiful tonight. I think I'll remember the way you looked tonight for the rest of my life."

I try to shut the words out, but I feel them wrapping around my chest all the same.

I don't know how long we lie together like that, only that some-time later, sleep finally comes and there's a stillness in me when I let it claim me.

~

I wake up to the feeling of warmth and sunlight. Strong arms surround me, holding me, keeping me safe. It's not a feeling that I'm used to—I've been alone for so long, never allowing myself to need anyone to give me that safety and comfort. As I let myself lie there in Raph's arms, I let him do all of those things. I tell myself it's because I'm barely awake, but part of me knows it's because I'm tired of the cold, my body craves his warmth and in that moment, I let myself give in to that. I don't allow myself to think about what's happening or what will happen. I shut out the questions and rational thoughts, because it feels like none of those things belong in this moment.

I shift in his arms so that I'm facing him and when he opens those vivid blue eyes, I forget to breathe for a moment.

Neither of us says anything for a long while as we lie there in each other's arms, gazes locked, bodies entwined, and it's probably the most intimate thing I've ever experienced in my entire life.

The morning sun is streaming in through the floor to ceiling windows, touching everything with its warmth. But Raph glows with a light all of his own. Everything about him is golden—the perfect hue of his golden skin, his sexily dishevelled ash blond hair like a halo surrounding him and that smile, which in that moment, is devoid of its usual arrogance, is so beautiful, that it's impossible to look at without losing all coherent thought.

I didn't realize how much I'd been working to block out the effect that he has on me, until I let myself feel it all in that moment. His very presence makes every fiber in my being come alive and everywhere we touch, I feel the fire. Like that very first day on the beach, I get the feeling like I've been sleep walking until now and looking at him is like waking up.

I realize that I, on the other hand, must look like an utter mess. I'm still wearing the red dress from last night. But I'm also still sporting last night's make-up and I can bet that the smoky eye look has probably now turned into more of a panda-eye look. But the way that Raph is looking at me, those heated blue eyes traveling every inch of my face, as if trying to memorize every detail, makes me forget about all of that just then.

I remember his words from last night—*you're so goddamn beautiful, Jaz, it's almost unreal.*

I've always thought that about him but I couldn't even begin to imagine that he thought the same about me. Suddenly, the memory of everything that he said to me last night comes flooding back and I don't think I can lie there with him a minute longer without feeling like I'm going to burst into flames or something equally embarrassing.

"I should probably jump in the shower and wash this gunk off my face," I say finally, breaking the silence.

A mischievous grin plays on those sensuous lips and before he can make a lewd remark, I leap out of my bed and head straight for my en-suite, shutting the door firmly behind me. Yeah, I'm definitely in need of a cold shower.

~

*W*hen I emerge from the bathroom, freshly showered and feeling a little more rational, I find Raph stretched out on my bed, looking like he's also just showered and changed last night's tux for a grey t-shirt and faded jeans.

My gaze falls on my open sketchbook that Raph is leafing through. Usually I'd be uncomfortable with someone looking at my sketches— they're personal, reflections of memories which are sacred to me. But Raph already saw my painting of Rockford Cape that day in the art studio and as he studies the sketches of the same scene, I don't feel any discomfort.

"You really are one hell of an artist," he says, as he looks up to find me watching him.

"Thanks," I reply, feeling the usual embarrassment at the compliment.

"No—really. It sounds insane, but it's like I can almost feel the wind and the sea breeze when I look at these sketches."

"That does sound insane," I scoff, although an art teacher in one of my previous high schools once told me something similar.

"I think it probably has to do with your powers—like you've always felt the connection, although you didn't know what it was," he says thoughtfully.

His insightfulness surprises me. I realize that he's probably right. I get the sense that my life before this place was nothing but a shadow, a faded image of the true picture. That before this place, I was nothing but a ghost—wandering through life, but not really living. I tell myself that it's the vivid colors and breathtaking landscapes of this world that makes me feel alive. But something inside me knows that it's not just those things. That the face before me now, so beautiful that it's almost unreal, has something to do with it, too. Raph's very presence makes every fiber in my being come alive and the thought is so frightening, that I can't allow myself to even think it.

I've been trying all morning not to think about what happened last night, but as Raph's eyes lock onto mine just then, it's impossible to keep the thoughts out of my mind. I don't know what any of it means. I wanted the truth from Raph, I asked him for it, hated him for not being able to tell me. But now that he has, I have no idea what to do with it, and I get the sense that neither does he.

I fiddle with the hem of my sleeve, feeling suddenly awkward, because now that I'm thinking about Raph's words from last night, I have no idea what to say. But I'm saved from having to say anything because Raph is already speaking.

"I want to see this place. Will you take me?" he asks.

At first I don't know what he's asking, but as my gaze falls back to the sketch of Rockford Cape, I get it, although I have no idea how he thinks I can take him there.

"Magnus told me that only Dynasty heads have keys to the portal. Why else do you think I'm still stuck here?" I reply.

That last part seems to cast a shadow over those luminous blue eyes for a moment, but it's swept away with a rather smug looking smile as he digs something out of his jeans pocket.

"I swiped the St. Tristan key last night. Hopefully, I can get it back to the vault before anyone notices."

My eyes widen as I gape at the golden key laying in Raph's palm. The engraving of the sun on the bow is near identical to the row of suns tattooed on Raph's side. A million conflicting thoughts and feelings race through me. This key is my way home, back to Earth. Back to my life. If someone had asked me a couple of months ago if I wanted my old life back, I'd have said yes in a heartbeat. Now ... now, I don't know anything anymore.

But that's not what Raph is asking me. He's asking me to take him to the one place that for so long has been my anchor. The place that is most sacred to me. I'd never felt the urge to share it with anyone else before, but just then, I can't deny that something inside me does want him to see it. I've walked that familiar stretch of coastline each year alone for the past ten years, but now I want to walk along that shore with him by my side. The realization is insane, but undeniable all the same.

Some part of me recalls Magnus's warning about Earth not being safe for me anymore. I consider telling Raph, but remember Magnus' words about the fact that the other Dynasties didn't even know about this supposed threat. Not that I really know anything about it either. In fact, some part of me still doesn't even believe that it's true. Still, I don't think Magnus will be very happy about this little outing.

"Wait, isn't it forbidden to go to Earth without special permission from the Dynasty heads?" I find myself asking.

Raph just waves a hand dismissively.

"What they don't know ..." He flashes me another wicked grin and the last of my resistance falls away. Damn those dimples.

"Okay," I say finally.

Raph smiles back at me and it's not that arrogant smile which is infuriatingly beautiful but a small, intimate smile, which feels like it's meant for me and me alone and it makes his beauty all the more devastating.

He gets up then and holds the key out in front of him. At first nothing happens but I can sense Raph's focus and then I can feel the air around me shifting like it did that day in the abandoned playground when Magnus opened the portal last.

The atmosphere splits open and I can't believe my eyes. I'd seen this happen once before, but the sight is still such a shock to my system. What feels like a storm blows through my bedroom and I let Raph take my hand and lead me into the portal.

Starlight and rainbows surround us and I clutch onto Raph for dear life as we fall through the breath-taking spectrum of the vast universe.

The last time I did this, I was scared out of my mind, but Raph's arms are tight around me, holding me to him, as if he might never let go and the fear that I'd once felt is replaced by his warmth, his light and this time, I let myself feel it as he leads me through the void between our two worlds.

*I*t was morning when we left Eden, but it's twilight when we reach Earth, although the journey feels like it lasted only a few minutes. I don't even try to figure out how the whole inter-dimensional travel thing works.

But I'm glad for the twilight because Rockford Cape has always been the most beautiful at sunset. The sky is a glorious mix of blue and violet, with steaks of pink against the backdrop as twilight descends on the rickety pier. The amusement park's lights reflect off the calm waters, making the scene look almost magical, although not in an otherworldly way. The scene is breathtaking in its natural beauty.

Beside me, I can feel Raph's excitement and wonder. He quite literally seems like a kid at an amusement park.

We're on our second round of this ridiculous fishing game where you have to pick out prizes with a fishing rod that I used to love so much when I was a kid. It hits me then how surreal all of this is. Never in my wildest imagination could I have thought that I'd be standing here with Raph, playing tacky amusement park games and enjoying myself more than I have in a long time.

We ride on the Ferris wheel where Raph finds the dizzying view from the top exhilarating, whereas I quake at the height. Then he humors me by going on the ghost train with me which used to scare me shitless when I was a kid, but as I got older, realized was nothing more than a track lined with glow in the dark skeletons and plastic mannequins dressed as witches. We gorge on cotton candy, popcorn and hot dogs and then go back to playing a couple more games.

The whole thing is so normal, so human, that I could almost imagine that we're just two normal teenagers on a date. But of course, we're not, and there's nothing normal about Raph. I don't fail to notice the looks that people are giving him, which reminds me of that. It's similar to the look that people were giving Magnus when he came to Rodeo Ricky's that night a few months ago—as if they can sense that Raph is totally out of place here, in this world. As if they can sense that there's something about this guy that makes the very air around him come alive.

But it's more than just that, most people, mostly female, are openly gawking at him. As if they can't help but look at him in the same way that they wouldn't be able to help being drawn to an impossibly bright flash of light. They have no idea who he is, but it's as if some primal part of them can sense the power and air of regal authority that surrounds him. As if there is some age-old instinct inside them, compelling them to bow down and worship the god walking among them. Raph certainly looks the part, too, with his halo of golden blonde hair, tall powerfully muscled body, face like an angel and those impossibly blue eyes. Hell, it's impossible *not* to think that he's some kind of higher being.

The looks are disconcerting to say the least, but Raph doesn't seem to notice, or at least he pretends not to. He's spent his entire life being the center of attention and under constant scrutiny. The stares don't seem to faze him at all. I used to find it arrogant, but now I think I find it admirable—his ability to stay unaffected in the face of such scrutiny.

Despite enjoying myself, Magnus's warning eats away at the back of my mind and I swear there are some moments when I can feel eyes on us, watching. But I brush the paranoia away. The only people watching are the people gawking at Raph and as disconcerting as that might be, it's hardly dangerous.

Raph hands me the fuzzy teddy bear that he's just won.

"What's this for?" I ask, examining the stuffed animal dubiously.

"Birthday present."

"It's not my birthday," I reply dryly.

He flashes me a wicked grin.

"I know it's not."

My eyebrows raise in surprise. I'm pretty sure I haven't told anyone when my birthday is. Only Magnus knew and that was from getting his hands on my birth certificate.

"How do you know when my birthday is? Right. I remember. You're a stalker."

He laughs in response.

"It's pretty hard not to notice when someone has the exact same birthday as me."

If I had been surprised earlier, now I'm utterly shocked.

"What? *You have the same birthday as me?*"

"The 31st of March, down to the very second."

"That's … more than a little bizarre," I reply.

His smile only grows wider.

"I think it's fate trying to tell us that we're made for each other." His tone is light, but I wonder if he's not entirely joking.

Not knowing how to respond to that, or to the totally creepy fact that Raph and I were apparently born at exactly the same time, *down to the very second* as he says, I shift my attention to the fuzzy bear that I'm clutching. I eye the angel wings on the bear's back and its blue eyes, and I shoot Raph a dry look which he returns with one of feigned innocence.

"Is this meant to be you?" I ask, quirking an eyebrow at him.

"No—why? Do you think there's something angelic about my perfect face?" he asks with a cocky grin.

I roll my eyes.

"Don't flatter yourself." I lie because I definitely did think the first time I saw him that he looked exactly how I thought an angel might.

"I think we both know that there is nothing angelic about you."

His grin turns wicked, and I regret my words because I'm now flushing so hard, I feel like my face is on fire.

"Hmm. I don't think you've given me the chance to show you just how un-angelic I can be … *yet.*"

The promise in his words sends a thrill racing through me, although I try to stamp down on it. I'm well aware that despite all that he confessed to me last night, apart from holding me as we slept and again as we hurtled through the depths of time and space, he hasn't made a single attempt to touch me or to kiss me. I try not to think about it because something inside me knows that when he does kiss me again, this time, he won't stop. The thought of his lips moving on mine, for real this time, makes heat pool in my core and I so should not be feeling this way right in the middle of a goddamn amusement park.

I can sense the anticipation building in both of us. The dull ache as sweet as it is almost painful, until the tension between us is so thick, that I'm almost choking on it. I'm too aware of every movement, every accidental brush of his hand against mine, every breath that he takes a few inches too close. I feel like I'm about to come out of my skin by the time we reach the photo booth near the pier entrance.

I find myself thinking of the strip of photographs that was now lost along with all of the other memories of my mom. Raph notices the change in my expression and tugs at my hand gently.

"I think we should make some new memories," he says as he pulls me into the booth. I don't have the chance to object because the next thing I know, I'm sitting on his lap in the cramped booth and his arm is firmly around my waist.

I shift on his lap and I don't miss the way the bulge in his jeans hardens. I'm embarrassed as hell, but the burning look in those blue eyes, sears away any thought or feeling that isn't about his lips on mine or his hands on my body. *God, what is happening to me?*

He leans forward and just as I think he's going to kiss me, he lowers those impossibly long golden lashes, shielding me from the intensity of his burning gaze as he feeds some coins into the slot next to the screen. I groan inwardly in frustration and part of me thinks he's doing this on purpose, teasing me almost.

Four flashes go off in succession as we sit there, our faces inches from each other's, our gazes locked. Neither one of us even bothering to pose for the photographs. I wonder if they'll even develop properly given all the fire and heat I can feel in the booth right now.

The last flash goes off but neither one of us moves. Raph's eyes are like twin flames as he raises a hand to cup my cheek and I feel the touch like a brand. He leans closer again but again, it's not to kiss me. At least not on my lips.

I feel his lips against my neck, at the sensitive spot where my pulse is hammering against my skin and my fingers are digging into his shoulders as he trails open mouthed kisses all along the side of my neck. He lets out a groan as he seems to breathe me in and it's got to be the sexiest sound that I've ever heard in my entire life. The moan that comes out of my own mouth is one of equal abandon, because I can barely think past the feeling of his lips licking and sucking the sensitive skin along my neck in a way that tells me exactly what it will feel like to have him do that to my lips and other places, too.

It's impossible to remember that we're still sitting in a photo booth in the middle of an amusement park, as my fingers find their way into his hair. I grip onto those silky strands and bring his head closer to my skin because nothing feels close enough. I can feel a shudder race through his powerful body as I move on his lap again, the softest part of me pressing down on the hardest part of him. I'm aware of the tremor racing through me and the way his body quakes as his hands travel over mine. Even through our clothing, I can feel the fire in his touch. The ache inside me is almost painful now, and I'm clutching at him to try to ease that ache, although I have no idea how.

He curses as I press down on him again and his arms around me tighten as he shifts me so that I'm straddling him. From this angle, I can feel just how equally affected he is. He thrusts upwards at the same time as pulling me closer, so that his hard length presses into the building ache at my center. I gasp at the contact and I think I lose all coherent thought.

"Is this what you want, baby?" His voice is gruff and I can't even form words, let alone answer.

I want him to kiss me and I can sense that he knows it, too. But I was right about him teasing me or at least making the ache between us build enough so that when he does actually kiss me, I know that the universe will probably explode.

A loud buzzing sound goes off, signalling that our prints are ready. I couldn't care less because all I want is for Raph's lips to keep moving on my skin.

But Raph just chuckles as he pulls away, and grabs the strip of photographs.

What the hell just happened?

I slowly return to my senses and as I step out of the booth. I'm mortified when I look down at my dishevelled clothing and even more so when Raph steps out of the booth. His golden hair is sticking up and mussed, as if someone was just running their fingers through it. *Yeah, me*—I remind myself. That was me in there pulling at his hair, grinding almost shamelessly against him. Those breathy moans were also mine, coming out of my mouth as I reveled in the feeling of Raph's lips and tongue working on my throat. I can barely believe that those sensations were real or that I was the one feeling them, but Raph … Raph does something to me that makes every fiber in my body come alive with feelings and sensations I've never experienced before in my entire life.

Raph flashes me a wicked smile that tells me he knows exactly what I'm thinking and how shaken I feel, but the slightly dazed look in those vivid blue eyes tells me that he's equally affected.

I expect him to tease me then, but instead, he takes my hand in a surprisingly sweet gesture.

"Walk with me," he says.

I let my fingers intertwine with his and nod because I still don't think I'm able to speak.

He doesn't let go of my hand as he lets me lead him away from the pier and along the familiar stretch of coastline.

The beach is deserted apart from a few stragglers at the edge of the pier and I feel the familiar calm settling over me as I look out at the last rays of sunlight disappearing behind the violet and pink horizon.

Being here with him, sharing this place with him that is so sacred to me, is frighteningly intimate. I'm terrified to realize that not only do I trust him enough to share this with him, but I also want him here with me, beside me. That after years of walking this shore alone, and being content with that, I want someone walking it with me and never in a million years could I have imagined that the someone would be Raphael St. Tristan. The guy who, up until a few weeks ago, was the only real enemy I've ever had.

"At the risk of sounding lame, I don't think I've had so much fun in a long time," Raph says from beside me.

"Ditto," I reply. "I love amusement parks, this one in particular, for reasons that you know."

"I've never been to one before." I'm not sure why Raph's words surprise me.

"Don't they have amusement parks in Eden?" I ask.

"Sure, they do." He shrugs then.

"But I didn't really have time for that kind of thing growing up—or at least my father didn't think so."

I feel a pang of sadness at that and I remember what he told me last night about his life not being his own and what it meant to be the heir to the throne. I realize that he hadn't had much of a childhood at all—another part of him which is a mirror of a part of me, my own childhood ripped away when I was seven. But at least I had those seven years with my mom, whereas it seems like Raph didn't have a childhood at all.

"So, thank you for sharing this place with me," he says finally; he looks humbled in a way that I don't think I've ever seen before.

He lets loose a long breath as he looks out at the sun dipping lower behind the horizon.

"I've watched Earth from afar so many times, but this is the first time I've been down here. I used to think that nothing could be more beautiful than Eden but there are colors here on Earth that I've never seen, colors that don't exist on Eden."

His words surprise me because I had thought the same about Eden. But as I follow his gaze out over the horizon, I see those hues of deep pink and purple that perhaps I hadn't seen on Eden.

"Do you want to try shifting the day into night? It's close enough to sundown that it won't disturb the natural cycle," he says and something occurs to me then.

"How does it all work? Magnus only mentioned that the day is by the hand of the St. Tristan Dynasty, the night is by the hand of the Evenstar Dynasty and the other Dynasties watch over everything in between." I'd never really thought about it before, mostly because I was trying not to get too caught up in the alternative realm that was Eden, but there was no denying that it had happened regardless.

"Well, everything on both planets runs its own cycle—night, day, sunrise, sunset, winter, spring, summer, fall—you get the point.

"It's not like one of us is constantly on watch, manually shifting the seasons or making the sun rise every morning. But it's by our power, the power of the Seraph, of the Dynasties, that it does happen.

"When things become imbalanced or something throws the cycle off, then as keepers of the elements, that's when we're made to intervene to restore the balance."

I nod, although part of me still doesn't understand fully. This is all still so new to me—only a few months ago, I had no idea that any of this even existed.

"So, do you want to give it a try?" Raph asks then.

I hesitate for a moment, but I don't see the harm.

I wait to hear his instructions but instead I feel him stepping closer to me from behind, until I feel the solidity of his chest flush against my back. His warmth and closeness play havoc with my senses, and it's a wonder I'm able to stay standing.

He reaches out and takes my hand in his, stretching our arms out towards the horizon.

"Find the connection." The feel of his breath against my ear sends a thrill racing down my spine, but I force myself to focus.

I find that connection, the one I've felt inside me for as long as I can remember and I feel it take over my senses.

I feel the pull of the moon just beyond sight, the stars just beyond reach and I draw them both closer. Just like that day in elements class, it feels like some primal part of me knows what to do. The connection is dizzying, the power in my veins throbs. The intensity of the power is frightening, and exhilarating at the same time.

Raph's fingers entwine with mine and suddenly I can feel his own connection to the daylight. The sheer power that he has over it takes my breath away and I'm reminded of exactly who and what he is. I'm reminded of the sheer force of him. A god in every sense of the word.

He sweeps the sunlight away, just as I coax the darkness forward, our powers perfectly in sync. The connection that I feel between us in that moment shakes me to the core. I've never felt so *close* to someone in my entire life, so connected, and I'm certain there's no other feeling like this in the entire universe. The feeling is so alien, so new, yet at the same time, it feels as ancient as time itself, as primal as my deepest desires.

In that moment, with our powers fused together, it's as if we're one person. Like two halves of a whole snapping into place with such finality, that it's almost frightening. It feels like I've been wandering through the universe for an age, lost, searching for something and in this moment, I've finally found that lost fragment of myself. It's *him*.

In that moment, he isn't the heir of the St. Tristan Dynasty and I'm not the heir of the Evenstar Dynasty, we're nothing but the power of day and night breathing side by side. Breathing as one. There is no him, there is no me. There's only *us*.

I watch through wide eyes as the last of the sunlight disappears behind the horizon, as the moon appears and as a blanket of stars descend on the now midnight blue sky.

Once night settles fully over the scene, we both let go of the connection. I don't realize how much effort I'd been exerting until I hear my own ragged breathing as I try to catch my breath. But I know that breathlessness is from that universe shattering connection that I'd just felt with Raph, too.

I'm suddenly aware of my own body again. I can feel Raph's eyes on me. When I turn to him, he's looking at me with something like wonder and something else I've glimpsed before, but never allowed myself to acknowledge.

I don't have time to, either, because my thoughts are jolted when I feel the pattering of rain against my skin. Raph is equally surprised and we both look up to see the heavens opening as sheets of rain blanket us both.

"Was that you?" Raph asks through the sound of the rain.

"No—definitely not. Maybe it's Baron up there telling us to get our asses back home."

We're both laughing then, as the rain falls in thick sheets around us. The water soaks through my clothes and every inch of my skin is slick with rain. I tilt my face up to let the rain wash over my cheeks, and when I turn back to Raph, all laughter is gone from his face. Those vivid blue eyes blaze into mine and even though I'm now totally soaked and freezing, I can still feel the heat of his gaze and every inch of my skin burns under it.

He moves closer to me, brushing my soaked hair away from my face and I think I stop breathing altogether when I feel his breath against my cheek, against my lips.

The air is hushed, still, as if waiting for something. Time itself seems to have stopped and I feel the same stillness in my own body, every fiber hushed in anticipation. It feels like the universe itself is watching as we stand there, Raph's lips a hair's breadth away from mine, the rain falling around us.

"What are you doing?" I ask then, my words barely a whisper in the inch of space between us.

This time, he answers. I feel the words on my lips and they wrap themselves around my chest like a vice.

"I'm kissing you."

Then Raph's lips meet mine and whatever else I'd been thinking suddenly doesn't matter anymore. Nothing matters anymore but this kiss. This moment.

Just like that day in the forest, it's barely a kiss at first. Just his lips brushing softly against mine and just like that day in the forest, I feel the touch in every part of my body. White light explodes behind my closed eyelids and every pore in my body is awakened by the sensation.

Before I can even think, I'm kissing him back with an intensity that frightens me. His arms around me are both strong, yet terrifyingly gentle, as he slides his hand up my spine, in a caress that causes my body to tremble. He buries his hand in my hair, and I hear a moan escape my lips as he deepens the kiss.

Some part of me is terrified and I can hear the whisper of danger echoing through my mind. This kiss, this touch is taking me to a place from which I know I can't return. But it's impossible to think of anything other than the intensity of the sensations whirling around us in that moment, threatening to consume us both.

I open myself up to him, and he makes that low sound in the back of his throat as he explores my mouth, his tongue slicking over mine, moving against it in the most intimate caress. I realize faintly that I'm clutching onto him as tightly as he's grasping for me.

My mind is swimming in the torrent of emotion that is carrying us away and everywhere we touch, sparks arch between us. I've never kissed like this before, never been kissed like this before—it's insane and at the same time, beautiful in its intensity. Too frightening to contain, too fierce to control.

I can feel the fine tremor that has overtaken Raph's body, the way the same tremor has taken hold of mine and neither of us seems to be in control of ourselves anymore. The kisses are too much, yet not nearly enough.

Raph's hands travel to my waist, to my hips and the urge to be closer to him is irresistible, undeniable. He lifts me in an effortless motion and I wrap my legs around his waist. I hear myself gasp as he rolls his hips into the softest part of me and I'm whimpering as he crushes the center of me against his hard length. Heat flares in my core at the contact, and I can feel the shudder quaking through Raph's powerful body. The rain pours over us, blankets us. But neither of us seems to care.

Raph's lips brush against mine again and again with such passion and deep heart-wrenching emotion, that I can feel something inside me shattering at the deep rooted knowledge that nothing this good can ever be right. Nothing this intense can ever last. Even the brightest stars burn out. But as all the pent up longing and emotion that we'd both denied since that first day on the beach in Arcadia washes over us, drowning us, it's almost impossible to remember caution or reason. It's impossible to think of the consequences of indulging in this kind of earth shattering passion, for allowing ourselves to fall into the chasm that's gaping before us. I can't remember the hate that I once felt for him and the equal hate that he has felt for me. Except the way that he's kissing me, the way that he's touching me, makes me think now that perhaps it hadn't been hate at all.

His hands are everywhere, as if he can't touch enough of me, can't hold me hard enough and everywhere he touches, my skin burns and awakens. He is the fire and I throw myself into it.

We're both gasping for air like two divers resurfacing when we break away from each other. He's still holding me against his body and my legs are still wrapped around his waist when he touches his forehead to mine. My lips feel swollen and still tingle with the ghost of his kisses. My skin feels raw and aches at the absence of his touch.

Raph's eyes are locked onto mine, his chest rising and falling rapidly. The emotion smouldering in the depths of those midnight blue eyes convince me that all those months, it hadn't been hate that I thought he was feeling. It hadn't been hate at all.

I draw a shuddering breath as I try to speak then.

"Raph ..."

My voice is barely a ragged whisper and I trail off because I have no idea what to say in the wake of everything that came before.

But he smiles then, a small smile that wraps itself around my heart. There's something like wonder in his eyes, so fragile and so at odds with that icy glare that I saw that first day on the beach, that it takes my breath away.

"Say it again," he says.

I don't know what he means.

"That's the first time you've ever said my name to me." The realization that it's true, hits me then, too.

"Not asshole, not prick …"

I let out a laugh, and it sounds shaky as hell, because my senses are still fried from those kisses.

"Or dickhead, or fucker …" I add, which only makes his smile widen.

That smile turns wicked as he nips the bottom of my lip with his teeth.

"I want you to say it again. But next time, I want you to be screaming it when I …"

He whispers something in my ear that sends shivers through my body and makes me feel like I'm going to burst into flames.

"Let's go home," he says, the promise of that whisper in his eyes.

I remember where I am and a few months ago there was no way anything could drag me back through that portal and back to that world. But now … now the only place I want to be is in these arms. As foolish as that might sound, and as much as I don't want to think of that place as home, I find myself nodding in response and when I open my mouth, it's to tell him to take me home.

I take one last look at the night sky above us, and it seems like even the stars are smiling down on us.

The moment we crash through the portal, Raph's lips are on mine again and this time, the first touch is anything but soft and tentative.

I'm aware that my bedroom is dark and of my back hitting the plush rug in front of the fireplace, but not much else as Raph kisses me with a hunger that shakes me to the core. He devours my lips and I meet his hunger with equal intensity.

Distantly, I can sense him setting the fireplace ablaze as he covers my trembling body with his powerful one. He breaks the kiss only long enough to tug off his soaked shirt and my mouth goes dry at the sight of his bare body. Every single part of him is corded with muscle. His chest and abs are ripped like a diamond, so defined, that I can see shadows against his golden skin from where the muscles cut. My gaze lands on the row of suns tattooed on the side of his left rib that I'd seen once before and again, I can't help but think how freaking sexy those tattoos are.

It's not like I hadn't noticed Raph's physical frame many times before, but the sight of that large body over mine makes me realize just how big and powerful he is and how small my frame is in comparison. The sight thrills me in a way which sends delicious shivers down my spine. I want him, I want him so much, and I let myself feel all of that just then.

He reaches out to touch his fingertips to my cheek in an achingly tender caress, which a few months ago, I could never have believed he'd be capable of. But I'd been wrong about him, wrong about that hate which I knew now was not hate at all. But something far deeper, something far more dangerous.

The tremors racking my body are telling me that I should be terrified, but I know that it's more than just fear racing through me because I can almost taste the desire in the very air I'm breathing. Mine or his, it's impossible to tell.

His eyes lock onto mine, dark with hunger and a need that takes my breath away and his words have an equal effect.

"God, Jaz, you're so goddamn beautiful. I want you so much, I feel like I can't even breathe when I look at you."

His words echo my own feelings, his desire mirrors my own and the connection that I feel to the elements seems like nothing compared to the one that I feel when I look at that impossibly perfect face. His beauty is utterly devastating and for a second, I can't quite make myself believe that he's real. That this is real.

Raph's fingers move from my cheek, trailing down the side of my neck, until his hand finally rests on my chest. I know that he can feel my heart beating wildly and when I raise a shaky hand to his smooth chest, I can feel the running stag clamor of his heart, too.

"Your heart is beating so fast right now, Jaz," he whispers, his voice sounding hoarse.

"So is yours," I reply softly.

He smiles then, that heartbreakingly intimate smile that I know no one in this entire universe has seen but me.

"I want to touch you so badly, Jaz. Will you let me?" The plea melts away the fear and doubt, because although I know he can sense just how much I want him, he still asks for my permission.

I don't trust myself to speak, so I plant a kiss on his smooth chest instead, right over where his heart is jackhammering like crazy. I nod up at him and I feel the shudder that races through his powerful body.

I hear the way his breath hitches as he leans down to kiss me again. But this time, the kiss is different. The way his lips touch mine is like nothing I've ever experienced before. As limited as my kissing experience might be, I had no idea that a person could even be kissed like this—the awe, the tenderness, the reverence, all of it washes over me and I feel the kiss like a punch to my chest. Painful and exquisite, all at once.

I feel myself losing grip on all thought when Raph's lips begin their descent. He lifts my body enough to remove my soaked t-shirt and he plants a delicate kiss on my shoulder as he gently eases both bra straps down. I feel him reach around me and with expert fingers, he unclasps the back. A moment later, my bra joins my t-shirt on the floor somewhere.

I'm now entirely naked from the waist up and I've never felt more vulnerable in my entire life. Raph pulls back and his eyes travel the length of my bare skin, from the peaks of my breasts to the valley of my bare stomach below. I feel the fire in his gaze, the hunger in his eyes, so deep and all-consuming, that it's almost frightening. But I can feel how he's holding himself back, controlling that desire. Part of me doesn't want him to, the foolish part of me that's as hungry for him as he is for me, wants to unleash all that he is and I want to burn in that fire.

The flames burning in the fireplace encase Raph's golden body with its glow but I realize that Raph himself is glowing, too. His skin is radiating its own light and the sight is almost too beautiful to watch without coming apart.

"You're glowing," I say softly.

Our gazes lock and I meet his eyes unflinchingly, because when I say my next words, I want him to feel it in every fiber of his being.

"Touch me."

The plea snaps whatever leash that Raph had been holding himself back with and like a beast freed of its tether, his body covers mine again. His mouth captures my breast and I hear myself cry out at the new and unfamiliar sensations raging through me. His hand grips my waist as he rolls his hips into mine, the hard length of him pressing against the softest part of me. Each thrust of his hips elicits a moan from my lips. I can feel the vibration of his responding groan against my breast as he continues to suck and lick at the soft skin.

His free hand comes up to cup my other breast, and the rough pads of his fingers against the softness, is almost too much to bear. I'm gasping out his name and I can feel his smile against my abdomen as he travels lower down my body. He wanted me to say his name again and he sure as hell is making it happen.

He pauses when he reaches the waistband of my jeans. His fingers hover over the button, but he looks back at me and waits. The silent request tugs at my chest and I can only nod in response, not trusting myself to speak.

My jeans are off in less than a second and I'm aware that the only piece of clothing left covering my body is the thin scrap of lace around my waist.

His hands tremble at my waist as he lowers the fabric, and I know he can feel me trembling, too. He catches the lace with his teeth and I don't think I've ever seen anything so sexy as he works the material down my thighs.

I know that he can sense my apprehension when that last piece of clothing joins the rest on the floor, because he slows down then, trailing soft kisses along the inside of my thigh. His kisses are traveling higher and soon his mouth will touch me where no other person has ever been. The thought terrifies me, but the want overpowers the fear, because I do want him. I want him so much.

"I've wanted to do this since the first moment I saw you on that beach," he says, and when I look down, I know I'm wrong about the sight of his teeth around my panties being the sexiest sight I'd ever seen, because the sight of that beautiful face between my legs, exceeds that by far.

His eyes are fixed onto the center of me, and he lets out a shuddering breath.

"God, Jaz, you're so damn beautiful, every part of you."

I don't get a chance to respond, because a split second later I feel his mouth on me and the world, hell the entire universe disappears, leaving only the feeling of his mouth licking and sucking at the most intimate part of me. His mouth moves with a hunger that brands me, claims me and I let him lay that claim, because I want every inch of me to belong to him and only him.

My back arches clean off the plush rug as his mouth closes on the throbbing bud at the center of me, and I feel like I'm coming out of my own skin. I feel his groan of approval vibrating through me and I can't think past the feeling of his mouth on me, working me until I'm at a fever pitch, every inch of my skin burning.

When his finger thrusts inside me, I think I forget my own name and when his tongue slips inside me to replace it, I remember only his. I'm breathing it out over and over as the tension inside me mounts, until my body can't contain it anymore.

I'm still crying out his name when his mouth covers mine, devouring the sound as my body shudders and shakes uncontrollably. He holds me through it, his tongue caressing mine in the same way that it had just been caressing the most intimate part of me, and I can taste myself on his tongue as I kiss him back with utter abandon.

I collapse in his arms and he drops delicate kisses along my jaw, down the side of my neck as I struggle to piece myself back together. But he's there with me, holding me, and although it feels like I've just lost my own sanity, the feel of his warmth, of his solid arms around me, makes me feel safe.

Eventually, he carries me to my bed. The soft covers feel heavenly against my naked skin. But not as good as the feel of his arms around my waist as he pulls me against his side. I glance up at him and his expression looks like he's just had his mind blown, but that doesn't make sense because I'm the one who just lost my mind in all of these crazy sensations.

Something occurs to me then, and I suddenly feel awkward as hell. Because this is the first time I've ever done anything like this, so I have no idea how to reciprocate.

"What about—"

But he doesn't let me finish, cutting me off with a kiss deep enough to remind me what his mouth, his tongue felt like in other places.

"I wanted to touch you first, Jaz. Tonight is all about you," he says when he breaks away.

Our gazes lock for a long moment, and I feel like I'm losing my grip on the universe again. Nothing exists outside this world that we've created.

I rest my hand on his chest then, my fingers touching the hard smoothness of his skin.

"Is it always like this?" I find myself asking. "I feel like I'm going to burst into flames every time I look at you," I confess.

He smiles, but his eyes are serious, midnight blue and dark with emotion.

"No, baby. It's never been like this for me before."

He pulls me closer to him, his chin resting on top of my hair and I can feel him breathing me in.

"God, Jaz, what are you doing to me?" He lets out a shuddering breath and I want to ask him the same thing, because I feel like I can't even think straight right now.

We lie like that for what seems like forever, but at the same time not long enough.

Then I feel his mouth curling into a smile against my hair, just as I'm about to drift off to sleep.

"I love it when you say my name, Jaz."

Embarrassment floods me and I lift my arm to deliver a punch squarely to his rock hard gut. But he catches my fist in his hand and quick as a snake, he thrusts forward and shifts me onto my back again.

His lips crash onto mine and although I've only just pieced myself back together, I let him unravel me all over again.

26

*W*hen Monday morning comes, I find myself slipping out of my room soundlessly, not wanting to wake Raph. I leave for class much too early and it's because where it really matters, I'm one hell of a coward.

The memory of Raph's mouth on me, not just on my lips, but on every part of my body, is seared into my mind. The first time on the plush rug in front of the fireplace, the second time before we both finally succumb to sleep, once more in the middle of the night and again when we both woke up on Sunday morning.

Then there was the whole of Sunday when we spent the whole day in my bed. What started off as an innocent plan to watch movies all day, turned out to be not quite so innocent, with Raph making me cry out his damn name way too many times. I'd been dying to touch him, to make him lose his sanity in the same way that he had made me lose my mind, but he kept telling me he could wait, that it was all about me, although the way his body trembled and the naked pleasure in his eyes told me that he had enjoyed every minute of it as much as I had, if not more.

I flush as I remember the feel of those sensuous lips against the most intimate parts of me and the way I'd come apart against those lips, over and over again. I let out a groan of frustration as I make my way to campus, suddenly feeling like I need another cold shower.

But as undeniably pleasurable as each moment has been, it feels like all of it happened in some isolated world that we had created all for ourselves, a world where it didn't matter who and what Raph was, a world where his throne and the duties and obligations that came with it, didn't exist. But it's back to reality now and in the cold light of day, I can't ignore the questions, the doubts that I've kept at bay since Friday night when Raph spoke those words to me that seemed to steal away all sanity and reason.

I kick myself for letting any of this happen. I should've stayed away from Raph, I shouldn't have accepted his truce or his offer to help me. That way, we would've stayed enemies, because things were so much simpler when I believed that we hated each other.

I should've stayed clear of him when he told me that he didn't want me, that he couldn't want me, that none of this could ever matter because apart from the not wanting me part, the rest of it is still true.

"What happened to you this weekend?" Dani asks, as we settle into first period, thankfully not a class that I share with Raph.

"I tried calling and I texted you a few times because you seemed kind of upset when you left the Fall Ball on Friday."

I consider lying, but I decide against it, because Dani is my friend, the first one I'd made in this place and I want to confide in her.

"Oh, Dan," I sigh. "So much has gone down since then."

Dani looks intrigued and she raises an eyebrow expectantly.

I tell her everything that happened, and although I keep my voice down so only she can hear, she's far less subtle with her exclamations.

I keep the bedroom parts brief, but I can still feel my face burning once I've finished.

Dani is silent for a long moment.

"So, Raph really *went down on you?* More than once?" she asks finally.

"Dani!" I cry out in frustration. "Is that really the only part that matters?"

"Hell yes, it is," she replies quickly.

"You are one lucky girl," she adds. "I don't think there's a girl here that wouldn't love to swap places with you right now."

"Well, they're welcome to because I have no idea what to do with this mess," I reply, covering my face with my hand.

Dani's face turns somber then.

"I don't know what you should do either. I mean, it's great that Raph finally came out and admitted what everyone with eyes and ears has known since that first day you stepped on campus. More than great.

"But you're right—it's way more complicated than that. Raph isn't just any guy—he's a Dynasty heir, *the heir to the goddamn throne*. He's up to his eyeballs in obligations and duties. He's been raised in a certain way, taught to disregard what he wants for the sake of his Dynasty, what his throne needs him to do."

"Thanks, Dan, that makes me feel a hell of a lot better," I grumble. She's speaking with such knowledge and conviction, that some part of me wonders if she's maybe talking about more than just Raph here, if maybe it's the same for Lance, but to a lesser extent.

"What I mean is, Raph must really feel something fierce for you if he's willing to step out like this."

"But what if it's just another piece on the side for him. He told me that he and Layla have this sick understanding where he basically gets to screw around with whoever he wants, but none of that changes who they are to each other. She's his *betrothed*, Dan. Everyone expects them to be together and one day, she's going to be his queen."

I feel the stabbing pain at my chest when I say the words out loud, and the realization of what I've just gotten myself into crashes over me like a tidal wave.

Dani's face softens as she covers my hand in hers.

"If you really believe that you're just another piece on the side for Raph, then you wouldn't have let all that happen between you this past weekend. No way, Jazmine. I know you. I know that you believe there's something more to it than just that."

I did, one hundred percent, believe that on Friday night but now … now, in the cold light of day, I'm not so sure.

"I don't know anything anymore," I say then.

"Okay, well don't jump to conclusions until you do know for sure," she says and I can make myself agree with that at least.

~

*M*y resolve to keep an open mind quickly wavers when Raph walks into my second period class with Layla on his heels. The sight of them together used to make my stomach twist, but now it makes me feel so completely sick, that I'm finding it hard to stay seated at my desk. Because all I want to do is get the hell out of here and as far away as possible from the sight of Raph and Layla together.

The realization that I felt crashing over me earlier, returns with a vengeance. What the hell had I been thinking, letting myself get involved with Raph? A guy who, a few months ago was solely responsible for making my life a living hell, a guy who is clearly betrothed to the most beautiful girl I've ever seen in real life and who, coincidentally, hates my guts.

My eyes land on Layla's all too perfect face and I can almost imagine her with a crown on her head, sitting beside Raph's throne— his queen. That is who she's destined to be, and me? I'm nothing more than just another foolish girl who let Raph into her panties. It's my own fault, though, because I knew what I was getting myself into. I knew that I was way out of my depths with this guy, that his promise to break me was no idle threat because even if I do now believe that it isn't his intention, it doesn't change the fact that I know, deep down, that he will.

There's no other way this could end. I don't know anything about dating or even hooking up with guys. My total inexperience means that Raphael St. Tristan does indeed have the ability to break my naïve little heart, if I don't start seeing sense this very second.

I force myself to face that painful reality and school my face blank, despite the churning in my gut.

But when Raph's vivid blue eyes lock onto mine, that reality wavers, because although I search for any sign of regret, I don't see anything of the sort. Instead he's looking at me as if I'm the only person in the room, hell, maybe even the only person in the entire universe. Dani isn't in this class with me, but if she were, I know she'd be throwing me one of her pointed looks right now.

Still, I keep my guard up when instead of following Layla to the front row, he walks towards where I'm sitting. The desk beside me magically empties and Raph drops down into it.

"Jaz." He greets me with that heart stopping smile and when my gaze falls on those sensuous lips, all I can think about is the wicked things that those lips, that tongue did to my body all weekend long.

The smirk on Raph's face tells me he knows exactly what I'm thinking and that he's thinking of exactly the same thing, too.

"Hey," I manage, keeping my tone casual.

A small frown forms on his face as he assesses mine.

He leans over to me and the feel of his mouth so close to my ear causes shivers to race through my spine.

"I woke up this morning thinking it was going to be the best Monday morning I've had in a long time, but I was bitterly disappointed when I realized that I was all alone in that big bed of yours," he whispers.

I force my erratic heartbeat to calm. I need to keep my head and it's proving almost impossible with Raph whispering in my ear.

"I had to get to class early," I lie and even I can hear how lame that excuse is.

I don't turn around to see Raph's reaction, but from the corner of my eye, I don't miss the way his frown deepens.

Thankfully, I'm saved by Professor Hoxton, who hands out a surprise quiz, which means that we'll have to spend the rest of the class in silence.

It doesn't stop Raph from burning a hole into me all the way through class, though, as those impossibly blue eyes turn to study my profile more than just a few times. I can sense him trying to read me, but that's the last thing I want.

When the bell rings, I grab my things hurriedly and head for the door without a second look back. I'm halfway down the hallway when I feel Raph's hand closing around my arm. Dammit.

I school my face into a neutral expression as I turn slowly to face him. But his expression is nowhere near as calm. He looks confused and there's something else mixed in there, too ... hurt? But that doesn't make sense because I can't let myself believe that he'd actually be hurt by anything that I could do to him, regardless of all that he's said to me.

"Is ... is something wrong, Jaz?" he asks tentatively, searching my face.

I work to keep him from seeing anything in it which might give me away.

"No, no—of course not," I reply. "I've just got a really busy day today," I add quickly.

He searches my face for another moment and he looks like he might try to push the subject, but nods slightly instead.

"Okay," he says finally.

"You coming to lunch?" he asks, looking at me expectantly.

"No—I have to drop some books off at the library, then see my art professor before next period," I lie again.

I don't give Raph a chance to object, as I turn on my heel and walk away, practically running from him.

I avoid him for the rest of the day. I ignore his confused looks, which turn into concern and then finally anger. I ignore the impulse to throw myself into his arms and kiss him in front of the entire class, so that everyone here knows that he's mine. I tell myself that the impulse is a crazy one, because of course, he's not mine and nor will he ever be mine. I need to accept that and forget everything that happened this weekend and I need to do it fast.

27

*S*overeign Hall is as still as a tomb when I get in after class. I know that Raph usually has soccer practice on Monday afternoons, so I'm safe for another few hours. I don't want to think about what's going to happen when he gets home, when he knocks on my door tonight.

Needing to work off the agitation that has been building inside me all day, I dig around in my wardrobe for my swimwear, feeling like a few laps in the pool should do the trick. Unfortunately, other than my now replaced Regency issued black one piece, my swimwear consists only of bikinis. I grab the first pair that I see—red and nicely cut. Not that it matters, because there's no one home to see anyway.

The water in the heated pool feels amazing against my tense muscles and I feel the tension slipping away with each lap. I'm probably on my fifth lap when I notice someone standing over the far edge of the pool.

My stomach sinks when I realize it's Raph, and at the same time, my heart speeds up, as I take in the sight of him. The soft pool lights reflect against his golden skin and every inch of him is ripped like a dream. My mind plays unwanted images in my head of the sight of that powerfully muscled body above mine, the feel of his rock hard chest crushed against my breasts and I'm glad I'm submerged in water, otherwise I think my skin will burst into flames.

The look in Raph's eyes makes me still completely. Those midnight blue eyes are clouded over and pissed, very pissed.

"Hi," I say lamely.

"Care to explain why you've been avoiding me all day?" he asks, crossing his arms over his ridiculously chiseled chest in a way that makes his arm muscles bulge.

For a moment, I consider trying to deny it. But then I realize it's no use. One, because he's clearly not going to believe me and two, because it's probably better for us to get this out of the way now, so that we can go back to, well whatever it was we were before all that happened between us this past weekend.

"I don't think this is such a good idea," I say finally, still feeling totally lame because the words are a total understatement. Raph had been right that day in the forest when he said this was a mistake. He'd been right to try to stop it. It was my fault for pushing him, for making him tell me what he was wise enough to know could never matter.

But his face just tells me that he doesn't agree with that at all.

He doesn't say anything, though, diving cleanly into the pool instead. He surfaces after a moment and I can feel my body tensing as he swims towards me.

He stops a few inches in front of me and the closeness is not doing great things for my self-control.

"Is that so?" he ask finally, quirking an eyebrow.

I force myself to swallow.

"Yeah, it is. I mean—I think you had the right idea about this being a mistake. Because—you know nothing can ever come of this. So, maybe we should just stop now before things get—"

He cuts me off then as his head dips and his lips make contact with the side of my throat. I think I let out a moan as he trails those open mouthed kisses along my neck which drive me insane with need and make my skin come alive at the same time.

My hands grab onto his shoulders instinctively, my fingers digging into his skin as he licks and sucks at the sensitive spot where my pulse is hammering beneath the surface.

"The only mistake was not doing this the first moment I saw you on that damned beach." He speaks the words against my skin and I shiver at the sensation it causes.

When he pulls away, his eyes blaze into mine and the hunger inside me is reflected in them.

Still, I try to hold onto the resolve that's fast slipping away.

"Raph ... I've never ... I don't do this ..." My words are as incoherent as my thoughts. But Raph hears them.

He cups my cheek with his hand and the hunger blazing in his eyes turns into something deeper, a different type of fire, with the ability to incinerate my entire universe, if I let it.

"I know, Jaz."

I let out a long breath then.

"You can have any girl you want and I know what you're used to ... I can't measure up to that and I can't let myself do this, when I know there are other—"

He cuts me off. "You have *no idea*, Jaz. I've never wanted anyone the way I want you. I've been with other girls, yes. But none of them ever meant anything to me. I don't even think I really wanted them. I just wanted to distract myself, I was just trying to find something to fill the void. But none of them ever could."

He drops his gaze and shakes his head almost ruefully.

"I guess I was just searching for something, although I had no idea what until you came along."

His words leave me breathless and when his impossibly blue eyes lock onto mine again, I think I stop breathing altogether.

"I don't know how I know this, but I'm certain that I'll never want anyone the way I want you. No other girl can even come close, Jaz. Not one."

Those words floor me and I can feel the last of my resistance being burned away under the intensity of his gaze.

"We can't," I say again in a last attempt to hold onto reason, but I hear the weakness in my own words.

"This—it's wrong. You were right—we can't want each other like this."

"We can't," he replies, drawing even closer, until his bare chest is pressed up against my breasts, with only the thin material of my bikini top separating us.

"But we do."

I back away from him in an attempt to distance myself from that all-consuming fire, but he follows me until my back hits the tile of the pool wall and there's nowhere else for me to go.

"Do you want me, Jaz?" he whispers, as he trails featherlight kisses along the outer shell of my ear, along my jaw line.

I clamp my lips shut to stop myself from answering, because I know the answer won't be the right one.

Beneath the waterline, I feel his hands move from my waist, down to my hip and further still until he's cupping the most intimate part of me, the part that he and he alone now knows only too well. His free hand closes around one of my thighs and I think I stop breathing when he hitches that thigh higher so that my leg curls around his waist.

All thoughts sweep out of my mind and I feel like I'm coming out of my skin as those skillful fingers draw aside my bikini and thrust inside me. My back arches against the tiled wall at the sensation and I cry out his name at the same time as he groans into my neck.

He repeats the question again, this time with his fingers buried deep inside me.

"Do you want me, Jaz?"

"Yes," I gasp out before I can stop myself, because who the hell am I fooling. I do want him, I want him more than I've ever wanted anything in my entire life. More than could possibly be right, more than could ever make sense.

I feel his lips curve against the corner of my lips and he nips my bottom lip with his teeth before his mouth crashes into mine. There's not a single protest left in me as his fingers move inside me at the same rhythm as his tongue moves against mine. Distantly, I'm aware that we're in the glass-walled natatorium; anyone could walk in and see us. Hell, they don't even have to walk in because the show would be visible through the glass walls. But I'm too far gone to care. Way too far gone. And there's something wickedly thrilling about the prospect. I'm surprised at myself for the thrill, but then again, Raph awakens parts of me that I hadn't even known existed. He told me once that I had turned his world upside down, but he was wrong—it's he who has turned mine, making it come alive in a way that makes me sure I wasn't really living before I met him. The thought is a frightening one, because I don't know how I can ever give that up, how I can ever give *him* up.

"God, Jaz, you feel so good, it's almost unreal." He groans against the skin at the base of my throat. He lifts his head and locks his gaze onto mine. The heat in those eyes, the hunger burning in them as he watches me slipping closer and closer to the edge, undoes me and when I finally fall off it, he devours the sound of his name coming from my lips. My inner muscles, my whole universe contracts around him and Raph lets out a tortured groan. He curses and a shudder rolls through his body as mine shakes with release. "Fuck, baby, that feels so hot. You're as tight as a dream."

Like the other times before, he holds me to him as I piece myself back together. But this time, I want him to come apart, too.

I move so that his back is to the tiled wall now and a few inches to the left, so that he's up against the tiled bench just above the waterline.

"Do you want me?" I ask him the same question, and the responding hunger in his kiss should be answer enough. But I want more.

"Do you?" I ask again.

He presses his forehead against mine and his breathless answer takes my own breath away.

"I want you so much, Jaz, I think I'm losing my mind. I want you more than I want my next breath."

"Then show me how much you want me," I say, feeling brazen and reckless because the way that he just made me come apart, just seems to have stripped away the last of my inhibition.

He understands what I mean and the answering heat in his gaze makes it difficult for me to remember that I'm trying to make him come apart and not the other way around.

With one swift motion, he lifts himself onto the tiled bench and guides my hand beneath the waistband of his swim shorts to find him all too ready for me.

My fingers close around his hard length, and as he eases his swim shorts down, I hear my own breath hitch at the sight of him. My mouth goes dry for a second because I can't quite believe what I'm seeing is real. He smirks at my expression and that spurs me into action.

I have no experience in this whatsoever. But Raph knows that, too, so he guides my hand along his length, once, twice. His hips twitch with each pass and the pleasure in his face, along with the groan that rumbles from somewhere deep in the back of his throat, is the hottest thing I think I've ever seen.

He doesn't have to guide me when I lower my lips to the tip of him, as my hand closes around the base.

He curses as my lips make contact, and I can feel the shudder rolling through his body as my head dips lower, until the tip of him hits the back of my throat. He's too big for me to take the full length, but the sounds he makes with each pass of my mouth along his length tells me that it doesn't matter.

His hand cups my cheek for a second in a tender gesture which makes my chest tighten, and when his fingers touch the edges of my lips which are curled around him, his eyes darken with an emotion that steals my breath.

"You're so goddamn beautiful like this, Jaz." His voice is hoarse, husky in a way that sends delicious shivers down my spine.

His hand finds its way into my hair then, gripping onto the wet strands as he guides my head over his length. The tugging sensation against my scalp causes shivers to race through my spine and when his hips begin to thrust upwards to meet my strokes, I think I lose all coherent thought.

I look up at his face as I work him closer to the edge and what I find is a look of pure male ecstasy. His head is thrown back against the tile wall, his lips parted as he watches me taking him deeper into my mouth. Our gazes lock and I don't think I've been more turned on in my entire life. The pure need in Raph's gaze, the sounds he's making and the way that his powerful body trembles under my touch, makes me feel undeniably powerful, like I could get him to do just about anything right now, every inch of him at my mercy.

I let out a moan which vibrates against him, and his eyes cloud over with an even deeper desire. He thrusts even deeper and he lets out another groan. His skin is glowing in the dim light and it feels like he's going to burst into flame at any minute.

"Jaz, I'm close … god, baby—" His voice is so guttural, that I barely recognize it just then.

He tries to move my head away but I don't let him. I want to feel him come apart inside me, and a second later, he does. His large body shudders and quakes as the release hits him, and the feeling of his hand gripping tighter against my scalp as he pulses in my mouth is intoxicating.

He lifts me clean out of the water then and positions me so that I'm straddling him. He surprises me when he pulls my head down to his, his lips claiming mine, even though I still have the taste of him in my mouth. He doesn't seem to care, though, as his tongue spears into me and he kisses me until we're both breathless, until neither of us can ever again deny how much we want each other.

"Where are we going?" I ask Raph, a few days later, as we walk out of last period physics.

It's late afternoon, but overhead, the sun is already sinking low in the horizon. The shorter days signal the shift from autumn to winter and I can't quite believe that I've managed to survive an entire season at Regency.

Raph takes my hand in his and as we walk hand in hand through the campus grounds, like it's the most natural thing in the world, it hits me how surreal all of this is. If someone had told me at the beginning of the semester that this is how we'd end up, I would've laughed my ass off. After telling them to screw off, that is.

"I was thinking that we should start up your elements training again," he replies, as we head further away from the main campus buildings and towards the training fields.

After that almost kiss in the forest and everything that happened since, needless to say, elements training with Raph had been out of the question.

I nod in agreement as we finally reach the vast training field.

Raph drops his backpack down on the grass at the edge of the field and I follow suit. He turns to me with a thoughtful expression, as if debating something in his mind.

"I'm thinking that maybe we should try something different," he says finally.

"Okay …" I reply, although I'm not sure what he means.

I follow him to the center of the field and I expect him to run through the usual routine of talking me through how to connect with the elements. Instead, he stands facing me, as if we're about to duel.

His next words confirm that's exactly what he's proposing and I can feel my body bristling in alarm. It's one thing to face off against Layla but dueling with Raph is an entirely different ball game.

"I'm not so sure this is such a good idea …" I begin to say.

He flashes me that arrogant smile in response, which never fails to irritate the life out of me, even now.

"You scared, Jaz?" he asks.

Bastard. The challenge in his tone is clear and he knows me well enough to know that I'm not one to back down from a challenge. Especially not one from him.

"No," I reply curtly. "I just don't think it would be a fair match."

His gaze softens then.

"The power that you unleashed in that duel with Layla? I've never seen anything like it, Jaz. I told you as much that day. You don't need to be taught how to connect with the elements anymore; even I can see how deep that connection runs inside you. What you need now is to learn how to duel with it."

I let out a long sigh then.

"What for? It's not like I'll ever have to fight in an actual duel. Unless you count the training duels in elements class," I reply with a shrug.

In truth, I have no idea why students here even learn how to *duel.* I get why they need to learn how to use their elemental powers, but even then, as Raph has told me before, the elements usually run just fine on their own, unless there's some kind of imbalance which requires the Seraph to step in. This dueling thing seems to be a hangover from a previous age. An odd tradition referred to in the pages of my Eden history textbook.

But something in Raph's expression makes me wonder.

"You never know when it might come in useful," is his only reply. His eyes are unreadable, but I feel a slither of discomfort nonetheless.

I don't get the opportunity to respond, though, as he turns and heads to his end of the field.

I guess that means we're dueling then.

Memories of that duel between Raph and Baron that I'd witnessed during my first few days at Regency flood my mind, and I say a silent prayer to the powers that be that I won't come to regret this.

Not that I believe for a second that Raph would intentionally hurt me. At least not anymore. But I've seen how he fights. I've witnessed his raw power. The most powerful Seraph in his generation and I'm certain that he could incinerate me in the blink of an eye, even without meaning to.

Despite my apprehension, I feel a familiar wave of adrenaline rushing through my veins as I stand facing Raph from the opposite side of the field.

Overhead, the late autumn sunset paints the sky with hues of pink and purple, casting an almost magical glow on the lush green field.

I'm aware of other students crossing the campus grounds and on the other sports fields in the distance, but as I focus my senses, the entire universe narrows to just the two of us. As if we're the only two people in the entire universe, with the elements surrounding us, our only allies. A whisper of premonition runs through me and for a split second, it feels like the very universe itself is watching, waiting. As if it's been waiting for this moment since the beginning of time itself.

I sweep the ridiculous thought away, but the whisper of fate in my veins remains.

I expect him to make the first move. But he waits with the patience of a predator. My eyes lock with his momentarily and what I see there isn't the face that I'm certain I, and I alone know. It's the face of the heir to the throne of Eden. The face that everyone else in this world sees. The face that every single one of his opponents must see. It's no wonder that no one is able to beat him.

Like a veil dropping, there isn't even a hint of what I know lies beneath that mask. There is only the heir and as he stands there on the field, it is with the air of the crown that is his by birthright.

He read something in my expression, even across the distance. Because in an instant, that mask falters.

"You okay, Jaz?" His voice carries over to me across the vast field.

I pull myself together. Putting steel in my spine as I meet his gaze unflinchingly, I remind myself that I'm no damsel in distress or wilting flower. I'm a *fucking badass*. I didn't let Raph get the better of me when we were enemies and I sure as hell won't let him win now, even though his kisses make me feel like I'm going to *faint* every time.

"I'm fine," I reply, flashing him a smirk which I know will set his temper alight. "Just don't try to take it easy on me."

His responding grin is nothing short of wicked.

"I wasn't planning to."

And with that, the duel begins.

I open with a tornado which I'm pretty damn proud of. But Raph makes quick work of dissipating it until it's nothing more than a gust of wind. *Bastard*.

He counters with an almighty heat storm which feels like it's about to burn through my skin. I barely manage to summon a rainstorm in time to stop myself from bursting into flames.

Then we're *really fighting*. No holds barred. Any pretence of politeness falling away, and I fucking love it.

We match each other blow for blow, countering and attacking seamlessly, as if we've been opponents for a lifetime. As if we were created for this very purpose. The field quakes as every season, every element known to the universe is unleashed over the vast field. The sight would be terrifying, if I wasn't so fully immersed in it.

When our powers clash, it's raw, primal, all-consuming. Just like that night on Rockford Cape, it's like two halves of a whole snapping together, as seamless and as ancient as day shifting into night. He is my equal and I'm his.

But there is one key advantage that Raph has over me. His skills are honed, refined. He knows his way around a duel and he executes each move with tactical precision. He knows each move I'm going to make before I make it, and he knows exactly how to neutralize and counter against it.

It's in this that Raph really shines, and I know with certainty that raw power will never be enough to best him. Because Raph was made for this, and it's for this reason that he is undefeated.

Still, I'm not about to let him win so easily. I don't know how long we stay locked in battle. I lose all track of time and space as we clash against each other, but I'm certain that it's longer than his duel with Baron.

I feel my body tiring, weakening. But gathering my last ounce of strength, I focus on the call of the darkness. That same power I felt in that duel with Layla. The sky above the field darkens and I'm not entirely sure if it's the natural cycle of night descending on the campus grounds, or if it's my own power bringing it forth.

Either way, tapping into that power, so potent in my own veins, feels exhilarating and terrifying all at once. Nothing can describe it. Nothing can come close to it.

I feel the shadows gathering around me and for a moment I'm scared to unleash them. But as I lock eyes with Raph across the field, the fear dissipates. The look in his eyes tells me he knows exactly what I'm about to unleash and that he's capable of withstanding it all. He knows everything I'm capable of and he wants it all.

I let go then, the shadows rushing out of me like a tsunami covering the entire universe and for a split second, there is nothing but darkness.

Then in that darkness, I see a flash of light. Growing brighter and brighter with each passing second, until it consumes the darkness. Until not a single shadow remains.

When the darkness clears, I see Raph standing a few steps away, moving to my side of the field. He's encased in the afterglow of the daylight he's just unleashed, but I can feel him shielding me from the burn.

The light dims, then finally fades into the night as he holds out his hand to me.

I take it, and for a moment neither of us speaks as we stand there at the center of the decimated field, our ragged breaths filling the space between us.

There's something like wonder in his eyes and I'm certain it's mirrored in my own.

The silence is shattered by the sound of loud applause, ringing out through the field.

I'd been so immersed in the duel, that I hadn't even noticed the crowd that seems to have gathered around the edges of the vast field. Raph seems equally surprised as he takes in the cluster of students surrounding us.

He turns back to me with a grin.

"Not bad, Jaz."

"I second that," Baron's voice travels over to us as he jogs across the field in his soccer uniform, Lance and Keller in tow.

"So, this is why you missed soccer practice today? So that you could get your ass almost handed to you by Jazmine?" Lance adds with a smirk.

I hold back a chuckle at that, as Raph shoots Lance a look of death.

"It wasn't that close," Raph grumbles.

"It was pretty damn close," Keller interjects, flashing me a wicked smile.

"Yeah, and I thought your duel with Layla was badass. This one was fucking incredible." Baron says, grinning at me.

"It looks like Raph might finally have met his match," Keller says to Baron, with a knowing look as they grin at each other.

Raph turns back to me, all laughter gone from his face. His eyes darken to a midnight blue as they lock onto mine.

"Yeah," he says, quietly. "I guess I have."

He kisses me then. In front of the other Dynasty heirs, in front of the entire crowd.

I close my eyes and kiss him back, not caring that everyone is watching and at the same time, feeling like we're the only two people in the entire universe.

I know with an unshakeable certainty that I'll never again stand in a room full of people and still feel alone. Because among the faceless crowd, Raph will always be there. The missing piece of my universe that I didn't even know I'd been searching for. But now that I've found it, I'm certain that I'll never again feel whole without it.

The next couple of weeks feel like they belong to someone else's life; because my life has been this cold, desolate thing with loss as the only overpowering constant. But now, when I wake up every morning, it's to the feel of strong arms around me, warmth flooding me and when I lie in bed at night, it's to the feel of Raph's body moving against mine, his lips on mine and on every other part of my body, including the most intimate parts that he and he alone knows.

The only overpowering constant now is how much I want him. I thought that the torrent of desire would fade after the first week but it hasn't, not even a fraction. I can't seem to get enough of him—the feel of his lips against mine, the taste of him in my mouth. I can sense that it's the same for him, too, his crazed need for me seems to only get stronger each day. He can't seem to keep his hands off me, can't seem to stop kissing me.

In the midst of that insane need, there is also an aching tenderness which makes me feel like I'm standing on the edge of a cliff, looking down at a deathly drop which would most definitely shatter me into a million pieces, if there isn't anyone there to catch me at the bottom.

Sometimes he has those nightmares of his mother that tear him awake, panting in the middle of the night. But I'm there and the way that he holds me each time, makes me feel like I'm the only one who can make those shadows go away.

But it feels like there's something deeper that draws us together, too. We train together almost every day after Raph's soccer practice. Dueling against each other, honing our skills. Predictably, he beats me every time. But it's always close and every duel is a reminder of how perfectly we fit together on an almost primal level. Equals in almost every way. As seamless and as natural as day shifting into night.

The rational part of me knows that this can't possibly last. There is no happy ending here. At least not for me. But the way that Raph looks at me ... as if I'm all that matters in this world, in this universe, makes it difficult to remember that stark truth. Because that truth does still exist. In some ways, everything has changed between us but in other ways, nothing has.

Raph is still the heir to the throne, he still has his future planned out for him. A future which includes his betrothal to Layla. We don't speak about it, but that truth is there and with the passing of each day, I can feel it growing closer and closer, like a storm looming on the horizon.

"You excited for winter break?" Dani asks as we walk out of second period.

"I love the holidays—it is winter season after all, and no one does winter break like the Aspen Dynasty," Keller replies.

I hadn't even thought about it, although I knew it was coming up because Magnus called me a few days ago to arrange for me to be collected so that I could spend winter break at the Evenstar palace.

"I guess it'll be nice to get a break," I say. End of semester exams have been kicking my ass lately.

A stab of disappointment hits me when I realize that winter break will mean two weeks of being away from Raph. The Evenstar palace isn't far from the St. Tristan palace by any means, but I doubt Magnus would approve of Raph sharing my bed there, especially because he has no idea that we're now ...

My train of thought stops there when I realize that I still have no idea what Raph and I are to each other. There are a few things which Raph and I have yet to do—one is to talk about what exactly is happening between us, which makes me utterly foolish. Because it makes me no different from all those other girls who are all too willing to jump into bed with Raph, knowing that he wants nothing more than to satisfy his base desires.

There have been no such other girls since that first kiss between us, though, and some part of me suspects, a while before that, too. But the thought is of little comfort. It's the same foolishness that has stopped me from bringing up the subject because I'm terrified of the answer. Raph told me that night after the Fall Ball that it's about more than just that with us. But I still have no idea what that even means or exactly how much *more* there is, because surely, there isn't anything more that he *can* give me. His words return to me then—*my life, it doesn't belong to me, it belongs to my Dynasty, to my throne.*

I'm suddenly not looking forward to winter break. Not at all. Raph would be in his palace, under his father's watch, being reminded of all the duties, all the obligations that make him who he is, the throne that his life belongs to.

"There's a big Dynasty Winter Ball each year which the Aspen Dynasty hosts. Mostly, it's just spending time with family though," Keller says.

"My little brothers terrorize everyone in sight. The Oaknorth Dynasty are pretty close to the Aspen Dynasty, so they spend a lot of time on our estate. You're free to come along with Lance, if you want, Dani."

Dani flushes in response.

"Not sure about that. Lance and I are taking things slow still. But my folks live in one of the worker residences of the Aldebran estate, so I'll be close by."

Keller rolls her eyes.

"The Aldebran Dynasty usually keep to themselves during the holidays.

"The St. Tristan Dynasty and the Delphine Dynasty though …"

Keller cuts off mid-sentence when she realizes what she's about to say. But I get the gist.

My stomach twists painfully when I realize that with the close links between the St. Tristan Dynasty and the Delphine Dynasty, Layla would likely be spending a considerable amount of time at the St. Tristan palace over the holidays, playing happy families with Raph. Being alone with Raph. He assured me that there's nothing going on between them. But who am I kidding—he may not love her, but she's still the most stunning girl I've ever seen in real life and she's made it clear that she still wants Raph.

No hot-blooded male would be able to resist that and although Raph has never spoken about that period of time he spent trying to make things work with Layla for the sake of duty, it doesn't take a genius to figure out that it must have involved physical contact—kissing, touching, *having sex*. The thought of his hands on her, his lips on her—those same hands and lips which are on my body every night, makes me feel so sick, that it's an effort to keep walking.

"Hey—you okay?" Dani asks, noticing the change in my demeanor.

I let out a long sigh in an attempt to calm the paranoia raging inside me.

"Yeah, I just realized that Raph and I probably won't see each other much during the holidays," I manage to reply.

Understanding dawns on Dani's face.

"You're worried about Layla," she says knowingly, and I wonder how in the relatively short period of time that I've known this girl, she's now able to read me so well.

"Yeah. I mean he told me that he doesn't love her. I know that there's nothing like that going on between them anymore. But we haven't really talked about that side of things much more than that ..."

A mischievous glint sparks in Keller's eyes just then. Some part of me has been uncomfortable with talking about Raph and me in front of Keller at first, but she's made it clear that although she and Layla have been friends since they were kids, she's a neutral party. Raph is also her friend and I was surprised to learn that she thinks of me as one, too.

"Uh huh, too much fucking and not enough talking," she says and I flush crimson in response.

Dani chuckles, but she knows the deal. Because that's the other thing that Raph and I haven't yet done, aside from talking about what's happening between us. Even though most nights we would be clawing at each other, desperate to get closer, I could sense him holding himself back, keeping some part of himself leashed.

If I'm honest with myself, I'd admit that I want more than anything to break that leash and I can sense that he knows that it's what I want, too. But still, he keeps himself reigned back, always stopping before we get that far. Even when I can feel his body quite literally quake with the effort, and I can see the all-consuming desire darkening those vivid blue eyes until they're almost black. I know it has something to do with the fact that he knows I've never taken that step before, that he would be my first. But some paranoid part of me wonders if there's more to it than just that.

"They haven't actually done that," Dani says on my behalf.

"The fucking, I mean," she clarifies when Keller looks confused. Because although the walls in Sovereign Hall are thick, I know that some nights they must be able to hear the sounds we're both making from my room.

Keller's eyes widen almost comically.

"Hang on, wait. You're kidding me, right?"

I'm still bright red, and although I feel ridiculously embarrassed, I manage to shake my head.

"No. Fucking. Way. All this time that Raph's been up in your bed and he hasn't even tried to go there?"

I shake my head again and Dani, as she always does whenever she asks me this same question, looks as disbelieving as Keller.

"Damn, Jazmine …" she trails off and she looks like she wants to say something more, but is holding herself back.

"What?" I ask.

Keller just shakes her head.

"I've just never known Raph to go without," she says.

"Don't get me wrong, I love Raph like a brother, but we all know that he's not exactly one for self-restraint and who can blame him? Hot girls offer it to him on a plate, he takes it. Only Baron can top his record."

I feel sick to my stomach now, and I don't want to ask the next question, but I do anyway.

"You think he's …" I can't even finish the sentence without feeling like I'm going to vomit.

Keller's eyes widen again.

"No—no. Of course not…." She trails off.

"At least, I don't think so. I mean, anyone with eyes and ears can see that Raph is totally sprung on you, I've never seen his royal highness like this. Ever. I mean Baron's having the time of his life teasing Raph about how whipped he is.

"But this is just so unlike him, that I don't really know what to make of it."

Keller looks at me thoughtfully.

"If he's willing to wait for you, then it must be because he feels something really fierce for you," she says.

"So you should have nothing to worry about with Layla."

I try not to feel the hope growing inside me at her words.

"Except, Jethro St. Tristan was quite clear about Raph's betrothal and that hasn't changed as far as I know," I reply pointedly.

Keller's expression turns somber then.

"I'm not going to lie to you, Jazmine. You don't need me to tell you how complicated and fucking messy this whole thing is. That's what comes with getting involved with a Dynasty heir …"

Dani's eyes flicker with something like understanding, and some part of me thinks that must be why she's taking it slow with Lance, being careful, whereas I've been so totally foolish.

"Raph in particular, because he's the heir to the throne. He's always had the most pressure on him. But something tells me that if he's as serious about you as I think he is, then nothing will stop him from being with you."

I want to believe her, but I can't quite let myself. I'm reminded of my own warnings to myself back when I still had some sense in me, before Raph's lips stole that sense away. The warning that I'm way out of my depth with Raph. If I'm honest with myself, I'll admit that somewhere along the road, I've taken a wrong turn—I've let myself get involved with a guy who is, in all likelihood, going to break me in two, just like he promised to do that very first day.

My warnings seem to disappear into vapor, though, when Raph rounds the corner, looking sexy as hell in his white shirt, dark grey Regency blazer and black tie. I didn't think I had a thing for guys in uniform. But clearly, I do. Despite my best efforts, I can't help but notice how insanely beautiful this guy is. His ash blonde hair, perfectly mussed, his vivid blue eyes, those perfectly chiseled features, coupled with those dimples, could make even a nun leave her calling. He flashes that devastatingly beautiful smile which makes him look like how I think an angel might. Except I know there's nothing angelic about that wicked mouth of his. Nothing angelic at all.

"Hey, Jaz," he says, dropping a kiss squarely on my mouth. My face flames, but there isn't a hint of embarrassment in Raph's. It's another thing that makes me believe that there is really more to this. Because far from trying to hide it, he doesn't seem to care who knows about us. In fact, it almost seems like he wants everyone to know that he's laid claim on me, that I'm his and his alone.

Baron, who I hadn't realized was with Raph, makes a gagging sound from behind him.

"Get a room," he quips.

"No, wait. On second thought, your room is down the hall from mine, so it's not like that's any better."

"Shut up, B," Raph growls.

Keller and Dani chuckle at that. Baron turns to Dani then.

"Hey, Dani, I hear you're going to be spending the holidays in my neck of the woods."

Dani flushes in response.

"Yeah, I'll be visiting my parents at the workers' residences."

"That's cool," he replies with a smile.

My eyes travel from Dani to Baron and back again, the cogs in my mind turning. Beside me, I can feel Raph and Keller doing the same thing.

"Anyway, let's hit the cafeteria. I'm starved," Baron says, seemingly oblivious.

Raph hangs back as Keller and Dani follow Baron.

"We'll catch up with you guys," he says.

Baron rolls his eyes, as does Keller. Dani shoots me a wicked grin.

I turn to Raph, and I see that Dani's look wasn't unwarranted. I know that look. Those were definitely bedroom eyes. We're in the middle of the school day, standing right in the middle of a busy hallway, but I still feel the thrill racing down my spine at that look and the promise within it.

Before I can object, Raph pulls me into an empty classroom and locks the door behind us. I don't know who makes the first move and it doesn't even matter, because next thing I know, our lips are crashing together, our tongues intertwined.

Raph lifts me up so that I'm sitting on one of the desks and he positions himself between my legs. I gasp at the feel of his hard length against the center of me, and he lets out that sexy as hell groan as he rolls his hips against the pressure building inside me.

"God, Jaz, I can't even get through two classes without feeling like I'll lose my goddamn mind if I don't get my hands on you," he says against the skin at my neck. The rawness of his words and the way he growls them into my mouth sends shivers down my spine.

He reaches between us, his hand reaching up underneath my skirt. He growls again in approval at what he finds there. I should be embarrassed at the clear evidence of my arousal, but the need I feel whenever Raph's lips are on mine, or when his hands are on me, never leave room for anything else but that hunger.

"I love how much you want me, baby," he says, referring to that evidence, that very damp evidence.

"I want you inside me," I say unabashedly. A few weeks ago, I'd have been mortified at those words coming out of my mouth. But ever since this thing between us started, I've become aware of this whole other side of me. This side that Raph has awakened and only he could invoke in me.

He complies with my plea and his fingers plunge inside me in an instant. My back arches and I claw at his shoulders as I wrap my legs tighter around his waist.

"Oh, god, Jaz, you're so beautiful when you're like this."

He trails kisses along my neck then, kissing and sucking at the sensitive skin.

"Your cheeks flushed, your perfect little mouth parted like that. Those fucking beautiful eyes of yours cloudy with how much you want this, how much you want me."

His words do something to me, because every single one of them are true. If there was a mirror in here right now, I'm sure that's exactly what I'd see.

I don't know what makes me say these next words. Maybe it was something to do with Keller's words earlier or just the fact that I can never get enough of Raph, and how much I want him.

"I meant that I want you inside me for real, Raph," I whisper.

I feel a shudder roll through his body and he lets out a tortured groan, which is a good sign. But his hand stills completely. In fact, his entire body seems to lock up.

The sensations raging through my body are abruptly cut off as Raph steps away from me. I try not to jump to conclusions, but I can't help but feel stung.

Raph is a picture of conflict. His jaw is working and his eyes darken with some emotion that's almost frightening in its intensity.

"Don't—don't you want to?" I ask, although I kick myself for sounding so pathetic, for being so pathetic. God, here I am just another foolish girl offering herself up on a plate to Raphael St. Tristan. In an empty classroom no less—real classy. Except he doesn't seem to be into it. Not at all.

Heat flashes in his eyes and as quick as lightning, he takes my face in his hands. His lips meet mine, but this time the kiss is achingly tender, like that reverent kiss he gave me that night after coming back from Rockford Cape.

The kiss makes me feel like he's reaching right inside my chest and squeezing the beating muscle inside. It's that powerful. Every doubt, every question is swept from my mind. At least just for that moment. Because this isn't just any kiss. You wouldn't kiss someone like this who you were just screwing with—kissing with lust, desire, hunger? Yes. But not like this. This kiss means something and I feel that meaning wrap itself around my heart.

When he pulls away, his eyes are as dark as midnight, as he touches his forehead to mine.

"God, you have no idea how much I want to be inside you," he says, and his words send a delicious thrill along my skin.

"I want to be inside you so bad, that I can't even think straight half the time, and when we're lying in that bed of yours, my body on yours … it takes *everything* I have, every last bit of self-control to stop myself from burying myself deep inside you."

I gasp at the intensity of the words, because although I did sense the effort he had to exert at controlling himself all those times, hearing him say it out loud is entirely different.

He sees the question in my eyes and saves me from having to ask it.

"But I want to wait until you're ready. Really ready."

His answer floors me and I feel like I can't breathe for a second.

"Trust me, my dick hates me for it, but I …"

He trails off and I suddenly get that feeling again that I'm teetering on the edge of a cliff, but this time, I feel like he's there next to me.

He doesn't finish the sentence, though. What he says instead is enough. At least for now.

"It's never been like this for me, Jaz. You think I've done this a thousand times before, but I haven't—not like this. I don't want to mess this up. I'm so goddamn terrified of messing this up."

He looks uncertain, shy almost, in a way that's so at odds with his usual air of confidence. That uncertainty does something to me and I reach out for him then, kissing him with more emotion than is safe for me, letting him inside me in another way, which I know is far, far more dangerous.

I manage to get through the rest of the final week of the semester without insecurity rearing its ugly head again. But of course, it had to wait until the last day of semester to appear.

"Hey, Jazmine, how's it going?"

I turn from my locker to see Devon stop in front of me as he passes by.

Other than seeing him in calculus, I haven't really spoken to him since that night of the Fall Ball. He hasn't brought up going out again in any of those brief conversations in class, and he hasn't tried to text or call. I'm certain it has everything to do with Raph's less than subtle exhibitions of the claim that he's staked on me and of course, god only knows what kind of warnings Raph's been doling out to his team in the locker rooms. Because every time a member of the soccer team passes me, they fix their eyes directly on the floor, as if they're scared out of their minds that they'll turn to stone if they so much as look at me the wrong way or just scared out of their minds of Raph more likely.

"Hi, I'm good, you?" I reply politely.

Devon fidgets for a moment and suddenly I feel awkward.

Because part of me does feel bad about agreeing to go with him to that party after the Gramercie game and to the Fall Ball, when my mind was on Raph. But I was in denial back then and Raph had made it clear he didn't want me. In hindsight, I should've known that it couldn't have turned out any other way between Raph and me. That from that first moment on the beach, we were headed on a collision course right into each other's arms. As wrong as that might be.

"I'm okay," Devon replies, and the awkwardness dissipates as we talk about class and the holidays. I'd forgotten how easy going and nice Devon is. Although I didn't really get a chance to get to know him that well, it must've been part of the reason why I, for a moment, thought that I might want to.

"Anyway, I should get going. But it was nice talking to you. It got kind of awkward back then after the Fall Ball, but you're a great girl, Jazmine, I hope we can be friends," he says finally.

"Sure," I reply casually. "I'm glad we got a chance to catch up, too," I add honestly. "I wanted to speak to you after the Fall Ball to explain things, but I thought you'd be mad at me, you know because of what happened afterwards with Raph …" I trail off and kick myself for mentioning it.

Devon's expression falters for a second, but he flashes another easy smile.

"Don't worry about it. I knew what I was getting myself into. I kind of suspected there was more to it between you guys, even if nothing was going on at the time. I mean Raph wouldn't just go around warning every guy in school off a girl unless he's wanting to stake his claim."

I feel a surprising warmth at those words, because it reminds me that whatever it is that Raph feels for me, it goes further back than I had let myself acknowledge.

Devon seems to be deciding on whether to say something, and I eye him curiously.

"Take care of yourself, Jazmine. Like I said, you're a nice girl—too good to be Raph's latest slam piece."

There's no malice in his words, just genuine, friendly concern. But the words are crude all the same, and I feel sick at the thought.

Is that what everyone in school thinks of me? *Raph's latest slam piece?* I don't usually give a crap about what other people think, but I can't deny that the label stings. More so than the outcast label he'd slapped on me that first day I walked on campus. In fact, I'd trade this label for that one in a heartbeat.

I realize how naïve I've been. As much as I try to deny it, I like Raph's public displays of affection, the unabashed way he stops to kiss me in the middle of a crowded hallway or in the cafeteria, not caring who's looking. I thought it was his way of showing everyone that he doesn't care who knows about us. But all its showing people is that I'm Raph's latest piece on the side in what is a sickeningly long line of girls. Of course, everyone here knows that Raph is still betrothed to Layla and that any other girl is just his entertainment on the side. But she's his queen. Always has been, always will be.

I tell myself to calm down, though, because I'm jumping to conclusions here. I remind myself of those moments when Raph and I are alone and he's looking at me as if … as if I'm the only person in the entire universe that matters. I remind myself of the way he kisses me, that tells me there's so much more to this thing between us than just lust. If that's all he wants from me, he wouldn't be waiting until *I'm* ready to have sex, he'd have made that move already and no matter how much I try to deny it, I know deep down that I'm in so deep with him, that I would have let him. Hell, I offered it to him on a plate just a couple of days ago and still he wants to wait.

But the doubts don't disappear entirely, because I also still remember what Raph told me before our first kiss—that none of this could ever really matter. With all that has happened since, the passion burning away my reason, the hunger blinding me to reality, I seem to have forgotten the cold hard truth, or at least shoved it aside whenever it reared its ugly head, like I'm trying to do right this very minute.

I'm saved from having to say anything because I feel Raph's presence behind me. He fixes that icy glare on Devon, the one that he fixed on me that very first day on the beach, the one that reminds me what we were to each other back then and perhaps what we should have kept being, if either of us had any sense.

"Hey, Raph."

"Devon," Raph replies coolly.

Devon gets the message.

"See you, Jaz," he says, as he begins backing away. "Take care of yourself," he says again, referring back to what he said earlier. He doesn't have to. The words are emblazoned in my mind.

But I don't let any of those insecurities show in my face as I turn to Raph. I stiffen a little when he kisses me lightly. But thankfully, not enough for Raph to sense that something's wrong.

"What did Devon want?" he asks, point blank. His possessiveness would be endearing, if it wasn't for the fact that Devon's earlier words are still ringing in my mind. Four words in particular—*Raph's latest slam piece.*

"Nothing. He just wanted to catch up," I reply casually.

Some part of me wants to confront him right here and now about this latest label. But another part of me is telling me that I shouldn't care what other people think of what's happening between us, as long as Raph and I know the truth about what we are to each other. *And what is that exactly?* The cruel voice in the back of my mind whispers. But I shove it aside because the middle of a school hallway is not the time and the place to be having this conversation.

"So what, you two are best friends now?" Raph, however, doesn't seem to be so concerned about causing a scene.

It's not the first time Raph's acted jealous. Hell, he starts growling at Baron like a caveman whenever he finds us hanging out together in the kitchen some mornings. As much as I try to deny it, I usually like the feeling that he cares enough to get jealous. But right now, it just pisses me off. Because who the hell is he to get jealous when the list of girls that he's been with is probably longer than Santa's freaking Christmas list and I've only ever been with one guy—him. Only him. Plus, there's the fact that he's still *betrothed.* As in promised to marry someone else.

This time, I can't keep the frown from my face, but Raph interprets it as me being pissed about his cave man ways.

He lets out a long breath.

"Sorry, Jaz. You know I can't think straight whenever any other asshole gets within two feet of you."

He pulls a face of exaggerated repentance, which makes me laugh, despite my mood. God, I must be demented.

"So, you're the only asshole who gets to come near me?" I keep my tone light, but the words aren't exactly a joke.

"Hell, yes," he replies, throwing an arm around my shoulders as we walk out of the main building. "Because I'm *your* asshole."

I don't want those words to mean anything, but I'm stupid and foolish, so they do. I still haven't forgotten about Devon's words. I know that Raph and I are going to need to have this conversation, but that same foolish part of me delays the inevitable.

And as he leans down to touch his lips against mine again, I don't feel like talking at all.

"And you're mine, Jaz," he murmurs against my lips. "All mine."

The words wrap themselves around me and just for that moment, I let myself believe it.

~

I'm rummaging in the fridge for a snack when I hear the front doors open. The guys all have an end of semester soccer meeting, so I expect to see Keller or Ivy walk in. Layla has a useful knack of avoiding me when I'm downstairs, although I don't miss her death stares at school.

Unfortunately, Layla's avoidance tactic doesn't seem to be working today, because it's she who walks in through those doors.

But when she fixes her eyes on me from across the reception hall, I get the feeling that this run-in is a very deliberate one.

I school my face blank and ignore her completely as I close the fridge door. Suddenly, I'm not so hungry. But before I can make a beeline for the stairs, Layla intercepts me.

"How's it going, Jazmine?" she asks.

I blink in surprise, because this girl hasn't said a single civil word to me since I arrived in Eden and now she's asking me how I'm doing? Bizarre is an understatement.

"Fine," I reply evenly. But I narrow my eyes in suspicion, because I'm not convinced by her seemingly neutral manner. Not convinced at all.

And I'm right not to be, because from her next words, it's apparent that her claws are definitely still out.

"Fine? I would've thought you'd be more than fine. I mean with all that time that Raph's been spending in your bed ... a slut like you must be having the time of her life."

I picture myself pulling chunks of golden hair out of her pretty little head and gouging those pretty green eyes out, but I stop myself. She isn't worth it.

I've been expecting this confrontation since that night of the Fall Ball. In fact, now that I think about it, I'm surprised it hasn't happened sooner. Layla must be losing her touch. Whatever. I don't have time for it.

I let out a sigh and move to step past her. She doesn't let me go that easily.

"Get out of my face, Layla," I say through gritted teeth, trying to hold onto whatever self-control I have left.

"I'm not finished with you, slut," she replies with a sickening smile.

I roll my eyes, although I can feel my patience waning. Fast.

"Okay. What? Why don't you just get all those insults that you've clearly been saving up off your chest. I promise I'll try to keep a straight face."

Layla's eyes narrow in response, and her voice is eerily calm when she opens her mouth next, although her words are far more lethal.

"You know, as much as I'd like to do that, I don't think I need to. You know what you are—I don't need to tell you."

"Oh, yeah and what am I?" I ask, although the last thing I want is for her to answer.

"You're a shiny new toy that's just happened to catch Raph's attention—for now. This ... fascination of his? It's temporary."

I try to block out her words but I feel them cut into flesh all
the same.

"He'll play with you for a while, use you to keep himself entertained. Raph loves the chase and life can get pretty boring for us
Dynasty heirs with all these rules and obligations—not that you'd
know, because you're not really one of us.

"Then he'll toss you aside once he's bored of you. Just like all the
others. I'm sure you're not foolish enough to think that there haven't
been other girls before you—many, many girls before you. I mean, I
don't blame those girls, or you, for that matter. It's probably good
while it lasts, in fact ..."

She flashes me a wicked smile which makes my stomach churn.

"From my own personal experience, I know just how *good* it is. So.
Very. Good."

If I felt sick before, then I'm pretty sure that now I'm on the verge
of throwing up.

The look she gives me is almost sympathetic.

"That is, until it ends. Because it *always* ends. There's no other
possibility.

"Raph knows, just like I know, just like every damn person on this
entire planet knows, that Raph is *mine* and *I'm his*. Always has been,
always will be.

"It doesn't matter who he warms his bed with and equally, it
doesn't matter who's in mine. Because at the end of it all, he'll be on
that throne and I'll be right there next to him. That's how this fairy
tale ends."

She studies my expression, and as much as I try to, I can't keep the
devastation from showing through.

"But you knew that already, didn't you, Jazmine? If I didn't think
you were such a worthless slut, I'd feel sorry for you. Life after Raph
gets bored with you? Well, I think you know what that's going to feel
like, in fact, I think it keeps you up at night.

"I get it, though. Raph—well, he's the personification of the element that he lords over. Like the sun itself. When his attention is on you, it's like having the sun beaming down on you, but when it's gone ... well, he can cast quite a shadow."

Layla pauses then for effect.

"But who knows, I *could* be wrong. It's unlikely. But I could be. Raph *could* decide that you're entertaining enough to keep you around in the long term. But even if he does, you'll always just be a girl to warm his bed at night. During the day, in all the ways that really matter, it'll be *me* by his side and you'll have to watch from the gutter where you belong, as he rules Eden with me beside him.

"You'll be nothing more than Raph's dirty little secret. Just like you were your daddy's. Because Raph may not care who knows about you right now, but it will be an entirely different matter when he ascends to the throne. Ironic, isn't it? You going from being one king's dirty little secret to another's?"

I tell myself her words are poison. Lies. But they hit home all the same, because they echo the doubts, the insecurities that have been raging in my own mind since that first kiss. Still, because I'm foolish, I still try to deny it.

"Shut up, Layla. You don't know what you're talking about and you sure as hell don't know Raph—"

She cuts me off with a mocking laugh.

"What? I don't know Raph the way you do?" She flashes me a cruel smile.

"Oh, honey, you're right about that. I don't know him the way you do—I know him better," she says.

"I've known Raph his entire life. You've known him for two minutes.

"Raph's all messed up because of his mommy issues. He goes through these phases where he hates his privileged life, hates his Dynasty, hates his throne, hates his father and all the pressures he puts on him. But at the end of it all, Raph was raised for that throne. Privilege, duty, obligation—it's all that Raph knows. It's what makes him who he is.

"If you really knew him, knew just how sick and twisted he is, then you'd stay the hell away from him. Raph is his father's son. Anyone who believes otherwise is a fool—are you a fool, Jaz?"

It's a rhetorical question but I answer it in my own mind anyway. Yes. I've been a fool. I am a fool.

I've been working hard to keep my face from showing just how deep Layla's words are cutting, but I can't hide it now and to my horror, I can feel the moisture pooling in my eyes. From the gleeful look on Layla's face, she sees it, too.

I'm saved from breaking down right in front of this girl who hates the very air I breathe, and who's just torn up any last shred of hope, when the front door swings open.

Raph, Baron and Lance walk through. Their eyes dart between me and Layla and I'm sure they sense the tension. Raph's eyes go to me instantly, but I don't stick around to hear what he has to say.

Without another word, I turn and run up those stairs, away from Raph, from Layla, from the rest of the Dynasty heirs and their sick and twisted world that I want no part of.

❧

*I*t takes Raph all of two minutes after I step through the threshold, to follow me into my room.

I sense him come through the door. But I keep my back to him as I attempt to compose myself. I busy my hands with finishing my packing before the car that Magnus has sent for me comes to collect me later that evening.

Raph says nothing at first, but I sense him coming towards me. His strong arms wrap around my waist, and for a second, I let myself lean back against his chest, let myself feel his warmth, let myself feel his strength.

He drops a kiss to my shoulder, and when he breaths me in, I think I feel my chest crack, because I've always loved how much he seems to love the very scent of me, like he needs it more than he needs air to breathe. I'm reminded of that night on the beach after the Gramercie game, when he held me just like this, and told me afterwards that he didn't want me. If I'd been smart, I'd have walked away right then and there.

Layla's words are still playing themselves in my mind and I feel sick to my stomach. He told me once that he didn't have more to give, that it wasn't his to give, but I'd carried on regardless, willing to take whatever pieces of him I could have. I never thought that I'd be this girl—the bit on the side.

But I guess that's what I've become and the thought of it makes me want to jump in the nearest shower and wash every trace of Raph off me. What makes it more sickening is the fact that I'm probably just living up to everyone's expectations. Raph, Dani and Keller know the truth, but everyone else probably still thinks that it makes perfect sense that someone with my past would jump into bed with Raph the first opportunity she got, even if the guy basically treated me like shit for those first few weeks. It's so pathetic, I would laugh, if I didn't feel like crying.

I find a sliver of resolve from somewhere deep inside me, and force myself to step away.

"What's wrong, Jaz?" Raph asks gently.

I don't answer him because I don't know where to start. We haven't really talked about what the hell is happening between us since that day in the pool, and even then, there wasn't much talking. I've been too busy letting Raph strip me of my senses. I'm not going to let that happen now.

Maybe I didn't think it was the right time to talk about this earlier, after Devon's words to me. But after what Layla just said? It sure as hell is the time now.

"What am I to you, Raph?" I ask simply.

Raph's face softens and I feel like clawing my eyes out, so I can't see that tenderness in his eyes.

"You're mine, Jaz." He repeats those words from earlier, reaching out to touch his fingers to my cheek. Layla's words ring in my mind then—Raph belongs to her and she belongs to him. Layla is his. Not me.

I jerk back before he can make contact and his eyes cloud over. I tell myself not to care and when I speak again, I throw words at him like chips of ice.

"Your what? Your latest fling? Your piece on the side? Or better yet, as people at school seem to be calling me—your *latest slam piece*."

Raph's eyes flare, and he looks furious. I can practically feel the air around him heating with white rage.

"*My what?* Who the fuck said that?"

His anger is good in a way, because it means he had no idea about any of it and that it wasn't his intention for people to see me that way at all. But still, it does little to ease the burning inside me.

"It doesn't matter because it's what I am, isn't it? Your latest bit of entertainment, until you get bored with me?"

To his credit, Raph looks distraught at my words. Furious but distraught.

Raph takes a deep breath, in what seems to be an attempt to calm himself.

"Is this about what I just saw downstairs? Did Layla say something to you?" he asks evenly.

My temper rises and everything that I've been holding back these past weeks comes rising to the surface with it.

"Maybe it is, but she didn't say anything that I haven't already been thinking about—for a while now."

"And what's that?" he demands, his anger barely in check now.

"The fact that all those weeks ago you told me that you can't actually be with me in the way that really matters, in the way that you think I deserve because your life doesn't belong to you and there's nothing more you *can* give me. But despite all of that, I ignore all sense and reason and I still let you climb into bed with me every night, let you kiss me, touch me, even though it can never be anything more than just that. God, I must seem so pathetic right now. I bet you've heard this so many times before from all of those other girls who jumped into bed with you in the past, knowing full well that it can never be about anything more than just sex."

Raph catches me by the shoulders and locks his eyes directly onto mine.

"Is that what you think this is?" he asks.

I don't answer him. I don't think I need to.

"You have *no idea*." He leans his forehead against mine and this time I'm too tired to push him away.

He lets out a long breath, closing his eyes for a second as if gathering strength from somewhere inside himself.

"What I feel for you, Jaz? It scares the *shit* out of me."

His voice sounds hoarse with emotion and for a moment everything inside me stills. For a moment, I feel like I can't even breathe.

His words floor me and I know I feel the same way. But despite how much I want that to be enough—it isn't. It doesn't make Layla's words any less true.

"But it doesn't change the truth of what you told me before—that none of this can ever matter."

"I know that's what I said. But now ..."

He shakes his head.

"Now, it feels like it's the *only* thing that matters."

His words echo my own feelings towards him to such an extent, that it's almost frightening.

"I told you before that my entire future was planned out for me from the moment I was born. My life was meant to be fucking perfect, but every day I lived it before you, felt like I was alive but not really living.

"You weren't part of the plan, Jaz. For the first time in my life, I have no idea what the hell is going to happen. But I've never felt so alive. Being with you, wanting you, has made me come alive. *You* make me come alive.

"I can't even pretend that this isn't a mess. But it's a fucking beautiful mess ... and I don't know how I know this, but I'm certain that I'll *never* be able to give this up."

I open my mouth to say something, but close it again, because I can't think of a single objection. Devon's words, Layla's words, my own warnings, none of it seems to matter anymore and that cliff that I have been standing on the edge of? I've fallen right off it. But I was wrong to be scared, because Raph is there to catch me, and he's here now. With me.

"I told you before that my life doesn't belong to me, it belongs to my Dynasty, to my throne. But I don't know how that can be true anymore because I'm certain that from the first moment I saw you on that beach, *I've belonged to you.*"

Layla was wrong about him, I let myself think then. Raph isn't his father's son. He's his own person with his own choices—and *he belongs to me.*

I have no words that can even come close to what I want to say. So, I kiss him instead and I know he can feel the meaning of my unspoken words in that kiss by the way his powerful body quakes with the impact of it.

All my life I've been running. Drifting from one place to another like a ghost. But as Raph's arms tighten around me, holding me so close to him as if he's terrified at the very thought of me leaving, I feel something that I've never felt before. Like after all those years of running, of searching for something, although I never knew what, I've found it. I've found where I belong—and it's here. With him. In these arms, and I don't have to run anymore.

He leans his forehead against mine, his hands cupping my cheeks and when he speaks, it's with those endless blue eyes locked onto mine, looking into my very core and his words mirror everything that I feel there.

"I told you on that first night that you didn't belong here. But it was only because I knew from that first moment exactly where you belong. You don't need to run anymore because *you belong with me now, Jaz.* You always have."

All the doubts, all the questions just fade away. For good this time, leaving only the two of us in the vastness of time and space.

"I've been hearing about how well you've been settling into life at Regency Mount," Magnus says as we have breakfast on one of the garden terraces. It's in the middle of winter but he heats the air around us to make it pleasant enough.

I can't help but remember that only a few months ago, we were sitting in this very same place. Magnus telling me that I was about to be shipped off to a boarding school full of royal brats and me wanting more than anything to go back to Earth. But now … now, things are undeniably different. In that relatively short space of time, I feel like I've lived more than I had in all of my seventeen years on Earth and I know that it has something to do with something I'm certain Magnus knows nothing about. Or more accurately, *someone*.

But the way that Magnus is eyeing me, makes me wonder. Jethro told me at the Fall Ball that he had eyes and ears all over Regency. I wonder if that's the case for all the Dynasty heads.

I find it hard to meet Magnus's eyes as he studies me across the breakfast table.

I grasp for something to say to distract him from just *how well* I have been settling in at Regency.

"You mentioned that you've been heading a lot of missions lately—does it have anything to do with what you told me before? About Earth not being safe for me anymore?"

That does the trick, because Magnus becomes instantly wary at the question.

"Yes," he replies simply.

"Care to elaborate?" I ask, quirking an eyebrow and now I really do want to know. I've been so immersed in all the drama at Regency, that Magnus's warnings from when he first dragged me through that portal have fallen by the wayside. In hindsight, I see how warped my priorities have become—life in danger or guy drama. Which is more important? But Magnus's determination to keep me in the dark has made the threat feel so distant, that it's easy to forget that it exists at all.

It also reminds me just how much my life has changed these past few months. I feel like if I look in the mirror right now, really look, I might not even be able to recognize myself. Whether that's a good or bad thing, I've yet to decide.

"You know I can't," he says flatly.

"But it's my life that's supposedly in danger there—or were you just saying that to keep me here? Because when I—" I stop abruptly before I let slip that Raph had stolen the St. Tristan key so that we could take a little forbidden field trip to Earth just to spend an afternoon at the beach. I know that Magnus would be furious, but nothing happened while we were there. Not a single hint of danger. Something gnaws at the back of my mind, as I remember that feeling of being watched. I brush the thought away just as I had that day, because like I told myself then, it was clearly nothing more than paranoia.

Magnus looks back at me expectantly. Waiting for me to finish. Dammit.

"Because I don't see any danger from where I'm sitting," I finish lamely.

"That's as it should be. It is essential that state threats are dealt with sensitively and confidentially. As I told you before, this matter in particular, is something that not even the other Dynasties know about."

Alarm whispers through me at those words. *State threats?* That sounds pretty serious.

"One day, when you're dealing with such matters, you'll understand."

I scoff at that.

"Just because I haven't tried to run off back to Earth yet doesn't mean I'm now ready and willing to take up the mantle as heir to the Evenstar Dynasty or whatever else you want me to be."

Something flickers in the depths of Magnus's eyes and I feel myself bristle at what I see there.

"When the time comes, Jazmine, you will have little choice and I have every belief that you will be ready."

I roll my eyes. These people and their propensity to take away choices.

"Then I don't think you know me very well," I retort.

Magnus's eyes grow thoughtful.

"No, I think it's quite the contrary—it's you who doesn't know yourself very well."

I stare back at him blankly. What the hell is that supposed to mean?

"You're destined for great things, Jazmine. In time, you'll realize that."

I think he must be talking about his hopes for me to succeed him as the head of the Evenstar Dynasty, something I can't even imagine myself doing. But there's something about the way he's looking at me which makes me think there's more to it.

"Care to elaborate on that one, too?"

"Yes."

My optimism at his words is short lived.

"When the time is right."

I let out a groan of frustration.

"Do you always have to speak in these mysterious riddles?"

He flashes me an amused smile, and I take that as a cue to ask more questions, although I don't think Magnus is likely to answer them.

"How about swapping some of those riddles for the truth?"

The amused look disappears instantly.

"The truth, when revealed at the wrong time, is a dangerous thing, Jazmine."

His words aren't entirely wrong, but the look in his eyes makes me think that there are far more dangerous things on the horizon than just some wrongly timed truths.

⁓

"What are we doing here?" I ask Magnus later that afternoon as we stand at the center of a large court-yard on the palace grounds, overlooking the wide expanse of rocky coast beneath.

"I've been hearing great things from Professor Roman about your progress with elements training, so I'd like to see for myself," he replies.

"You're a natural it seems. Just like I said you would be. Hardly surprising given your heritage. Your father was certainly the best in his generation."

I feel my body bristle at the mention of my father. I haven't really allowed myself to dwell on it since arriving on Eden and I've made it pretty damn clear to everyone around me that it's not a topic for conversation. But I know it's something that I won't be able to avoid forever. I'm just hoping to delay the inevitable for a while longer, I guess.

Magnus gestures to the center of the courtyard expectantly and I gape at him in response.

"You want me to duel with you?" I ask, which earns me a bemused smile.

"My dueling days are long behind me, I'm afraid. But I would like to see how your powers have developed and help you along, if I can."

It's clear from his expression that he has no idea exactly who is responsible for my progress to date and I keep it that way, because something tells me that he won't be pleased to learn the truth.

I take a deep breath and make my way towards the center of the courtyard, with Magnus walking beside me.

We start with unleashing shadows, Magnus letting me show him what I know before he precedes to show me how to hone my skills.

I see from the flashes of pride in his expression, that he's pleased with what he sees and despite myself, I feel a strange rush of warmth at that. It's been such a long time since I've felt anything like it. Before my mom died, I remember feeling something similar whenever she used to gush over my drawings, but I'd been so young then, the memories merely ghosts in my own mind.

"You have raw power. In fact, I've never seen anything like it," Magnus says, as we take a break from the latest round.

"But you'll need more than that in a duel. You need to control the shadows instead of letting them control you. The darkness should be at your beck and call, ready to act on your command."

I feel my brow furrowing in response. What is it with everyone here and dueling? Magnus seems to have the same enthusiasm for it as Raph does and while admittedly, I've come to enjoy dueling, I still don't see why everyone here seems to think it's so important. I suppose it's a way of displaying power. But I've never been one for showing off.

Still, I can't deny that Magnus's tuition is already helping. Raph may be the best in this generation, but Magnus's experience and wisdom is invaluable, and while Raph's training has been instrumental in my progress, Magnus is able to teach me to perfect the powers that Raph himself doesn't possess. Namely the power over the night. The power of our bloodline.

"Again," Magnus says, gesturing for me to continue, but this time, with a tighter leash on the shadows.

We continue to train for what feels like hours and I lose all track of time until the sun dips low into the horizon, signaling the shift of day to night.

I look up at the sky above as Magnus allows me another pause.

The ghost of the crescent moon and the stars above grow more prominent in the darkening sky, and I feel the familiar call in my veins.

Magnus is silent as he stands beside me, but I know he can feel it, too.

"Take my hand," he says as we stand there, side by side, looking out at the horizon.

I feel his power flow into me and my own flowing into him as we silently paint the horizon with night.

It's not like that night at Rockford Cape when Raph and I shared our powers. This connection completes some other part of me in a different way.

As night descends on this part of Eden, in that moment, I feel the connection to the only family I have left in the entire universe and suddenly that universe becomes a little less lonely for it.

~

"*I*t's been okay so far, I guess. Magnus trained with me earlier and he says that he wants us to keep training together while I'm home for winter break.

"But he's being his usual cryptic self and every time he looks at me, I get the feeling that he knows exactly what's been going on at Regency these past few months ..."

I'm sprawled out on the big ass bed in my equally big ass bedroom, talking to Dani on my cell later that night.

"You mean about you and Raph?" Dani supplies.

"Yeah, Magnus has this all seeing, all knowing thing about him that gives me the creeps sometimes," I reply.

Dani snorts in response.

"Does it matter if he knows?" she asks me then.

I can't seem to answer that straight away. Raph's words to me on that last day of semester has floored me and has changed everything between us. But it doesn't make things any less complicated between us. Quite the contrary, in fact, and I'm not about to plunge head first into the mess that is surely to follow once Jethro St. Tristan finds out. I have a feeling that Magnus would be less than thrilled, too. Despite wanting desperately to hear those words from Raph, I knew from the moment he said them what the fall out would be and I guess I'm just afraid of the consequences. For him more than for myself.

I thought that once everything was out in the open, and I knew where I stood with Raph, things would be clearer, easier. But it seems like as soon as we get past one hurdle, another one just appears in its place. As soon as one question is answered, another more difficult one is posed. I wonder why everything has to be so hard when it comes to Raph. I tell myself that it's because it's worth having. But I wonder for a second whether I'm just fooling myself again.

"I don't know," I answer truthfully, letting out a long breath.

Dani doesn't push it, and I change the subject quickly.

"So, how's things with your folks?" I ask.

"It's great, I've missed them, so it's nice to be home," she replies. She goes on to tell me about her jam sessions with her dad. Apparently, he's an amazing guitar player and taught Dani all she knows about music.

I lie back and listen to her talk enthusiastically about home and her family. I'm reminded of my own memories with my mom, her teaching me how to pick up a paintbrush for the first time, how to mix colors and the wonder that I felt when she showed me all those things. I feel a pang of wistfulness, but I don't feel bitter. If anything, hearing Dani talk about her family is strangely comforting. It reminds me that loss isn't the only thing that exists in the universe.

"Have you seen Baron around?" I ask after a while.

"No, the Aldebran estate is pretty big, so I doubt I'll bump into him," she replies. I hear a pause in there somewhere but I don't read anything into it. Why would Dani need to lie about bumping into Baron?

"You seeing Raph tonight?" she asks then.

"Yeah, he called earlier to say he's coming later tonight."

My cell vibrates against my ear then, telling me I've got a message. Speak of the devil.

"Gotta go, Dan. Raph's here," I say, as I climb off the bed and head out of my bedroom.

"Okay, don't do anything I wouldn't do," she replies breezily.

"Likewise," I say almost absently.

Dani lets out a weary sigh, but we've both hung up before I can make heads or tails of it. Weird. I make a mental note to prod her later.

I text Raph and tell him to meet me by the side entrance. It's late, so Magnus should be asleep, as should most of the staff. But I don't want to risk anyone seeing Raph waltz in through the main entrance hall.

He has a wry smile on his face when I greet him at the east wing entrance.

"If I didn't know better, I'd say you were sneaking me in," Raph says.

I roll my eyes in response.

"Just get in here."

He drops a lingering kiss on my lips, which suddenly makes me want to get him back to my bedroom as soon as possible. But I pull away after a few moments, fully conscious that we're still standing in the middle of the service kitchen.

I turn on my heel and motion for Raph to follow me, but I don't miss his responding smirk.

The good thing about living in a palace is that the place is so damn huge and the walls so thick, that I'm sure Magnus won't even sense Raph's presence here tonight. I don't know where Magnus's quarters are, but I'm pretty sure it's not in the same wing as mine. Perfect. I know from Baron and Keller's complaints, that Raph and I aren't always as discreet as we like to believe and the thought of Magnus being awakened by the sound of us in the middle of the night is more than mortifying.

When we get back to my room, I flop down on the bed and Raph stretches out beside me. I turn on my side to look up at him as he props his head up on his elbow. My room is dark, apart from the soft glow of the bedside lamp, but still Raph's beauty is devastating. God, I wonder for the hundredth time if there will ever come a time when I can look at him without feeling like the breath has been punched out of my lungs and he's looking at me as if he's wondering the same thing about me.

I notice that his expression seems pre-occupied, though, his eyes a darker shade than usual.

"What's wrong?" I ask gently.

He doesn't answer for a moment, reaching out to touch his finger-tips to my cheek instead. I lean in to the touch and cover his hand with my own.

Something flickers in the depths of those midnight blue eyes, but I can't read it and a moment later it's gone, replaced by that heart stopping smile that always makes my insides feel weak.

"Nothing. I've just missed you," he replies. I search his expression but the earlier troubled look is gone or at least well hidden. I've forgotten just how good Raph is at that. When we first met, his face had been as impenetrable as ice, giving nothing away and now although there's not a trace of that ice in his gaze, it's just as unread-able. But I don't know why that surprises me. After all, Raph was raised for life in the public eye—shielding himself, veiling his true emotions is a necessary skill that he must've been taught to master from the day he was born.

"Why don't you tell me what's up? You look like something's bugging you," he adds. I know what he's doing, but I don't want to push him about what's on his mind, if he's not ready. Now that he's back home, he must have a hundred different things to deal with and then of course, there's his father. I know from the nights that we've stayed up talking just how much Raph dislikes being around him and the constant pressures he puts on Raph.

I let out a long sigh.

"Magnus just keeps dropping these not so subtle hints about this great big future planned for me as heir or head or whatever of the Evenstar Dynasty. He keeps talking all this crap about me being destined for greatness but of course, he won't actually tell me what he means, because the guy seems to speak exclusively in riddles and

I'm meant to just trust that the truth will come out at the right time."

Raph's gaze flickers, but again, I can't decipher that look. He takes my hand, and entwines his fingers with mine.

"People underestimate just how destructive the truth can be if revealed at the wrong time," he says quietly. I eye him curiously, but still I can't read him.

I let out a frustrated groan.

"Not you, too."

He grins at me, some of that earlier tension I sensed in him, fading.

For a moment, I consider telling him about Magnus's warnings that Earth isn't safe for me anymore, even though its meant to be some Evenstar Dynasty top secret. But I decide against it. It's not like Magnus has even given me enough to go on and Raph already seems like he has a lot on his mind, without me adding to it.

His expression turns serious again as he lets out a long sigh.

"We should talk about the Winter Ball ..." He trails off, his frown deepening. I wonder if this is what's been on his mind. Because it sure as hell has been on mine. I've tried not to think about it, but it looms on the horizon like a dark storm cloud.

We haven't even touched on the subject until now. The proverbial elephant in the room. But we both know what's expected of Raph. Going to that ball with Layla is a given. Only a couple of weeks ago, the very thought of it would have made me feel sick. But now ... now it feels like it doesn't really matter. Because I know what he wants. I know who he belongs to. I replay Raph's words to me that last day of semester—*I'm certain that from the first moment I saw you on that beach, I've belonged to you*, and it feels more than enough. At least for now. One step at a time.

Our gazes lock then and the look in those endlessly blue eyes tells me everything I need to know. He would walk into that ball with me on his arm with the entire world watching, without a second thought, if I asked him to.

But I won't. Because I care about him enough to know he's not ready for the consequences of that, and if I'm honest, neither am I.

"You know I would—" he starts to say, as if reading my thoughts. But I don't let him continue.

"I know," I reply simply, brushing my fingertips against his jawline. "I know you would."

He brings his hand up to close over mine and as ever, his touch sears me.

"You don't need to prove anything to me. Not right now."

"Jaz—" he begins to object, but I don't let him.

"One step at a time," I say.

He's silent for a long moment, his eyes searching mine.

"One step at a time," he repeats finally.

I shift to lie on my back, although I keep my fingers entwined with his by my side as we fall into silence, both of us lost in our own thoughts.

When I turn back to Raph, his expression is clouded.

"You haven't … you haven't changed your mind about us, have you?" he asks then. The uncertainty in his eyes tugs at my chest and I want nothing more than to tell him exactly just how impossible it is that I would ever change my mind about him. That I would ever stop feeling this way for him.

But I'm a coward and I can't seem to make myself say those words. So, I tell him with my lips against his instead. He kisses me back with equal intensity and keeps kissing me until we're clawing at each other, his hips grinding mercilessly against the softest part of me and I'm gasping at the waves of pleasure coursing through me.

His t-shirt and jeans come off and they join my discarded clothes somewhere on the floor. Then I find myself straddling him, wearing nothing but my bra, although the lacy material leaves little to the imagination.

I hear his breath hitch, as I reach behind me and unclasp the thin back strap. A second later I'm entirely bare. A few months ago, I'd have felt frighteningly vulnerable and embarrassed but with Raph, the want and need that I feel for him leaves room for little else. He awakens a side of me that I know didn't exist before him. This brazen person that I become whenever Raph's hands are on me, is someone that he alone seems to have created.

His eyes darken with barely repressed hunger as his hands travel from my hips to my sides, caressing the sensitive skin there with a featherlight touch. His touch achingly tender in contrast to the bruising desire I see in his eyes.

He's looking at me with that awe and reverence which steals my breath even before he speaks those words which always feel like a punch in the chest whenever he says them.

"God, Jaz, you're so beautiful."

His hands finally move to cup my aching breasts and I hear a breathy moan escape my lips at the contact, followed by his responding groan which is sexy as hell.

Even through the thin material of his boxer shorts, I can feel him hard as granite beneath me and I don't even seem to be in control of my own body as my hips press down on that hardness.

He curses and his hips thrust up to meet mine as I grind against him, desperate to sate the throbbing at my center.

"Fuck, baby, that feels so good," he grinds out.

It does. It feels so damn good. But it's not enough. I want him inside me. I want to claw at him until we're so joined together, that nothing can tear us apart.

I can feel from the way his hard length is throbbing beneath me and the almost palpable waves of desire coursing from him, that he wants the same thing.

His hand moves from my breast, and the absence of his touch there makes me ache for his warmth. But the ache is quickly replaced by a deeper need as his hand travels down, past my abdomen, then lower still. When his finger spears through my tight passage, my skin burns with that need, until I feel like I'm about to burst into flame.

"More ..." I gasp out, as the burning need inside me builds, stripping away all sense and reason. Raph's responding growl is like fuel to the fire raging inside me.

When he adds another finger, the feeling of fullness makes me cry out and my whole universe narrows to the feel of them thrusting inside me at a rhythm which takes me closer and closer to the edge. The way he's watching me as I take that pleasure that he's giving me, undoes me completely and when our eyes lock, the intimacy is almost too much to bear.

I can feel the aching bud at my center throbbing with need, swollen and pulsing painfully, burning away any sliver of inhibition left in me. I can see from the wicked look in those midnight blue eyes, that Raph knows exactly the desperation that he's driving me to.

My breathing grows ragged until I'm panting, whimpering and finally pleading.

"Please ..." I gasp out as I grind down on his hand in an attempt to sate the need throbbing at my center.

Raph curses as he pulls me forward, until my body is flush with his, my breasts crushing against the rock hard expanse of his chest. His hands grab the sides of my face and his mouth crashes onto mine. I open myself up to him instantly and his tongue spears into my mouth so deep, it feels as if he's trying to devour me, brand me, claim me and I'm only too willing to let him.

We're both gasping for air when he breaks the kiss and his eyes lock directly onto mine, looking into my very core.

"You don't *ever* have to beg me for anything, baby. Everything I am is *yours*." His voice sounds so guttural, that I can barely recognize it and for a moment, I find it hard to breathe. I want him. I want him so much, that it feels like I might die from the sheer intensity of that desire.

I want to beg him to bury himself deep inside me until there's nothing separating us, until our bodies are so fused together, that nothing can possibly exist but him and me.

But before I can open my mouth to voice what we both seem to want, he's lifting me forward in one swift motion until I'm hovering over his face. I don't even have a chance to object, because a second later his tongue slices through the center of me. My back arches and I think I see stars.

His groan of approval vibrates through my body and I'm utterly helpless against the torrent of pleasure coursing through my body, pulling me under until I'm gasping for breath. My hips move of their own volition, rocking sensually against Raph's wicked mouth.

That skillful tongue works me to the edge, devouring me like a man starved and when it slips inside me, I can only cry out as I lose every single one of my senses.

When the waves of pleasure finally subside, I kiss my way down the rock hard expanse of Raph's golden chest, down to his equally hard abs and further down still to the even harder muscle throbbing beneath. I can feel just how affected Raph is by that trail of fire in the way his powerful body quakes under my lips.

My mouth waters shamelessly at the sight of him and in the same way as he devoured me, I do the same. The way that his body rocks under my touch and the sexy masculine sounds that he makes, sends shivers of pleasure through my own body and when he begins to thrust and his hand forms a fist around my hair, I think I lose my mind at the same time he loses his.

Sometime later, we're lying blissfully in each other's arms and I wish for a moment that it can always be like this, that the world outside the one that we've created can just disappear.

My hand finds its way to the side of Raph's left rib where the row of intertwined suns is etched into his golden skin.

"What does this tattoo mean?" I find myself asking, as my fingers trace the outline of the intertwined rays.

"It's a symbol of the St. Tristan Dynasty," he replies quietly. "I got it as a reminder of who and what my life belonged to."

I feel a cold chill racing through me at his words, a reminder of who and what Raph is. A reminder of all that is against us.

"But that was before you," he says.

"You're mine now, Jaz and ... I'll do whatever it takes to keep you."

Those luminous blue eyes lock onto mine and when I take in the perfect contours of his impossibly beautiful face, for a moment I feel like I can't breathe. This guy—this infuriatingly arrogant and complicated, yet impossibly perfect, impossibly beautiful and frighteningly powerful guy is *mine*. He can have anyone. Any goddamn girl in this entire world most likely, but he wants me—and I want him. More than I've ever wanted anything in my entire life. And I can't quite make myself believe it's real.

Something inside me makes me hold onto Raph tighter, because I can't shake the strange feeling descending on my shoulders, the thought that nothing this good, nothing this intense can ever last. Even the brightest stars burn out.

Raph seems to sense something in me, because his arms tighten around me, too. He leans his forehead against mine, his hand cupping my cheek and when he speaks, his eyes are locked directly onto mine, those impossibly blue eyes burning into me.

"What are you doing to me, Jaz?" he asks.

I want to ask the same thing about him. But I already know exactly what he's done and what he's continuing to do to me. The thought is terrifying, but when I'm with Raph, I don't feel that fear.

I find myself remembering Raph's words to me on my first day in Eden, telling me that I didn't belong here and how I had believed that. But we'd both been wrong. Because whenever I'm in Raph's arms, the sense of belonging that washes over me is so intense, that there's no question in my mind that I'm exactly where I belong, that I can finally stop searching for that place to belong because I've finally found it and it's here. With him.

He kisses me again, and because neither of us can ever seem to get enough, we devour each other all over again.

3 2

I wake up to the feeling of featherlight kisses along the sensitive skin of my inner thigh and when those kisses travel higher, any remnants of sleep clouding my senses disappear completely.

I'm fully awake when Raph's sensuous lips meet that sensitive bud at my center. He positions my legs wider on top of his shoulders and my back arches at the sensations that it causes.

I can feel his lips curve in a smile against the most intimate part of me, as I cry out his name over and over.

So loud, that I don't hear the door open.

A cough alerts me to the presence of someone in the room and I almost scream, as I frantically grasp at the blankets to cover my body. My very naked body.

I gape in shock at Magnus standing at the threshold of my bedroom door and I think I'm dying with each second that passes, as he assesses the scene.

Me naked in bed. Raph in between my legs. I don't think I've ever been so mortified in my entire life.

Magnus, to his credit, is completely calm. But he looks far from pleased.

I can't even bring myself to look at Raph for fear that I'm going to burst into flames from embarrassment.

"Raphael," Magnus says, finally.

Raph, to his own credit, keeps his facial expression completely neutral. So it's only me who's dying of embarrassment here, clearly.

"Magnus," Raph replies, evenly.

"Jazmine, I've just come to let you know that breakfast is ready downstairs, if you're hungry."

Magnus's eyes travel to Raph then.

"Judging from what I've just seen, I doubt you're still hungry, Raphael," he adds dryly.

Someone kill me now.

Before either of us can respond to that. Magnus makes his swift exit.

Raph bursts out in laughter an instant later, but I'm not laughing. Not at all. I swat him away as he tries to kiss me. Without another word, I fly into my walk-in closet and throw on some clothes. I go for the most modest clothes that I can find, although in light of what Magnus has just seen, I doubt it will make a difference.

Thankfully, Raph's fully dressed when I come out but he's still wearing that shit-eating grin.

"Well, that's one way for people to find out," he says, flashing me a wicked smile which earns him a solid punch directly to his mid-section.

~

Magnus says nothing and I'm equally silent as I eat my breakfast as fast as I possibly can. I have no doubt that I'll probably get indigestion after this.

But I'd rather that than having to withstand Magnus dissecting me with that those all-knowing eyes for a second longer than I have to.

I'm glad that I managed to send Raph on his way, even after he tried to insist that he should come to breakfast to explain to Magnus. I couldn't think of anything worse. But this deafening silence is ten times worse. I've never had to deal with this awkward parental disapproval after being found in a less than innocent position with a guy. I almost feel like a normal teenager. But of course, I'm not and even more so, neither is Raph.

Magnus finally speaks, and when he does, I find myself wishing for the silence again.

"Do you know what it is that you're doing with Raphael St. Tristan?" he asks calmly.

I stare at him blankly because there's so much in that question and I don't know what he's actually asking. So I go for the simplest answer that I can.

"Yes."

Magnus raises an eyebrow.

"You can't possibly know, Jazmine," he replies simply.

"What is that supposed to mean, *Magnus?*" I retort. But he keeps that unshakeable calm. Damn he's good.

"It means that you have no idea of the full implications of your and Raph's actions."

I bristle at that.

"Is this you trying to have the sex talk with me?" I snap. "Because I'm a little too old for that, I think. Maybe you shouldn't have waited until I was seventeen to bother to find me." I know that last part isn't true—Magnus has told me that he didn't found out about me until just before my father's death. But still, I'm trying to distract him from digging deeper into this thing between Raph and me.

He doesn't take the bait.

"No. I expect that you have adequate knowledge about such things," he replies dryly.

"This is about something far more serious. I told you before that the St. Tristan Dynasty and the Evenstar Dynasty are the two sovereign Dynasties. The rule of Eden has always fallen to one of the two.

"As such, these two sovereign Dynasties have always been the furthest apart, just like the elements that they lord over. Night and day, the sun and the moon. Opposites and rivals in almost every way. You're playing with fire here, Jazmine. You have no idea of the full implications," he says again.

"Well, why don't you tell me then?" I snap. I'm sick of Magnus's cryptic words and for once, I just want him to tell me the whole damn truth, whether he thinks it's the right time or not. But of course, he doesn't.

"All you need to know is that you cannot trust Raphael. He is a St. Tristan, heir to the St. Tristan Dynasty no less, and he is his father's son."

These last words echo Layla's and I feel my blood turn cold at hearing them. I force myself to block out the whisper of doubt racing through me. Because I do trust Raph. I hadn't realized just how much I've come to trust him until now, as Magnus forces me to question it.

"Raph is not his father's son. He's his own person. You don't know him," I reply evenly.

Magnus's eyes grow troubled then.

"No, Jazmine. It's you who doesn't know. Raphael's … allure when it comes to the opposite sex is no secret. But not everything is as it seems. The St. Tristan Dynasty is toxic."

His words make my temper flare. The only other member of the St. Tristan Dynasty I've met is Jethro and I couldn't agree with Magnus more when it comes to him. But he's wrong about Raph.

"Is this the part where you take away my cell, ground me for life and tell me never to see Raph again?" I ask flatly, although I'm fiercely hoping not.

Magnus just shakes his head wearily.

"I have no right to exercise that kind of authority over you, Jazmine."

"Damn right," I retort.

"But I can only hope that you'll listen to me. You cannot trust him, Jazmine. The St. Tristan Dynasty is poison and every single member of it is a snake."

I don't excuse myself as I get up, shoving my chair back as I walk away. I can't listen to another word from Magnus and I tell myself it's because I trust Raph and nothing that Magnus says can ever change that.

33

*U*nlike the Fall Ball, the Winter Ball isn't only for Regency Mount students. It's for all of the Dynasties and nobles, so it's a much grander affair.

Although it's been a relatively mild winter so far, the Aspen estate is covered in a thick blanket of snow for the occasion and of course, the snow is real.

But it's not just the snow covered landscape that steals my breath or the grand manor house, because at the center of the vast estate grounds, there is what looks like an actual *ice castle*, which appears to have been erected especially for the event.

Orbs of pale blue light float high above the rafters of the vast ball-room which is made of pure ice. When I walk into that ballroom, I feel like I'm walking right into a storybook painting.

"Impressed?" I turn to see Keller coming up behind me, looking awesome in her silver and white dress. Amidst the backdrop of the ice palace, she looks like the snow queen from those children's stories herself. She's totally in her element.

I remember thinking when I first met this girl that she was all attitude and cold as ice. But I was totally wrong, just like I'd been wrong about a lot of things when it came to Eden and to the Dynasty heirs.

I return her beaming smile with a wide grin of my own.

"Impressed is an understatement," I reply.

"Did you do all of this yourself?"

"Of course not!"

"She had help from us."

I blink once, twice. At first, I think I'm seeing things, because there's a young boy now standing on each side of Keller, both of whom look identical. From their light brown hair to their deep grey eyes, so much like Keller's, but with a spark of mischief entirely their own, and even down to their identical silver bow ties. Twins.

Keller rolls her eyes.

"Jazmine, meet Leo and Jael, my little brothers, a.k.a, the Aspen terrors."

Leo and Jael each flash me a smile. Leo's is slightly shy, whereas Jael's is both mischievous and brazen. Both boys are handsome, even for their age but I can tell that Jael is the one to watch out for. He'll be breaking hearts left, right and center when he grows up, no doubt.

"Hi, Jazmine," Jael replies, with that daredevil smile.

"Wanna dance?"

My eyebrows shoot up as Keller claps her little brother around the back of his head.

"Aren't you a little young?" I reply, with a grin.

"No. I'll be eleven in a few months," he says, with unwavering confidence.

"Quit being such a menace," Keller groans.

"Okay, forget the dance. How about a date instead?"

This time, I can't help but laugh in response, and Keller is equally amused.

"I'm sorry but I'm seeing someone right now," I reply, once the laughter has subsided.

Jael looks genuinely disappointed.

"Speaking of which, where is your date?" Keller asks then, looking around for Raph, although she's not going to find him because despite his many protests, I'd insisted that he should still go with Layla, like his father wanted.

It was probably a crazy decision on my part. But after Magnus's less than glowing reaction to finding Raph and me together, I'm convinced more than ever that the big reveal about our relationship would definitely need to wait. Showing up together to a ball with all the Dynasties and nobles watching would be like breaking the news with a sledgehammer. I don't know much about politics or Dynasty life, but breaking it to Raph's father by making such a public statement definitely doesn't seem like a good idea.

I don't even mind that he's going with Layla. I realized the other day, when Magnus challenged me about it, that I really do trust Raph. I know with every fiber in my being just how deep his feelings for me run and he's made it clear to me, that no other girl even exists for him. He's mine and for now, that's enough. The public declarations and all of the consequences flowing from that, can wait.

"I sort of convinced him that we shouldn't go together," I reply casually.

Keller's eyes widen in response.

"Why the hell did you do that?"

"Because I don't think either of us is ready for that and ... I trust him," I reply evenly.

She seems to be thinking that over for a moment, then flashes me a smile.

"Good for you," she replies finally, which reinforces my belief that I've done the right thing.

That feeling doesn't last long, though, because a second later, Raph makes his entrance and right by his side is Layla.

All eyes turn to them as they walk through the ornate entrance carved entirely of ice. Raph looks devastatingly handsome in a white suit jacket and black tailored trousers. Layla is wearing a shimmering ice blue gown which makes my own black and silver dress look plain in comparison. Individually, they're both undoubtedly model beautiful and stunning, but together they glow with an almost ethereal light. Any fool can see how perfect they look together and suddenly

I'm not feeling so good about my decision. But I remind myself that I could have stopped this from happening, if I had only said the word.

I'm comforted somewhat by the clear look of displeasure on Raph's face as he enters the ballroom and by how his eyes search for me, softening instantly when they find me.

"Speak of the devil," Keller says.

Jael's eyes follow Keller's and my gazes to the entrance and his mouth drops open.

"Wait—is *Raph* your boyfriend?" he asks.

I hadn't really thought of us in terms of labels, but …

"Yeah, I guess he is," I reply with a faint smile.

Jael frowns then.

"That can't be right because—"

He breaks off mid-sentence, and I notice Leo cutting him a warning look.

Keller and I eye the twins curiously.

"But you remember what we heard mom and dad saying …" Jael says.

"Have you two been eavesdropping on mom and dad's conversations again?" Keller demands, looking annoyed.

Leo grabs Jael's arm suddenly.

"Gotta go," he blurts, turning to make a run for it and making sure to drag Jael with him.

"Wait—" I call out, but they're out of earshot in a split second. Damn, those two are fast.

"What the hell was that?" I ask, as I turn back to Keller. She only shrugs dismissively, probably used to her little brothers' antics. But I'm not and Jael's words have left me feeling more than just a little curious.

"There's been a flurry of Dynasty sessions and advisory meetings lately. Something's going on in the Dynasty chambers, I guess, but who knows? They keep most things strictly confidential behind those doors—well except for when my little brothers happen to eavesdrop on my mom's meetings in her study or when they go snooping through her papers."

The whisper of curiosity grows louder in my mind, but I don't have time to ponder on it though, because a moment later, I feel a muscled arm curling around my waist.

"You look so beautiful tonight," Raph's voice in my ear sends shivers down my spine. But I'm well aware of where we are and of the eyes on us. I jerk away instantly and Keller stifles a grin. Raph, however, doesn't look amused.

"I hate this," he says with a sigh.

Thankfully, I'm saved from having to come up with a response as Baron bounds over with Lance in tow. I look across the ballroom to see Ivy standing with Layla among a group of nobles. But no Dani. She mentioned that she probably wouldn't come, even though Lance did ask her to go. She seemed pretty elusive about her reasons, though, and it's definitely something I plan on grilling her about later.

"Where are your dates?" Keller asks, eyeing Baron and Lance.

"Or did you two finally admit how crazy you are about each other and decide to come together?"

"Ha. Ha." Baron replies, rolling his eyes.

"If you must know, I'm taking a break from all this dating business," he adds.

Keller's eyes look like they're about to fall out of her head. Raph looks equally baffled, and I'm pretty sure my expression is similarly confused.

"You don't *date* girls—you only sleep with them, remember?" Keller says slowly, as if she's talking to a lost child.

Baron looks genuinely offended, which baffles everyone even more, because he's usually so proud of this reputation when it comes to the opposite sex.

But he doesn't say anything, stalking off to the other side of the ballroom instead.

"What's up with him?" Keller asks.

Lance just shrugs.

"He's been acting really weird since the beginning of winter break."

I notice Lance's own downcast expression then.

"I guess Dani decided not to come along then?" I ask.

"Yeah, she said she had stuff to do with her parents, but I'm not sure if there was some other reason, too. We haven't had a chance to speak much lately."

"She probably is just busy with her parents," I say. "It definitely sounded that way when I spoke to her last anyway."

Lance's frown eases a bit at that. He turns to talk to Keller, and Raph takes the opportunity to pull me aside.

"Are you sure you're okay with this?" he asks, his eyes searching mine.

This is definitely not the time or the place to be having this conversation. Especially when I can feel Jethro's eyes on us from across the ice ballroom, watching us like a hawk. I'm also all too aware of Magnus's watchful gaze and the troubled expression on his face. I stifle the groan of frustration working its way up my throat.

I told Raph that Magnus has been less than pleased about finding us together. I didn't go into any detail about why exactly. I certainly didn't repeat Magnus's words about the St. Tristan Dynasty being toxic and not to be trusted. But I got the feeling that I didn't need to. I may be new to this world and the web of power and politics that weaves it together, but Raph certainly isn't. He clearly doesn't seem to care about any of that at the moment, though.

"I'm fine," I reply, forcing myself to meet those vivid blue eyes, schooling my face blank.

His frown deepens and he opens his mouth to say something, but I don't let him. I need to get as far away from him as possible right now, otherwise I'm certain that I won't be able to stop myself from kissing him right in the middle of the ballroom, with the entire goddamn world watching.

"I'm going to go check on Baron," I say finally, moving to walk away. Thankfully, Raph doesn't follow, but I feel his eyes on me every step of the way.

"How about you ask me to dance?" I ask, as I reach Baron on the other side of the ballroom. His expression lightens, and he holds his hand out to lead me across the ballroom in a waltz.

I see Raph across the dance floor, finally deciding to play along as he leads Layla in a waltz. Except, as I watch them together, it's diffi-cult to remember that he is only just playing along. God, I hate how perfect they look together. Like a golden prince and his princess, right out of a fairy tale.

I turn back to Baron, because if I let myself look at Raph and Layla together for a minute longer, I won't be able to stop myself from scratching my own eyes out.

"So, what's up with this break from dating thing?" I ask.

He lets out a long sigh.

"I guess I'm just tired of people thinking that's all there is to me," he replies. There's no sign of his usual carefree expression. I'm surprised by it, but at the same time, glad for him.

"That's good," I say gently, and he smiles slightly in response.

We're silent for a long while as Baron continues to lead us through the waltz.

"What made you finally trust Raph?" he asks finally. The question surprises me, and I'm not sure of the answer at first.

"I guess it's because he showed me that there's more to him than the arrogant prick that he makes himself out to be," I reply.

Baron flashes a grin at that, which makes me break into a smile, too.

My expression turns solemn then.

"Whoever she is, she's a lucky girl," I say. I don't know what makes me say that. But I guess I just figure that it has to be because he's finally found someone worth taking that step for. I have no idea who, or whether I'm jumping to conclusions. I don't think I am, though—because I know from experience that it's only when you feel some-thing fierce for someone that you'd risk losing yourself just to find them.

Baron looks surprised by my knowing words, but he smiles in response. The waltz ends, and as I walk off the dance floor, I'm inter-cepted by a group of nobles who tell me they knew my father. I'm not entirely comfortable with the conversation, but I do the best I can to veil my emotions the way that everyone here seems to do so well.

When I finally manage to excuse myself from the group, I'm intercepted by another and the night goes on like that. Magnus comes to join me on a few occasions, and he seems to be glad that I'm getting the hang of this meeting and greeting the nobles thing. But the whole thing is entirely exhausting.

I'm glad that it keeps me distracted from having to look at Raph and Layla all night, though. I hadn't thought about how difficult it would be for me to actually see them together like this—entertaining the courtiers, totally in their element. Whenever I catch a glimpse of Raph, there's not a hint of his earlier displeasure, so it's either gone entirely or just very well hidden. I tell myself it's because he's been trained since birth to play this part. It reminds me that this is his life; he's made for these grand balls and the opulent ceremonies that go with them. Layla hangs dutifully on his arm, like any good queen would, and it makes me wonder what in the hell I've gotten myself into. Because just as Raph was born for this, so was Layla. I wasn't. And although Raph had told me once before that I do belong here and that I belong with him, doubt still gnaws at the back of my mind.

It's nearing the end of the night, when a strikingly beautiful woman who I recognize from that first ceremony, and from my Eden politics book, introduces herself. She shares so many of Keller's features, that I know who she is, even before she says her name.

"It's an honor to finally meet you properly, Jazmine," she says and unlike disingenuous words and barely veiled looks of disapproval that have been directed my way from some of the other nobles, she seems entirely genuine.

"Vega Aspen, head of the Aspen Dynasty." She holds out a hand to me, which I take willingly.

"I believe you've become quite good friends with my daughter, Keller."

"Yeah, Keller's great," I reply with a smile.

"I'm glad to see it—our two Dynasties have always been close allies. Your father and I were good friends. He was like a brother to me."

Her expression grows sad at those last words, and again I'm uncomfortable at the mention of my father.

"You have his eyes," she says, after a moment. "It's like I can almost see him looking out through them."

"Magnus told me the same thing," I manage to say.

"Your father was a great king, Jazmine. One of the best kings to ever sit on the throne of Eden," she says.

"One day, I hope that you'll be able to follow in his footsteps."

I don't think I hear those last words correctly. Because they make no sense.

"Raph's next in line to the throne," I finally manage to reply. I never did give it any thought as to how the whole sovereign Dynasty thing works. Magnus told me that the rule of Eden always falls to one of the sovereign Dynasties. My father had been the last king, but Raph is next in line to the throne. I'm guessing that the crown probably alternates from one sovereign Dynasty to another. That the St. Tristan Dynasty and the Evenstar Dynasty take turns at taking the throne. It's the most logical explanation. But something about Vega's expression makes me think there might be more to it than just that.

My mind starts racing then and I get an image of a thousand jigsaw pieces laying before me. Fragments, suspicions, words. But I can't make sense of it, I can't put the pieces together and every fiber in my being is screaming at me not to.

I realize that I'm just staring at Vega in utter confusion, as her expression grows even more troubled. My stomach churns as my discomfort levels soar to new heights, and I can feel my heartbeat pounding painfully in my chest, making it difficult to breathe.

"Magnus hasn't told you?" she asks finally.

"Told me what?" I demand, any vestige of politeness out the window.

Vega shakes her head.

"It's not common knowledge yet, but I would've thought that Magnus might have at least mentioned it to you by now."

"Please, can you just tell me what the hell you're talking about? Because Magnus sure as hell hasn't said anything to me. But that's no surprise because keeping me in the dark seems to be his favorite past time." I'm fully aware that I'm being rude now, and that this woman doesn't deserve to be on the receiving end. But I'm too confused and alarmed to care. A bad combination.

"It's not my place to tell you," she replies regretfully, and I think I'm going to scream in frustration.

"You should speak to Magnus," she adds, then walks away before I can say anything else.

Damn right I'm going to speak to Magnus.

I look around the ballroom which is already emptying. Jethro's icy gaze lands on me as I cross the ballroom, but Raph is nowhere in sight and neither is Layla. But that's not who I'm looking for just then.

I find Magnus across the ballroom and when I march over to him, I can see that he's either been watching the entire exchange between me and Vega, or my face is just that pissed.

"We need to talk. Now," I say bluntly.

Magnus doesn't say anything because he already knows. He searches my face for what seems like an eternity and I meet his gaze with a merciless one of my own.

"Okay," he says finally.

"Let's go back to the palace. There is something you need to know."

I should be glad to hear those words, but they have a ring of finality to them that only deepens the sickening feeling of dread in my gut. As I walk out of the ice palace into the dark night, the chill in my bones only grows colder and I'm certain at this point that I don't want to hear whatever it is that Magnus is about to tell me.

34

I'm sitting across from Magnus in what appears to be his study. The large wood paneled room is dark, apart from the light of the fire blazing in the large fireplace at the center.

Neither of us says a word as Magnus stares into that fire, as if it might give him the right words to tell me whatever it is that he needs to tell me.

I don't force those words, because whatever they are, I know I don't want to hear them. Not at all.

But he turns to me, and says them anyway.

"I told you before that the rule of Eden has always fallen to one of the two sovereign Dynasties. The St. Tristan Dynasty and the Evenstar Dynasty."

"Yeah, so there's some kind of rota where the throne alternates between the two sovereign Dynasties." I speak my own assumption out loud, then hoping that in doing so, it will make it true. Only when I do speak it out loud, I realize just how ridiculous it sounds.

"No," Magnus replies simply, and my world grinds to a halt as I wait for him to shatter it.

"The crown has always fallen to the eldest sovereign heir—the first heir from the St. Tristan Dynasty and the Evenstar Dynasty to reach their eighteenth birthday, ascends to the throne."

The churning in my stomach intensifies, until I feel like I might throw up all over the polished wood floors.

I remember that day at the amusement park. Raph telling me that we have the exact same birthday—*down to the very second*.

Magnus is watching my face and the look in his, tells me that he can see I already know. But he says it anyway.

"You and Raph share the same birthday, Jazmine. Down to the very second.

"Your father didn't know about you, no one knew about you. So, from the moment Raph was born, it was always assumed that he would be next in line to the throne.

"When the Dynasties first found out about you, everything about you was a mystery. We had no idea who you were, let alone what day you were born. There was always the possibility, of course, that you'd be older than Raph. But even if you were, it was always assumed that because your blood is tainted with human blood, whilst you could take up your rightful place as heir to the Evenstar Dynasty, ascending to the throne was out of the question," he continues.

"But when I obtained your birth certificate, I discovered that you were born on the same day as Raph, at exactly the same second. A true phenomenon, which could not be ignored.

"I told only the Evenstar Dynasty's closest allies at first. But somehow, Jethro also found out. The Dynasties have since been examining the laws of Eden and debating in secret for months, as to what needs to be done. Nothing like this has happened in centuries, let alone in any of our lifetimes. It was resolved that no one should find out about this phenomenon, until it was decided what must be done."

"Raph knew," I find myself saying, almost involuntarily, my voice barely a whisper in the dimly lit room.

Magnus's eyes turn to me.

"Yes, he must have. I don't doubt that Jethro would have told him."

I get that image of a thousand jigsaw pieces scattered in front of me again and I still have no idea how to put them together. The way that Keller's little brothers ran off after Jael's surprise at Raph and me being together; Magnus's own warnings and Jethro's less than pleasant words to me at the Fall Ball.

"What—what does this mean?" I ask, although I'm certain I don't want to know the answer.

"It means, Jazmine, that something must take place, which hasn't taken place in Eden for centuries. It means that nature itself requires that there must be a Crown Trial."

"What the hell is a Crown Trial?" I demand, although my voice is shaky, because my whole universe feels like it's spinning right now.

"It's a duel—you against Raph. For the throne," he replies simply and the universe that had just been spinning? It comes crashing down around me, shattering into a million pieces.

"For the throne?" I sputter.

I shoot up to stand on my feet, as the torrent of emotions raging inside me threatens to pull me under. Hell, I'm already drowning.

"*I don't want the damn throne* and I'm sure as hell not about to fight Raph for it."

Magnus's eyes grow even more troubled then.

"You must do this, Jazmine. You see, the laws of nature may be cruel and they may be harsh in the same way that storms can wipe out entire cities and famines can decimate a nation, but they are necessary in order to keep the balance. Even the slightest upset in that balance can have consequences beyond anything which anyone can even comprehend. The laws cannot be broken and they require a Crown Trial to determine which sovereign heir will next ascend to the throne."

"*Fuck* the laws," I reply, I'm aware that I'm shouting. I'm aware of the manic desperation that must be shining in my eyes right now. But I don't care.

"There is *no way in hell* that I'm doing this and I don't believe for a second that the universe will come crashing down just because I don't."

But Magnus only shakes his head in response.

"You don't understand, Jazmine, even the slightest crack in the foundations can cause the entire world to shatter. Both worlds.

"A phenomenon like this has the power to change the entire universe. The Crown Trial must take place, or we risk both worlds falling out of balance."

I stare back at Magnus for a long moment. The only sound in the dead silence is my own ragged breathing.

"You knew this was going to happen, even before you brought me here," I say finally. "You knew and yet you still brought me here. You knew, but even when I asked, you wouldn't tell me. You just kept the truth hidden from me out of some twisted belief that I wasn't ready to know it."

Magnus's eyes widen, and his expression is aghast.

"No—*of course, I didn't know then*. I told you that I only found out about this phenomenon when I obtained your birth certificate and even then, I couldn't be certain as to the consequences. No one could. It has only just been determined what should be done."

"But you suspected? You knew that there was always a possibility that it could come to this?" I ask flatly.

"Yes," Magnus replies simply. He doesn't say anything else. But he doesn't need to.

Anger washes over me, white hot fury sweeping away any sense and reason, until it's all I can see. It's only when I feel the trust being swept away with that storm, that I realize it was ever there at all. The realization feels like a punch to the stomach. Had I been that lonely and desperate for family, that I had grown to trust this total stranger? Grown to care for him in a way that I hadn't felt since my mom died? I feel sick at the very thought. I've let myself get dragged into this, let myself be lied to and manipulated, let myself be used as a pawn in this twisted web of power that these Dynasties seemed to be locked in.

"I'm so sorry, Jazmine, I didn't mean for you to find out this way and I wish that this didn't have to happen. But it does and I have every faith in you that when the time comes, you will have the courage to do what it takes."

"No." My voice sounds as cold as the ice creeping into my core. I trusted you and you've been lying to me all this time—hiding things from me which I sure as hell deserved to know from the very beginning. The part about Earth not being safe for me—is that a lie, too?"

"No, Jazmine. Of course, it isn't."

"So are you going to finally tell me why?" I demand.

"I can't. It's more than just a danger to your life, Jazmine. The need to protect this world from the knowledge of this threat is greater than your need to know about it," he replies simply, which only adds fuel to the fire burning in my chest.

"Why should I even believe you? Why should I believe a single word that comes out of your mouth? Why the hell should I even trust you?"

Magnus's calm seems to snap, and for a moment, I can almost feel the waves of anger rolling off.

"I'm your blood, Jazmine. Everything I've done so far has been for my son's memory, your father, and for you, Jazmine. I'm the only one you can trust." He says these last words distinctly, and he doesn't have to say anything else, because my mind is already there.

My initial rage has been so all-consuming, that I hadn't even considered all the other far reaching consequences of this universe-shattering revelation. Or perhaps that was the reason why I had chosen to focus my rage solely on Magnus, so that I don't have to think about Raph.

But I'm helpless against the torrent of those thoughts swirling inside me now, the doubts screaming in my mind, the storm threatening to pull me under.

"I told you that you couldn't trust him, Jazmine," Magnus says, as he sees the storm raging in my eyes.

His words feel like a punch to my gut, but I don't believe them. I can't.

"I don't know what you're talking about." My voice is barely a ragged whisper in the darkness.

"Raphael has been raised from birth to take the throne. The desire for the crown ingrained in his very being—it's who Jethro made him to be. *It's who he is.* And Raphael knew this whole time that it might come to this. He must have known, because his father certainly knew —that one day, you could take from him what he's been raised to want all his life, at *all costs*."

Images of my first duel with Raph rush into my mind. The way he'd seemed so closed off when I questioned him as to why I'd ever need to know how to fight in a duel. We'd trained together almost every day since. My powers are as familiar to him as his own. He knows every move I make before I make it.

Maybe that was the point. Something in my mind whispers, but I can't bring myself to hear it.

I'm shaking my head, backing away from the spot where I'd been standing frozen. I can't listen to these words, I can't hear them, I can't think about what they mean. Every fiber in my being is telling me that they can't possibly be true. Not when every time I close my eyes, I can only see the way that Raph looks at me when we're lying together, as if I'm the only thing that matters in this entire universe. Not his throne, not his Dynasty, not his betrothal. But me.

The troubled look in Magnus's eyes deepens as he regards me.

"Don't lie to yourself, Jazmine. You're stronger than that."

His words feel like a stab to the chest, and all I can do is turn away from those truths threatening to swallow me whole, and run.

I hear Magnus calling after me, but I don't stop. I keep running until the cool night air hits my burning lungs.

I've never driven on Eden, but I don't even think twice as I get into one of the waiting cars in the palace courtyard and it isn't any different from my limited experience of driving on Earth.

I tell myself to calm down as I drive the short distance to the St. Tristan palace. I don't know anything for sure. Raph will explain. He'll tell me that it's not true. He'll tell me that Magnus is wrong—wrong about the Crown Trials or at the very least, wrong about Raph's intentions.

I play Raph's words over in my mind in an attempt to stop myself from breaking down entirely.

I'm certain that from the first moment I saw you on that beach, I've belonged to you.

You're mine now, Jaz and ... I'll do whatever it takes to keep you.

I hold onto those words, because they're all I have left.

he St. Tristan palace is still as a tomb when I arrive. The doorman doesn't so much as bat an eyelash at my arrival and I get the impression that girls visiting Raph at all times of night is far from an unusual occurrence. I try to remind myself that it's no longer the case. Raph hasn't so much as looked at another girl since this thing between us started. But the sickening feeling in my gut only deepens.

I follow the doorman's directions to the west wing of the first floor, through the seemingly never ending marble corridor, my steps echoing ominously through the darkness. I finally reach the large double doors at the end of the hallway. One of the doors is open a crack, but for a moment I can't make myself go through it.

Get it together, I tell myself.

I raise my hand to knock, but then I catch a glimpse of something through the crack of the door which stills every fiber in my being. I can barely make it out at first—a flash of skin, a gasp, a breathy moan.

Terror washes over me and my mind is screaming at me not to open that door. But I don't listen.

The door swings open and for what seems like an eternity, I just stare … and stare … and stare.

Shimmering ice blue material lying discarded on the marble floor. A dress.

My eyes follow the trail to a thin scrap of white lace on the floor, then another.

When I raise my eyes to the large silk-sheeted bed, for a moment my mind can't comprehend what I'm seeing. That traitorous muscle in my chest refuses to accept it.

I close my eyes and open them again, thinking that the image will disappear, that it's not real. But it doesn't disappear.

Layla's naked body straddling Raph's is real. So real, that I think I feel my heart stop at the sight of it and I want to scratch my own eyes out to stop myself from seeing any more of it. Everything about this nightmare is real—from the sight of Raph's naked torso leaning back against the wide headboard, to the sight of Layla's naked breasts pressed up against his chest.

His hands are gripping her forearms and his eyes are locked onto hers. I can't see the look in them, but I don't need to. I know only too well how those midnight blue eyes look when they're dark with desire, with need, with passion, and I've been a fool to think that any of that was real when those eyes looked at me.

For a moment, I can feel the ghost of his touch, those hands on my skin, touching my body and I let out a tortured cry which sounds pathetic, even in my own ears.

They turn to me and the sick realization dawns on me that they must have been so caught up in each other, that they hadn't even realized I was standing here.

They see me now, though. Shock flares in Raph's eyes. But I tear my gaze away from his face after a split second. I can't bear to look at him. I can't even bear to breathe the same air as him.

My gaze lands on Layla, and the gleam of triumph in those cruel eyes makes me gag on reflex, as bile rises in my throat.

We stand there frozen, like pillars of salt, for what seems like an eternity and the universe feels like it has narrowed, so that we're the only three people to exist in it. I was a fool to let Raph make me feel in those intimate moments like we were the only two people in the vastness of time and space. It has never been just the two of us. Layla has been there all along, and those moments—they were all lies.

I hear Keller's words repeating themselves in my head.

I've just never known Raph to go without.

I know now that he hasn't been going without. Not at all. It becomes clear to me, why he never took that step with me—because he didn't need to. Didn't want to. He had Layla for that, and she is all that matters. It's always been her.

Raph and I have never used the word *love*. I'd always been too much of a coward to voice just how fierce my feelings for him had become, and I realize that perhaps it was also because some part of me knew that love was too weak a word for what I felt for him. I'd hoped that it was the same for him, too, and the words that he has spoken to me, well, they went far and above just love.

But I was wrong—about his words at least. Those words were lies and it's clear now why he has never used the word love with me. As simple as that word is, it holds a meaning that could never be faked the way he was faking with me. He told me once that he didn't love Layla. But it's clear now that I've been a fool to believe him.

I feel the realization like a knife to the chest, but I force myself to accept it, even if it kills a part of me.

Raph is the first to move. He pushes away from Layla and leaps off the bed. As he approaches me, I can see that he's not totally naked, from the waist down at least. But the mental image of Layla unbuttoning his black suit trousers then removing them, just causes my stomach to twist even tighter.

"Jaz—" His voice is low and I can hear the distress in it, but I can't let him speak. I can't let him get those words out. Because Magnus had been right about him—he is toxic and every single word out of his mouth, poison.

And what could he possibly say to restore the breath to my lungs? What could he possibly do to piece that traitorous muscle in my chest back together? Nothing he can say can ever make any of this go away. He will never be able to make this right.

But it's my fault too—I knew from the very first touch, the very first look, that Raph would most likely shatter my heart into a million pieces and break me in two. Hell, he had promised on that very first night to do the latter. But I haven't listened to my own warnings, or indeed his. I've been foolish and blind.

I can see perfectly clearly now. I came here looking for answers and I sure as hell have them. Not the answers my stupid heart was hoping for, but I was foolish to think it would turn out any other way. Layla had been right when she told me that there was only one ending to this fairy tale and it wasn't a happily ever after for me. Not at all.

"Shut up!" I cry out.

He opens his mouth again, but I make sure he closes it.

"*Just shut the fuck up.* I don't want to fucking hear it."

He moves forward another step, but I don't let him come any closer.

"Don't you dare touch me, don't you dare come anywhere near me."

I'm shouting so loud, that Raph stops dead in his tracks and I'm surprised no one has come in to see what the hell is going on already. I can feel Layla's gleeful eyes on me. But I ignore her completely.

I'm so angry, that I'm shaking, every fiber in my body buzzing with adrenaline. I can feel my eyes burning, fierce with pain. But I'm too angry to feel ashamed, too angry to care. I take a deep breath, struggling to breathe through the feeling in my chest which feels like a bomb is exploding inside it and I've let Raph past my defenses to plant the bomb there. It was only a matter of time before it detonated.

Maybe I should ask him to explain himself. Maybe I should beg him to tell me what I'm seeing is some horrible misunderstanding. But I don't. Because that part of me is dead now, leaving only a block of ice in its place.

I finally meet his gaze and I feel nothing. Because a block of ice can't feel and when I speak, my voice is as cold as the arctic wind, as cold as Raph's own gaze that first moment we met. I know now that was his true self. Not the guy who made me feel safe, made me feel like I'd finally found somewhere to belong. Not the guy who kissed me with such awe and reverence, that it felt like I was all that mattered in the entire universe, who told me that I was all that mattered and that he belonged only to me. No—that guy didn't exist. He was nothing but a lie. All of it was a lie.

I should get the hell out of here. Now. Something inside me needs to hear the words from his own mouth. I need to hear him say it.

"I just want to know one thing."

Raph's eyes flinch at my words, at my tone, but they don't look away. Good. I want him to see just how dead he is to me now.

"Did you know about the Crown Trial?"

Something flickers in the depths of Raph's eyes, but still he doesn't look away.

"Yes," Raph replies simply, and the fragments of the shattered universe that had been lying at my feet earlier? They're swept away into the darkness, never to be pieced back together again. Devastation is an understatement. The pieces of the puzzle that I'd been desperately trying to put together, fall into place, but the image is too horrific to even look at.

If the world ended right now, I doubt I'd even notice, because it feels like it already has and nothing, *nothing* will ever be the same.

He's opening his mouth to speak, but I cut him off again by holding a hand up. I'm not screaming this time, but I don't need to. Because the look in my eyes is clear enough.

"Was that the reason why? Was that the real reason why you tried to drive me away and then why you tried to get close to me in the first place?" It should hurt me to ask these questions, but I don't let it hurt. I can already feel the numbness settling over me, and soon I pray, I'll feel nothing at all.

Raph doesn't answer, but the flash of guilt that I see in the depths of those heartbreakingly blue eyes, is enough. This time, I don't need to hear the words, because that look tells me all I need to know.

He finally drops his gaze, unable to look me in the eye for a second longer. I'm glad, because I don't want him to see the lone tear slipping down my cheek.

Layla sees it, though, and her responding laugh echoes through the silence. My gaze falls on her naked body still lounging on Raph's bed like she owns it, which is fitting, because in all the ways that matter, she does. Just like she owns him.

I'm certain that from that first moment I saw you on that beach, I've belonged to you. Raph's unwelcome words play themselves over in my mind and I feel like ripping off both my ears, so that I can never again hear any of his lies.

"Did you really believe that Raph was into you for real?" Layla asks, the delight ringing in her voice.

She quirks a perfectly shaped eyebrow, as she examines the devastation on my face.

"Oh, you did. How...."

Her lips curl into a cruel smile.

"Foolish," she says finally, and I have no response, because she's right.

It's that same foolishness that makes me look back at Raph. Hope can be a stubborn thing and that one last grain of hope inside me wants him to say something. Anything to make the clawing in my chest go away. But he doesn't. He's as silent as a pillar of stone. He won't even look at me.

That last ember of hope dies and I'm finally able to move. This time when I turn and run, Raph doesn't ask me to stay. This time, there's nothing he can possibly say to make me stop running.

I'm almost at the car next to the palace gates when I hear footsteps crunching on the gravel behind me.

Every fiber of my being stiffens, but when I turn around, it isn't Raph approaching and I don't know whether to be relieved or bitterly disappointed.

"I warned you to stay the hell away from Raph," Layla says to me.

I don't even know why I reply. But I have nothing left to lose now, anyway.

"You warned me about being Raph's latest fling. Not about *this*—

not that he was ..." I can't even make myself finish the sentence as my insides start heaving.

"I warned you that you have no idea how sick and twisted he is," she replies coldly. "You should've listened."

There isn't a single protest left inside me because she's right—I should've stayed away from Raph. But I didn't listen. Not to my own warnings or those from the people who know him far better than I ever did.

I should get in the car and get the hell away from this place, although I have no idea where I can go to escape the Dynasties and their twisted world. But something keeps me rooted on the spot, as if the masochist in me wants Layla to twist the knife in deeper.

"Raph was raised to want nothing else but that throne. It's who he is. No matter how much Raph may resent his father's hand in his life, nothing can change the fact, that it's that hand that's molded him from birth for that crown.

"When your existence was revealed and when you were found and brought back here to Eden, well, you can only imagine the lengths that Raph was willing to go to in order to protect what he's been raised to desire above all else, at all costs.

"First the plan was to make your life so miserable here on Eden, to break you so badly, that you'd go running back to that trailer park back on Earth. But then it was discovered that the laws require the Crown Trials to actually take place, and there was no way around it. So the plan changed somewhat, and Raph would need to break you in an entirely different way—in a way far more wicked, if you ask me."

She flashes me a radiant smile which would have been beautiful, if it wasn't so twisted.

"It may have been his father's will, but Raph sure as hell executed it with perfection. Raph's always been *so good* at getting girls to fall head over heels for him, until they'd sell their own soul just to get a taste of him. Except in your case, it wasn't just your soul, it was your claim to the throne, too."

I'm reminded of Jethro's words to me at the Fall Ball, that Raph is next in line to the throne and nothing would change that. I'd thought that he must have been referring to Raph's betrothal, but I know now that it was about far more than just that. It was about something far more twisted. I feel sick to my stomach and I'm surprised at my ability to keep myself from vomiting all over the gravel courtyard.

"I have to admit, Jazmine, I'm disappointed in you. I thought for a moment there that you would have more sense than to let Raph toy with you like that. But I was wrong—you're just as foolish as all of those other girls, all too willing to open their legs for Raph. But who can blame you, Raph sure as hell knows how to use his hands and that wicked tongue of his to strip a girl of all of her senses."

If there was anything left inside my chest, it's decimated right in that very moment and distantly, I can feel my hand gripping onto the handle of the car door, just to keep from doubling over.

"Too bad you didn't get the pleasure of getting acquainted with his dick, too—because that would have really sealed the deal."

"Go to hell, Layla," I manage to say finally, my words barely a ragged whisper in the night.

"I'm going to ignore that, along with everything else I hate about you and I'm going to grant you this one small mercy. From one enemy to another."

She holds something out to me then and my entire body stills as my gaze lands on the golden key in her hand.

"Where—where did you get that?" I gasp out.

"Does it matter?" she replies.

"All you need to know is that it's your ticket out of here."

I stare at the key in her palm, the moonlight glinting off it like a promise of salvation from this hell that I've been plunged into. I used to think my life on Earth was hell, that trailer park and all of the other temporary homes and faceless foster parents before it. But I was wrong. I'd trade that loneliness and loss for this devastation clawing at my chest in a heartbeat. Layla seems to know it, too.

"Take it—get the hell out of Eden and never look back."

I don't ask any questions, I don't hesitate for a moment longer. I reach out and take that key from Layla's hand instead. The irony hits me. Magnus has lied to me. Raph has lied to me. But Layla has been open and consistent about her hatred of me from the start. She's been the only honest person here in this web of deception.

I don't know how to open a portal. But having watched Magnus and Raph do it, some primal part of me already knows. I let that part of me take over as the air around me shifts and splits open to reveal the universe beyond.

For a moment Magnus's warnings about Earth not being safe, enter my mind. But I brush it away. Magnus lied to me. How could I trust anything he's ever said to me and even if it is true, I'd much rather the shadow of that unknown danger, than the very real one in this place. It isn't just the St. Tristan Dynasty that's toxic, this entire world is poison.

This world is a mirror of Earth, Magnus once told me. If only I'd known then just how right he was. This place may have seemed beautiful, vibrant and vivid in a way that my life on Earth never was. But it's just as ugly.

The beauty is nothing but a deception. It draws you in with promises of hope that creep into your soul. But it's all lies. All of it. The danger that lurks beneath that beauty is like the thorns beneath the bloom of a rose, like poison from the sweetest forbidden fruit. Now, I know how those human myths about Eden were formed. Eden itself is the forbidden fruit and I had been foolish enough to taste it.

As I stand at the entrance of the portal and take one last look back at the St. Tristan Palace, some part of me hesitates for a moment. But the palace is as still as a tomb and Raph is nowhere in sight. I don't know why that still has the ability to slice through my chest, not when any remaining connections with Eden have already been burned away in the devastation that I've just emerged from.

Raph once told me that the throne was all he was raised to ever want, *at all costs*. I should have listened. Because in the midst of his web of lies, that was the one truth.

I step into the portal, I do just as Layla said—I get the hell out of this poisonous world and I don't look back.

ALSO BY MJ PRINCE

Coming soon...

Dynasty Volume II: Shattered Heir

Can't get enough of Eden? Then sign up to MJ's newsletter to get all the latest release news for **Shattered Heir**, freebies and advance copies.

SIGN UP here: http://mjprinceauthor.com/dynasty-updates/

Each subscriber will get an exclusive **BONUS** scene of **Secret Heir** told from Raph's POV!

Alternatively, leave a review on amazon.com or goodreads.com and send your email address to contact@mjprinceauthor.com to receive the bonus scene!

...Welcome to Eden...

mjprinceauthor.com

ABOUT MJ PRINCE

New Adult and Young Adult author, sometimes artist, sometimes lawyer, often a dreamer and a hopeless romantic but a die hard bookworm *at all times*.

STALK ME ON SOCIAL MEDIA...

Twitter: @mjprinceauthor
Facebook: @mjprinceauthor
Catch sneak peaks on Wattpad:
https://www.wattpad.com/user/mjprince_author
Get insight on my visual inspiration on Pininterest:
https://www.pinterest.co.uk/mjprinceauthor/
Follow me on tumblr for general mental unloading whilst writing:
https://mjprinceauthor.tumblr.com/
Check out my reading list and reviews on Goodreads:
https://www.goodreads.com/user/show/73038198-mj-prince
Sign up to get all the latest release news for **Dynasty Volume II: Shattered Heir**, freebies, advance reader copies and a chance to win Dynasty swag: **SIGN UP here:** http://mjprinceauthor.com/dynasty-updates/

...Welcome to Eden...

mjprinceauthor.com
contact@mjprinceauthor.com

ACKNOWLEDGMENTS

I grew up with an unhealthy obsession for YA novels. LJ Smith was my all time fave and I could never get enough. I also had a great love for classic literature (I've read Great Expectations and Wuthering Heights one too many times) and I was a huge William Shakespeare fangirl. An eclectic mix, I know!

Finally taking the plunge and writing my first novel has been amazing experience and I couldn't be happier with the world that I've created within these pages. I hope that my readers enjoy being immersed in Eden and the world of the Dynasty heirs just as much as I enjoyed creating it.

The journey to publication has been a huge learning curve. After receiving a contract offer from a small press for this novel, I realised that I'm way too much of a control freak to hand over the reigns at this stage so I decided to go it alone and I've enjoyed every minute of it. I want to thank everyone in the huge indie community who has helped bring Eden to life.

Thank you to: my main beta reader, Shalini Gopal, you've been a big influence on a couple of scenes in this novel and I truly appreciate your input and feedback; Evelyn Guy of Indie Edit Guy for your excellent editing services; Indie Sage for the on point PR service, I couldn't have asked for a better release promo campaign; and the reviewers and bloggers who helped make the release of this book such a success.

Last, but by no means least, thank you to all my readers. You make all the late nights and missed social events so worth it!